SYLVIA TOWNSEND WARNER

(1893–1978) was born in Harrow, the daughter of George Townsend Warner, housemaster and Head of the Modern Side of Harrow. As a student of music she became interested in research in the music of the fifteenth and sixteenth centuries, and spent ten years of her life as one of the four editors of the ten-volume compilation *Tudor Church Music*. In 1925 she published her first book of verse, *The Espalier*. With the publication of the novels *Lolly Willowes* in 1926, *Mr Fortune's Maggot* and *The True Heart* in the two following years, she achieved immediate recognition. The short stories she contributed to the *New Yorker* for over forty years established her reputation on both sides of the Atlantic.

In 1929 Sylvia Townsend Warner visited New York as guest critic for the *Herald Tribune*. In the 1930s she was a member of the Executive Committee of the Association of Writers for Intellectual Liberty and was a representative for the Congress of Madrid in 1937, thus witnessing the Spanish Civil War at first hand.

In all, Sylvia Townsend Warner published seven novels, four volumes of poetry, a volume of essays, and eight volumes of short stories. Her biography of T. H. White, published in 1967, was acclaimed in the *Guardian* as one of the two most outstanding biographies to have appeared since the war.

A writer of formidable imaginative power, each of Sylvia Townsend Warner's novels is a new departure, ranging from the revolutionary Paris of 1848 in *Summer Will Show* (1936), a 14th-century Abbey in *The Corner That Held Them* (1943) to the South Seas Island of *Mr Fortune's Maggot*, and 19th-century rural Essex in *The True Heart*.

Sylvia Townsend Warner lived most of her adult life with her close companion Valentine Ackland, in Dorset, then in Norfolk and later in Dorset once again where she died on 1 May 1978, at the age of eighty-four.

SUMMER WILL SHOW

By

Sylvia Townsend
Warner

With a New Introduction by
CLAIRE HARMAN

*'Winter will shake, Spring will try,
Summer will show if you'll live or die.'*

PENGUIN BOOKS – VIRAGO PRESS

To
Valentine Ackland

PENGUIN BOOKS
Viking Penguin Inc., 40 West 23rd Street,
New York, New York 10010, U.S.A.
Penguin Books Ltd, Harmondsworth,
Middlesex, England
Penguin Books Australia Ltd, Ringwood,
Victoria, Australia
Penguin Books Canada Limited, 2801 John Street,
Markham, Ontario, Canada L3R 1B4
Penguin Books (N.Z.) Ltd, 182–190 Wairau Road,
Auckland 10, New Zealand

First published in Great Britain by Chatto & Windus 1936
First published in the United States of America by The Viking Press 1936
This edition first published in Great Britain by Virago Press Limited 1987
Published in Penguin Books 1987

Copyright Viking Penguin Inc., 1936
Copyright renewed Sylvia Townsend Warner, 1964
Introduction copyright © Claire Harman, 1987
All rights reserved

Printed in Finland
by Werner Söderström Oy

Set in Fournier

INTRODUCTION

'It must have been in 1920 or 21, for I was still in my gaunt flat over the furrier in the Bayswater Road and totally engaged in *Tudor Church Music*, that I said to a young man called Robert Firebrace that I had invented a person: an early Victorian young lady of means with a secret passion for pugilism; ...
He asked what she looked like and I replied without hesitation: Smooth fair hair, tall, reserved, very ladylike. She's called Sophia Willoughby.'*

Twelve years later, on a visit to Paris, Sylvia Townsend Warner found that she wanted to write a novel about the 1848 revolutions. Sophia and Minna Lemuel, who had also been invented in advance, 'started up and rushed into it'. A fanciful beginning, perhaps, but there was nothing fanciful about the novel they were rushing into, *Summer Will Show*.

Summer Will Show was published in Britain in the autumn of 1936, when Sylvia Townsend Warner and her companion Valentine Ackland were about to depart for Barcelona. They were going to Spain in support of the Spanish Government in the Civil War, taking up a three-week job with the Red Cross. They had both joined the Communist Party in 1935 and were committed and active members of it. Practical ones, too, never glory-hunters. In 1932, however, when *Summer Will Show* was begun, Sylvia Townsend Warner's interest in communism was academic. Fascism in Europe was not yet a conspicuous terror; National Socialism had not taken over Germany, nor Franco Spain. Sylvia's life at the time was ruled more by love and pot-boiling than by love and politics. Her story of the young lady aristocrat who ends up on the other side of the barricades,

*Sylvia Townsend Warner, 'A note on *Summer Will Show*', *Letters*, p. 39. Chatto & Windus, 1982.

saying 'I have changed my ideas. I do not think as I did', was written during a period when the author's own political ideas were crystalising out.

An interesting point in *Summer Will Show* is that Sophia Willoughby is not changed so much as defined by her experiences. The English lady communist in the June revolution in Paris is the same cool and austere person as the English lady landowner surveying her tomatoes in Dorset. What is different is that she has purpose, a direction; her actions are dictated by personal commitments rather than by duty. For the lady landowner, 'Duties came out of thought, one after another, swift as bees coming out of a hive'. 'Behind every love or respect stood a monitorial reason, and one's emotions were the expression of a bargaining between demand and supply, a sort of political economy.' Sophia Willoughby had functions to perform, she was a wife and mother as well as landed gentry, but divested one by one of functions, set free from 'a world policed by oughts', what is she left with but herself; impotent, barrened, a free woman. And what use, the novel asks, is that?

'It was boring to be a woman, nothing that one did had any meat in it.' Freedom presents itself to Sophia as a void to be filled up: religion, ambition, travel, learning, she considers and rejects them all. Her gestures of defiance misfire; riding to hounds during her period of mourning Sophia discovers 'a growing impression that she was out on false pretences, having in reality an assignation with the fox'. What is a woman to do whom death and destiny have contrived to make free? St. Paul provides one ready answer and it is only a matter of chance that Sophia is prevented from carrying out her eventual choice of action; to seek out her estranged husband, to replace her dead children, to tie herself back down to a purpose.

It is freedom on a different plane that Sophia Willoughby needs. She has dreamed of leading a 'wild, romantic life . . . unsexed and unpersoned', a dream that lives up badly to the brief chance it is given on a journey back from Cornwall alone, but the virtue of having had the dream impresses itself:

In a space no longer than it takes to open one's eyes she was back in her accustomed life, in a leap was transferred to daylight from darkness. And yet, as by the mere closing of eyelids, one can surmise a darkness stranger than any star has pierced, a darkness of no light which only the blind can truly possess, she knew that by a moment's flick of the mind she could levant into a personal darkness, an unknown aspect of Sophia as truly hers as one may call the mysterious sheltering darkness of one's eyelid one's own.

The relationship between Sophia and Minna Lemuel is the backbone of the story and Minna's influence from Blandamer, Sophia's family home in Dorset, to the barricades, is all-pervading. Minna is one of Sylvia Townsend Warner's most charming creations, observed at length and with a remarkable attention to gesture, tone of voice, the actress tricks that make her at once 'the world's wiliest baggage' and a genuine innocent, 'completely humble and sincere'. When, at the beginning of Part II, we are plunged into Minna's narrative of escape from the pogrom in Lithuania, Sylvia Townsend Warner achieves an important coup; having told us that Minna is a spell-binder, she makes her one. The narrative, with its complete change of pace and tone, pushes the reader into that Parisian drawing-room with Sophia. One is, for its duration, more of a listener than a reader.

The teller of tales, the dramatist and visionary is also a charlatan. Ageing, unbeautiful, unscrupulous, 'her principles were so inconsistent that to all intents and purposes she had no principles at all'. As Sophia's former husband's former mistress, Minna was known as nothing better than a Jewish strumpet and even when Sophia later loves Minna herself, she can find little to admire, 'for what good qualities she had must be accepted with their opposites, an inconsequential pell-mell of wheat and tares'. It is this, indeed, which is Minna's attraction:

One could love her freely, unadmonished and unblackmailed by any merits of mind or body. She made no more demands upon one's moral approval than a cat, she was not even a good mouser. One could love her for the only sufficient reason that one chose to.

Frederick's wife and Frederick's mistress have no further need of Frederick. Their *ménage à deux* thrives on poverty and ill-luck, the incongruity of their friendship, defiance of convention, defiance of the revolution even, if it gets in the way. The February revolution is nothing to Sophia, merely an affair of foreign politics, something standing between her and a decent restaurant. While the streets are in uproar, Sophia is seated on a pink sofa, wrapt in an extraordinary colloquy with Minna which lasts a whole day and leaves them bound together in a 'fathomless' intimacy. The intimacy, the unanimity of their relationship and its essentially interior nature is symbolised in the portrait which the student Dury paints of them, the title of which would serve as a description of the whole book, 'A Conversation Between Two Women'.

The conversation acquires a peculiar intensity, that of lovers, but remains veiled sexually. Lesbianism was not Sylvia Townsend Warner's theme in this book, though at points it seems implicit. What the author is glorifying in Sophia and Minna is love freed from any rationale, a sort of anarchism. Not all women who loose themselves from being 'kept'—in or out of marriage—are suddenly lesbians. Not all revolutionaries are communists, although Sophia is.

Summer Will Show is an unillusioned book, remarkable in a political novel. Idealists and exploiters of ideals are viewed in the same clear light. There is no sentimentalisation or romanticising of the cause Sophia espouses, indeed she doesn't even do anything so definite as espousing it and is not ever completely accepted by the people she chooses to help. There is no glorious revolutionary halo around the part she has to play, nor round her—we are not spared her slightly acid feelings of having been snubbed by the real revolutionaries. This is part of what makes *Summer Will Show* a really remarkable historical novel. The ordinariness of historical events, even revolutions, is conveyed intact; there is not a breath of quaintness or 'period feel' to the writing. As in Sylvia Townsend Warner's later novels, *After the Death of Don Juan*, *The Flint Anchor* and, especially, *The Corner That Held Them*, there is a complete identification with the period, a contemporary feel which goes far beyond the scope of historical accuracy to a sense of historical actuality.

Sylvia Townsend Warner had read histories and memoirs of the 1848 revolutions only to find that they differed wildly: 'Legitimists, Orleanists, Republicans all told incompatible versions of the same events, and several times didn't even agree on dates. But their prejudices made them what I needed. It was from one of these that I read how Marie-Amelie urged poor Louis-Philippe to go out and confront the mobs, adding, "Je vous benirai du haut du balcon". I reflected that this nonsense coincided with the Communist Manifesto, and this shaped the argument of the book.'* Haven't we heard this before? Not quite: 'I am slaving away at the Revolution of '48. Do you know how many books I have read and annotated in the last six weeks? Twenty-seven, old fellow, and in spite of that I have managed to write ten pages.' Flaubert and his annotations for *L'Education sentimentale* might well have intimidated another author but Sylvia Townsend Warner, having made a few admiring curtseys to the old man, succeeds in keeping his novel and hers well away from each other. There is indeed more Balzac than Flaubert evident in *Summer Will Show*.

Sophia Willoughby is in Paris from February 1848, the eve of the first uprising, the one which brought in the Provisional Government, till the second insurrection in June. It was a

*Sylvia Townsend Warner, *Letters*, p. 40.

period during which revolutionary zeal was seen to degenerate into chaos. Universal suffrage was declared, slaves freed in the colonies, but in the city Parisians starved, there was no work, only the mockery of the National Workshops which Albert, a working-class man co-opted onto the government, was called upon to organise. His only noticably successful project was to employ 12,000 men in demolishing a small hill. The provinces, impoverished and hungry after the two dreadful harvests of 1846 and 1847, were in danger of using their new votes to re-elect their former overlords, so their Government, dedicated to the will of the people, postponed all elections indefinitely. This atmosphere of compromised ideals and misfiring liberties is admirably dramatised in *Summer Will Show*; Aunt Léocadie, the Legitimist, is a glorious portrait of cautious impassivity, attending a concert in aid of the wounded revolutionaries in a carriage from which the armorial bearings have been removed, 'a tactful concession to the people whose heart was in the right place though their king, as yet, was not'. '"It is one's duty to help these poor wounded creatures"', Léocadie declares. '"Whatever their opinions they bled to free us of a tyrant. And a quantity of them were wounded by accident."' Frederick Willoughby, the non-political man who moves with the times, is reported towards the end of the book to have sided with the Bonapartists. Gaston, the fanatic who stage-manages an atro-city in February, has no place in the June revolution. Sylvia Townsend Warner presents us with a large array of types and humours in the book. The Romantic movement is not very flatteringly represented by the lachrymose Wlodomir McGusty and the soulful Dorset doctor's wife, Mrs Hervey. The new type of revolutionaries are characteristically silent and phleg-matic; the communist Martin, his sister and Ingelbrecht, the theorist of revolution, are shown to have rather grim and acid characters which seem to testify to the seriousness of their intent, the depth of their perception of the political situation. Minna Lemuel herself is part of the demonstration. Her type of revolutionary is, as Ingelbrecht points out, a thing of the past, a romantic revolutionary in a communist revolution, whose effectiveness is seen to diminish drastically during the course of the action. It is Minna's protégée, Sophia, for whom the new revolution has some use.

Summer Will Show is a novel with a strong undertow of imagery. Much of its force is poetic as much as dramatic. The first part, with its leisurely-paced opening so different in style from Sylvia Townsend Warner's earlier novels, is a *tour de force* of narrative skills and a subtle evocation of place and character. It is, I think, as good a piece of sustained writing as can be found in any of Sylvia Townsend Warner's books, the visit to the lime-kiln, the arrival of the blackamoor Caspar Rathbone and the smallpox deaths of Sophia's children leaving the strongest possible impressions, yet innocent of melodrama. Images accumulate their effect throughout the book; the chestnut trees which have lost their flowers and are 'brooding, given over to the concern of ripening their burden of fruit' are at first a symbol of maternal pride to Sophia, later an omen which she failed to recognise, and by the end of the book will take on another significance. The portrait of Sophia's grandfather, too, provides ironically flexible interpretations: 'with his gun and supple wet-nosed retriever he seemed to be watching through the endless bronze dusk of an autumnal evening, paused on the brink of his spinney and listening with contemplative pleasure to the steps of the poacher within'. The poacher seems at first to Sophia to be her husband Frederick— in the long term it proves to be Sophia herself.

With Sophia's arrival in France and, at the start of Part II, Minna's introduction into the narrative, there is a switching of tone which nicely conveys the foreignness of both Sophia's surroundings and her behaviour, which she feels now owes nothing to convention. She is unfixed, floating, and her impressions of Paris are similarly snatchy, taken in almost against her will. She arrives as a visitor, forced to negotiate the riotous streets of a foreign capital in order to find her husband, but her purpose evaporates quickly as she is drawn into another life, or rather, towards another life, for she remains throughout the book at one remove or more from what she perceives to be a different sort of existence, as when watching Minna in the mirror Sophia sees her 'as though in the innocence of a different world'. Though it is a world she cannot yet inhabit completely, Sophia's observations achieve a remarkable objectivity. She sees things just as they are. It is the clear sight of a disburdened mind:

The houses with their pale dirty faces had the vivacious appearance of town children. This one was trimmed with lemon colour, that with blue, beyond the arabesqued façade of the wineshop was the sober nut-coloured door of the watchmaker. All his clocks were ticking, but one could scarcely hear them for the song of the canaries caged in the first-floor window under the scroll saying *Midwife*. From the watch-maker's darted a very small kitten, prancing sideways on stiff legs. Sophia stooped to caress it, and noticed that attached to the tartan ribbon round its neck was a tin medal dedicating it to the care of the Virgin and Saint Joseph. But it escaped from her hand and capered on towards the butcher's shop where a woman wearing a claret-coloured shawl stood conversing with the grey-haired proprietress over whose solid bosom and heliotrope gown was tied a muffler of the brightest acid-blue.

The clear sight, the detachment of the heroine gives Sylvia Townsend Warner an ideal vehicle for observing one side of the 1848 revolutions from many angles. It is not issues she is interested in but how they affect people, and no two seem to have identical perceptions or goals. Even the communist Ingelbrecht is alone in his ideas: 'seeming to trot on some intent personal errand, true to his own laws and oblivious of all else'. This makes *Summer Will Show* an alarmingly realistic political novel. Sophia is happy with Minna and her raggle-taggle of followers, but they are not themselves happy; Minna is all too pleased to exercise a talent for theft, picking up old iron to fuel the communists' ammunitions factory, although she fears communists and hasn't given a thought to the further end of her action, 'their billet in limb or heart or brain'. Guitermann, the impoverished Jewish musician, falls victim to a galloping consumption, but we are snatched out of a graphic and terrifying description of his death by his landlady's bitter reproaches: 'Just our luck that he should move in and die! I told my man that he had paid the rent in advance but he had only paid me one-half of it . . . for us there is nothing but living. We are tough, we cannot die so easily as these artists.'

'With what desolation of the spirit one beholds the dream made flesh' says Minna as she watches the barricades go up from her balcony, and when she is bequeathed a farm in the countryside she decides not to visit it, not because of the personal danger involved—the provinces were fomenting a counter-revolution against the city—but because she doesn't want to be disappointed by it, wants it to remain her beautiful dream. It is not the dreamers, though, who survive the chaos and desperate aimlessness of the revolution when it comes, nor is there any value attached to their ideals retrospectively. Léocadie, the arch-survivor, dismisses them as a sort of aberration: '"It is people like you and me, Sophie, who have never done a day's work in our lives, who wonder, and meditate on society, and ask ourselves what good we can do in the world."' Sophia rejects this view of things and the ending of the book, though left open, is positive in tone, although this may have more to do with 1936 than with 1848. The ultimate message is a bleak one, expressed in the centre of the book in an image of the Seine: 'However much blood might flow into that river, no tincture, no composition could possibly result. Blood would not mix with that cold vein of nature. And leaning on the balustrade Sophia thought how, through every city, some river flows, bearing its witness against the human delusion.'

Claire Harman, Manchester, 1986

I

IT was on this very day—the thirteenth of July—and in just such weather that Sophia Willoughby had been taken to see the Duke of Wellington. At ten o'clock precisely the open barouche came to the door, and Sophia, who had been dressed and ready and punctual, it seemed for hours, ran down the steps to admire the turn-out. Walking stiffly, her legs well apart in order not to crumple the fluted frills of her long white muslin drawers, she had inspected the vehicle and the horses from all sides. Her scrutiny was searching, a child's exacting curiosity, sharpened and stiffened by the consciousness of being an heiress, the point advancing on the future, as it were, of that magnificent triangle in which Mr and Mrs Aspen of Blandamer House, Dorset, England, made up the other two apices.

But even under her eyes there was nothing to be found amiss. The wheels were spotless, Henry's white silk calves were blamelessly symmetrical (and that was her doing, since only two days before she had pointed out that the stuffing of his left leg extended quite an inch farther down than that of his right leg), every button winked in the sun, cockades and nosegays were spruce as they could be. Moreover, John coachman had remembered to shave the back of his neck. This array of man-flesh was highly gratifying, but it was the horse-flesh that fuelled her greatest satisfaction. The two chestnuts had never looked better. Pools of reflected light gleamed on their shining flanks with a lustre like treacle, it was a deep physical pleasure to see the veins on their close-clipped bellies, they tossed their proud heads in the air, and their snorts of well-being mingled with the fine clatter of bits.

And then Mamma and Papa had come from the house, Mamma wearing a new dress of shot silk, a bonnet with feathers, a lace scarf, and purple kid gloves. The sunlight flashed, sudden as a viper's bite, from the gold half-hunter watch opened in Papa's hand.

' Augusta, it is seven minutes past ten precisely.'

The footman arranged the shawl round Mamma's feet, shut the door, and sprang up behind ; and the barouche, with its grand freight of the Aspen triangle, rolled down the drive towards the west gate of the park.

Now, down the same drive, walked she, Sophia Willoughby of Blandamer House, Dorset, England, and the new Damian and Augusta ran before her, bowling a hoop between them. The same sun burned unconsumed overhead, and, thanks to the good forestry of Job Saunders, scarcely a tree was missing from that avenue of lime and beech whose shade had spattered the barouche party with hot and cold. 1826, 1847—twenty-one years to a day—a majority's measure.

How little the place had changed ! The drive a trifle mossier, perhaps, the trees in the park holding out a larger shade under which the sheep might gather from the sun, and this year the lime-blossom not quite so forward. But I . . . I am changed indeed from that proud and happy child, sitting between Mamma smelling of orris root and Papa smelling of Russian Eau de Cologne, and going to see the Great Duke.

And a sense of what was due to her position made her heave a sigh.

As though her thoughts had walked into the sun again, a feeling of pride and well-being swept her on from the melancholy which befitted her. Glancing from side to side she acknowledged the added richness and maturity which twenty-one years had bestowed upon her property, and her mind busied itself with the improvements which she could and should bring about before the new Damian came of age.

Further plantations, an improved breed of cows at the home farm, the lake dredged and a walk of mown grass and willow trees carried round it, the library windows enriched with coloured glass, and a more respectable tenantry—to these schemes and others time and income should be adjusted. For now the Aspen triangle was reversed, and she, the hind apex, propelled forward its front of Damian and Augusta, even as now she was propelling them towards the lime-kiln.

During the early spring they had developed whooping-cough, and the remnants of the disease still hung about them. Sophia's own whooping-cough had been dealt with by the traditional method of being dangled over a lime-kiln to inhale the fumes; she could recollect the exciting experience, and the hands of the man who had lifted her up—hard hairy hands, powdered with lime, the fingers with their broken nails meeting on her bosom under the fur-edged tippet. Her whooping-cough had come in winter, and had been a matter of a week or two. All her due childish ailments had been after that fashion: thoroughly taken, and swiftly dismissed, like the whippings which had fallen to her lot.

For all that doctors and valetudinarian ladies might say,

Sophia held by old-fashioned manners with children. Crusts, cold water, cold rooms, scanty clothing, rough romping games to harden them, philosophical conversations to enlarge their minds. She herself had been brought up under the dispensation of *Émile*, and it had answered admirably. Walking swiftly under the gashes of sunlight that striped the avenue, she smiled to think that the stables and sheepfolds and kennels of Blandamer House had not produced a more vigorous or better-trained animal than she.

She slowed her steps, turning to the children's nurse, who was already lagging behind.

' Hannah, I am positive that the lime fumes are what the children need. I only regret that we have not done it before.'

' Yes, madam. They do seem better to-day, certainly. Under Providence.'

Fool ! thought Sophia with decision. And as though her father had spoken, a voice said within her, a voice from the Regency penetrating into mid-century, ' That, my dear, is what you may expect, if you choose your maid-servants from Sunday School families.'

' I should have done it before,' she reasserted.

The system which had strengthened her childhood she had faithfully imposed upon her children, in every case of doubt consulting the practice of her father, and doing as he would have done. It was a pity (for many reasons it was a pity) that she was not a man ; for then she could have known with more assurance how Papa would have brought up a boy. Before Damian could walk he had been given a go-cart and a goat—a goat which had also supplied the nursery with milk. As soon as his legs could straddle a pony, a pony was his. But for all her care she had not yet succeeded in striking a spark of horsemanship from the boy, and he was fast turning into that most ignoble type of rider : a rider who knows how to avoid falling off. Damian had been given a miniature tool-chest, and encouraged to visit the carpenter's shop ; he had a little gun, and a fishing-rod, and a stretch of the park had been levelled into a cricket pitch, where Damian might play with the village boys ; but for all she could do, he remained childish. Nor was there any hope that the criticism or scorn of his play-fellows would spur him on to greater daring, since his peculiar charm of confidingness and affability made him an idol among those of whom she designed him to be the leader. Only last week she had met little Larkins coming up the back drive with a young owl which Master Damian had been scared to take from the nest for himself.

She commandeered the bird, and as soon as he was out of sight tossed it up into the air. Then she had sought out Damian.

' Damian ! Bill Larkins has brought your young owl. But if you cannot get a bird for yourself you cannot be fit to keep it, so I have let it go.'

The child sighed.

' O dear ! I wanted it for Sister.'

It had been difficult to turn away, so ravaging had been the sudden impulse to caress him, to bow down the lids of those clear hazel eyes with a kiss. She had to be careful not to make a pet of Damian. Every one seemed irresistibly moved to indulge and befriend him ; pliable and affectionate, he lent himself to cosseting, just as his sleek brown curls twined themselves round the fingers of any hand that rested on his head. But petting would do him no good, it would be no true kindness to the child, for soon he must go to school, and he must not go there a milksop. He should have gone this year, but Doctor Hervey said he was still too delicate. The hardening system, so admirable, so well-proved and well-accredited, so successful in her own case, did not apply so perfectly to her children. On the nursery door the notches recording her own growth from year to year were still visible; and year by year Damian and Augusta fell short of them.

The clatter of the hoop-stick had failed. Looking out from her thoughts she saw that the children played no longer. Hannah was carrying the hoop, and the boy and the girl walked staidly beside her. Their cropped hair (Augusta's hair had been cropped to make it grow more strongly) showed the hollows in their slender necks. They had sloping shoulders, both of them. Their father had just such shoulders; yet he was vigorous enough, when he liked to bestir himself. The two forward apices of the Aspen triangle looked much too much like Willoughbies, at that moment; and she was glad of the lodge gates and the road beyond. It would be hotter there, but the change of surroundings would free the current of her thoughts, fretting so uselessly round the fact of her husband.

Here, when they had been driving to see the Duke, the barouche had passed a cluster of the villagers of Blandamer Abbotts, those who, being too childish or too infirm to walk to the route along which he would pass, had gathered about the gates of Blandamer House for the minor spectacle of the Squire and his Lady and the little Miss; and as the lodge gates had swung open a shrill fragmentary cheer had been raised. Papa bowed, Mamma bowed, Sophia bowed repeatedly until Papa had bidden her not to ape grand manners. A flush of confusion at the rebuke had been submerged in the more thorough flush of being suddenly tossed out into the full heat of the sun, and Mamma had put up a sunshade. Now the sun fell upon her with the same emphasis.

Augusta said, ' I think this road was nicer when the may was in bloom.'

' Much nicer,' the boy replied. ' And look at that chestnut tree. It is quite ugly now that there are no more flowers.'

' I disdain July,' the girl remarked, with something of her mother's decision.

The chestnut trees grew at the north-west corner of the park, so massive that they completely dwarfed the heavy stone wall that bounded it. Under their bulk of foliage it shrank to the value of a wicker paling. In the July sun their green was dark and formidable. They have lost their flowers, thought Sophia. I like them better so. Her mind, clumsy at anything like a metaphor, dwelt heavy and slow on the trees, and under the shade of her straw bonnet she blinked her eyes as though dazzled. The chestnuts had outgrown their flowers, rather, and now stood up against the full strength of the summer, unbedizened, dark, castellated, brooding, given over to the concern of ripening their burden of fruit. Like me, exactly, she thought. I admire them, and I am glad to resemble them. I am done with blossoming, done with ornament and admiration. I live for my children— a good life, the life my heart would have chosen.

Out here, where the road ran among the large swelling fields, it was as though one were in a different world from that bounded by the park wall. Only an occasional hedgerow elm or elder-bush shadowed the road. The grass banks were whitened with dust, and the flowers that grew there, chalk-white milfoil, and fever-few, looked like spattered handfuls of a thicker dust. The sun flashed on the flints in the fields, the loose straws on a rick glittered like shreds of glass. It was the landscape that Sophia had known all her life long. She liked it for acquaintance' sake, but knew that it was ugly. The land was poor, its bones showed through, its long history of seed-time and harvest had starved it, it had the cowed ungainly outlines of a woman gone lean with over-much childbearing. Except for the park-lands of Blandamer House it was unwooded, and the hills where the sheep-walks lay had none of the dignity of proper hills, they were round-shouldered slouching hummocks. However, it was all familiar to her, and a considerable part of it belonged to her, and did its duty and was productive. Just as she desired a more respectable tenantry, Sophia might have desired a more suave and fertile landscape; but in the depth of her heart she knew that one was as unimprovable as the other, and the consciousness of having no illusions made her content with what she had.

Now, by a thicket of elder and dog-roses, the path that led to the lime-kiln branched off. It ran on a grassy ridge between two fields. On the one side was a crop of barley, ripening well, but poor in straw. The poppies growing among it made the green of the barley seem almost sea-blue by contrast. On the other side was a turnip field. Two men were hoeing there, their hoes ringing against the flints. As the party from the house filed along the ridge the younger of the men turned round and came towards them, pulling his forelock. The sweat stood on his burned skin, his shirt clung damply to his shoulders. Tucked in at the back of his collar was a wad of dock-leaves, wilted and discoloured.

' Good-day, madam. Good-day, little master and miss. Here's a fine day for your walk.'

The children hesitated politely, embarrassed to see such a hot man so close.

' How the little master do grow ! '

' Go on, children,' said Sophia.

So that's the excuse you make to leave off working, she thought to herself. If the children had come out with Hannah only, the rogue would have talked for half an hour. She turned to look back. The man was still standing idle ; catching her eye he pulled his forelock again, but at the persistence of her look he went back to his work.

After two more fields the path ran into the stony track that led uphill to the lime-kiln. The cleft in the hillside was filled with elder-bushes and blackthorns. The children, who had been silent in the fields, began to chatter again now that they were shaded from the sun. At intervals they coughed. Twice the party had to halt for a coughing-fit to be got over. Sophia, chafing at all this dawdling, and obliged to make some answer to Hannah's chit-chat, and grievings, and condolences, felt a rising exasperation. It was one thing to live for one's children : another to go walks with them, and converse with their nurse-maid. She pined for something decisive, for the moment when she should exercise her authority. Thankfully she stepped from the climbing track to the small grassy platform where, in a nook of the hills, the lime-kiln stood.

' But where's the man ? ' cried Hannah. ' O madam, how unfortunate if he's not here ! '

' Of course he's here. There he is.'

She called to him, and heard with pleasure her voice carry its command over the silent hillside. The man did not raise his head. He was sitting on the grass by the kiln, with his arms crossed on his knees, and his head bowed, as though he were asleep. She advanced alone across the grassy platform, and only when her shadow fell across him did he raise his head. She noticed how dilated his pupils were, and that as he rose to his feet he staggered.

' You should not fall asleep in the sun, my man.'

He raised his head and stared at her. His face twitched, he swallowed, as though his throat were too stiff for him to speak. He has been drinking overnight, she thought. However, she must make the best of him ; having got the children to the kiln she must carry out her purpose, whether this fellow were sober or no.

' I have brought my children here, to breathe the lime fumes,' she said, speaking slowly to drive the words into his head. ' Is the kiln working ? '

' Kiln be working, mum.'

She beckoned to Hannah to bring forward the children, who were hanging back, frightened. Hannah began to comfort them, and their faces grew paler.

' It won't hurt, my lamb, now don't get into a fuss. It's nothing, it will be over in a minute, it won't hurt you. I dare say you'll like the smell, and you'll be able to see inside, and all. Why, you'll quite enjoy it.'

' Children, come here.'

She seated herself on the grass, composedly, as though in smoothing her silk skirts she would allay their fears. Impressed by her dignity they stood before her, their faces stupid with heat, but docile and calm, now that they were under her spell.

'Damian, do you remember the lesson on lime in your Natural Science?'

'Yes, Mamma.'

'Then tell Augusta what you remember of it.'

Damian turned to Augusta with a company smile.

'There are two sorts of lime, Augusta. One is slacked lime, and that is dug into the fields. The other is quicklime, and that is more interesting, I think. It is hot, burning hot. Once a man who was drunk fell into a pit of quicklime, and when he was pulled out his face, his hands, everything, was burned right away.'

Augusta's mouth opened appreciatively.

'And another time a poor little cat fell in. And all its hair was burned off, and——'

'No! O Damian! Mamma!'

'You foolish baby, do you suppose I would bring you here to be hurt?'

She took the child in her arms, and held her close. With Augusta's wet eyelashes scrabbling softly against her cheek she continued,

'And, Damian, do you remember why lime is spread on the soil?'

'To kill insects, Mamma?'

'Yes, and to purify it. Lime purifies the ground, and purifies the air. That is why I had the Pond Cottages lime-washed after the fever had been there. That is why all our cow-sheds are lime-washed every six months. And that is why I have brought you and Augusta here to snuff up the fumes from this lime-kiln. The smell of the burning lime will go into your lungs, and strengthen and purify them, so that you will be cured of your coughs. Now do you understand?'

'Yes, Mamma.'

'And you, Augusta, have you understood?'

Against her neck Augusta's head nodded drowsily. She yawned, stretched herself, and sidled down into her mother's lap; in another moment she would have been asleep if a fit of coughing had not waked her.

Hannah had not listened to the lesson in Natural Science. She was fanning herself with her pocket-handkerchief, and looking with disapproval at the man of the lime-kiln, every now and then drawing in her breath and shaking her head. For he had sunk down on to the grass again, and sat in his former attitude, sprawling there, in a way that was not respectful to gentry. Stepping to his side she prodded him swiftly, and whispered,

'Can't you get up? Don't you know you're wanted?'

He answered her prod with an oath, but rose the moment after.

'You're drunk, you beast!' she whispered. But for all her scorn and reprobation, her class loyalty made her add,

'Pull yourself together, lad. Don't you know that this is Mrs Willoughby? Better not let *her* see you in this state.'

'I bain't drunk. How can I afford to be drunk before midday? But I've got a headache as would split a stone. What do they want of me?'

' She told you. You're to hold the children over the kiln, so's they can breathe it. Here! Wipe your hands on the grass and do up your shirt a bit. What's that on your wrists ? '

' Bug sores.'

Now all together they walked towards the kiln, moving slowly under the weight of the sun. To Hannah's religious mind it seemed as though they were advancing towards an altar of Moloch. Not that she had any doubts as to the rightness of the proceedings ; she also had grown up in the knowledge that lime fumes were good for whooping-cough. But the conjunction of fire, children, and this solemn advance upon the kiln made her remember Moloch. The look of the kiln, too, was ecclesiastical in a heathen way. Squarely built of stone, solidly emerging from the turf, its walls were blackened and ruddied with stains of burning ; and above the vent the fumes trembled upon the air, glassy, flickering, spiritual, as though they were rising up from the power of a mysterious altar.

They seemed to be a long time marching towards it, falling, with every slow step, deeper into its domain of heat and heavy odour. The man went in front. Following him went Sophia with a child on either side, and Hannah walked after.

' If you will stand on the steps,' said Sophia, ' we will lift the children up to you. Now, Damian, you can go first. Shut your eyes, and breathe deeply.'

Returned to earth, Damian whispered to Augusta,

' I looked.'

' What is it like ? Is it like hell ? ' she asked softly.

There was no time to hear, for now in her turn she was taken hold of, and hoisted towards the man's grasp. She gave a sudden cry, wriggled, and made her escape.

'What is it, Augusta? You are not afraid, surely? Damian was not afraid.'

The child's face was pale, but her look was less of fear than of some suspicion and bewilderment in which she was deeply absorbed.

'Mamma! I don't quite like the man. He's so queer.'

'But he's the kiln-man. His work makes him look like that.'

Her face working in an attempt to find words, the child whispered,

'It's not him that I mind. But there's something about him so very auspicious.'

At the second hoisting she made no resistance; and whether the man had overheard her or no, he knew his place well enough to show no consciousness of her words. Standing priest-like and impassive upon the steps, his head and shoulders dark against the background of trembling air, he stretched out his arms for the light burden, and Augusta was held above the opening of the kiln.

Her face, lit by the flickering fires below, wore the same bewildered and cogitative expression, and her eyes did not open for a single glance of curiosity for what was beneath.

'Why didn't you look?' enquired Damian. 'Were you afraid?'

'I forgot.'

'Miss Augusta kept her eyes shut as she was told,' improved the overhearing Hannah. 'Miss Augusta behaved properly, and God will cure her cough because she was obedient.'

Lost in her musing dream, the child stood pale and unhearing.

The man having been given the shilling for his pains, and dismissed from their world, the little party moved away, slowly and religiously as they approached. No one spoke. Sophia was the first to rouse herself. The fumes must have made us sleepy, she thought, suddenly conscious that there was something odd, something pompous and bewitched about the way they were all behaving. And she began to walk faster, and to sweep her glance this way and that over the wide view from the terrace of the hill.

At the entrance of the lane she looked back. The man was standing where they had left him, staring after them. Hannah looked back too.

' How he stares, madam ! But no wonder. He might be here year in, year out, and scarcely be visited by a soul, let alone little gentry children. He'll think of this till supper-time, I dare say.'

Sophia nodded her assent. Even as she did so, her mind glancing casually at the lot of the lime-kiln man, she received a sudden and violent impression that, however fixedly he had stared after them, and stared still, he did not really see them, and that their coming was already wiped from his mind like a dream. . . . A fancy, and she disliked fancies. . . . But even before she had time to rebuke it Damian coughed, and her thoughts were tilted back again to what was actual.

What childishness to have expected that the children would be cured of their coughs immediately. She was no wiser than a poor papist, that would hope to nail up a waxen leg or a goitre before a shrine, like dead vermin nailed up on a gamekeeper's tree. Walking ahead, listening for coughs, she began to reason herself into common sense, damping down her present fears by a reckoning of what illnesses the children had already been through, what remained for them yet to combat. It should be comforting to know how greatly the former outnumbered the latter. Damian aged nine, Augusta aged seven, might be looked upon as scarred and salted veterans in these wars of youth. It is best to get such things over early in life, every one was agreed as to that. Later on they might affect the constitution, and certainly interfered with schooling. So she might count herself lucky among mothers.

'Excuse me, madam, but the children are rather tired. I think it would be best for them to sit in the shade for a while.'

The sycamore by the gate between the two fields made a small separate world of shade in the glaring whitish landscape. In its shelter the two children stood islanded, looking out on the brightness all round as though they were looking from a fortress on some beleaguering danger. They had drawn close together, and stood in silence, their bright eyes flickering in their pale faces, their bony knees seeming years older than their thin legs. Augusta loosened her straw bonnet; as it fell back it showed her hair, plastered dark and limp on her forehead.

'Certainly, Hannah. Let us rest by all means. I expect you are tired too.'

'Oh no, madam.'

However, she retreated with alacrity to the shade of the sycamore, sat down, spread out her skirts for the children to sit on, and took out her knitting.

' Hannah, my head thumps,' said Damian.

' Never mind, dear.   It will soon be better.'

From a neighbouring field a bull blared.   The noise, so thick and shrill and dully furious, seemed the very voice of the midday heat.   It was as though the sun thrust its voice from the heavens.   The cows in the meadow went on feeding, whisking their tails against the flies that pestered them, and snatching at the herbage.   The bull blared again and again, and the cows cropped on, un-interested.   Sensible cows, thought Sophia.   She was tearing up grasses also, and mechanically stripping off the *Loves-me*, *Loves-me-not* seed-heads.   This waiting irked her, this waiting for the next cough.   She disliked sitting down in the middle of a walk, she disliked any kind of dawdling.   A slow and rigid thinker, to sit still and contemplate was an anguish to her.   Presently she jumped to her feet, saying,

' Children, I shall walk on.   You can stay here with Hannah until you have rested enough, then you can walk slowly to the end of the path.   Meanwhile, I shall have reached home, and sent the carriage to bring you the rest of the way.'

I wonder how Hannah will like listening to that bull, she thought with amusement, as she climbed the stile, and set out briskly along the grass ridge.   But the amusement faded from her mind, and with a few more steps she was teased by cares again.   Suppose the lime-kiln treatment did not work, what was she to try next ?   And presently there would be that boy from the West Indies that Uncle Julius was send-ing.   True, he would not be in the house for more than a week, but in that week a number of things might go wrong, he might tease Augusta, or corrupt Damian.   For however necessary it was to be broad-minded about negroes and half-castes, the necessity to be broad-minded about bastards was not so imperative; and now she half wished that she had not undertaken to look after the brat. Well, it was another responsibility, another care—and she straightened her shoulders, and walked more erectly, feeling herself with every step deepening her hold upon the earth that she trod upon and owned, and resolutely absorbing the rays of the down-beating sun. It was an extraordinary thing that she, who had been so strong all her life, should have given birth to two such delicate children. Nor was Frederick delicate either, though he had fussed inordinately about his health. No, the delicacy was not inherited. It was struck out in the conjunction of the parents, it was the worst, the only enduring result of that deplorable mating.

She could still hear the bull blaring—a furious monotonous cry, a wail almost, ringing through the unmoved country-side. It was Dymond's bull, she supposed, not a good beast, at any time, and ageing. Dymond must be spoken to. A place in service must be found for Topp's eldest girl, who was doing herself no good, hanging about among the farm-hands. Mamma's tomb must be scrubbed again, and a room (the red dressing-room would do) made ready for that Caspar, Gaspar, whatever the child was called. She was a landowner, and a mother, and every day there was more to do, more to oversee the doing of. Duties came out of thought, one after another, swift as bees coming out of a hive. She was a mother, and a landowner; but fortunately, she need no longer be counted among the wives.

Now she saw her hand as it had been eighteen months ago,

a hand whitened with winter and indoor living, holding the quill that moved swiftly and decisively over the paper. She could see the very look of the four pages, neatly filled with her even Italian script, and her signature, exactly filling the calculated space at the bottom of the fourth page—the four pages on which she had stated to her husband her exact reasons for wishing not to live with him again, her exact decision never to do so. She could remember everything : the look of the winter room, the fire rosy on the white marble hearth, the yellow flames of the candles she had lit, and the uncurtained window reflecting them, presenting its illusion of bright fire and sallow candle-flames alight in the dusky February garden where the evergreens bent toppling under the rainy wind. She could remember the dress she wore, the bracelet on her wrist with its staring onyx, the new scratch, raw and blatant, on the green leather of the escritoire. With a veer of wind the rain had spattered against the windows, and on that streaming surface the reflection of the fire and the candle-flames had brightened. She could re-member the smell of the sealing-wax, and the exact imprint of the seal, and the look of the letter, lying sealed, stamped, and addressed, on the summit of the other letters she had written that afternoon.

> Frederick Willoughby, Esquire.
> Hôtel de l'Étoile,
> rue Ste Anne,
> Paris.

So clear, so authentic was the recollection that walking along the road between the dusty hedgerows and the parched fields she yet had a feeling of a rainy afternoon and of the safe pleasure of being within doors by a fire. It was only what she had said that she could not remember. Out of all that letter, so swimmingly written, so clear-headedly willed, that letter which was to decide the remainder of her life, she could not remember a single phrase, a single sentence.

If I had been jealous, thought Sophia, if the last angry embers of love had smouldered in me when I wrote, I should remember my letter still. And if there had been a twinge of hope left, I should have kept a copy of it. But as it was, I wrote it as one writes a business letter, a letter dismissing a servant, or refusing an application.

Now the lodge gates had swung to behind her, and the shade of the avenue dappled her progress. I go to my house, she said to herself, alone. I rule and order it alone. And no one doubts my sufficiency, no one questions my right to live as I do. I am far safer than if I were a widow. For at my age, and in my position, I should be pestered with people wanting to marry me, I should have to live as cautiously as a girl. But now I can stand up, and extend my shade, my suzerainty, unquestioned as a tree. No cloistered fool of a nun could live freer from the onslaught of love than I, and no queen have a more absolute sway.

She turned off to the stables, to order the carriage which was to fetch Hannah and the children. While the horse was being put in she stood by, making desultory conversation with the coachman, and looking round the stable-yard. Here she had run as a child, to strut over the cobbles with her legs apart in an imitation of old Daniel, to plunge her bare arm into the bins of corn and oats, to sniff saddle-soap and the bottles of liniment and horse-medicine, to dabble in the buckets and, when no one was looking, to lick the polished metal on the harness, so cold and sleek to the tongue. Again she felt the sense of escape; for here everything was clean, bare, and sensible; there was no untidiness, and no doubt. Her horses (she did not admit it but the thought was there) were everything that her children should have been: strong, smooth-skinned, well-trained, well-bred. The texture of the muzzle searching her hand for sugar, so delicately smooth, so dry and warm and supple, satisfied something in her flesh which the kisses of her children left unappeased. To them she responded with tenderness, with pity, with conscience, with a complicated anguish of anxiety, devotion and solici-tude. Even in bending to kiss Damian the thought would spring up: *His forehead is very hot. Has he a fever?* But to this contact her own vigorous well-being could respond with an immediate and untrammelled satisfaction.

At the stroke of the stable-clock the pigeons flew off with a whirr. In a moment, even while the vibrations of the metal still hung on the midday stillness, they would fly back to the roof and sit sunning there; but she was bidden away. What next to do? Dymond's bull, Topp's girl, Mamma's tomb. . . .

Mamma's tomb came into the province of the gardener. He was in the tomato house pinching off the lesser fruits. A good servant, she thought, watching how unerringly he nipped away the poor, the imperfect, the superfluous growths. A heavy smell, spiced and pungent, flowed from the vines, and from his hands. The sun beat through the glass upon the white-washed wall, the shadows of the vines with their dangling fruits were sharply patterned. The grey-green foliage was hung with swags of orange and scarlet fruit.

' A good yield, Brewster. Better than last year, I think.'

He nodded, and said in a voice that, for all his years of service in England, retained its Scottish whine,

' There'll be too many, I'm thinking, for the house to eat them.'

He seemed to be reproaching her for living alone, for not keeping up the state which his tomatoes, his peaches, his melons and nectarines, deserved. She countered him swiftly.

' In that case, the rest can be sold.'

It might not be genteel to sell one's superfluous fruit. Neither was it genteel to live apart from one's husband. But the one and the other was sensible, was rational, was concordant with Sophia's views as to the conduct of life. Brewster had intended no reproach, she could see that now, for it was without any reservation that he began to speak of a fruiterer in Weymouth who would make a good offer. It was foolish of her to have thought that he would reproach her. She lived singularly uncriticised by her household, so calmly enforcing her will upon them that they felt themselves supported by it. Every inch of Sophia's body, tall, well-made, well-finished, her upright carriage, her direct gaze, her slow, rather loud voice and clear enunciation, warded off criticism.

' Good. Then you will see to that this afternoon, Brewster.'

' Yes, madam.'

Mamma's tomb had been troublesome from the first, owing to Mamma's odd wish that a weeping willow should be planted over it. The willow dripped, cast its leaves, and stained the white marble. Moreover, in Sophia's opinion, it looked rather silly and sentimental. It was strange how Mamma, in her two years of widowhood, had remodelled her character, on that first flood of forsaken tears sailing off into a new existence of being fashionably feeling. She had read poetry, she had read novels. She had covered pages of hot-pressed lilac paper with meditations and threnodies of her own composition, and had pressed mournful flowers between the pages. Refusing carriage exercise, she had taken to wandering about the garden in the evenings, and at her bidding an arbour had been put up, where she could sit in the dusk, catching colds and looking at the moon. When fetched indoors by Sophia, instead of knitting or embroidering, she would play the piano—not very well, since she had not touched the keys since her marriage except to play quadrilles and waltzes—but with prolonged enjoyment and great expressiveness. She became as finicking as a girl over her meals, grew thin, developed a cough, and declared on the slightest provocation her intention of dying as soon as possible of a broken heart; and after two years of this conduct she had done so, withering mysteriously, with the strongest resemblance to a snapped-off flower that could have been achieved by human suggestibility and human obstinacy.

Sophia had watched this behaviour with bewilderment, embarrassment, and disapproval. It was not new to her that people could behave like this. At her boarding-school several of the young ladies had complied with all the dictates of fashion in being romantic and sentimental, and during the short season in London in which she met and married

Frederick she had worn the prevailing mode of feeling as duly as she had worn flowers in her hair. One was foolish, and the other was messy; but while they were the mode it would have been eccentric not to make a show of compliance. Mamma had approved her demeanour, Papa, philosophically, had approved her compliance; but there had never been, at any point of the Aspen triangle, the slightest yielding of heart to these whims of behaviour and feeling. Sophia might gaze at the moon as much as she thought fit; but she gazed at it through the drawing-room windows. Sophia might visit a waterfall, or a ruin; but she must change her stockings and have some hot wine when she returned. Sophia might refuse her food, pine, burst into unexpected tears, copy poetry into albums and keep pet doves, while her marriage was being arranged and her trousseau ordered; but once married it was understood that she would put away these extravagancies and settle down into the realities of life once more.

No one had understood this more whole-heartedly than Sophia, and in the second week of her honeymoon, as she and Frederick strolled under the archway of their twelfth Rhine castle, she had come to a sudden decision to cut short their travels and return to Blandamer House, where the settling down could be more effectively put into action. Seated upon a block of crumbling masonry and prodding the earth with the tip of her parasol, she listened to Frederick reading aloud legends of robber barons and mysterious maidens. It had taken another week to move him: legends by day and roulette and the opera-house in the evening made up a life that Frederick was loth to relinquish; but at last, seated in their travelling carriage on the deck of the Channel boat, she beheld the chalk cliffs of Kent whose whiteness promised her the chalk downs of Dorset. She could not turn to her husband to express her pleasure, since he was walking up and down with his cigar; but indeed she had not needed to; her pleasure was sufficient without expression.

Already she had been quite well able to do without Frederick; and returning to her father's house, she seemed to be bringing her husband with her like one of the objects of art which she had bought on her travels. Inevitably a return to sensible real life meant a return to Blandamer. The Willoughby house, too large and traditionally splendid for the Willoughby means, was let on a long lease to a Person from the North who had made a fortune during the wars. Edward Willoughby and his wife, flourishing on the rental in London, had no mind to encourage a younger brother and his country wife to settle near by. A visit or two had shown Sophia that she was not popular with them, and hearing them speak of the Person from the North, she had suspected that to them she had seemed socially little better than he, since to a mind so elegant as Mrs Edward Willoughby's the production of military small-clothes and the ownership of an estate in the West Indies were almost equally commercial and suspect. Conscious of this, she had determined to make a country gentleman of Frederick; and since he would one day or other share with her the ownership of Blandamer, it seemed to her, and to Papa too, sufficiently conscious of that dowry of debts which Frederick had brought to the marriage, proper that her husband should begin at once to accustom himself to the life which the course of time would entail upon him.

So they had settled down. To her this process meant

arranging the west wing as their peculiar domain, teaching the servants to address her as Madam instead of Miss, holding her own with Mamma, choosing her clothes for herself, and awaiting the birth of her first child. Now, looking back upon those years, she could admit that for Frederick things might not have been so easy. Re-rooted in her old life, the more strongly settled there by the additional weight of marriage and maternity, she had watched Frederick fidget—at first watching with compunction, then with annoyance, at last with indifference. Then, scarcely noticing his absence, she had let him go again. Frederick was in Northamptonshire, staying with friends for the shooting season; Frederick was at Brighton for his health; Frederick was at Aix-les-Bains being a companion to an uncle from whom he had expectations. From these absences he would return, affable, wearing new clothes and laden with gifts, to admire the growth of his children, to exercise his riding horse, to lounge and twiddle through a spell of bad weather until he went off again. Sometimes, taking pity on his aimlessness, she would put aside her work and play a match of billiards with him ; she was a better player than he, though not so well in practice, and their rivalry under these circumstances was almost the only thing that made their relations real and living. Meanwhile Mamma ate, slept, netted, and fondled her grandchildren, and Papa, suddenly grown old, laid every day more and more of the cares of the estate upon Sophia's shoulders. In the evenings, before the tea-equipage was brought to the drawing-room, the four would play whist together, and Sophia and her father would beat Frederick and Mamma.

She was too haughty to deny herself that luxury of the

proud-minded—a sense of justice. Justice made her admit that things were not too easy for Frederick. And on the day when the growing sympathy of the neighbourhood for that poor neglected young Mrs Willoughby first penetrated the calm of Blandamer, it had been natural for her to reply that no sensible person could expect Frederick to stay perpetually tied to her apron-strings. Resenting this first waft of criticism, she had written to her husband encouraging him to prolong his stay at Aix. Frederick immediately returned. Sophia engaged lodgings in Mayfair, provided herself with clothes of the latest fashion, and took him off for a month of gaiety, leaving behind her full and exact directions of everything that should be done in the nursery, the home farm, the Sunday School and the hot-houses during her absence. With the same method and resolution she had arranged four weeks of exemplary fashion and enjoyment—dinners, balls, break-fast-drums, the races, the opera, Hyde Park and the hair-dresser; and during the first week she had as unflinchingly stormed her sister-in-law for introductions and invitations. But this had not been necessary, after all; Frederick knew already every man, woman, and head-waiter they encountered.

Filling her diary with careful accounts of everything seen, done, heard, and visited, Sophia had thought to herself, as day after day was written down and disposed of, Once back at Blandamer I can be happy and sensible again; and it was with a feeling of nearing the winning-post that she left her farewell cards, paid the bills, and dropped kid gloves and bon-bon boxes into the waste-paper basket.

That visit to London had done much to stay local criticism.

The pity due to a neglected wife faltered before the aspect of such a fashionably dressed young woman who had heard Grisi and seen Vestris. But the excursion, so well calculated to circumvent the doubts of others, had done as much, or more, to breed uneasiness in herself. Heretofore an absent Frederick had been a shadowy creature, a something dismissed to wander in exile from the real life and centre of life at Blandamer, to drink watered milk and eat stale vegetables, breathe bad air, and keep unhealthy hours. Now the place of this spectre was taken by the Frederick she had seen in London, a Frederick popular, sought-after, light-hearted, affable, open-handed and probably open-hearted—her satellite of Blandamer changed to a separate and self-lit star.

A weaker or an idler woman might have been jealous; a woman in love would certainly have been so. Indifference and responsibility preserved her from any sharper pang than annoyance, and the grim admission that the current opinion as to her pitiable state must be, in the eyes of the world, well-founded. Papa's death, the growth and illnesses of her children, the cholera, the potato disease, and Mamma's strange florescence of widowhood distracted her attention from the increasing frequency and length of her husband's absences, his uneasy behaviour, half-frivolous, and half-servile, when he was with her. Even when she knew for certain that he had been many times unfaithful to her, and was again neck-deep in an adultery, she was not jealous. She was furious.

Her fury had been intensified by his choice of a woman.

For even to Dorset the name of Minna Lemuel had made its way. Had the husband of Mrs Willoughby chosen with no other end than to be scandalous, he could not have chosen better. A byword, half actress, half strumpet; a Jewess; a nonsensical creature bedizened with airs of prophecy, who trailed across Europe with a tag-rag of poets, revolutionaries, musicians and circus-riders snuffing at her heels, like an escaped bitch with a procession of mongrels after her; and ugly; and old, as old as Frederick or older—this was the woman whom Frederick had elected to fall in love with, joining in the tag-rag procession, and not even king in that outrageous court, not even able to dismiss the mongrels, and take the creature into keeping.

Her fury lasted still. Walking swiftly and heedlessly, she had made her way from the tomato house to the park. And now she stood under the wasp-droning shade of a lime tree with a dozen sheep staring at her. The leader moved a step nearer, the others shuffled after it. She must have been here a long while for their timid curiosity to have brought them so close. If I were to speak as I feel, she thought, eyeing them sardonically, how you would scatter! She kept silence, silent as she had been from the moment she first heard the news, scornfully silent before the sheepishness of mankind. For all that any one knew Mrs Willoughby was still patiently and unresentfully awaiting her husband's return from the Continent.

It was fortunate that Mamma's death had taken place when it did—before Sophia's discovery of Minna Lemuel. Mamma —a rather stupid and trifling woman, the slave of her grand-children, the gull of any village slut who chose to wear a tattered bodice and lose a husband, amply deceived by her son-in-law, and constantly buying tender greenhouse rarities which turned out to be chickweed—had yet been able to

keep her daughter almost in awe by a power of reading the
most carefully concealed thoughts.   From the moment when
Sophia had first suspected Frederick, Mamma had known of
it; and though not a word had been spoken, Sophia was
made aware of Mamma's knowledge.   For a shawl had been
handed like a shelter ;   a ' Thank you, my dear,' at the passing
of a cup of tea had murmured : ' My poor forsaken child, I
know all, and feel for you as only a mother can ' ;   a second
glass of port accepted with, ' Well, Sophia, since you insist,'
had said : ' But you always were headstrong.'   And day by
day Sophia had felt herself more like some strong rustic
animal entangled in a net.   The net was never drawn close.
She had but to stamp or bellow a little, and it shrank to the
silken twist of Mamma's netting, which had again trailed off
that black silk lap and needed to be picked up.   With the
rather pompous disapproval of a strong character, Sophia
deplored her mother's feminine intuition.   It was too subtle,
it was the insight of a slave.   Exercised upon her childhood
it had fostered her with subtle attentions, gratifying her wishes
before she herself was aware of them.   But slaves, it is well
known, make the most admirable attendants to young
children.

So it was a good thing that Mamma had died, her silken
net sinking into the grave after her as a dead leaf is drawn
under the mould by earthworms, before the first, the only
and final rupture with Frederick.   Even after the funeral
Sophia had walked cautiously, suspecting the net might be
trailing still, that, put away among gloves, or her own baby
clothes, or in letter-case or jewel-case, she might find a letter
from Mamma, saying what only impregnable death would

give her the daring to say, condoling or counselling. Such a letter, and most of all, a letter of counsel, was a thing to dread. For Sophia respected death, that final and heavily material power, as greatly as she despised finesse and feminine intuition; and however little the living mother had been honoured, the dead mother was another matter. But there was nothing either of sympathy or counsel. Mamma had betaken herself bag and baggage to the grave, even the lilac-paged albums were inscribed: To be Burned Unread after my Death. Nothing had been left over except a packet of letters that slipped through the lining of an old dressing-case, letters written by Mamma to Papa shortly before their marriage. Sophia had read them, a little guiltily, carrying them to the stale window-light of the winter dusk, for to light candles would have illuminated the act into an impropriety. But she had not read long. They were cold and insipid, reading them was like eating jelly.

The sheep were within a hand's-breadth now, and her fury had died down. She was glad. She had no wish to feel anger when anger was so unavailing. Of the two moods possible to her, such rage, and the icy disdain in which her letter to Frederick had been written, she preferred disdain. It was more dignified, and it allowed her to get on with her work. For now all her passion of life should be poured into what she had to do: bring up her children, order the house and the estate, govern the village. That should be enough, surely, for any woman who had outgrown her follies; and cool enough now to smile at herself, she considered what small half-hearted follies hers had been. For though while Frederick was wooing her she had been quite thoroughly and properly in love with him, from the day of the marriage she had known without illusion what lay before her : respectable married life with its ordered contacts and separations, the attentive acceptance that a married woman should feel for a man who must be made allowances for, a man much like other men—a compromise that one might hope would in time solidify into something positive and convenient. Nor, from these soberly chilling ashes, had the sudden explosion even of Minna Lemuel raised up a flame of that folly of loving too well. It was not that Frederick had ceased to love her, but that he should love such a one as Minna, that had tormented her, and must be at intervals her torment still.

Over her luncheon of cold chicken and claret, Sophia found herself pondering the conduct of Uncle Julius Rathbone with unexpected approval. Julius Rathbone was her father's half-brother. At her father's death she had, so to speak, inherited him, and with the inheritance had come something of Papa's masculine tolerance. Julius was part-owner and manager of the estate in the West Indies which supplied the Aspen wealth; and twice a year or so he sent large consignments of guava jelly, molasses, preserved pineapple, and rum. These were for general family consumption, and so were the portraits of his elegant sharp-nosed wife and his three plain daughters. Other consignments were of a kind more confidential— accounts of his scrapes, financial and amatory; and now he was entrusting to Sophia his illegitimate son, a half-caste. '*He is now fourteen years old*,' wrote Uncle Julius, '*and I do not want him to get false ideas into his head. I should be very grateful if you could place him in some moderate establishment where he could receive a sound commercial education.*' Then,

as though with a waving of the hand, the letter had turned
to a more detailed account of the guava jellies, etc., which
would accompany the boy across the Atlantic, and ended with
' *your dear Aunt, as usual, sends her fondest love, and so do the
Girls.*'

It was scarcely a matter in which she could consult with
people of her own standing, even had she felt inclined to do
so. She told her solicitor to advertise the requirements, and
send the answers to her. They came in hundreds, it seemed
as though England's chief industry was keeping boarding-
schools where religion and tuition had united to put into the
heads of bastards all the suitable ideas and no false ones.
Most of the prospectuses came from Yorkshire, but finally
she settled upon a school in Cornwall; and though Uncle
Julius had begged her not to put herself out in any way,
Sophia could do nothing without becoming conscientious
and determined to do it thoroughly, so workmanly pride as
well as humaner considerations made her travel to Cornwall
to inspect the Trebennick Academy. It was a tall house
standing alone on a sweep of moorland, having on one side
of it a lean garden filled with cabbages. The moorland
sloped to a valley, and on the opposite slope, against the sky-
line, was a prick-eared church with a well-filled graveyard.
She saw the Trebennick Academy on an April afternoon, but
unless a gardener's eye were to find it in the condition of the
cabbages, there was no sign of spring in the landscape. Stones
of various sizes were tumbled over the moor, rusty bracken
was plastered against them by the winter's rain, and a fine
mist limpened the folds of her pelisse and bloomed her gloves.
The air was such as she had never smelt before, very fresh and

smelling of earth. Her first impression was one of distaste, almost of fear; and that evening, coughing over the peat-fire of the Half Moon Inn, she all but decided against the Trebennick Academy. Yet on the morrow, smelling again that fresh, earth-scented air, she found herself queerly in love with the place, and reluctant to leave it so slightly tasted, as when a child she had felt reluctant to leave, half-eaten, some pot of stolen jam.

There was no doubt that, in some unsuspected way, she could have been very happy at Trebennick. That air, so pure and earthy, absolved one back into animal, washed off all recollection of responsibilities; one waft of wind there would blow away the cares from one's mind, the petticoats from one's legs, demolish all the muffle of imposed personality loaded upon one by other people, leaving one free, swift, un-burdened as a fox. At intervals during the summer Sophia had found herself betrayed by fancy into Cornwall, and lead-ing there a wild romantic life in which, unsexed and un-personed, she rode, sat in inns, slept in a bracken bed among the rocks, bathed naked in swift-running brooks, knocked people down, outwitted shadowy enemies, poached one night with gipsies, in another went a keeper's round with a gun under her arm. Out of these rhapsodies she would fall as suddenly as she had fallen into them, and without a moment's pause go on with what she was doing: a memorandum for the bailiff, a letter to the dressmaker, the paper boat her hands had been folding and fastening for Augusta to sail on the pond. In a space no longer than it takes to open one's eyes she was back in her accustomed life, in a leap was transferred to daylight from darkness. And yet, as by the mere closing

of eyelids, one can surmise a darkness stranger than any star
has pierced, a darkness of no light which only the blind can
truly possess, she knew that by a moment's flick of the mind
she could levant into a personal darkness, an unknown aspect
of Sophia as truly hers as one may call the mysterious shelter-
ing darkness of one's eyelid one's own.

However well a life in Cornwall might suit her (not,
though, that it was a life that the real and waking Sophia
could anywhere find), seeing Caspar she doubted if the
Trebennick Academy could possibly do for him. She had
arranged her mind before his coming, telling herself that
black blood is stronger than that of the white races, that the
boy would bear little or no resemblance to Julius, and might
well be no more than a woolly negro. But the boy who
stepped from the carriage and walked towards her up the
sunlit steps might have come, not from any surmisable
country, but from a star, and before his extreme beauty
and grace she felt her mouth opening like that of any
bumpkin.

Could this beauty be for her sight alone? She heard a
servant whisper, 'What a little blackamoor!' Fools! she
said to herself; and like one with something at stake she
awaited the moment when her children should be introduced
to the newcomer.

The minds of Damian and Augusta had also been arranged
beforehand. They had been told something of the colour
question, and of the rational humanitarianism which forbids
that any race should toil as slaves when they would toil more
readily as servants; they had been told, more practically, not
to stare and not to be shy. They had also been told (though

the question of bastardy had been left undiscussed) not to be too familiar.

Augusta's conduct was all that could have been asked of her. She had come forward prettily, said her greetings, held out her hand, glanced with her blue eyes as though they beheld nothing out of the ordinary. Damian had both stared and been shy, but his conduct had better pleased his mother. It was obvious that the arrival of this dusky piece of romance had stirred him deeply; and Sophia found herself moved towards her son not as a child but as a companion. His admiration corroborated hers, sanctioned it almost; she was knit to Damian, not by the common bond that tethers a mother to her child, but by the first intimation of that stronger link that time might forge, the close tremulous excited dependence of the woman upon the male she has brought forth. Flying out into the future, launched there the faster by the weighted impetus of her practical character, she decided that Caspar must be present, and honoured, too, at Damian's coming of age.

Meanwhile the two boys were walking across the lawn, Damian a little stiffly holding the newcomer's hand.

Augusta's carefully adjusted sigh intimated that she wished to receive attention.

'How do you like Caspar? Do you think you will be friends with him?'

'I like him very much. Is he a heathen?'

'No, of course not.'

'Oh!'

Regret was implied.

'Did you want him to be a heathen, Augusta?'

'No, not exactly.   But if he had been I had a plan, that's all.'

'To convert him ? '

Sophia's voice had gone a little dry.   Once again Papa's
cool shade had neared her, remarking on what one might
expect if one chose the nurse for respectable piety.   Religion
was all very well, and a certain amount of it was necessary,
no doubt, if only to comply with custom.   Papa himself
would have been the first to agree to that.   But Sophia did
not wish her children to be too religious.   Untimely piety,
not only in story-books, allured untimely deaths.

'No.'

'Why did you want him to be a heathen, then, my
darling ? '

Augusta did not answer.   She fidgeted, and stared across
the lawn.   Suddenly she began to cry.

'My love, my little one, what is it ?   What is the matter ?
Don't you feel well ? '

'Mamma, Mamma !   Don't let us ever go to that place
again.'

'The lime-kiln ? '

There was no doubt in Sophia's mind as to what place
Augusta meant.   The child's long shudders vibrated against
her bosom, this life she encompassed with her anxious arms
was separate and inarticulate to her as an animal's, it was
as though the fiddle should suddenly take a personal life
upon it, wailing against the player's shoulder.

'Of course we won't go there again if it frightens you.
There will be no need to go.   Your cough is almost cured,
isn't it ? '

Though a child be born, nursed, the creature and study

of endless nourishing days, she thought, it is never one's
own to understand. Its every movement bruises one, is as
terrifying and incomprehensible as the first movement in the
womb, as alien as that first announcement of a separate life.
And as though it were her own mysterious pain she rocked
and comforted, Sophia rocked and comforted her child. Her
mind, despairingly detached from her emotions, surveyed the
lawn before her, noticed that a bough had withered on the
copper beech and must be lopped off, wondered when
Damian and Caspar would come in sight again, beheld
Caspar's little trunk being lifted from the carriage, recol-
lected the list of clothes that were considered necessary by
the Trebennick Academy, revised her own supplementary
list, and wondered again if it would be right to send the boy
there. But if one cannot understand even one's own children,
how hope to judge best for the bastard of one's half-uncle
and some unknown quadroon, passionate and servile, her
gold ear-rings swinging proudly, and the marks of the lash
maybe on her back ?

And how hope, her thought went on, to trace or elicit the
connection in Augusta's mind between Caspar being a heathen
and the visit to the lime-kiln ? No, no, distraction was the
only hope : to be busy, to do the next thing, and the next
thing. And already Damian and the half-caste were in sight,
and the child in her arms wept no longer.

During the week that Caspar stayed at Blandamer the
household disapprobation hardened, and behind it, rearing
up like a range of further mountains, ice-summits of the neigh-
bourhood's disapproval disclosed themselves. That the child
should be viewed askance because he was coloured and a

stranger was no more than natural; but he had more than that to call down wrath. He was not more black than vivid, not more of a stranger than of a phoenix.

Every one who came in contact with him—and no one could keep away—must need call out some achievement, as people prod monkeys at a fair; and then, angered by the brilliant response, sulk, grumble, and belittle it. The boy could ride. The groom took him from Damian's pony, mounted him on the bay mare and set him at a jump. Over and over the boy went, and cantering back, slid off the excited beast like a silk shawl dropping to the ground. Roger went off snarling and talking of circus-riders. Mr Foscot, the curate of the next parish, who came once a week when the weather was fine to give Damian swimming lessons, challenged the visitor to dive. From the first plunge Caspar came up discoloured and quivering, his body aghast at the chilly lake-water; but for all that, being anxious to please, and vain, he dived repeatedly, and in swimming outstripped the curate, looking back from the end of the course, his chattering teeth displayed in a smile of pleasure at having done well. Mr Foscot praised him duly; but also admonished him against staying in the water too long, since to do so would be bad for Damian and inconsiderate.

Mr Harwood, the rector, also noticed the boy, enquiring if he knew his catechism. Caspar had never heard of the catechism. 'I don't know what Church he belongs to,' Sophia had interposed, coldly. Mr Harwood was well enough in his proper place, in his restored Gothic, cushioned by her supplies of red felt and green velvet; and admirable in the parish; but this interview took place in her dining-room.

'I am a Protestant, please.'

'Then you should know your catechism, my boy.'

Damian only was privy to what followed. Not till later in Caspar's visit did Sophia hear how, having borrowed Damian's Prayer Book and learned the catechism by heart, adding several collects as a gratuity, Caspar, accompanied by Damian, called upon Mr Harwood and insisted upon a hearing.

'Very glib, remarkable quickness,' the rector had added, telling this story. 'But such facility—I expect, Mrs Willoughby, that you share my opinion—is not altogether desirable. Light come, light go, you know.'

Seeing her frown he added that he preferred Damian's type of mind. But even this sop did not appease Sophia ; and with irony she amused herself by taking the old man to the conservatory and picking him a bouquet of her gaudiest and most delicate tropical plants. 'I am afraid these are all I can offer you,' she said. 'There are no violets left.' But, delighted and admiring, he did not perceive the insinuation.

With the same shortsighted partisanship all the household set themselves to match one boy against the other. And Caspar was always the readier, the more agile, the more daring. Each new feat increased their bile against him. They seemed bent on calling out his best in order to trample on it.

But Damian showed only the purest delight in the successes of the elder boy, and if Caspar had had no other gifts his music would have been enough to birdlime the English child. He had brought a small beribboned guitar on which he accompanied his ditties, singing in a thrilling oversweet treble, forgetful of himself, as a bird sings, his slender fingers clawing the wires with the pattering agility of a bird's footing. He sang every evening, sitting on the terrace, his head leaning against the balustrade, his eyes half-closed, singing hymns and love-songs and melancholy negro rants, his fingers pattering over the dry wires. And Damian, like an entranced dog, would sit as close as possible, his lips moving with the singer's, his whole being rapt and intent. Sophia lacked the instinct of music, Caspar's songs were apt to be particularly irritating to her since she could not understand the words. But she was glad to make one of the music party, soothed by the sight of her child's pleasure, caressed by the outer wave-lengths of a world into which she could not enter; and while the music lasted she would stay, gazing at the picture the children made—the picture of two white cherubs and a black.

Often she told herself that it was impossible to dismiss this being to the Trebennick Academy. Yet she did nothing. With Caspar's coming something came into her life which supplanted all her disciplined and voluntary efficiency, a kind of unbinding spell which worked upon her lullingly as the scent of some opiate flower. His beauty—a bloom of youth and of youth only—his character, so pliable, sweet and shallow, and the wide-open flattery which he gave to her, all worked her into a holiday frame of mind. It was not possible, while Caspar was in the house, to do anything but enjoy: enjoy the ample summer weather, the smooth striped lawns over which they strolled, the waving of the full-flourished boughs, the baskets of warm raspberries, the clematis pattern of stars, the smooth-running gait of her household, the sweet cry of one crystal dish jarred against another, the duskier bloom coming upon the outdoor peaches along the south wall, her children's laughter, the cool amethysts she clasped about her neck. Seeing Caspar unharmed by slights and snubs, she troubled herself no more about them; and the sense of being superior to such foolish things heightened her pleasure, seeming to make her move more grandly and freely above their pettiness, as though she were invulnerable as one of those vast white clouds that ambled so nobly overhead. It was all a dream, it could not last, soon her anxious days would repossess her—and surely Augusta had a little snuffle, one sneeze would bring down this enchanted world about her ears; but till the sneeze, till the crash, she would lie basking, trouble herself about that place in Cornwall no more than Caspar troubled himself.

So, doing nothing, too deep in living for action, she swam through the week of the visit until its last day. Then her warm world was rent away from her by a sudden outcry of anger from Damian. The three were playing on the lawn, and she jumped up and ran through the opened french window, alert with anger at this threat to her content, furious and ready to pounce. Like a hawk she was on them. Augusta was in tears, Damian was pulling her hair. She heard the half-caste implore, his voice urgent with fear. ' Don't be angry, don't quarrel, loveys. Oh, don't ! '

' What's all this ? '

They were silent, Augusta checking her tears with surprise at the sudden onslaught.

' Caspar ! Were you teasing them ? Is this your fault ? ' He shook his head despairingly.

' What has happened ? '

Still he did not answer, wringing his small hands and casting deploring looks from one child to the other. Then Augusta began to weep again.

'Horrid Damian, hateful boy! You are a bad brother, you hurt me.'

'Hold your tongue, silly!'

'You did hurt me, you did, you did! You pulled my hair, and it's given me a headache, and you aren't sorry in the least, for you didn't stop, even when Caspar begged you. Caspar is a fool. He ought to have knocked you down. But he can do nothing, he can only play his silly guitar.'

She turned to the half-caste, and tried to make a face at him, but more tears ruined the attempt. He had come towards her on his knees, and with a cry of sympathy began to stroke the jangled curls.

'Go away! I don't want you. You're *black*!'

'Augusta!'

But before the word was out of Sophia's mouth Damian hurled himself upon his sister, scratching and buffeting her.

'How dare you, Augusta, how dare you? I'll kill you for that. Caspar is my friend, and he isn't black, and I'll kill you for saying so.'

'Black, black! He is black. A blackamoor! And he's not a proper boy either, he's only a bastard. Harlowe said so. I heard her. A black bastard, that's all your Caspar is.'

She railed out of the tumult of Damian's assault, her cropped hair tangled over her face, wet with spittle, a furious fighting mane, which she shook over her flushed cheeks. A long scratch leaped out on her arm, and began to bleed. Damian thrust his face against hers, snarling, speechless with rage.

It was all Sophia could do to unclench their combat. Raging herself, locked into a stone of anger, she hauled them towards the house.

'Kneel down,' she commanded, trembling with fury, forcing them down with hands that were like stone against their slight shaken flesh. 'Stay there and quiet yourselves.'

After that struggle under the midday sun the shaded air of her sitting-room was cold as a tomb. She trembled as she sat down behind her desk, entrenching herself as against two savage animals. Presently she took her Commonplace Book, and began turning over the pages. The children knelt quietly now, subdued by the austere cool of the shaded room. Under her lashes she saw that they had begun to exchange glances, allied again, now that they had her wrath to look forward to.

'Listen.

'*On Tuesday last, Samuel Turvey, a boy of nine years of age, apprentice to a chimney-sweep, was suffocated in the chimney of a house at Worksop. His master declares that the boy, having gone a little way up the chimney, called down that he was wedged, and could go no further. As he had shown sullenness before, and refused other chimneys, a fire of damp straw was kindled on the hearth, in order that he might be obliged to mount. He still expostulated, though he was heard attempting to go further. To the horror of those present, his body then fell to the hearth, he having been rendered unconscious by the smoke, and loosing his hold.*

Plucked from the fire he was discovered to be badly burned,
and died the same day in the workhouse infirmary.'

She read coldly and slowly. After a pause she asked,

' Do you understand that ? '

' Yes, Mamma.'

' Would you like to be a chimney-sweep ? '

' No, Mamma.'

The boy's answer was mechanical. He knelt and trembled,
his face was ashen, every now and then it quivered. Her
words had fallen on ears almost deaf, he was still absorbed
in the bodily aftermath of the quarrel. Augusta cried out,

' What a horrible wicked man ! '

' He had his living to make. And chimneys have to be
swept. And some chimneys are so built that a brush cannot
be put up them, so a boy must go instead. Only it happens
that I am rich, and so such things do not happen to you or
your brother.'

It was difficult to speak. Her own wrath still kept her
throat clenched, her tongue heavy. Her hand trembled,
clattering the paper of the book. She laid it aside, and hid
the shaking hands in the folds of her shawl. Outside,
shrunken in the violent sunlight, she could see Caspar,
standing where they had left him, staring at his shadow with
hanging head. The gardener's boy was shearing the edges
of the lawn, glancing sometimes over his shoulder at the
half-caste, eyeing him with a complacent gulping grin as
though the child were a penny spectacle at a fair.

' On just such a morning as this, some unfortunate child
has been driven up a dark chimney. And you—you can find
nothing better to do than quarrel like wild beasts. Worse !

For no animal quarrels without reason, for food, or for supremacy. Be ashamed of yourselves. Now, get up. Go to Hannah, and tell her to put you both to bed, and to draw the blinds. There you shall spend the rest of the day.'

They glanced at each other, as though consulting, and rose. Lagging, they moved towards the door. Then Damian turned back.

' But Caspar. I must say good-bye to him.'

' No.'

An hour later Hannah came to say that the boy was still weeping. Sophia shook her head. A profound disgust and weariness held her back from yielding.

' But I am afraid it will make him ill, madam. He does take on so. Now Miss Augusta—she's asleep.'

Sophia shook away the plea. He is always ill, she thought, bitterly impatient ; and going to the medicine chest she mixed a sedative. Hannah carried it off, divided in her mind between pity for her nursling and gratification at any sundrance between the white child and the coloured.

The table was laid for two, and during luncheon Sophia kept the conversation upon the Trebennick Academy. Still locked in cold rage, she spoke to Caspar severely and practically, explaining that if he wished to gain favour with his teachers and fellows it would not do to play the guitar, dance or sing. The carriage appeared before the windows, the small luggage was loaded on, it was time to start. In the hall the boy hesitated, looked round questioningly. ' Your cousins are in disgrace,' she said, and he followed her submissively, hanging his head.

During the journey she spoke little, thought little, still

brooding furiously over the morning's incident. Arriving at
Exeter, naked there of the dignity which clothed her on the
platform of her own railway station, she was for a moment
aware of herself as a spectacle: an English lady travelling
with a little black boy. Her mind waved a grim acknow-
ledgment towards Uncle Julius Rathbone, who managed the
affairs of his heart so competently. At St Austell the railway
ceased, for the rest of the journey they must drive. They
drove in a small closed waggonette, cold as the tomb. It
was strange to look out of this mouldy box and see the
blazing landscape through which they moved. Armies of
ravelled late-summer foxgloves grew beside the stone walls;
as the day wore on their purple turned melancholy and dis-
coloured against the hues of a flaming sunset. She leaned
her head out of the window, interrogating the air, searching
for the romance of her previous visit. It was there still, but
the long summer's warmth had changed it, and now it was
turned from an excitement to a menace. With something
like fear she felt that her body was heavy, her mind slow, that
she was strong and helpless as a stone, strong only to be
trampled on and to endure. The boy beside her, so quick,
so vulnerable, was better equipped for life than she. Now
she would have been glad to talk to him, would have clutched
at any expedient which might carry her away from this
obsession of being cold and heavy and helpless; but he was
listless, half-asleep, and doleful, gone crumpled and dead as
suddenly as a tropical blossom.

' Here is Caspar Rathbone,' she said at last, standing before
the smouldering peat-fire which seemed to be identical with
the fire she had noticed on Mr Gulliver's hearth six months

ago. She had done her errand, now she could say good-bye, drive back to the Half Moon, fall exhausted into the strange uncomfortable bed. It was all something done by rote, done before and quite unreal. As she looked back from the waggonette, and saw that Caspar had already been swallowed up by the Trebennick Academy, the sense of doom and pre-destination which had, all the journey long, rested so leaden upon her sharpened suddenly into the thought: *The child will die there. I shall never see him again.* But this a moment after she drove out as sentiment; and she knew also that, even without this expunging explanation, she could not, for the life of her, have turned back then to rescue him, or to make any attempt to turn destiny aside, so deeply had this hallucination of puppetry and rote enforced itself upon her.

Shivering and stupefied, she sat alone in the dining-parlour of the Half Moon Inn, unable to eat the food set down before her. ' I believe I am going to be ill,' she said to herself; and rousing, she ordered a glass of hot brandy-and-water. It was cold before she remembered to drink it; and having drunk it she sat on, staring at a glass picture of Britannia, and a bunch of dying foxgloves in a white jug, sat until a tap on the door aroused her as though with a thunder-clap, and the landlady came in, awkward and timid, to say that it was past midnight, and would the lady be sitting up much longer.

Almost the next thing that she knew was another tap, which roused her to morning, and the recollection that of the day's two eastward trains from St Austell she was catching the earlier. The boxlike waggonette was waiting for her, it had spent the night at Trebennick also, the same ravelled foxgloves awaited her along the hilly winding roads. But yesterday's cloud had evaporated. With renewed delight she smelt the exciting soulless air, and watched the shaggy contours of the hills. She was in Cornwall, unknown, and without responsibilities. Her body rejoiced and grew impatient, chafing at the joggling waggonette; and telling the man he should spare his horse she alighted, and walked up a hill. The rough road underfoot delighted her, the dust flew up like an incense, the light of morning seemed spilled on the lonely country for her alone. At St Austell she paid off the man, and saw her dressing-case put in the office. She would travel by the later train. It would harm neither man-flesh nor horse-flesh to make two journeys to the station. Thence she went on to a tobacconist, and bought some cheroots. She had four hours to spend, four hours in which her soul could be at liberty.

Any road would do, and the road she chose took her out of the town, and past a slated farmhouse under a group of sycamores, and over a suddenly humped stone bridge. The stream was small, brilliant and swift-running; she left the road and followed it through the steep small fields towards a dome of rough moorland. Here, scrambling over the last stone wall, she sat down in the sun, settled herself against an outcrop of granite, and lay basking, stripping bracken fronds between her fingers, and listening to the chatter of the brook. Its waters were exquisitely cold and sweet. She drank, at first from her hand, then, stretching herself along the warm turf, from the stream itself, where the water arched, glassy and smooth, over a rock. It ran so strongly that at the first essay she plunged her mouth too deeply into the flow, and spattered her face and hair. She was hungry now, and glad of the parcel of sandwiches put up by the Half Moon Inn. Then she took out a cheroot, lit it, and began to smoke. It was not such a good cheroot as those she had stolen, long ago, from Papa's cabinet. But it was passable, and had this advantage over the others, that she would not be whipped for it.

The cheroot was half finished when a company of gipsies crossed the shoulder of the moor, not seeing her in her shelter of rock and fern. They loped along in single file, picking their way over the waste as though they followed a scent. They were at home in the landscape like animals. Yet though I should like to stay here for ever, she thought, spreading out her palms to feel the sun, I should never want to be a gipsy. But I would build a house here, no larger than that ruined cottage I passed, live alone, and do everything for myself. Perhaps a woman coming in to do the cooking and make the bed. But everything else I would do, and at night sit by a fire of wood that I had chopped myself. Her mind went back to the hours she had spent with old Saunders, the estate woodman, and to the day when, suddenly yielding to her persuasions, he had allowed her to fell a tree. The noise of the axe chiming through the silent plantation was in her ears, and the cry and harsh rustle of the falling tree. That afternoon her parents had given a dinner-party, and she had been allowed to sit with the ladies in the drawing-room, pulling the silk mittens over her blistered palms, thinking to herself, To-day I felled a tree. Saunders, no wonder, had kept his own counsel, and no one else had ever known. Now she went the round of her woods with young Saunders, nodding her agreement as he chalked the trees due for felling ;

but still her glance could find the mossy hollow whence the root of her tree had been stubbed out. 'For it is my own mark I want to leave,' she exclaimed, striking her hand against the rock. 'Not always to work my will through others.'

She had still more than an hour of liberty before she must remember the second train and walk back; yet already a liberty in which she had nothing to do was irksome to her. Should she walk further, paddle her feet in the stream? The one was pointless, the other childish. It was boring to be a woman, nothing that one did had any meat in it. And her peculiar freedom, well-incomed, dis-husbanded, seemed now only to increase the impotence of her life. Free as she might be to do as she pleased, all her doings were barrened. Should she have her horse saddled in the middle of the night, ride through the dark and the rough weather till morning, she rode to no end. Should she enforce her will over convention, go out into her woods and cut down another tree, the deed would only be granted to her on the terms that it was a woman's whim, a nonsense to be tidied up as soon as possible by the responsible part of the world. If she were to shoot a poacher, the Justices of the Peace would huddle it away as an accident. Yes, they would say that she was frightened, a timid female acting in fear of her life. She could do nothing out of doors, a woman's sphere was the home. Yet there, what could she do to appease her desire to leave a mark? The cook made the jams, which anyhow were eaten by the following summer, she had no talent for painting in watercolours, and certainly she could not write a novel. Needlework and embroidery? Often her long-ing had turned to these, and fingering the quilts and bed-hangings worked by the bygone women of her race she had most passionately envied them their power to leave behind them something solid and respectable, envied them the solace which could accompany them through the long idleness of a woman's life. Her bureaux were filled with beginnings: lace-pillows with rusty pins, crumpled canvases with half a parrot's wing embroidered; but her hands, so strong and shapely, could not manage a needle, bungled and grew weak before their natural employment.

In thoughts like these her last hour of liberty trailed by, and at last she was glad to get up, shake out her skirts, tie on her bonnet and go. The stream kept her company down the valley, an idle influence, turning no mill-wheels, running happily to waste. She had drunk of it; but she could not drink of its brilliant peace.

During the journey she stared sometimes at the landscape through the mesh of her veil, sometimes at the mesh itself, eyeing this needle-run entanglement as though it were something alien and inexplicable, a puzzle set before her in a dream. At Exeter a young woman got into the carriage who carried a baby and was in tears. As soon as the train started she broke into conversation. Her talk was perfectly insipid, alternately self-pity and brag, and Sophia found herself listening with pleasure, glad of any distraction from her own thoughts. For any forward thinking travelled only to boredom, and she would not let her thoughts turn backward, lest they should recall the events of yesterday, the iron sense of doom which had so oppressed her, that terrifying evening at the Half Moon Inn.

Mrs Henry Woolby, daughter of the late Canon Pawsey,

lasted till Dorchester, where Sophia got out, hearing as she did so that life was so cruelly full of partings, and that Mrs Woolby's address was 7 Marine Terrace, Dawlish.

Her groom was beside her, holding the dressing-case. She turned to give him her ticket.

' Good-evening, Roger. Is all well ? '

She heard him catch his breath, and now looked at him. His face was flushed, she thought he had been drinking.

. ' Master Damian, madam, and Miss Augusta. They're queer.'

' What ? '

' Miss Augusta, madam, she was took queer late last night. And this morning Master Damian was queer, too.'

' Has the doctor been sent for ? '

' Yes, madam. Grew fetched him this morning.'

' What did he say ? '

' I'm sure I don't know, madam. But I understand he said it might be the smallpox.'

She saw again the blank face of the Trebennick Academy, the staring sunset, the empty porch whence Caspar had already been whisked. But it was not he whom she would never see again. It was her own children, the fruit of her forsaken womb.

Once I am at the house, she thought, driving between the ripened cornfields, I can get to work. I am only a little late, four hours' delay cannot count for so much. Already she felt the need to exculpate herself; and since destiny cannot be wheedled, and since in any crisis her nature turned, not to God but to destiny, she would brazen it out. Yet in turning rather to destiny she was like one who seeks shelter.

God, an enormous darkness, hung looped over half her sky, an ever-present menace, a cloud waiting to break. In the antipodes of God was destiny, was reason—a small classical temple in a clear far-off light, just such a temple as shone opposed to a stormcloud in the landscape by Claude Lorraine that all her life long had hung in the dining-room. Small and ghostly were the serene figures that ministered there, a different breed to the anxious pilgrims who in the foreground rested under the gnarled tree, turning, some to the far-off temple, some to the cloud where lightnings already flashed. God was a cloud, lightnings were round about his seat; and though the children must pray to Jesus, and Mrs Willoughby support the Church of England, Sophia, even in her childhood, had disliked God exactly as she disliked adders, earthquakes, revolutions—anything that lurked and was deadly, any adversary that walked in darkness. For God, her being knew, meant her no good. He had something against her, she was not one of those in whom he delighted. Now in his cloud he had come suddenly close, had reared up close behind her—at her back, as usual, for God was not an honest British pugilist. But once at the house, she thought —and already the carriage was turning in at the lodge gate— she could get to work.

Seeing the children, all her sense of competence fell off her. They were not her children who lay there, her children biddable and comprehensible. They were the fever's children, they were possessed; devils had entered into them, and looked with burning sullen glare from their heavy eyes. A devil strengthened Augusta's hand to strike at her when she bent down to smooth the damp curls; a devil with a thick

strange voice answered her from Damian's mouth—mocking
her with answers at random.

The doctor was there, waiting for her arrival. He had
sent for a Mrs Kerridge, who would do everything, who
understood these cases.

' The less you see them,' said he, ' the better.'

' Infection ? I don't fear it. I never catch anything,' she
answered.

He shook his head. ' Even so, a stranger is best. In any
fever, the essential is discipline.'

His voice was grim, but his eyes pitied her.

' Have you no one to be with you ? ' he said.

She shook her head. She knew what would come next—
a hint, an enquiry, about Frederick. She put out her will
and stopped it. Later that evening, wearing a flustered
mixture of everyday clothes and a best pelisse and gloves,
came the doctor's wife—a flimsy little boarding-school
creature, much too young and genteel, thought Sophia, to
be any good to the broad-backed bottle-nosed doctor, a man
as stolidly cunning as his hairy-legged hunter. And she
could hear the conversation between them. ' You must go,
my dear. You're at home in a drawing-room, you'll under-
stand her better than I.' And then, ' Oh no, Henry, I
couldn't dare such a thing. I'm far too shy.' However, the
faculty had prescribed her—or perhaps she was the pink
colouring. Anyhow, there she sat, crumpling a lace pocket-
handkerchief, staring at Sophia and hurriedly averting her
gaze to the tea-urn. ' I do so feel for you. It is so terrible
that you should be alone,' was as far as she got. Yet, silly,
common, timid as she might be, there was a certain reviving

quality about her company. Like a glass of *eau sucrée*, thought Sophia. It is deplorable that one should find solace in such wash, yet in that year of being finished in Paris under the guardianship of great-aunt Léocadie she had often found pleasure in *eau sucrée*. And those were beautiful eyes, eyes that could be admired without any social embarrassment, for eyes are enfranchised from any question of breeding, a variety of flesh so specialised as to transcend what else conditions a face into being well-bred or common, worn, a precious jewel, in any head. The lips might simper, the hands twist uneasily ; but the beautiful eyes dwelt on her with an attention beyond curiosity or adulation. I never want to see you again— thought Sophia, duly begging her visitor to stay a little longer—but I shall never forget your eyes.

But she was gone, almost running from the room after a sudden awkward embrace. ' Mrs Willoughby, I can't express to you how I feel ! ' Hot, a little roughened, her lips had been like those of a child. ' She might be in love with me,' said Sophia, picking up the childish glove, so creased and warm. ' Now I suppose she will go home and dash off some verses in her album. For she certainly keeps an album. Poor little creature, she must get out of these sentimental ways if she is to be a doctor's wife.' And putting away the glove in a drawer, she wrote in her notebook a memorandum that to-morrow a glove must be returned, flowers sent to Mrs Hervey. Left to herself again, the terrors of her situation— strange that a chit like this should have been able to keep them at bay—thundered back on her again, and God was again a louring cloud, and she must do all she could to establish herself as methodical and undismayed.

The clock struck eleven, its calm silver voice suddenly enlarging the expanse of the empty room. She looked up, raising her forehead from her hand, opening her eyes. She stared about her, searching for a bunch of dying foxgloves in a white jar. Her being had sunk back to the previous night: she was again in the sitting-room of the Half Moon Inn with the lamplight hot on her cold sweating forehead and the moths flying in at the open window, she was locked in the same desperate cold trance. But now she knew what it was that oppressed her so deathlily. Not Caspar's death, nor her own, but the death of her children had breathed so cold on her. For they would die, they would die! And through what untold stretches of time she must stumble, bearing the load of this knowledge, while yet they lived. Every minute was there to be lived through, methodical as the bricks in a prison wall. There could be no escape from this torment until despair came after it. How long did it take for a child to die of smallpox? A week, perhaps, or longer. Everything would go on, the fields be reaped, fruit ripen, meals appear and be taken away. The grass would grow, stealthily the grass would grow, as it grows on lawns, as it grows on graves. Two days ago, while her children had been quarrelling, the lawn had been mown and its edges sheared. It would need to be mown again, once, twice, before they were dead. For a blade of grass cannot be turned aside, any more than the scythe death swings so steadily, so skilfully. With this to come, with this to endure before its coming, how could she pass the time until the death of her children? There was nothing she could do. Mrs Kerridge was perfectly qualified, could take charge of everything in the sickroom. The laundrymaid could wash bed-linen, the cook could make gruel, the housemaid empty slops, the scullion scour dishes. Every one else was provided for, had something to do to pass the time, some service to mitigate their care. But for her, the mother, there was nothing. She must wait, idle and alone.

Treading like a thief she went through her house so strange to her, and up the stairs, and along the passage to the night nursery door. A chink of light shone from under it, there was no sound within. They are dead already, she thought, waiting outside. But no, they were asleep, in a sound sleep, the two of them, a sleep that would do them good. Being so well asleep, she might open the door, steal in, look at them? But then they might waken, and the good of their sleep be undone. She must stay outside. Shivering and burning she waited, and down in the hall the clock ticked. Suddenly there was a whimper, a stir, a weak melancholy whining that seemed as though it must go on for ever. She turned the handle, and went in. Mrs Kerridge, enormous in the candle-light, was bending over Augusta's cot. She turned, and moved heavily and noiselessly towards the door, her finger to her lips.

' How are they ? '

' The boy's asleep. The girl has just wakened, she's fretful. But I don't mind that, that's a good sign.'

' Let me come to her.'

' No, madam. It's best not. Maybe she wouldn't know you. If she did, she'd fret worse. She's thirsty, you see. Best leave her alone, and she'll go off again.'

The door was closed upon her, she stood again in the

passage, listening to that endless whine. At last, sighing like some oppressed animal, she turned and went obediently downstairs. Stupid with anguish she unlocked the garden door, and walked up and down the lawn, looking at the dim wavering light from the night nursery windows. Once the shadow of Mrs Kerridge crossed the blind, slow and towering.

It seemed on the morrow that every one she encountered had only two things to say : first, the children's illness ; next, fine weather for the harvest. Even Doctor Hervey, patting his horse's neck, sunk in a final silence which rebuffed any further question from her, and yet apparently unable to mount and leave her, must needs at last say, ' Splendid weather, this. Just what the farmers want. If only it lasts.'

It seemed as though it would last for ever, as though the unmoving air were a block of heat set down on the earth. Time could scarcely press its way through it, the minute-hand of the clock flagged, seemed wavering to a standstill. All the windows stood open, but no refreshment came in. Through the country-side, on the burning upland fields, the harvest was being reaped, the men, stooping, sickle in hand, worked like automatons, only pausing at the hedgerows to gather another handful of docks to plaster under their sweaty shirts. For such God-sent weather as this was not to be wasted. The overseers were among the men, seeing to it that they kept to their labour. To and fro from the cornfields trailed little processions of women, carrying water, or cold tea. Into some fields a farmer might cause a cask of soured cider to be carried. But this was a dubious measure. Though at first the men might seem to work the better for it, by the end of the day half a dozen of the weaker would be lying under the hedge, writhing and powerless with colic.

The trees of the park, heavily mustering, cut off the world of the Aspens from the drought of the working world. Deep in the branches the wood-pigeons cooed. Shoots of iridescent spray filled the greenhouses, the little fountain plashed, at dusk the flower-beds were watered. But thirst was in this world also. From the night nursery sounded the endless weak wail of the children, craving for the water that their treatment denied them. Mrs Kerridge, who knew everything, knew that fever patients must not be allowed to drink beyond a regulated allowance. A little wine they might have, a little warm soup ; but not water lest, the fever being for a moment checked, the eruption should be driven inward.

For five days the heat never slackened, and only on the sixth day did a thin brownish vapour begin to steal up from the westward, muffling the sun as it lowered. With dusk, a furtive wind got up, stirring the hot air. All day long Sophia had been framing in her mind the letter which must be sent to Frederick. It must be sent, it was a matter of propriety, of self-respect. Yet the day was over, and she had not set pen to paper. It was not wounded pride that prevented her. She had more pride than the pride that had been wounded, she was proud as a woman as well as proud as a wife ; and woman's pride knew that it had more to suffer by Frederick's absence than by his recall. Were he not to come, people would talk, would surmise. Already they must be doing so ; their silence before her was the index of how they prated behind her back. That Mrs Willoughby's children should be in danger of death and that Mr Willoughby should remain on the Continent would drag her through a shame far deeper, far more sullying than the private disgrace of having beckoned him to return.

But the summons pride would have sent, envy kept back. Too well she knew what the quality of Frederick's grief would be; how naturally, how purely his sorrow would run, how spontaneously he would feel all that she must feel with anguish, with difficulty and torment. He would melt, where she must be ground small. His heart's-blood would run freely, where hers stagnated like old Seneca's. For as she had given birth to her children, she would lose them : with throe after sickening throe, with effort, and humiliation, with clumsy, furious, disgraceful striving, with hideous afterbirth of all her hopes. But for Frederick it would be all an emotion, a something that afterwards music could call up, or the first snowdrops, or a page of poetry. And lanced for his spirit's health by the death of his children, he would go back, quiveringly consolable, to be comforted by Minna Lemuel.

But write I will, she said to herself. There was the escritoire, and the inkstand, and the mother-of-pearl blotter which she had used when last she wrote to Frederick. I will write, and Roger shall take in the letter the first thing to-morrow morning. But the room was heavy with her resentment, she would walk in the park a little, to clear her head.

The light shone from the nursery windows, the wailing cry hung on her hearing. She turned her back, and walked swiftly across the parched turf, her glance on the ground, walking without direction. Presently she knew that the glimmer of water was before her. She had come to the boat-house by the lake. A screen of poplars grew beside it, the hot wind stirred them, slightly, raspingly, as though it were a cat's tongue, licking. Against the piles of the boat-house the water slapped, lightly and rhythmically. Then, in a moment, as though a hand had grasped their trunks and shaken them, the poplars swayed violently, bending almost to earth, struggling to rear again against the grip of air that held them, and a wave, and a second wave, smacked against the echoing boat-house, and staring into the water she saw a brilliant sword of lightning strike up at her.

In a moment the thunder-clap was about her ears. She turned and ran, remembering only her children's terror of thunderstorms. In the distance between the lake and the house the rain had come, drenching her to the skin. Into the house and up the stairs the lightning pursued her, brandishing before her steps. But the house was silent, they must still be asleep.

As she pushed open the heavy door, a voice came into her hearing.

'Don't drop me, don't drop me! I will keep my eyes shut, I promise not to look. Oh! . . . Burning! That's hell, Sister! But I didn't look, I kept my eyes shut. Don't drop me! I saw nothing, only those hairy arms. O Devil, don't drop me. *That's Satan, you know.* For in six days the Lord made heaven and earth, thy man-servant and thy maid-servant, thy cattle and all the stranger that is within thy gates. No! For in six days the Lord made heaven and earth . . . Don't drop me, don't drop me! My mouth's hot. I looked at hell with my mouth, my mouth's burning. Hannah!

Come and take hell out of my mouth, take it out, I say!
And our mouths shall show forth thy praise. For in six
days . . . Three sixes are eighteen, are eighteen, four sixes
are twenty-four, five sixes are hairy. In among the hairs are
spots, like little hot mouths. Don't drop me, *don't drop me*!'

His hands were fastened, that he might not tear himself to
pieces. His face and neck were covered with sores, sores
were on his eyelids, sealing up his eyes. His hair stood out,
stiff and bristling, as though the fever had singed it. Out of
this horrible body, speckled with sores, swollen as though
the poison within might at any moment explode it, the clear
childish voice bubbled senseless as the tinkle of a fountain.

'Poor little lamb,' said Mrs Kerridge, tightening the bed-
clothes with her bleak hands. 'It's wonderful how he keeps
on about hell. But they often do, children. Not that they
know what they're talking about, you know, for they don't.
You couldn't expect that.'

Sophia turned to the other bed. Out of the circle of the
candle-light, its semi-darkness was lanced by the quivering
blue flare of the lightning. Augusta lay there unstirring,
unafraid. Her mouth was open and she snored, and choked
with phlegm. As the lightning flickered out and the thunder
pealed, putting out the noise of her breath, she seemed to go
under like some one drowning, wearily rising to the surface
again with the ensuing silence.

Mrs Kerridge had followed Sophia, and stood behind her,
shaking her head slowly.

'She doesn't fight like her brother do.'

'I was afraid the storm would wake her. She is terrified
of thunderstorms.'

Mrs Kerridge did not answer.

Which of them will die first? The question rose to her lips, but she did not utter it. If the woman could say, she would not speak truly. No one ever spoke the truth in a sickroom. And they would both die, and since die they must, the sooner the better. For already her own children, the children she loved, were dead. This tinkling little maniac, corrupting under her eyes, this snoring choking slug that lay couched so slyly under the lightning, these were not her children. Her own life had ceased in them, they were fever's children, not hers. Through the smell of the vinegar she could smell the foulness of their disease. 'When did I love them last?' she asked herself. 'Not when I left them to go to Cornwall. I was ashamed of them then. When Caspar was here, yes, for then they were well. But mostly they have been a care to me, a thing that must always be tended, made allowances for, buttressed up, remedied. Like a wound in me that would never quite heal, that must perpetually be cleansed and dressed. No, I have scarcely ever had time to love them, my mind divided between pitying them as they were, and glorifying them as they would be; as they would be when all their ailments and deficiencies were fought through and done with. A devoted mother! That is what I have been, that is what people have said, will say, of me. But devotion is not love. It grovels, fears, forebodes, lies to itself or to others. Devotion is a spaniel's trick, it is what the animal feeling of a mother turns into when it is cowed. An animal instinct cowed, that is what I have chiefly known. And now that fails me. My children are dying, and all that I can truly say I feel is resentment that I have been made a fool of. Damian's chatter maddens me, I could not touch either of them without a shudder, though at this moment I could easily lay down my life for them. But that is not love, that is devotion, devotion exasperated to its last act, the spaniel driven mad.'

Mrs Kerridge's stare was gradually propelling her from the room. As the door closed she heard Damian's raving veer back to the lime-kiln again. The sullenness of one unjustly condemned took possession of her thoughts. What a doom, that whatever I have done for the best should turn into whips and scorpions! The lime-kiln that was to cure their whooping-cough is now a hell that he must dangle over, past help of any snatching. The lime-kiln. Under the uproar of the storm she recalled with feverish accuracy every step of that journey: how, setting out, her thoughts had been of that long-ago expedition to see the Duke of Wellington, thoughts turned by the sight of the chestnut tree to an upswelling of maternal pride. She had felt herself stand up, a fortress, drawing out of the earth, out of the past, the nourishment which should feed and forward her ripening children. Dull, brooding, disblossomed, the chestnut had been she. And so they had gone on, walking between the songless July hedges, and over the parched fields, where the hoes had chinked against the flints. Edmunds, leaving his work, had come fawning up, ready to snatch an excuse for idling and gossip even from her austere disapproval. Then leaving the fields, they had gone up the steep track to where the lime-kiln stood on its grassy plateau with the heated air trembling above it. He had been asleep, his head bowed on his knees, his hands dangling; even at their departure, as he had stood watching them go down the lane, he had seemed like one sleep-walking. In his attitude, in his fixed stare, he had been like one beholding a vision, some fixed and grim hallucination of fever. For all his stare, she had thought, it is as though he does not see us. Hannah had gossiped a little about him afterwards. A rough solitary man, she had said, choosing of his own accord that life of uncouth solitude, a stranger from across the county, without kith or kin, and going only to the alehouse to buy a bottle to take away. Yet it was said that women would go to him, stealing to him by night, guided by the red glare of his kiln upon the dark hillside. A foul-living man, Hannah said. Had she not noticed the sores upon his wrists?

In the space between the lightning blearing the window and shuddering out again, Sophia knew that it was to this man, to those arms, already opening in the sores of smallpox, that she had entrusted her children. Like the flash of lightning the certainty had dived into her heart and vanished, leaving only darkness. Without a falter her body went on its way, moving neatly and composedly through the sound of the thunder-clap; as though wound up like a toy it carried her up and down the long drawing-room, even remembering, so skilful the mechanical body is, to wring its hands. Some one was there, watching her. She did not know who, or care.

'Oh!'

At the trembling whine of terror she stopped, came to herself. There, pressed into a corner, holding out something in her gloved hands, was Mrs Hervey. Her drenched clothes hung limp on her, her hair dangled in streaks along her cheeks, her eyes were black with fear and her mouth was open. Now, in a sudden swoop like a terrified bird, she rushed forward and fell on her knees before Sophia.

'Oh, Mrs Willoughby, forgive me if I've done wrong! But I felt I had to come to you.'

With her gloved hands, slimy and cold, she had caught hold of Sophia's hand.

'I don't know what you'll think of me, coming like this. No one knows I'm here, I came in through the window. But I had to come.'

'You must have some wine. I'll fetch you some. Or would you rather have tea?'

'Oh, no, nothing! I implore you, don't trouble to fetch anything.'

'Here are some salts.'

When she returned with wine and biscuits, Sophia found the young woman sitting on the smallest chair in the room, snuffing at the vinaigrette. Though she was shaking from head to foot she had composed herself into a ladylike posture, and could stammer out her speech of, 'Oh, how very kind of you. No, not as much as that, if you please.'

'Drink it down,' said Sophia, and tilted the glass at her lips.

The wine was swallowed, biscuits were refused. The storm continued, a musketry of rain rattling against the windows. With so much noise around the house it seemed impossible that any conversation should ever take place. My children are dying, thought Sophia, and I must sit here, dosing this little ninny with port and waiting to hear what hysterical fool's errand brought her. Yet she felt no anger towards the downcast figure, so childish in its grown-up fripperies, so

nonsensical in its drenched elegance. You should be at home
and in bed, warm beside your snoring old husband, she
thought—a sudden dash of tenderness and amusement re-
deeming her dry misery, so that she was almost glad that
instead, Mrs Hervey was here, blown in at the window like
a draggled bird.

She filled the glass again.

But the bird had revived into a boarding-school miss,
and with exasperating gesture of refinement, waved it away.
Then, sitting bolt upright, and opening her eyes as though
that must precede opening her mouth, she began impres-
sively,

' I have done something that I know is very indiscreet.
I am quite prepared to be reproached for it.

' The wife of a medical man,' continued Mrs Hervey, ' is
in a very delicate position. Officially, she should know
nothing. But it is impossible to take *no* interest, especially
where one's feelings are engaged.'

If you were not so much on your best behaviour, thought
Sophia, you would be telling me that I know what husbands
are like, don't I. The eyes had no charm for her now. Too
disdainful for either a true word or a civil one, she set her
lips closer, and inclined her head for sole assent.

But her wrath had showed out. The young woman paled
and shrank.

' I have thought of you day and night, ever since that first
evening when your children were taken ill and my husband
sent me to you. You can't understand, and I can't express
it. It's more than pity, than sympathy, for I have heard
other people pitying you, people who know you better than

I, women with children of their own. But they don't feel as I do. But that's not it, that's not what I came here to say. I would not put myself forward to tell you that.'

She stopped on her flow of words as abruptly as a wren ceases in mid-song, and turned her face aside as though to hide her tears.

' Though that had been all you came for, I should be very grateful to you for coming.'

Stiff and sincere, the words once spoken seemed completely beside the point, and Sophia had the sensation that she had snubbed without meaning to. If snub it were, the young woman ignored it, preoccupied in nerving herself to speak again.

' Mrs Willoughby, when I came that evening, I came at my husband's bidding, and I came with a purpose. There was something I had to say to you. But I did not, I could not, say it. You did not guess.'

' I did,' said Sophia gently. ' You came because Doctor Hervey had told you to find out if I had sent for my husband.'

' And I wouldn't ! ' the girl cried out with something like exultation.

' And now, I suppose,' continued Sophia, ' you have been sent on the same errand ?

' No ! I have refused, I have told him, nothing would make me do it.'

' Why ? '

The look that answered this made her ashamed. Like a reflection of her shame a deep flush covered Mrs Hervey's face. Reddened as a schoolgirl in fault, she drew herself up and began to speak with something of her former stiffness.

'You have asked me why I have come, and no doubt my visit must seem ill-timed and peculiar. I told you that I was prepared for censure. This is my reason for coming.'

She held out a letter. It was addressed to Frederick in Doctor Hervey's handwriting.

'I stole it,' she said. In her voice there was almost reverence for such a deed, and the pupils of her eyes, suddenly enlarging, seemed to rush towards Sophia like two black moons falling through a cloud.

'He gave it to me yesterday, to post. And I have had it ever since.'

But we might be two schoolgirls, thought Sophia, two romantic misses, stolen from our white beds to exchange illicit comfits, and trembling lest amid this stage-rattling thunderstorm we should hear the footsteps of Mrs Goodchild. The letter, lying so calmly on her lap, seemed to have no real part in this to-do. Some other motive, violent and unexperienced as the emotions of youth, trembled undeclared between them.

'For why should all this be done behind your back?' exclaimed the girl passionately. 'What right have they to interfere, to discuss and plot, and settle what they think best to be done? As if, whatever happened, you could not stand alone, and judge for yourself! As if you needed a man!'

The letter fell to the floor as Sophia rose and leaned her arm upon the steady cold of the marble mantelshelf and shielded her face with her hand. There was something to be done, if she could but remember what, something practical, proper and immediate. She had been staring at a white china ornament, and now, as she shut her eyes, its small glittering point of light seemed to pierce through her eyelids, and to become the immutable focus upon which her thoughts must settle and determine. Slowly she composed herself, was presently all composure; and round her steadied mind she felt her flesh hanging cold and forlorn, as though in this conflict she had for ever abandoned it.

The girl had risen too. As Sophia turned to her she said, 'I see you want me to go. Forgive me.'

'There is nothing to forgive. You have acted very well. It is a long time since any one has dealt by me with such honesty. I wish I could answer your generous impulse with equal truth. But I am too old, too wary of the world, to match you.'

She stooped for the letter, and put it back into the unresisting hands.

'This must go. And Doctor Hervey must never know that you brought it here.'

The girl sighed.

'Your guess was right, or your instinct. I do not want my husband to return. But whether he comes or no will make little real difference to me. Mine is a spoilt marriage. Yours is not, and I cannot let you endanger it.'

The rain had ceased, the storm was retreating. Though the air resounded with the noise of water, it was with the drips splashing from the roof-gutters, or the moisture fitfully cascading from branches when the dying wind wagged them.

'I will have the horses put in, and you shall be driven back.'

'Let me walk,' said the girl.

Common sense and civility yielded as Sophia looked at her

guest. Unspeaking she picked up a shawl, and as though in some strange pre-ordered consent they left the house by the french window, and walked side by side down the avenue. Iced with the storm, the air was like the air of a new world, the darkness was like the virgin dusk of a new world emerging from chaos, slowly and blindly wheeling towards its first day. Far off the storm winked and muttered, but louder than its thunder was the sipping whistle, all around them, of the parched ground drinking the rain. Halfway down the avenue Sophia took the girl's hand. It was ungloved now, cold and wet, and lay in her clasp like a leaf. So, grave and unspeaking, linked childishly together they went on under the trees, their footsteps scarcely audible among the sounds of the heavily dripping rain and the drinking earth.

She returned alone to the empty lighted drawing-room, to Mrs Hervey's chair pulled forward, and the decanter and the glass and the biscuits. They must be put away, she thought, all traces of this extraordinary visit; and as she carried the wine and the biscuits to the pantry she found herself stiffening with a curious implacability. No! However touching, such escapades were intolerable. One could not have such young women frisking round one, babbling as to whether or no one needed a husband, declaring on one's behalf that one didn't. From a woman of the village she could have heard such words without offence. Down there, in that lowest class, sexual decorum could be kilted out of the way like an impeding petticoat; and Mary Bugler, whose husband was in jail, and Carry Westmacott, whose husband should be, might declare without offence that a woman was as good as a man, and better. In her own heart, too, unreproved, could lodge the conviction that a Sophia might well discard a Frederick, and in her life she had been ready, calmly enough, to put this into effect. But into words, never! Such things could be done, but not said. And was it for the doctor's wife, an immature little feather-pate, to pipe up in her treble voice, in her tones of provincial refinement, that Mrs Willoughby did not need Mr Willoughby?

Setting back the chair, glancing sharply about the room— last time she had left a glove—Sophia shook her head in condemnation. This visit had left no visible trace of Mrs Hervey. But in this room, the serene demonstration of how a lady of the upper classes spends her leisure amid flowers and books and arts, words had been spoken such as those walls had never heard before. And to hear her own thought voiced she, the lady of the room, had had to await the coming of this interloper, this social minnikin, this Thomasina Thumb who, riding on a cat and waving a bodkin, had come to be her champion.

The next morning she sent off a letter to Frederick, coldly annoyed with herself for neglecting an essential formality— for with the putting of pen to paper it had become no more than that. Absent or present, he could not affect her now. The servants would make his bed, serve his food; she, trained better than they in her particular service of hostess- ship, would entertain him, a guest for the funeral. And then he would be gone again, back to his Minna, the only trace of his visit some additional entries in the household books. For there can be no middle way, she thought, where extremes have been attempted; and Frederick, failing to be my husband, must now be to me less than an acquaintance.

'As if you needed a man.' Mrs Hervey's words renewed
themselves in her hearing, spoken with an indignant convic-
tion blazing against the soberer colouring of Sophia's own
view of the case : that she could get on better without one.
In some ways men were essential. One must have a coach-
man, a gardener, a doctor, a lawyer—even a clergyman.
These served their purpose and withdrew—some less briskly
than others, she reflected, seeing Mr Harwood walking up
the avenue. He had visited her daily, to enquire after the
children and offer, she supposed, spiritual consolation. Appa-
rently the presence of a clergyman of the Church of England
in her morning-room was consolation enough, as though,
like some moral vinaigrette he had but to be filled by a
Bishop, introduced, unstoppered, and gently waved about
the room, to diffuse a refreshing atmosphere. To visit
widows in their affliction, she thought, moving the decanter
towards him, was part of his duties. Possibly she was not
sufficiently a widow to call out his most reviving gales. But
indeed, beyond a pleasant civility and a rather tedious flow
of chit-chat, no more was to be expected of him. He gave
away very respectable soup, and preached sensible sermons,
and his cucumber frames were undoubtedly the most success-
ful in the village. What more to ask, except that he should
soon go away? She had often congratulated herself that
the parish was served by such a rational exponent of
Christianity.

To-day, of course, they discussed the storm.

'This cooler air,' said he, 'must certainly be of assistance
to your little invalids. We may, indeed, consider the storm
(since you tell me it did not alarm them) as providential. I

understand, too, that nearly all the corn was already cut, so that the harvest will not be endangered.'

Tithes, thought Sophia.

God was a cloud, lightnings were round about his seat. But Mr Harwood was unaware of this, and good manners forbade that she should hint it to him. Instead, she found herself thanking him warmly for his promise of balsam seed, well-ripened by the hot summer. If brought on under glass and transferred to a southern aspect, she should have a fine show of plants next summer.

For everything would go on, and she with it, broken on the wheeling year. Next summer would come, and she would walk in the silent garden, her black dress trailing, her empty heart stuffed up like an old rat-hole with insignificant cares, her ambition for seemliness and prosperity driving her on to oversee the pruning of trees, the trimming of hedges, the tillage of her lands, the increase of her stock. Urged and directed by her will, everything would go on, though to no end. The balsams would bloom, and she be proud of them.

If I were a man, she thought, I would plunge into dissipation.

What dissipation is to a man, religion is to a woman. Would it be possible to become a Roman Catholic and go into a convent ? No, never for her !—of the two alternatives dissipation seemed the more feasible. For though she could not imagine how it might be contrived, since both to wine and the love of man she opposed an immovably good head, yet, could a suitable dissipation be devised, she might find in herself a will for it ; but under no circumstances could she yield herself to **devot**ion. There was gaming, she remembered; that was possible to women. And for a moment she paused to consider herself contracted into an anguished ecstasy that the croupier's rake could thrust or gather. Gaming might do; yet in its very fever it was cold, and if she were to survive, she must be warmed—she so frigid to wine and the love of man. There was ambition. That should fit her, with her long-breathed resolution, her clear head and love of dominance. But how should a woman satisfy ambition unless acting upon and through a man?—and how control a man by resolution or reason, when any pretty face or leaning bosom could deflect him?

Far off stood the shade of Papa, speaking of philosophy and the calm joys of an elevated mind. True, Papa spoke also of the inconvenience of blue-stockings, pointing to his own mother as a model of all a daughter should be—Grand-mamma, thick, dumpy, and perfumed, her creaking stomacher rising and falling under her gloved and folded hands, saying, ' Come, little Sophia. You must not run about in the sun. Fetch your needlework, and sit by me.' Yet, avoiding blue-stockings, one might yet find some succour from Papa and intellectual pursuits—take up chemistry or archaeology, study languages, travel. A woman cannot travel alone, but two women may travel together; and Sophia for a moment beheld herself standing upon a bridge, a blue river beneath her, a romantic gabled golden town and purple mountains behind, and at her side, large-eyed and delighted and clutching a box of watercolour paints, Mrs Hervey.

O foolish vision! Even were not Mrs Hervey stoutly wedded to her apothecary, how could one long endure such a wavering mixture of impulse and impertinence, sensibility and false refinement?

It is because she was kind to me, she thought, that my mind turns to her. She is young, silly, and can do nothing, yet she came to me in kindness, offering to my aridity a refreshment not germane at all to what she really is, but a dew of being young and impulsive. Caspar is such another, if he were here I should cling to him, listen to his music, solace myself with his unconscious grace of being young, and malleable, and alive. Should I adopt him, bring him here in the stead of my children? A black heir to Blandamer? Impossible! Though I have will enough to enforce it, the resentment of those I force would hound him out, all but his actual black body. And indeed, could I long endure to have this pretty soft wagging black spaniel in the place of my children?

Most of the time it seemed to her inevitable that both children should die. Then, more irrational than the conviction of their doom, would come a conviction of their recovery. Hope would twitch her to her feet, set her running towards the night nursery where she should hear from Mrs Kerridge indubitable symptoms of a turn for the better. And halfway there fear would stay her, bidding her sit down again, continue what occupation she had, taste, as long as it might linger, the hope so exactly fellowed to the previous hopes which enquiry had demolished.

Damian, Mrs Kerridge and the doctor said, was making the better fight. Yet it was Damian who died first, collapsing suddenly, and dying with a little gasp like a breaking bubble. Two hours later Frederick entered the house. Sophia expected him, yet when the carriage came to the door she ran out by the long window, spying from behind a tree at the intruder, come so inopportunely upon her misery. Whoever it is, she thought, not recognising her own horses, I will not see him. I will hide.

A foreigner, her mind said, in the instant before recognition. He ran up the steps and stood talking to Johnson, who had opened the door. She advanced, slowly mounting the steps behind him, knowing herself unseen by him. She seemed to be stalking a prey, and on Johnson's countenance she read with how much surmise and excitement her household awaited this meeting.

Why doesn't he turn round, she thought. I cannot touch him, and I don't want to speak, lest my voice should break, and deliver me over to him.

'Here is Mrs Willoughby, sir.'

As though I were the coffee, she thought; and her lips were moving into a smile when he turned to her.

'Sophia!'

His voice had altered. There was a new note in it, he had lost his drawl. She said,

'Damian is dead. Do you know? I can't remember if he died before the carriage started for you.'

He bowed his head.

'Johnson has told me.'

She saw that the horses were sweating. They must go to the stables, life must continue.

'You will be tired with your journey. Come in.'

Now which chair will you take, she thought—your old one?

But he remained on his feet, walking up and down the

room, as though, again under that roof, the habit of his
former listless pacing piped its old tune to him. To the
window, and turning, to the portrait of Grandpapa Aspen,
and back to the window again, his advance and retreat
surveyed by that quiet old gentleman, who, as Gainsborough
had painted him, seemed with his gun and supple wet-nosed
retriever to be watching through the endless bronze dusk of
an autumnal evening, paused on the brink of his spinney and
listening with contemplative pleasure to the footsteps of the
poacher within. *Benjamin Aspen Esq. J.P.* stated the gold
letters below. It had sometimes occurred to Sophia that it
were as though Frederick, uneasily treading the Aspen estate,
were the tribute of yet another poacher offered up to the
implacable effigy. But now the poacher walked with a freer
gait, a liberated air ; and it was in this new manner, and in his
subtly altered tone of voice, that Frederick halted by her chair
and said,

'I will not make speeches, Sophia. But you must let me
say how grateful I am to you for sending for me, how much I
grieve that it is for this reason that you have had to break
your resolution.'

The moment for a reconciliation, she thought, with the
more bitterness and annoyance since her sense acknowledged
that never before had Frederick's demeanour expressed so
patently, not merely an acceptance of their irreconcilability,
but a will to it that might be equal to hers. She stared at his
dusty boots, and said sourly,

'There wasn't much hope, Frederick, nor is there for
Augusta. They neither have much stamina. The Wil-
loughby constitution, I suppose.'

To speak so was abominable, was the last thing she had wished to do. Nothing could retrieve the words, even had she not been too weary for an attempt. And feeling the blood labouring to her cheeks she sat unmoving, scorning to avert her shamed face, and fighting against a flood of self-pity.

'The devil of a disease.' He spoke as though thinking aloud, voicing a train of thought which her words had not pierced. 'Vaccination or not, it will get you if it has a mind to. And if you creep through it, it may leave a life not worth living.' He went on to speak, as a traveller might, of the women in Paris who earned a livelihood as mattress-pickers, women whom smallpox had blinded. 'They come from the Quinze-Vingts,' he said. 'A child leads them to the door, and fetches them again at the end of the day. One morning, one spring morning, I came across two of these women sitting on the floor of an empty bedroom in my hotel. The door was open, and I watched them for a little, thinking how quickly they separated the tufts of wool, and wondering that they should work so silently, for as you know it's queer to find two Parisians at work and not chattering. Their backs were towards me, but when I said good-day they turned. Then I saw their faces, so scarred that it would not have been possible to say if they were old women or girls of nineteen, and instead of eyes, hollow sockets and sores. Death is better than that, Sophia.'

How deeply changed he is, she thought. It is as though a stranger were speaking. That woman's influence, I suppose. But, disciplined by the recollection of her last, abominable speech, she thrust down the thought of Minna Lemuel, and enquired as a hostess, speaking of food and refreshment.

' May I see Augusta ? '

Of the two children Augusta had always been his favourite. More of an Aspen in character than the boy, it had been as though in her he wooed his last hope of her mother. An embarrassment of honour made Sophia turn away and talk to Mrs Kerridge while Frederick stood by the sick child's bed. He had entered the room, she noticed, with a little parcel in his hand ; and now, glancing over her shoulder, she saw that he had unpacked from it a white rose, very delicately contrived from feathers, light as thistledown and sleek as spun glass. The small hand, so roughened and polluted, opened vaguely at the contact, clutched the toy and crumpled it, and let it fall.

' Speak to her, Frederick. She can't see you, but she may recognise your voice.'

' *Ma fleur,*' he said. The small hand stirred on the coverlet, closed as though closing on the words, and presently fell open again.

After he had gone back to Paris and she was left alone with the leisure of the childless, those words, and the tone in which they were spoken, haunted her memory—according to her mood, an enigma, a nettle-sting, a caress. It was as though, at that moment, not Frederick but some one unknown to her had stood by the bed of her dying child and said, *Ma fleur.* That it was said with feeling, yes. Frederick had always been sincerely sentimental, had in the early days of their marriage melted his voice even to her. That it was said gravely, yes again. To have lost one child and know the other past keeping would darken any voice into gravity. But beyond this, and beyon' anything her mind could unquarry, there remained a quality, part innocence, part a deep sophistication in sorrow, that must still fascinate and still elude her. The voice of one acquainted with grief. Not, as Frederick had been, suddenly swept into its shadow, but one long acknowledging it, a voice tuned for a lifetime, and for centuries of inherited lifetimes, to that particular note, falling since the beginning of the world in that melancholy acquiescent cadence, falling as wave after wave brings its sigh, long-swelled, and silently carried, and at last spoken and quenched on the shore.

Modelled on that Minna's Jewish contralto, she told herself, angrily stopping her ears against those two grave harpnotes. Accomplished mountebank, no doubt she could manage her voice to any appropriate timbre; and Frederick, who was always a copy-cat, a weathercock to any breeze that tickled him, had heard the right intonation, and unwittingly reproduced it.

To judge by Frederick, Minna must be a model of decorum. Throughout the difficult visit, he was amiable, tactful, unobtrusive. If it were not the Jewess's good effect, she said to herself, she had at last the answer to her old wonder: why Frederick, displeasing as a husband, should be so much in demand as a guest, should be summoned to Lincolnshire and London, Suffolk and Aix-les-Bains. For undoubtedly he was at Blandamer as a guest.

She had dreaded the intimacy which bereavement might engender; but he, avoiding the thistly touch-me-not which encumbered her behaviour, had exactly preserved the distance that must be between them. She had sickened, foreseeing the easy flow of his grief; it had flowed, but not to splash her. She had quailed, forecasting the social awkwardness which the funeral, the visits of condolence, the assemblage of Aspens and Willoughbies concurring to stamp down the turves over the death of a next generation, must entail. Weariness of body and mind, the apathy, half-relief, half-despair, that follows on bereavement, had partly muffled her ; but even so, she had been conscious how well Frederick was managing, how deftly he had walked his slack rope between the head of the house and the outcast whose bag was ready packed, the tragedy once played out, for departure.

Correct as a mute, she told herself ; faultless as some town tragedian supplying at a moment's notice the place of a disabled actor in a company of barn-stormers ; polished and affable as the Prodigal may have been, returning to shame with his shamefully acquired graces the angry rustic integrity of the stay-at-home. A French polish !

His accent had improved, too. *Ma fleur.* The Frederick of their honeymoon, the heavy English dandy, sheltering behind her flounces with his, Damn it, Sophia, you must do the parley-vooing, had suppled his tongue as well as his wits. Were she to meet Minna, she must say, Madam, I congratulate you upon the progress in your pupil. But no doubt, with such a vast, such a cosmopolitan experience, you could scarcely fail with any sow's ear.

Thus, sooner or later, her thoughts brought her face to face with that woman, there to discharge her rage. Everything she saw, heard, did, in her solitary existence, and the solitariness of that existence itself, must remind her of the children she had lost. And remembering that loss, she must remember Frederick, and remembering, her candour must oblige her to remember how well he had behaved, detached, unobtrusive, unfailing. How when Mrs Kerridge, resorting more and more to her professional secret gin, had oversipped the mark and come raging downstairs, declaiming in a tipsy fury against that slut of a kitchen-maid who had again, and as a personal affront, forgotten the nutmeg, he had intercepted and silenced her, sluiced her into sobriety, and sent her trembling back to her duties again. How, at the post-funeral luncheon, he had kept talk going, by some legerdemain removing the conversation to Central Europe, and even while speaking of the liberation of Poland, managing to keep them all in a good temper. How, with that account of the blinded mattress-pickers, he had patched over the afterwards of her atrocious speech, and yet had avoided seeming to change the subject. In the midst of such recollections, swelling under them and exploding through them, her bitterness against him would break out, and all his good behaviour, his detachment, his unobtrusiveness, his readiness, would seem a lackey's virtues and no more.

For it was in dancing attendance on his harlot that he had learned these embellishments—dancing attendance on a harlot, a school how much more rigorous than a wife, his very improvement demonstrated. As in that *Ma fleur*, which for all she could do still rang in her head, Minna Lemuel's voice resounded, in everything he had said or done he had borne witness to Minna, trailed her invisible presence through the house. Every alteration in him made up a portrait of her. What had the old Frederick cared for the liberation of Poland? What would those blinded mattress-pickers have been to him but two scarecrows, to be run away from in disgust and fear ? But weak-minded and porous, he had yielded himself to his Minna, was saturated with her, and willy-nilly must exhale her, even in the house of his wife, even at the bedside of his child. It was as though she could smell Minna on him, as though he had brought bodily into the house the odour of his mistress.

But now he had rejoined her, and she was left alone in the leisure of the childless, to oversee her emptied house, methodically to destroy every remnant of her children, every toy and piece of childish apparel ; for in her raging loss she could tolerate no sentiment of keepsakes, and in the burning of the bedding, the scouring of the sickroom, she saw a symbol of what her heart should do. Frederick was back with Minna, and she was done with them both. Telling herself this, in the next moment she would relapse, every consideration other than this a blind road that turned her back to the death of the children. If she remembered them, she must remember Frederick ; and how remember Frederick without snuffing Minna ? The children, Frederick, Minna. Through this order her thoughts ran, and at Minna stayed, ignobly fascinated, ignobly curious, until the next explosion of bitterness hurled her into a rage that could not think at all.

Presently she began to dream of her. Minna driving with Frederick in a painted circus chariot would appear on the horizon of the desert, where she stood talking with Job Saunders the bailiff about a sowing of scarcity-root. The chariot would sweep nearer, bouncing lightly as a bubble over the ridges of sand, pass, and vanish, and presently re-appear, persistent as a gadfly. Or she would come on Minna alone, seated in her own morning-room, and suddenly know that she had been established there for weeks. Waking, she kept the sense of the dream's vividity; the time of day, the position of a glove, every word spoken, remained. But there was always one blank. However she might interrogate her memory, or try by a stratagem of suddenness to surprise it of its secret, Minna's visage still eluded her.

At last, rather than expose herself to such dreams, she abjured sleeping. For many successive nights she went to her bedroom only that her maid should undress her, and to rumple the bedclothes into a look of having been slept in. Then, after the house was silent, she would get up, dress herself, and creep downstairs, where, lighting one of her secret store of candles, she would read, or sort papers, or labour at one of those many unfinished pieces of needlework, or sometimes play a match of billiards with herself. Time went fast in these vigils, faster than it went by day, when a hundred insignificant duties nailed her down to this hour and that; and surprised that the night was over she would hear, beyond the curtained windows, the harsh bird-notes of autumn dawnings, and moving heavily with stiff cold limbs hid the traces of her vigil, and went back to her bed just before the household began to stir.

She had almost forgotten Mrs Hervey. That strange interview on the night of the thunderstorm seemed as irrelevant as the incident of a fever dream, leaving nothing behind it that could supply any link between her and the young woman in the over-feathered bonnet whom she saw in church on Sundays. It needed the coming of quarter-day, and the arrival of Doctor Hervey's bill, to revive its memory. Then,

finding her thoughts running on the doctor's wife, she gave
them free rein, since it was better to be teased by Mrs Hervey
than by Minna. A visiting acquaintance betwen them was
neither possible nor desirable ; although they had walked
hand in hand down the avenue, or rather because they had
done so, a civil basket of dessert pears or a hothouse melon
would be the properest acknowledgment of that evening
visit and the misguided impulse which had prompted it.

Yet having chosen the melon Sophia went on from the
hothouse to the stable, and left word there that the carriage
was to be ready at midday to drive her to Mrs Hervey's.

The Herveys lived at Long Blandamer, a village with
genteel pretensions enough to support half a dozen shops, a
neat Wesleyan chapel, and sufficient trim-fronted stucco
villas to provide a society of weekly card-parties. It re-
presented the new world, as Blandamer Abbots, with its
mud-walled cottages, tithe barn, and one great house, re-
presented the old. Sophia had been brought up to feel at
home in the one, and not in the other ; and even now she felt
a certain stiffening as the carriage, splashed with the mud of
country lanes, moved over the smooth turnpike, overtaking
groups of self-conscious young women or nursemaids towing
beribboned children and fat pug-dogs. Doctor Hervey's
house had a green-painted trellis over its white front, a
pocket-handkerchief lawn with a small conifer planted in its
centre, an enormous brass door-knocker, and a cast of the
Dying Gladiator turning his back on the road in what was
obviously the parlour window.

The door was opened, the card and the melon received ;
and after a considerable pause Roger came back with the

message that Mrs Ingleby would be so delighted if Mrs Willoughby would step in. The parlour was exactly as she had forecasted, but its occupant considerably more than she had bargained for.

My dear Mrs Willoughby, dear madam, my daughter will be so delighted, such a superb melon, inexpressibly grieved, doctor's orders, you know, her favourite fruit, condescension, necessity of a hot-bed, bereavement, this one more comfortable, a little refreshment . . . The stout matron pranced about the room, assailing her with chairs and unfinished sentences, the flutter of her cap-ribbons seeming to fill the little room.

Waiting for the moment when breath must fail her, Sophia was at last able to enquire,

' I hope Mrs Hervey is not ill.'

' Oh no, not in the least, only what is quite natural, you know, at such times. But she does not come down till the afternoons.'

Then, after glancing towards the Dying Gladiator as though to be assured of his inattention, the matron leant creaking forward, and whispered,

' My daughter is expecting, you know.   In April.'

It might be April now, she thought, beholding the landscape of fields and hedgerows that with easy flow swept her away from the stucco of Long Blandamer. It was one of those autumn days which seem to have the innocence of spring. She was glad to wash her senses in it, they needed such a lustration. She had left the doctor's house feeling as though she had escaped, and only just in time, from a dusty and airless closet. Yet in such a narrow den of gentility, and with such a mother, a young woman would bear a child.

Yes, and another, and another; and grow middle-aged, and grow old, and die, and be buried under a neat headstone, describing her as a beloved wife. But what other lot, said her thoughts scratching nearer home, need any woman look for? What difference, save a larger den and a quieter mother, between Mrs Hervey's lot and the lot designed for her? With angry reasonings she tried to shake herself free from the sense of intolerable flatness and tedium which Mrs Ingleby's excited confidence had evoked. It was as though, after long days in a court-house, she had heard amid the buzzing of flies and the shuffling of feet a sentence of death pronounced, or of that worst death, a life-long imprisonment; and, suddenly stabbed awake from the indifference of scorn and sickness, had realised that the doom had been pronounced upon her.

'*I will therefore that the younger women marry, bear children, guide the house. . . .*'

Though her children were dead, she was not freed from that sentence.

The horses were checked, the carriage drew to one side. She looked out, and saw, advancing through the village, hounds with their tails flickering like shadows on running water, the bright colours of hunting coats and horse-flesh. Tall on their shining mounts between the low-thatched cottages of the hamlet, the riders looked like beings of another race, of an angelic stature and nourishment. Behind them came a following of stragglers—men out of work and long-legged girls; and from a cottage door a woman darted, swiftly tying on a clean apron and calling to her children to follow her.

' I will hunt again ! ' exclaimed Sophia. And in that deter-
mination it seemed as though all her cares might be shaken
off, and Minna forgotten. She had not hunted since the
birth of the children, never easy in leaving them for her own
pleasure lest some harm should befall; and now, within three
months of her bereavement, to ride to hounds would be an
outrage. However, do it she would, and show openly to all
that knew covertly how destiny and death had combined to
make a free woman of her. The apostle had not included
hunting in his programme for the younger women.

But she must wait for a new habit, she had grown too
thin for the old. Three journeys to the county town to be
fitted took off the edge from her anticipation, and when at
last the morning came she was half-defeated before she set
out. She looked with envy at Roger the groom. It was his
first meet, that is to say the first to which he had gone
mounted; and as they rode down the village street she
glanced back and saw with amusement how he grinned from
side to side, collecting the eyes of his former foot companions,
draining their admiration like some tossed-off stirrup-cup.

His livery was the work of old Mr Trimlett, and it fitted
far better than her new habit. In every way Roger was to
be envied. But Roger's was a short-lived kingdom. In a
couple of hours he was riding home behind her, crestfallen,
blinking, and trying to pretend that it was the sharp wind
only that made his eyes water. At the first covert they had
drawn a blank; and while the hounds were snuffing and
scrambling through Duke's Gorse the wind-baffled bawls of
a farmer, arriving belatedly across country, signalled to them
too late that their fox had been lying out in the plough, and

had sneaked away. Meanwhile the new habit was irking her more and more, too easy on the shoulders, too tight under the arms; and increasingly conscious of the singularity of her behaviour, and galled by the false heartiness of the welcomes proffered her by the other riders, Sophia discovered in herself a growing impression that she was out on false pretences, having in reality an assignation with the fox. If you'd hunt *me*, she thought, looking round scornfully, I'd give you a run for your money. And before she was aware she had signalled to Roger, and was riding home.

Of its fashion, it was a good enough right and left. By hunting at all she had estranged the goodies, and by deserting she must scandalise the nimrods. She was rather pleased with herself for the thoroughness of this blunder, and for the rest of the day a queer elation floated her along. But that night, having gone to bed whistling, she dreamed again of Minna, and woke next morning to a blacker despair than she had ever known.

Steadfast as a bodily pain it endured all day, an anguish and a tedium. At the day's end she duly allowed herself to be undressed, and lay in her bed long enough to rumple it. Rising for her vigil she had no more feeling than on any other night that what she was doing was not perfectly prosaic and practical; and it was without any idea of a resorting to despair's approved poetry that she did what she had never done before—drew back her curtains, and opened the window, and stared out into the hollow darkness of the night.

Though such a thought did not visit her, it was a night well mated to her mind's night—a dead darkness, without wind or star. It was as though even the earth's motion had come to a stop, a spring run down, and the vast toy for ever stayed from its twirling. A card-case lay on the window-sill, and with an idle whim she picked it up and dropped it into the well of darkness outside. It seemed an endless while before the ground beneath sighed back its confirmation of her act. 'The force of gravity,' she remarked to the night; and suddenly the foolish words seemed to clinch her despair, shutting her up for ever in the residue of a life without joy, purpose or possible release; and wringing her dangled hands, she bowed herself over the sill, her mind circling downward like a plummet through a pit of misery, her body listening, as it were, to the pain of her breast crushed against the stone.

Opening her eyes at last, she found herself staring at a star; but a red, and angry and earthly one—the flare of the distant lime-kiln. Wrought by the day's desperation to a fantastic clear-headedness, she put on her outdoor clothes, saying aloud as she moved about the room, 'I will go to him, as those other women do. He robbed me of my children, he shall give me others.'

It seemed to her that she was in a perfectly rational frame of mind; and with detached self-approval she observed how methodically her wits were working, bidding her put on stout boots, visit the potting-shed for the old storm-lantern that hung there, and take the path across the park which would let her out by the wicket gate. Just as her lantern light made real to her only the patch of road on which her feet were set, her consciousness showed her only a moment's world: a gate to be opened, a thistle skirted, a bramble's clutch to be disentangled from her skirts.

The journey, so laggingly long on that July morning, was a short one now, and presently her lantern light showed her the glitter of water running shallow over stones, and that she had reached the bottom of the track which led to the lime-kiln. In the pale chalk mud she saw the large imprints of a man's feet, and all the path as it led upward was speckled with fallen leaves from the bushes, trampled in so that they made a pattern as of black marble inlaid on white. All through her journey she had kept her eyes on the ground. There had been no need for sight to rekindle in her mind the red and angry star she had seen from the window. Now she was treading on the level turf, harsh with winter, and the star was before her, a fluctuating and sullen glare, and the smell of the kiln caught her throat and dried it as though with terror.

She raised her lantern, and sent its light forward. A furze bush seemed to leap towards her, massive and threatening. In the darkness beyond she heard a rustle and the sound of something breathing, the noise of some startled animal making off. Still holding up her lantern she went on, and with a few more paces had caught him in her light. He was sitting on the ground, his back to the kiln for warmth, his arms folded, his eyes watching her advance. He made no move to get up, his features did not alter from their look of dull resentment.

She was out of breath with the climb, and the warmth and fumes of the place made her feel suddenly dizzy and unreal. She sat down on the ground, a few feet away from him, settling the lantern beside her. It shone on her ringed hand, and on the muddied hem of her crape flounces.

'You've walked hard,' said the man, after a pause. His voice was like his look : dull and proud.

Her limbs were trembling. The cold of the spongy ground was like a wound.

'This is a queer time for a lady like you to be out a-walking —for you are a lady, I reckon.'

With an effort she controlled her voice and said,

'I have some reason for it.'

'Aye ?' said the man. He spoke slowly, dragging out the word, so that it hardly condescended to be an enquiry.

'I have come here once before. But that was by day, and I brought my two children with me.'

He shifted himself a little, moving his back against the wall, luxuriously.

'Now they are dead. Dead of smallpox.'

His expression changed, though not to pity. Its sullenness strengthened to wrath, a change of countenance impersonal and senseless as a sudden reddening of that canopy of lurid and shadowy air beneath which he sat.

'Children do die hereabouts,' he said. 'There's the smallpox, and the typhus, and the cholera. There's the low fever, and the quick consumption. And there's starvation. Plenty of things for children to die of.'

'You speak with little pity, my man.'

'I'm like the gentry, then. Like the parsons, and the justices, and the lords and ladies. Like that proud besom down to Blandamer.'

He spoke with such savage intent that she leaped to her feet. But he had not moved, nor changed his look from its sullen dull pride.

' Plenty more children, they say, where the dead ones came from. If they die like cattle, the poor, they breed like cattle too. Plenty more children. That's what I say to you. Rich and poor can breed alike, I suppose.

' Eh ? ' he shouted, lumbering to his feet and thrusting his face into hers.

In her plunge to escape him she forgot her lantern. She stumbled in the darkness, thought he was upon her. But there was no footfall, no sound ; and at last she had to go back for her lantern, stooping to pick it up under the reach of his hand. He stood looking after her, she knew. His raging glance was like a goad on her back, driving her on into the darkness. As she reached the track she heard, shrill and fleering, the sound of a woman's laughter, a forced hysterical cackle that taunted her out of earshot.

All her life long Sophia heard it said that the labouring classes were insolent, mutinous and violent. She had agreed to this as to a matter of course, accepting the rightness of any legislation designed to keep them down, and in her own dealings with the poor at her gate going upon the assumption that even such apparently toothless animals as widows and Sunday School children should be given their pounds of tea or their buns through the bars. Yet until this evening she had never heard a speech that was not respectful. Even the Labourers' Rising of 1830 had shown itself to her as a procession of men wearing their best clothes, men with washed smocks and oily church-going heads. In those ranks she had recognised, reining in her pony to watch them go by, Harry Dymond the blacksmith, who but a week before had shod the pony, old Ironsides, who every summer presented her with a peeled and patterned elder-wand, Bill Cobb, who was engaged to the laundry-maid, Herring the smallholder, whose hedges she ransacked for white violets. Those of the village who knew her had pulled their forelocks, and the rest had followed suit, eyeing, with the Englishman's pleasure in a smart turn-out, the handsome girl-child and the bright-coated beast. That evening they had marched up the drive and arranged themselves in a semicircle before the house. Mamma had talked of Marie Antoinette, but Papa, tapping his snuff-box, had gone out and addressed them from the top of the steps, assuring them that their behaviour was foolish, and their throats, no doubt, after so much ill-advised shouting, dry. Whereupon he had returned to his Marsala, and a barrel of beer had been rolled out into the kitchen courtyard. This, apparently, had ended the matter, except for the laundry-maid, who presently began to go about red-eyed and weeping. Bill, said Mrs Perry the housekeeper, had gone too far. Bill had been transported, and that foolish Ellen should have been thankful for her mercies, and that she was not burnt in her bed, instead of crying into the starch.

Now, in the kilnman, the insolence of the labouring classes had been demonstrated. Oddly enough, the outrage had left her neither shocked nor angry. Indeed, it seemed to have done her good; for after the moment of terror had blown off she found herself tautened and stimulated, as though a well-administered slap in the face had roused her from a fainting-fit. Her blood ran living again, her wits revived, her natural vitality, which seemed to have died with the death of her children, returned to her, and once again thinking was a satisfaction, and the use of her limbs a pleasure. Not even the fact that a woman had been there in hiding, listening to her discomforture and laughing over it, could dash her strange sense of something triumphant in this ignominious escapade. ' His vixen with him ! ' she exclaimed, and heard her chuckle sound out over the silent field, coarse and free-hearted, a sound as kindred to the country night as an owl's tu-whoo, or the barking of a fox.

What strange loves those must be, up there on the hill, canopied by the wavering ruddied smoke : loves bitter and violent as the man's furious mind, but in the upleaping of that undaunted lust of a strength which could outface violence and bitterness.

Too rough a sire, perhaps, for the heir of Blandamer. But his words, plain and vile, had served her purpose, fathering a determination in her mind. Plenty more children, he had said. Rich and poor can breed alike. Fate should not defeat her, she would have a child yet. And having already a husband it was certainly best and most convenient that the child should be his. So she would go to Paris, fetch Frederick back if needs be, beguile him, at the barest, explain her purpose and strike a bargain. As other women could trudge up to the lime-kiln, Mrs Willoughby might go to Paris.

Though more prosaically. A wish, half truly, half ironically felt, arose in her that she could know what manner of love it was that would take one out on a November midnight to lie embracing on the soggy turf. But one could not hope for everything ; and what she wanted, what she must have, was a child.

So, on the night before her journey, she uncurtained her window once more, looked towards the ruddy star on the hillside, and nodded to it briefly, the acknowledgment one resolute rogue might give another. The determination set in her by the kilnman had never wavered or bleached into fantasy. It proved so sturdy that she had been able to delay, trusting it to carry the burden of various postponements—a visit to London to observe fashions and buy new clothes, the conclusion of a purchase of some land adjoining hers, the choice of a parson to replace Mr Harwood whose Michaelmas goose had carried him off, entertaining Caspar for the Christmas holidays. Seeing him she had remembered her fancy that the half-caste should step into the shoes of her dead children—a moment's scheme, a doting desperate fancy. He showed nothing to recommend him for her pug's place now, his Sambo charm smudged out by a violent cold in his head, his fingers too heavy with chilblains to twitch more than a few jangling notes from his guitar, his only pleasure to sit by the fire sucking lozenges.

Holding by the belief that she might choose her time, she had allowed time to slip through her fingers, pleased to feel that every day's delay increased the impetus of her dammed-up purpose; and when Harlowe slipped and sprained her wrist, Sophia, firmly bandaging that genteel white flesh, forgot to be annoyed at this further impediment, absorbed in the pleasure of doing something which she knew she did well. To travel without a maid was not possible. So she thought, till a few days without Harlowe's ministrations showed her that she could brush hair and lace stays quite as well as she could wind on a bandage, and then every con-

sideration seemed to point out the superior convenience of
travelling alone. Only the world was against it. But since
her visit to the lime-kiln Sophia was against the world.

Now it was the third week in February, and in her head
still sounded the clamour of bird-song which had rung down
the sun of her last day at Blandamer. In the space, proper
to well-managed journeys, between everything done and only
the journey to do, she had gone out for a walk, to be sud-
denly ravished into the first evening of spring. Drenched
with long rains, the meadows were green as emerald in the
level light. Clouds, like the dividing folds of a stage curtain
drawing up and aside, made all the sky dramatic. Every-
where around her was the excited chatter of running water,
every ditch and drain babbling and hastening. Large as toys
the birds sat on the bare boughs, or darted through the
watery, lake-still air. Their clamour was dazzling, the
counterpart to the ear of the brilliant gash of the sunset.

It was as though everything had combined to egg her on—
the hastening water and the acclaiming birds, the drama of
the clouds and the swell of the fields, where the sun's shadow-
play drew a sharper furrow. And to remember that all this
seeming concurrence was the accident of the day, and that
she amid all the fervid excitement and quickening of the hour
walked with her separate secret purpose doubled her proud
fever, her confidence, and her delight in thinking that now
at last her will should be unscabbarded and flash free.

On the next night, too, she was to remember the kilnman
and his ruddy signalling star, for then she was at sea, looking
towards the lights of Calais. It was a pleasure to be in
France again—a light-of-love country which, making no

claims on her esteem, was the more likeable and refreshing. That coastline in the dawn might look as English as it pleased, wear a church spire and be trimmed with ample woods; but it was France, a country where one went for pleasure, whose inhabitants, as the children's geography primer said, 'were very fond of dancing, wine, and the Pope.'

To this toy country toy trains had been added since her last visit; and it was with a confirming acquiescence that she learned at the station that owing to a mechanical misfortune the Paris train would not run until after midday. The train stood in the station, and an old woman with her head bound up in a spotted nightcap shook out a feather whisk from a compartment window. The driver leaned from the cab, conversing with a porter. At intervals he patted the engine with a soothing hand as though it might rear. Since there seemed nothing to stay her from wandering where she pleased, she walked along the track, feeling a cat's impulse to move into the fresh sunlight.

'I tell you,' said the porter, 'we must have a change. We've had altogether too much of the old pear lately. He fattens himself too much, that pear.'

'Fat or thin,' said the driver, 'they're all the same.'

Pear must be the station-master, she thought, sliding her glance along the bright rails. Monsieur Poire. It was exactly what a French official would be called. But the porter had pursued her, and now was observing that although there was no immediate danger, since the Paris train would be for some hours more stationary, yet the promenade she had chosen was not what one could call propitious, and was, in fact, forbidden to passengers.

'I will go and have breakfast,' she said, smiling, pleased with herself and with him for pleasing her. For he was young, light and nimble, his eyes were sleek black-currants, the glib grandeur of his speech was like the polish of a new toy, so that altogether the encounter was like nibbling up a crisp young radish.

Beau pays de France. She felt suddenly happy, lightened in spirits as though a wand had been waved over her. She knew, too, that she was looking handsome, and in her stately mourning, spirited ; that her gloves fitted her triumphantly, that she had not forgotten how to speak French. And though there was no one to admire her, she was quite content to admire herself—indeed, a great part of her high spirits and good-humour sprang from her solitary and unprotected state. What a mercy it was that Harlowe had sprained that wrist ! For with Harlowe tagging after me, she thought, clutching my dressing-case and mouthing with sea-sickness, there would have been no escape. I should not be rambling out for my breakfast, and looking forward to a whole fore-noon of picking up entertainment where I please. No ! I should be hunting for somewhere that could supply a good English cup of tea, or sitting in the waiting-room. And she had a vision of Harlowe covering the bench with a sheet of newspaper before she would risk her seat on it.

The air was still the air of early morning, the sky a very pale blue. Along the quayside was a crowd of fishing craft. Looking down on them she saw how, amidst a seemingly irreparable filth and untidiness, some one was intently busy at polishing one particular knob. The smell of the sea, melancholy like a whine, rose from the filthy clucking water.

Catches were being auctioned, and she listened for a while, holding her skirts about her, yawning with hunger and early rising.

But before breakfasting she must buy a newspaper, a great many newspapers. And over her coffee she read with the sharpened interest which the mind gives to what is passing and alien how a boatload of convicts had left Havre for Belle Isle, how a mayor had been decorated, how a bishop had preached a formidable sermon against secret societies, how Lady Normanby had attended a reception at the Hôtel Talleyrand, how M. Guizot had expressed his disapproval of banqueting. His speech was reported at length, but she did not read it very attentively, only smiling at his Liberal language which compelled him to refer to the throne as *le Fauteuil*. A good description of that well-stuffed prudent monarch. Sophia held due English views of the Orleans dynasty. It carried on the business well enough, no doubt, but it was not the Old Firm, and its concessions to democracy must certainly have impaired the quality of its teas and sugars. Local prejudice too had strengthened her feelings for the Old Firm. Had not Charles X come in exile to her own country, a fragment of history walking slowly between the primroses of the park of Lulworth Castle, walking there with Marie Antoinette's daughter, the man and woman out of the past pacing black as shadows under the spring sky, hearing the indifferent plaudits of the rooks, who had heard the roars of an acclaiming and a bloodthirsty people? After this, one naturally felt that Louis Philippe was rather tame.

But I did not come here to muse about Louis Philippe, she thought, brusquely tidying up her meditations, for with

the recollection of that exiled king at Lulworth Castle she
had been carried back to Dorset, and to Sophia Willoughby
of Blandamer, whose children were dead, whose husband ran
in the train of another woman—Sophia Willoughby, that
desperate female who had so little to lose that she was now
breakfasting alone in a foreign town, landed secretly there to
carry out her foray. She did not want to think too much
about the reason of her journey. The determination in her
was so strong that it was like an actual pain, she would avoid
while she might the pressure of a thought upon it. When she
reached Paris, she would face the situation ; but meanwhile,
this unexpected pause seemed tumbled into her lap for the
very purpose of truancy and refreshment, and so she would
make the most of it, as she had made the most of those stolen
hours in Cornwall.

Must every thought twist her back upon the loss of her
children, her stratagem to have children again ? She paid for
her breakfast, and walked out with determination to amuse
herself. And almost immediately she found herself invited to
think once more of Louis Philippe.

In a narrow street near the quayside there was a group of
fishers and working-men who stood watching a young man
who was drawing in chalk on a blank wall. He drew swiftly,
scraping his chalk over the masonry, and sometimes giving a
hasty scratch to his hatless curls, as though he would ferret
out the idea of the next line. He drew a tree, a fruit-tree, a
pear-tree, since it bore on every branch an enormous swelling
pear. Then he drew a man, a peasant, holding a pruning-
knife.

The crowd closed up, there were chuckles, and exclama-

tions of approval. The young man stood back with the
gesture of one who had said his say, and through a gap in the
crowd she saw what his completing strokes had been. For
now the outlined pears had been filled with features, and the
features were unmistakably of the cast of the Royal Family—
a big Louis Philippe pear in the centre of the tree, with all his
lesser pears around him.

The man darted back, and with a violent stroke sharpened
the outline of the pruning-knife. And the instant after he fell
to rubbing out the drawing, demolishing it as swiftly as he
had made it.

The crowd went on, vanishing as the drawing had
vanished, the artist was gone too, and she alone was left,
staring at a blank wall, her eyes and wits blinking still at the
rapidity of the performance. But there, neat as the answer to
a riddle, was the identity of the Monsieur Poire whom she had
taken to be the station-master. It was nice to have it so pat ;
but to her, a foreigner, of no significance. She knew the
French. A nation that must have, throne or arm-chair, its
king, if only to quarrel with.

She walked on, pleased with the adventure, thinking that
perhaps the only satisfactory way of life was to live for the
minute. According to that she should miss the train to Paris
as she had missed the other train, remaining while her
pleasure in them endured to wander through these streets,
whose gay pallor, whose sharp scents, unmodulated crashes
of fish into roasting coffee, printer's ink into tar, entertained
her like a fair and welcomed her like a nursery. There would
be insular company, too, did she need it. For now, the morn-
ing being more advanced, the debt-driven English colony

had begun to show itself : marketing mammas, crowned with righteous bonnets, large-faced, large-eyed schoolgirls giggling arm in arm, shabby-genteel old gentlemen carrying newspapers, and over one arm, a travelling-rug.

No, this train she dared not miss. To live for the minute . . . That was how these had begun, the improvident others of her race. And here was their end : a vacant exile, tedium and pretentiousness, and the years of idle dallying, staring across the Channel, waiting to see the English boat come in.

She began to tremble, to hate the interval of time before the Paris train started. Long before due time, she returned to the station, to make enquiries, to oversee, if need be, that train's departure. And throughout the journey she practised herself in the mood she must take and keep : a mood cool, artful, and determined. For now was no time for romance or enthusiasm. The kilnman's star, which had guided her so far, might prove a Jack-o'-lantern now. There must be nothing in her adventure that could be called adventurous, nothing visionary or overwrought, no sense of destiny to betray her. As other people go to Paris to buy gloves, she was going to Paris to bargain for a child. I must concentrate upon Frederick, she told herself; if possible, not even mention Minna, and certainly not see her. For if I did, my rage might overset me. And in any case it would be beneath my dignity.

The Hôtel Meurice was well calculated to reinforce these resolutions. It enfolded her with all its admonitions of her class and of her race. For here, of course, Papa and Mamma had stayed during her year of being finished in Paris under great-aunt Léocadie's supervision ; here she had first drunk champagne and put on a pearl necklace. The wine-waiter, having taken her order, hesitated at the door of her sitting-room, politely recognising. Though he had served so many of her nation, his dwelling eye implied she was too fine a figure to be forgotten, and with the confidence of a family servant he enquired after her parents.

' There must have been many changes in Paris since we were here.'

His glance towards the window seemed to indicate that a few changes might have taken place outside.

She lingered over her dinner, thinking that when she had finished she would go to bed, to sleep long on that solid French mattress, and refresh herself for the morrow. But the noise of the city resounding beyond the curtained windows excited her, and the dinner and the wine had given her a sense of festivity, so that now to go tamely to bed was not possible. But where to go, being a woman, and alone ? For a while she dallied with the idea of a long drive, and began to map out the route which should show her, enclosed like some Turk's bride in her moving box of darkness, the greatest display of light and animation ; but her knowledge of Paris failed her, or she had forgotten what once she knew, for it was not possible to remember which street debouched into which— and to show her ignorance would be amateurish, and perhaps injudicious.

' Well, at any rate,' she exclaimed, rising angrily, ' I suppose I may drive to visit my husband.' And with this in her mind she began to array herself as though for a battle, putting on her diamond rings, sleeking the bands of her hair, pinning her veil to fall becomingly. The mirror, being

French, must have learned flattery, but even so there was no
doubt that the severity of her mourning clothes became her
well, enhancing the faint pure doll's pink of her cheeks,
giving value to her small regular features, ennobling her
maypole stature. Once already to-day she had thought her-
self handsome ; but how far off that early morning seemed
she was not to know fully until she crossed the pavement to
get into the waiting cab. For now a small snow was falling,
fine as the woolly powder which falls from a springtime
poplar tree. It fell between her and the dirty brown face
of a woman who was selling mimosa and who, scenting a
foreigner, hurried forward, her earthy face peering behind the
soft golden plumes. On Sophia's skin at the same moment
fell the powdering snow and the soft tickle of the mimosa
blossom. The shaken pollen made her sneeze, the touch of
this cold and this soft falling together sent a thrill through
her flesh.

I am in Paris, she said to herself, suddenly warm and
happy, as though happiness had just fledged out on her.
And holding her foolish bunch of flowers, she leaned back
in the cab, touching her face with their softness, trying to
hold intact the mood of pleasure so unexpectedly alighted.
To her loneliness the flowers were almost like a person, a
Cinderella godmother alighting on her desolation and ashes
and assuring her that after all it would be possible for her to
dance at the King's palace that night. Twice to-day I have
felt handsome—twice to-day I have been happy—and with
that rarest happiness, at least it has been rare to me, a simple
hedgerow happiness that any one, a child or an old woman
shelling peas, might feel. Perhaps at last I am in the way

of it. For I know what I want, and that is a very simple thing—a child, a thing any one might have. It need not even be sent from the South of France, like this mimosa. But if I have a child, this time I must not spoil it all with fuss and ambition.

Yet, having a child, how not to fuss, how not to be stiffened into anxiety and watchfulness? And she was beginning to wonder if it would not be best to bring up this child in France, where the climate was easier, where there would be no pressure from outside, as at Blandamer there must be, to freeze her back into the awkward consciousness of being a wronged wife, when the cab stopped.

More expensive than it looks, she decided, scanning the rather dowdy façade, with its well-scrubbed paint and unobtrusive blazon. It was snowing more heavily now, and the concierge opened an umbrella as he came forward. Mr Willoughby had gone out.

Sophia heard the money in her purse clink, and her voice say,

' To Madame Lemuel's ? '

Most probably. He would enquire of his wife.

He came back, bowing, to say it was so.

' Good. Then I shall meet him there. Please tell my driver where to go.'

The weight of her bribe had made him so abundantly confidential that though she listened for the address she could not hear it. But it must be some way off, for the driver clicked to his horse as though to mettle it for a long journey.

You triple fool, she arraigned herself. For what could it

serve her to follow Frederick to the house of his mistress ?
How few hours ago was it that she had sealed up that final
determination not even to mention Minna, if the mention
could be avoided ?   And now, carried away by this ridiculous
impulse, she was allowing herself to be driven to the woman's
door.   Well, there was time to revise the error.   She would
pay off this cab, and immediately hire another for the return
journey.   And Heaven knows, she thought, trying to stiffen
herself with practical considerations, what I shall not have to
pay for this jaunt—for the bribe had been considerable, and
already her cab had crossed the river.

Except for visits to great-aunt Léocadie in the Faubourg
St Germain, Sophia knew the Left Bank only as a territory
into which one was taken to see something historical.   She
was at a loss in the narrow winding streets, and peered out
anxiously, looking for something to recognise, alarmed by
the sensation of being in an unknown place, and wondering
if it would be as easy as she had supposed to find that cab
for the journey back.   The streets were narrow, ill-paved
and ill-lit ; flares of light from street market or wineshop or
rowdy café lightened the darkness unconsolingly ; and then
with a twist to right or left, they were passing between high
walls with garden-doors in them, walls over which trees
stooped their empty branches ; or the solid shape of a dome
ballooned up.   Then a larger dome, parenting all these,
appeared, and with an effort of memory she recognised the
Panthéon.   The horse slackened its pace ; even when the
crest of the hill had been reached the driver's click and whip-
crack were half-hearted, a convention only, and hearing this
she knew that the street into which they turned must be the

journey's end. Rue de la Carabine, she saw, lettered on the wall. And at the next moment the cab had stopped.

It was a narrow street. The houses, old and tall, rose up cliff-like, their shutters banding the perspective. Along the bottom of this crevasse three or four private carriages were being slowly driven up and down, the sound of the horses' hoofs falling like stones pattered methodically into a well. A carriage which had arrived just before her cab was now moving off to join in the back and forth of the others ; its occupant, a consciously romantic figure in a flowing cloak, was hesitating on the threshold of a stone passage, from which a flight of stairs ascended ; but seeing her, he seemed to take it for granted that she also would enter, and stepped back to make way for her. There was a lamp burning just inside the door, and its light showed her a face that was faintly familiar. I do not know you as well as the wine-waiter, she thought ; but I do know you. His following presence propelled her up the creaking circling staircase. I am done for now, she said to herself, propelled upwards, flight after flight, towards the sound of voices. Fool ! And as though her mind dared not acknowledge the extent of such foolishness, it busied itself trying to recollect when and where she had seen the operatic gentleman of the cloak.

Yes. At an evening party, a rather grand evening party, given by one of Papa's *émigré* friends, who had returned with the Restoration. He had stood in a moody attitude near the harp, some one had told her that he wrote—or was it composed music?—his name began with . . . No. She could not recall his name. Halfway up the third flight she recalled that he had been described as a poet. Hollow with fear, and driven on by fear, like a child arriving at a party she saw lights, and heard voices, and smelled, swaying out on that cold and dirty staircase, the perfumes of civilised society. And here was the party, the party to which she had not been invited.

Some of the party had overflowed on to the landing, and stood grouped round the doorway, looking inward. If I can stay out here, she thought with a last flicker of hope, and let him go past, I can sneak down again unnoticed. And carefully laying down her absurd bunch of mimosa she began to fidget with her shoe-fastening.

' Please go on,' she said to the cloak, and heard her English accent ring out like a trumpet. The cloak bowed, and passed her. After what seemed hours of deception with the shoe-fastening, she looked up cautiously. The cloak was standing by the doorway, having opened a path into the room for her. The other door-keepers were regarding her with polite curiosity. She straightened herself, and their expressions changed to surprise at her height, as though, rising so fiercely tall and straight, she had presented them with a fixed bayonet. Like one large family, occupying one large family pew, and she arriving in the middle of the service, they manœuvred her in.

' A chair,' said some one. But shaking her head she wedged herself into a corner. If they will leave me alone— she thought. At that moment her bunch of mimosa was handed in after her.

She was in an ante-room, whose doors stood open upon the larger room beyond. Both rooms seemed incredibly crowded, though as she realised, furtively looking about her, this effect was due to the informal way in which people had grouped themselves, and to the extraordinary mixture of people present. Entering, her embarrassment had been given a final wrench by the impression that all the women were in full evening-dress; but now, among these islands of glittering silk and lace she noticed other figures, some habited, as she said to herself, 'like artists,' others patently of the working class. Immediately in front of her stood a bald-headed old gentleman, wearing a plaid rug over his shoulders. To her left she looked down upon the polished shoulders and swaying fan of a ballroom elegant. Beside her was a Jewish boy, a hump-back, with a face that hunger had sharpened into a painful beauty. He had moved aside to make way for her and, seeing her flowers, had smiled. Otherwise no one seemed inclined to take the least notice of her.

I may get out of it yet, she said to herself.

There was talk; but it was of a quality, hushed and hesitant, that suggested the talk that rises among people who are waiting through the indeterminate interval between one item of a concert and another. Perhaps it was a concert. In the farther room the strings of a harp had been plucked. For some while her unused ears could make little of what was being said; but as her nerves quieted, and the hope of keeping her anonymity crept higher, she began to prick her ears, saying to herself that Frederick's voice, at any rate, would emerge to her on its familiarity. But it was another voice that she first caught in the entirety of a sentence, a loud fulsome voice that said, speaking French with a German accent,

' Most beautiful Minna, we are here to be enchanted. Will

you not wave your wand, will you not tell us one of your
beautiful *Maerchen* ? '

Good God, what a menagerie! exclaimed Sophia to her-
self, disgusted at the speech and the manner. The little Jew
had turned his head and was looking at her compassionately.
Why, she wondered. She saw the bunch of mimosa
trembling in her grasp. For those words addressed to
Minna, *most beautiful Minna*, had brought her rival before her,
in a flash making real the hearsay hated one, stabbing into
her consciousness the knowledge that the woman lived and
breathed, and was in the very room.

The fulsome voice was lost among other voices making
the same request. That's Frederick! her mind cried out,
and forgot him in the next instant, hearing in reply the voice
whose ghost had spoken at her child's bedside, saying, *Ma
fleur*.

' No, not a fairy-tale. I have told so many. This, this
shall be a true story.'

See her she must. And in the jostle of rearrangement
which had followed the requesting voices, Sophia shifted her
place till she could see from the ante-room into the room
beyond. When she could hear again, Minna was already
speaking, leaning forward with her elbows on her knees,
her face propped between her hands—the attitude of one
crouched over a sleepy fire, watching the embers waste and
brighten and waste again.

II

'B<small>UT</small> the first thing I can remember is the lighting of a candle.

'It is night, the middle of the night it seems to me, waking as a child does into that different world, mysterious, unfathomable, which night is to a child. A separate world, as though one awoke in the depths of the sea. My father is there, moving softly in the dusky room. He speaks to himself in a language which I have never heard before, and coming to the hearth he takes up an ember with the tongs, and breathes on it, as though he were praying to it. At his breath it awakens and glows, and I see his face, and his lips moving amid his beard. Then with the ember he lights tall yellow candles; and as the flame straightens he straightens also, and begins to chant in the strange language, raising his hand to his forehead, bowing and making obeisance. On his forehead is a little box, and over his head is the praying towel.

'For it is the Sabbath candle he had lit, and alone, in the depth of the night, in secret, he is praying to the God of our race, and glorifying him.

'I cannot understand it, and yet I can understand it well enough to know that it is something secret and precious, a jewel that can only be taken out at night. Afterwards, how long afterwards I cannot remember, I spoke to him of what I had seen. Then he told me how we were of the chosen people, exiles from Jerusalem, captive in this world as the gold is captive in the rock and trodden underfoot by those who go to and fro. And he showed me a book, written in our holy language; and in that book, he said, were the stories of good Jewesses, faithful women: Jael, who slew Sisera, and Judith who slew Holophernes; Deborah, who led an army, and Esther, who saved a people.

' It seemed to me that their stories were written against the sky. For our house, our hovel, stood at the edge of a fir-forest, and those black stems and branches, leaning and jagged, line after line, were like the Hebrew letters in the book; and as I ran through the forest, picking up sticks and fir-cones for fuel, I used to make stories to myself, stories of Jewish women, reading them from the book of the trees.

' But that was in summer, an endless lifetime, when the sky was as blue as a cornflower, when I picked wild straw-berries, and sucked flowers for nectar, and heard the con-tented bleating of our goats as they ate the sweet pasture, and the endless drone of the insects in the forest. And as day and night were different worlds, so were winter and summer. But best of all I remember the first spring.

' In the night, the wind changed. I woke up, and heard a different voice, loud like the coming of an army, and yet thick and gentle, as though it wrapped one in velvet. I pinched my mother, and said, " What's that ? " She woke with a start, and lay still, listening and trembling. " It is the thaw-wind," she said, " blowing from Jerusalem. With the Holy One is mercy." And she gathered me closer, and fell asleep again, and the wind seemed like her snores, warm and kind.

' The wind brought rain, a soft brushing rain like tassels

of silk. The hard crust of snow was covered with little pits, and the goats bleated in the shed. The snow began to fall off the roof in great clods that smashed as they fell. Suddenly the flat grey sky was blue, was lofty, with shining clouds, and a bird flew past the door. When I ran out the snow wetted my feet. It was beginning to melt, and I kicked and danced until I had scrabbled a hole, and there at the bottom of the hole was the ground again, with the grasses squashed and stiff and earth-coloured. I knelt by the hole, and rubbed my cheek against the ground, and snuffed it. Then I looked up at the sky, and the clouds were going so fast and so lightly that I felt giddy, as though the earth were sliding away under me. I ran about, kicking the melting snow, and shouting little tags of Hebrew that I had learned from my father.

' Day after day the wind blew warm, and the snow melted, and the ground appeared, and thawed, and clucked like a hen, drinking the snow-water. Blades of new grass came up, and small bright flowers, flocks of birds came flying, and settled on the patches of cleared ground, or pecked at the glistening tree-trunks. My mother came out into the yard, shading her eyes with one hand, holding on her other arm my little brother, who blinked and sneezed. He had been born in the winter, this was the first time he had felt the sun. I tugged at her skirts. " Let us go for a walk, let us go a long way," I begged. " To-morrow," she said.

' But on the morrow we could not go out at all, for the wind had shifted, hail-storms flew by, one after another like a flight of screaming cranes whose wings stretched over the whole world. The ground was whitened with hailstones, and the birds lay under the bushes, frozen to death. But the spring could not be stopped now, it came back again, the sun shone, clouds of midges sprang up from nowhere, the bushes swayed like dancers, shadows rippled over the earth like running water.

' When we were out of doors my mother seemed a different woman, walking with a freer step, singing as she walked. She carried her baby on her back, slung in a shawl, and I, thinking always of the women of Jewry, fancied that she was like Judith's handmaid, carrying the tyrant's head over the hills of Bethulia. We went over the heath, farther than ever I had been. It was piebald with snow, and the pools of bog-water we passed, fringed with cat-ice, were so violently blue under the blue sky that I was almost afraid of them. There was colour, too, in the birch copses, as though the stems had been smeared with damson juice. By one of these copses my mother sat down to suckle her baby. The sun shone on her breast, and it was as though her ugly clothes had been thawed away from this smooth strong pushing flower. When the baby was quieted I heard, through the small noises of the wood, other far-off sounds—roarings and crashes. " The wolves are fighting ! " I cried out, but she shook her head. And presently we went on towards the sounds. If it is not wolves, I thought, it must be woodmen ; for now among the crashes that were as though a tree had fallen I heard yelling cries like the whine of a saw. And we came to the wood's end, and stood on the bank of a river.

' On either side it was still frozen, the arched ice rearing up above the water like opened jaws. But in the centre channel the current flowed furiously, and borne along on it,

jostling and crashing, turning over and over, grating together
with long harsh screams, were innumerable blocks of ice.
As the river flowed its strong swirling tongue licked furiously
at the icy margins, and undermined them, and with a shudder
and a roar of defeat another fragment would break away and
be swept downstream. It was like a battle. It was like a
victory. The rigid winter could stand no longer, it was
breaking up, its howls and vanquished threats swept past me,
its strongholds fell and were broken one against another, it
was routed at last.

'I wept with excitement, and my mother comforted me,
thinking I was afraid. But I could not explain what I felt,
though I knew it was not fear. For then I knew only the
wintry words of my race, such words as exile, and captivity,
and bondage. I had never heard the word Liberty. But it
was Liberty I acclaimed, seeing the river sweeping away its
fetters, tossing its free neck under the ruined yoke.'

She stopped abruptly, like the player lifting the bow from
the strings with a flourish. Murmurs of admiration arose.
She seemed to listen to them as the concerto player listens
to the strains of the orchestra he has quitted, half relaxing
from the stanza completed, half intent upon what lies before.
This is all quite right, her expression said; presently I shall
go on again. For she had raised her head, and now Sophia
could see her face. It was ugly, uglier than one could have
believed, hearing that voice. A discordant face, Sophia's mind
continued, analysing while it could, before the voice went
on again; for the features with their Jewish baroque, the
hooked nose, the crescent eyebrows and heavy eyelids, the
large full-lipped mouth, are florid, or should be; but the

hollow cheeks forbid them, and she is at once a heavy voluptuous cat and a starved one. Meanwhile she had omitted to look for Frederick. But it was too late, for Minna had begun to speak again.

'When the next spring came, I remembered the river. Another child had been born, my mother was busy, I seemed likely to beg in vain. And this spring, too, was not like the other. A weeping mist covered the land, a mist that brought pestilence. From the village, where I was not allowed to go, came the sound of the Christian church bell, tolling for the dead. Noemi, our neighbour, came to our house and told my mother that the Gentile women said that the pestilence had been seen on the heath, a troop of riders with lances, moving in the mist. My father looked up from his work. " Such tales are idolatrous," said he. " Do you, a good Jewess, believe them ? " " *I* do not believe them, Reb," she answered. " They sicken for their sins and their swine's flesh. But let them believe it, if they will. It is better than if they said we poisoned their wells."

' This story of the pestilence riding over the heath made me think better of my resolve that if my mother would not take me to the river I would find my way there alone. I began to pester my father, saying that though I was only a girl, I was the first-born. And at last he consented. But with him it was a different journey, for he walked fast, talking sometimes to himself but never to me. The air was raw and sunless, my feet hurt me and I almost wished that we had never come, until reaching the birch-wood I heard again those thunders and crashings. I ran on ahead, towards the sound, and came by myself to the river bank. A mist hung

over the water, flowing with the river, the glory of the year
before was not there. Then, as I looked, I saw that on the
hurried ice-blocks there were shapes, men and horses, half
frozen into the ice, half trailing in the water. And in the
ice were stains of blood. Last year, I remembered, it had
seemed like a battle, like a victory. Had there been blood
and corpses then, and had I forgotten them? The full river
seemed to flow more heavily, when ice-block struck against
ice-block they clanged like iron bells. My father, coming up
behind me, spoke to himself in Hebrew, and groaned. " Who
are they, Father? " " The wrathful, child, the proud, and
the enemies of God . . . So let thine enemies perish, O
Lord ! " He cried this out in a voice that rang above the
tumult of the river. Then he was silent for a long time,
shuddering and sighing like an animal. At last he told me
that there must have been a battle, perhaps a war, where,
who could tell ?—and that the bodies of the slain, caught in
the frost, may have been locked up winter-long, that now
with the thaw were being hurried to the sea.

' All the way home, and for long after, I pondered over
this thought, so new to me, that there were other people in
the world, people living so far off that they might fight and
perish and no word of it come to us, no splash of their blood.
I knew from the Book, and from stories, that there had been
peoples and nations ; but I thought they were all dead. I
was forbidden to go to the village, lest the children should
throw stones at me. Our household, and Noemi's and old
Baruch's, was Jewry, and the village the Gentiles. But now
these dead men had come into my world.

' Soon came more living. For that summer, staggering

over the heath and staring about them as if afraid, came a
troop of strangers, men, women and children. They carried
bundles and bits of household stuff, pots and pans flashing in
the sun, wicker baskets with hens in them : some led goats,
or a cow, and an old white horse drew a hooded cart that
rocked and jolted on the moorland track. I was picking
strawberries when I looked up and saw them ; and spilling
the fruit I leaped up and ran home, to tell this strange news.
" They are gipsies," my mother said. " Run, child, and
fetch in the washing." Somehow I had heard of gipsies, for
I said, " No, they are not gipsies. These people could never
dance." My father went a little way to where he could see
them, my mother following him. I saw her start, and wring
her hands as if in pity, and then they hastened forward
towards the strangers. My father embraced the foremost, an
old man whose bald head glistened with sweat, my mother
hurried to and fro among the women. I could hear her
voice, loud with excitement, exclaiming and condoling.

‘ For they were a settlement of Jews, who had been driven
out of their homes, and had come over the heath looking for
some place where they might live unmolested. That night,
and for many nights to come, they camped on our
meadow, and my mother fed them, and beat up herbs to
put on their blistered feet. Their goats quarrelled with ours,
their children played and quarrelled with us. In fancy, re-
membering their coming across the heath, I told myself that
they had come like Eliezer's embassy, with servants and
camels, to ask for me in marriage. In fact, since their poverty
was even more abject than ours, I lorded it over the new-
come children, and discovered the sweets of tyranny.’

She paused again, but this time gently, and with a sly smile.

And you must still savour them, thought Sophia, seeing that mournful dark glance flicker slowly over the listeners, as though numbering so many well-tied money-bags. Our ears are your ducats. You are exactly like a Jewish shop-keeper, the Jew who kept the antique shop at Mayence, staring, gloating round his shelves, with a joy in possession so absorbing that it was almost a kind of innocence. In a moment you should rub your hands, the shopkeeper's gesture.

At that moment the slowly flickering glance touched her, and rested. It showed no curiosity, only a kind of pondering attention. Then, as though in compliance, Minna's large supple hands gently caressed themselves together in the very gesture of her thought. Sophia started slightly. The glance, mournfully numbering, moved on. But answering Sophia's infinitesimal start of surprise there had been a smile—small, meek, and satisfied, the smile of a dutiful child. And again there had been no time to look for Frederick.

'My position among these children was the stronger, since my father, by his learning and orthodoxy, was looked up to by all the newcomers. He led them in prayer, he exhorted them to cherish our faith, he comforted and advised them. By the end of the summer many of the immigrants had built themselves huts out of the forest, and settled near us. I was delighted with this, seeing that it gave us company and consequence. I blamed my poor mother for narrow-heartedness, since she did not rejoice as much as I did. Bending over the loom she would sigh and shake her head ;

and among the clatter of the pedals I overheard such words
as these : " One or two they will suffer. But not a multi-
tude." And then she would weep, her tears falling on the
growing web. But for all these doubts, which I could see but
not understand, she did what she could for our neighbours,
our neighbours who were even poorer than ourselves.

' Perhaps because they had opened their hands, my parents
began to grow more prosperous. My father started a little
shop, selling such things as seed and candles and household
gear. Because the wares were good and cheap, people from
the village came to buy, saying always that they were cheated
and overcharged, but coming again. My mother baked cakes
for their Christian feast-days, cakes flavoured with caraways
or wild anise, and I, instead of gathering wood strawberries,
cherries, and cranberries for myself, gathered them to make
into jams, and the money from this little commerce was put
by for my wedding dowry. One day my father came back
from a journey to the town with a coloured bandbox con-
taining a wig for my mother. For when they had married
they had been too poor to buy such a thing, and my mother,
shaving her head as Jewish women must do on marriage, had
ever afterwards worn only a kerchief. Now she had a wig, a
grand, an honourable wig. It was of horsehair, dyed chestnut
colour, very voluminous and towering, and when she had
put it on all her friends came in to congratulate and admire.
My father, too, looked at her as though she were beautiful and
stately as Queen Esther. His face was full of pride and love.
But I hung back, awkward and alarmed ; for to me this wig
seemed ugly and, worse still, baleful and unlucky.

' Under these glaring tresses I saw for the first time how

pale and careworn my mother's face had grown since the
coming of these other Jews and our riches, so that I had lost
all sight, now, of the mother who had walked singing over
the heath and suckled her baby in the birch-wood.

' But these thoughts I kept to myself, only saying among
those of my own age that the wig was ugly, and that when I
married I would wear a kerchief or perhaps keep my long
hair. When I said such things as these my playmates tittered
and pretended to be shocked. I made them long speeches,
saying that Jewry must be freed, and that when I was older I
would lead them all back to Jerusalem. Some of the boys
jeered at me, saying that I did not know where Jerusalem was
(indeed, I did not), and that anyhow I was only a woman and
could do nothing but obey my husband. But mostly they
followed me, and when my speeches were too much for them
I wooed them back with a story. All my stories were of
freedom and the overthrowing of tyrants, and so led to my
speeches again. And when I tired of their listening faces I
would give them the slip, and go over the heath to the river
(for it was an easy walk now); and sitting on the river bank
I used to say, over and over again, David's words : *Turn our
captivity, O Lord, as the rivers in the south*. For I had never
forgotten my first sight of the river, so proud and turbulent,
bearing away its broken fetters. The river would understand
me when I spoke of Liberty.

' Eleven times since I was born the ice had crept over the
running river and thickened there. And now it was winter
again, midwinter, and a winter's evening dusk. Not since
the winter of the pestilence had there been such ruthless cold,
such famine and distress. The wolves came out in broad

daylight, at night they fought among themselves, ravening
for each other's flesh. Unknown birds flew over us in bands,
driven even out of their north by the cold. Whenever they
flew over, a storm followed.

'I was just coming across the yard from the outhouse,
where I had gone to carry our goats their feed, when I heard
footsteps, a man running and staggering along the frozen
path. The running man was my father. He had torn off his
mittens as though their weight would encumber him, I saw
his red hands flapping against the dusky white of the snow.
His mouth was open, he fetched his breath with groaning.
He fell down on the icy track, and was up again, and came
running on with his face bloodied. He did not see me where
I stood motionless in the dusk of the yard, but ran past me
and burst open the house door and staggered in. Before he
had spoken I heard my mother cry out, a wild despairing cry
that yet seemed to have a note of exultation in it, as though it
were recognising and embracing some terror long foreseen.
I went in after him, very slowly and quietly, as though in this
sweep of terror I must move as noiselessly as possible. He
was leaning over the table, his hands clenching it, and trem-
bling. He trembled, his back heaved up and down with his
struggles for breath, with every gasp he groaned with the
anguish of breathing. Mixed in with his groans were words.
Always the same words. "They're coming!" he said.
"They're coming!"'

'Wolves!' exclaimed Frederick.

'*Christians*.

'My mother with averted eyes as though she dared not
look at him was hurrying the younger children into their

coats and wrappings. The baby began to cry. "Hush!"
she whispered. I could scarcely hear the word, but it was
spoken with such vehemence that the child, a child at the
breast, understood, and lay still as a corpse. With arms that
seemed to have stretched into the wings of a vast bird she
gathered us together. "Come! Come quickly and softly!
We must hide in the forest." "The Book," said my father.
"The candlesticks. The holy things of Israel." There was
no expression on her face as she stood waiting, while tremb-
ling and fumbling he collected these together, and wrapped
them carefully in a cloth. When this was done she laid her
hand on his arm, persuading him towards the door. He
stopped. "The others," he said. "They must be warned.
I will go to them." For a moment her set face seemed
to fall apart in an explosion of rage and despair. But she
said no word, standing by the door with her baby in her
arms and her children about her. "I will go," I said.
"Send me!"

'Through the heavy dusk I ran from house to house.
Many houses were closed and shuttered, I had to bang and
shout to be admitted. I stopped only to say, "The Christians
are coming." It was all I knew. In every house it was the
same. A cry, a lamentation! And then the same desperate
haste, and smooth making ready to fly, as though, waking
and sleeping, winter and summer, a life-long, a nation-long,
this had been expected and rehearsed. I had reached the last
house when I saw the darkness suddenly changed to a pattern
of ruddy white and leaping black shadows; and turning, I
saw torches, flaring pine-knots, and a throng of people, black
and hurrying, and heard shouts, and laughter, and curses.

No need, at this last door, to cry that the Christians were coming.

'I heard them calling out my father's name, saying that he was a usurer, and my mother a witch. Then there was a scream. It was one of our goats, I thought; but Dinah, the woman of the last house, thrust a shawl over my head, pressing her hands over my ears, and some one took me by the arm and began to run with me. My head was muffled in the shawl, I could not untie the knot, I could only run, dragged on by this hand on my arm. Sometimes a bundle with sharp edges banged against my legs, I was jostled against, I lost my footing and stumbled, and was hauled up again, blinded and half smothered in the shawl. All round were people running. I heard their feet striving in the snow, the thud of large feet and the patter of small. And behind us came the pursuers, shouting and jeering like cattle-drivers. Suddenly at my side there was a scream like a flash of lightning, and the hand that dragged me forward let go, and I ran on alone, tearing at the knotted shawl.

'Something cold and rigid stopped my flight, and at the same moment I felt a stab in my arm, and the blood running. I thought it was the pike of the Christians, and I fell on the ground and lay still, waiting for the death-stroke. But nothing happened. The flying and the pursuing feet went past, but no one touched me; and presently, feeling about, I found that it was a bush that I had run against, wounding myself against a broken bough, sharp with ice. My hands were too numbed to unfasten the knot, but with my teeth I bit a hole in the shawl, and tore it open and thrust out my head.

' I was at the edge of the forest, all alone. I thought it
would be dark, but there was still a faint cringing daylight.
The voices and the footsteps were gone far off, the screaming
and shouting almost done. At longer and longer intervals
there would sound a long wavering cry, or a yelp of anguish ;
and as I listened I remembered how after a summer thunder-
storm I had often sat at the edge of the forest, watching the
world flash out in its new revived green, and hearing the
last drops of rain fall, splash, splash, here and there, till at
last they ceased altogether, or I had tired of counting them.
Summer or winter, then or now . . . both were equally real
or unreal to me, as I sat under the bush, waiting, since
slaughter had passed me by, for wolves or cold to make an
end of me. There was a smell of woodsmoke in the air, and
through my stupor this comforted me. My wits were so
scattered that even when I saw the flames rising on the sky,
and knew that it was our houses that burned, the scented
smoke was still my comfort. I moved, to settle myself deeper
under the bush where I should die. With the agony of that
movement I was driven alive again, crying out with pain,
struggling to my feet, and felled by the weight of my stiffened
blood. Like an animal gone mad I darted over the snow,
shaking myself and whining, and running hither and thither.
Presently, near the edge of the forest, I came on the body of
a woman—dead ; and further on the body of an old man—
dead, too ; and the bloodied tracks led me from there to
something that might have been man or woman or child—
but was only blood and a heap of trampled flesh. Like a
mad dog I ran from corpse to corpse, snuffing at them and
starting away. Darkness had fallen, but the blazing houses

gave me light—light enough to find at last a round thing like
a fallen bird's-nest, cold and stiff with frost, and rocking
lightly in the wind. It was my mother's wig. There was a
body near by, but not hers ; and searching over the trampled
snow I found at last the track of my father's feet, his by the
print of the broken heel. The tracks led back towards the
hamlet. He had turned, and gone back for me, his first-born.

' Now I knew where to perish. The Christians should see
that a Jewess could be no less faithful than a Jew. And while
I ran towards the blazing house my old fancies flared up, and
it seemed to me that not only should I die defying them, but
that my race should be avenged through me, since I would
certainly kill many of them before they killed me.

' I jumped over a smouldering paling, and ran between the
burning huts towards our own. As I came in sight I heard
a long crackling yell of acclamation. The Christian women
had come up, to watch the burning, and to rifle ; and now
as I neared them they all cried out : " See, the little Jewess !
How she runs, the Devil is after her ! Throw her into the
fire ! No ! Don't touch her ! She's mad ! Look at her
eyes. She's mad, and will bite us."

' I threw myself among them, and they gave way, shrink-
ing back, grabbing at me and letting go, as I struck at them
with fists and set teeth. But in an instant I was caught by
two fat strong hands, my shoulders caught, and my face
pressed into a fat black-draped belly that smelt of onions and
incense. It was the priest, who had come up with the women.
I kicked his shins, but he held me fast, and the women,
flocking up, took hold of my hands and feet, and over-
powered me.

' " Hold her, good Christians, hold her," he said, coughing because I had butted his belly. " God has sent her into our hands. We will keep her, and baptise her. Holy Church has always room for another soul." '

She paused, her eyes staring out from her rigid pose. There was a stir at the back of the room, but no one turned a head. Only when the heavy eyelids drooped over the staring eyes was there a faint sigh, a rustle and exhalation as though a field of corn that had stood all day in the breathless August drought had yielded to a breath of wind. Released from Minna's gaze, Sophia felt a sudden giddiness. I will not faint, she thought. A chair was slid towards her. She had forgotten that all this while she had stood. But she would not sit down. Glancing about, trying to ease her stiffened eyes, she saw that the ivory fan of the woman seated near her was snapped in two.

Still looking down, Minna seemed to be summoning a final cold to arise from the depths of a well at her feet. Her face became even paler, her body stiffened as though with frost, her lips narrowed. When she spoke her voice was cold and flat like a snowfield.

' I shall not forget what I suffered in the priest's house . . .'

But the stir at the back of the room, discreetly swelling, had now arched itself into an enquiring silence. Into that silence broke a preliminary cough, and a dull snuffling voice said,

' Excuse me, ladies and gentlemen. But the people in the street are demanding the carriages for their barricade.'

' What ? '

Without animation the concierge repeated,

' The people in the street are demanding the carriages for their barricade.'

' Good God ! ' exclaimed Frederick, speaking from the heart of England.

A sort of quenched scuffle arose. Skirts rustled, chairs thrust back squawked on the parquet, voices, hushed but prepared to rise in a minute, questioned and exclaimed. A lady with diamonds called ' Stanislas ! ', and the bald man whose shoulders were draped with a plaid shawl uttered a growl of satisfaction. For already the assembly had split into two parties, the one lightly alarmed, lightly enthusiastic, the other excited, class-conscious, and belligerent. The ill-dressed and the well-dressed, who had been sitting so surprisingly cheek by jowl, began to group themselves after their kind. When the lady with diamonds embraced Minna and cried out, ' Ah, my dear ! It has come at last, our revolution,' the camp of the ill-dressed showed no sympathy.

Nor, thought Sophia, sharply observing this turn of the evening's entertainment, did Minna. Her narrative and her spell broken by the concierge's announcement, she had put on for a moment the look of a cat made a fool of—a massive sultry fury. Rallying, she had matched the situation by a majestic rising to her feet, a lightening of her sombre mask, a deepened breathing and an opening of hands, as though welcoming a dayspring on her darkness. This was havocked by the embrace of the diamonded lady. For a second time baulked of the centre of the stage, she seemed about to turn her back on her audience, till, catching Sophia's faithful glance, she made a swift, a confidential grimace, walked towards her, and deflecting herself at a few steps' distance began to talk to the hump-backed little Jew.

Round her oblivion her guests assembled with a growing anxiety to make their farewells. The voices became louder, more unrestrained, above them soared the voice of the revolutionary diamond lady.

'Stanislas! We must give them our carriage. Tell the man.'

But the concierge had taken himself off.

'Isn't he there? Tiresome lout! Minna, my angel, we are going down to join in the Revolution.'

'Good night, countess.'

She might have been brushing off a fly. Shivering, frowning a little, she continued her conversation with the little Jew, laying her hand on his arm, seeming to compel herself to speak with animation.

'But, David, you must insist on a proper rehearsal. What does he think your music is? Vaudeville? And of course he can afford a second flute-player. The last of his wretched concerts I went to, I am sure he had hired at least a dozen drummers, all of them butchers or sergeant-majors. No! Either proper rehearsals, you must tell him, or you will take back the score.'

'There is a barricade in your street, Minna. And revolutions have no second flute-players to spare,' said the man with the shawl.

'Why not, Ingelbrecht? A revolution must have music to match it.'

'Street-songs. But not symphonies.'

'Symphonies! Are the people, a free people, to have

nothing better than a tune on the hurdy-gurdy ? My dear, the truth is, you don't like music.'

Her change of voice might have wheedled open a strong-box, and he smiled and grunted, pleased to have his lack of taste recognised. But the hump-backed boy, grown pale and dejected as though a sudden gale had nipped him, slid from her detaining hand and, coughing, began to wind a scarf round his long thin neck.

The room was emptying fast. The well-dressed party having deposited their farewells had gone, to bestow or to rescue their carriages. The others, talking much louder now, were preparing to follow. Worse manners, Sophia said to herself, I have never seen. However, I suppose that I may walk off without good-byeing, as casually as they. Indeed, since she had come unasked, she could scarcely do otherwise.

It was high time to go. In this emptying room it would not long be possible for Frederick to avoid meeting her eye. He must certainly have discovered her by now, but tactful, as at his last visit to Blandamer, he made no sign of recognition.

Between her and the door stood Minna, feeding the hump-back with cakes and hot wine. Are you the child who ran across the bloodied snow to kill the Christians ? Are you the prophetess, the brooding priestess of Liberty, who spoke with such passion of the enfranchised river ? Are you the woman so bitterly hated, my rival and overthrower ? Sophia stared at the sleek braids of black hair and the smooth milk-coffee coloured shoulders, the drooping yellow scarf lined with rather shabby ermine, the attitude of elegant single-hearted domesticity. She would never know, never know more ! And with a pang of the mind she realised that after this false move there was nothing left her but to go back to Blandamer immediately. Hours, ages ago, propelled up the stairs by the man in the cloak, she had recognised the false move, had seen with the chess-player's pang her queen abandoned in the centre of the board, irremediably exposed to capture. She, who had meant to play so cunningly, had lost the game like any tyro. And to-morrow, with what ignominy, she must retreat, without hope of a child, without hope of any re-habilitation in her own esteem, without hope of any future but one of futility, rage and regret; and without (with the honesty of despair she admitted it) any hope of knowing more about Minna. From all those dreams she had never been able to carry into waking a recollection of the dream-Minna's face; and from this real-life encounter she would depart as tantalised, as unfulfilled.

'Good night then, my dear,' said Minna to the hump-back.

Now was the moment. Straight as a ramrod, looking neither to right nor left, Sophia took a step towards the door.

'You look so tired. Please drink a little of this hot wine before you go.'

How much the taller I am, thought Sophia, looking down on that countenance of candour and solicitude. She saw her hand go out, accepting the wine.

The warm spiced scent, slightly resinous, as though the Jewess had mixed all the summer forests of her childhood in the cup, was like a caress. Round the first sip she felt her being close, haggard and hungry.

'Ah! That will do you good. You look better already.'

A creative possessiveness, a herb-wife's glorying in the

work of healing, glowed in the words, and in the melancholy attentive gaze. I must speak, thought Sophia, or in another moment she will be putting me to bed. In any case, for mere civility's sake, she must say something.

'You must be tired too. Your narration—it could not have moved us so much without fatiguing you.'

There was a gesture of acknowledgment, stately and resigned.

'Tell me . . . The river, and the forest, where were they?'

'In Lithuania. Almost on the track of the retreat from Moscow. I could tell you something of that, too, of the old man, a deserter from the Grand Army, always limping from his frostbite, who pitied me when I was in the priest's house. I will tell you, one day.'

'I wish you had not been interrupted.'

'I was sorry to lose such listening as yours. Yes, as yours. Did you not know that I was speaking to you?'

'I am leaving Paris to-morrow.'

With her words came a rush of cold air. A window, giving upon a balcony, had been opened.

'Let us look.'

With the cold air came the sound of voices, of picks striking upon stone. From the balcony they could look down upon the barricade a-building. Already it stretched almost across the street, a random barrier of sawn-off boughs bristling, tables and chairs piled together, a cab or two (Stanislas seemed to have preserved the carriage), a mangle and a bedstead. Round it was a group of men, some busy uprooting the paving-stones, others artistically rearranging the confusion of boughs and bedsteads, like demented furniture-removers. Except for these, the street was empty.

'But what is the object of putting it here?' exclaimed Sophia.

'Moral effect.' Frederick's voice answered her words, adding,

'Hullo, Sophia! How long have you been in Paris?'

She was saved from answering by a head interposed between them, and a young man's voice saying excitedly,

'I will tell you the object, Madame. Behind that barricade patriots will defend the cause of liberty, will defy the tyrant, will bleed and conquer.'

'They have been defying the tyrant all day, you know,' added Frederick.

'Gloriously!' exclaimed the young man. 'Ah, what a day! I was there, this morning, in the Place de la Concorde, when the processions converged, waves of indignant patriots advancing with majesty, workers who had left their toil, their humble homes, to oppose the threat to their liberties, to intimidate that worthless Guizot with the spectacle of their might. The *rappel* was beaten. But it was sounded for them. They marched to the drumbeat. The National Guards which it summoned either retreated before them or joined their ranks in sympathy. They met, these waves, before the Chamber of Deputies. They stood there, immovable, crying out with one voice for reform.'

'Some bold spirits climbed the railings,' said Frederick.

'It was a voice to strike terror into the heart of any tyrant,' continued the young man, raising his own. 'But they did not only speak. They acted. The dragoons were powerless

before them. In the Champs-Élysées the first barricade went
up. Trees were cut down, benches uprooted, the café-
keepers hastened to offer their chairs and tables. It was reared
in a moment, that first brave barricade.'

' An omnibus,' Frederick added, ' an omnibus, coming
from the Barrière de l'Étoile, was seized in an instant and
added to the barricade. An omnibus, you know, Sophia, is a
very considerable object. Think what an improvement an
omnibus or two would be, down there.'

The young man was certainly a windbag, and might be a rival.
But it seemed to Sophia that Frederick's malice was aimed at
Minna herself, who with averted head leaned on the balcony,
staring down at the work below. She had pretended not to
hear the words, but her body had crouched under them, de-
jectedly defensive. Jew-baiting. The word rushed into
Sophia's mind, and turning on Frederick, she said,

' As an omnibus is out of the question, I wish you would
get me a cab.'

Ill-considered words : not only laying her own claim on
his attentions, but by doing so seeming to dispute Minna's.

' Certainly, Sophia. If a cab is to be found to-night, you
shall have it. But it may take a little finding. You may even
have to walk.'

' I will bring a cab,' said the young man, pleased to get the
better of the Englishman, and ready to take up any challenge.
'Madame, with your permission, I will bring you a cab
immediately.'

Frederick's stalking footsteps were already descending the
stairs, the young man clattered after him. Dignity seen from
above cannot hold its own ; but ignoring this, the two men

issued from the door in simultaneous exclusiveness, and went off in opposite directions, Frederick pausing at the barricade to examine it and talk to the workers. He will hand round cigars and be a success, thought Sophia. The rightness of the guess deepened her hatred against him ; and hearing his easy laughter, his mellow flourishing farewells, she gritted her teeth with rage.

Never had she hated him so thoroughly. For now, she thought, for the first time in my life, I am in his power. He can do with me as he pleases, pity me as a fool or ridicule me as a jealous wife, come scolding after him as a village woman goes to the alehouse to rout home a drunken husband. *Let him try !*—said her will. But he had tried already, and succeeded. Already he had made of her—what all convenient wives should be—his stalking-horse, the malice of his words rebounding off her to Minna, her wifely petticoats the shield whence he could attack his mistress. That spluttering young man might be Frederick's butt, but scarcely his rival. And the thought shot up that if Frederick were jealous of any one, it was of her.

And why not ? No doubt it would be a painful sight to any man to see even the smallest attention, the smallest civility, a glass of hot wine and a couple of sentences, bestowed by the mistress upon the wife. And so he had addressed to her his belittling of the revolutionaries, making her seem a party, however silent, to what must wound Minna. Yes, that was natural enough, and he had done it deftly— what more obvious shift than to show a wife in as unpleasant colours as possible ? Yet, good Lord, he had had two years to do it in ! Could any man, even Frederick, be such a fool as to neglect that essential process until wife and mistress met ?

Yes, Frederick could be such a fool. Slothful and ease-loving, it might well be possible that he had not stirred himself to mention her till this moment. For the mention of an ignominious marriage, of an uncongenial wife, might come under the heading of a business conversation ; and she knew how cunning the stratagems of his inertia to put off such. Yet, being such a fool, she, by a superior foolery, had enabled him to remain a fool and still be victorious. He had not to put himself out in the least, he need not even labour his wits for a lie. By her insensate escapade she had given herself into his hands—a stick to beat a mistress with. Perhaps they had already quarrelled ; she knew nothing of their relations, Frederick's passion might have cooled long since. If that were so, how aptly she had arrived, led by his good star and her bad—an angry wife roaring after her prey. What easier than to retire behind those petticoats, stroll off politely and leave the two women to fight it out and dry each other's tears ? Considering the beautiful simplicity of the trick, it was difficult not to snort aloud with anger.

But then, did Minna know who she was ? She was not labelled Mrs Willoughby, not outwardly, for all the inward brandings of the Law and the Church and society.

Trapped in this new dilemma, she raised her head and looked at Minna.

The sleet had turned to a drizzling rain. The lamplight of the room behind them diamonded the raindrops on Minna's black hair, washed with sleek glimmerings her folded wet hands that drooped over the balustrade. Her shoulders twitched with cold, but the wrap of yellow satin and ermine dangled forgotten. With averted face she seemed to be studying the work in the street below. A barricade, presumably, was a sight to gladden any revolutionary heart, and Minna was a revolutionary; but every line of her figure spoke of dejection.

Why do you let yourself be made miserable by his taunts? asked Sophia's heart, angered to see this vital creature cast down. Or is this, too, a trick to gain my sympathy? For it was too soon to forget those glances of triumphant power, those smiles of satisfied strategy, which had filled the pauses of Minna's narrative; and not even this appearance of drowned cat could allay the suspicion of a ninth life lurking. But meanwhile not a paw moved out to encircle her, there seemed no possibility of twitch in that dispirited tail; and though the completeness of this appearance of misery should have warned, *Artist*, only curiosity held back Sophia's impulse to pity this desolation, succour and rally it.

Never in her life had she felt such curiosity or dreamed it possible. As though she had never opened her eyes before she stared at the averted head, the large eloquent hands, the thick, milk-coffee coloured throat that housed the siren voice. Her curiosity went beyond speculation, a thing not of the brain but in the blood. It burned in her like a furnace, with a steadfast compulsive heat that must presently catch Minna in its draught, hale her in, and devour her.

She was still staring when her hostess turned.

' You are getting very wet,' remarked Sophia.

' So are they,' she answered, pointing downwards to where, round the completed barricade, the builders were huddling

into its shelter. They had a brazier, and now a frying-pan
had been produced, and the sizzle of fat was audible. With
astonishment Sophia realised that the furniture-removers were
settling down for the night.

'I must send them some food and drink.'

Minna spoke listlessly, almost automatically. Surely it was
not like this that the devotees of liberty nourished its warriors?
As though the look of enquiry had spoken its satire. Minna
started.

'You think I am not very enthusiastic? I have not given
them my carriage, I have not exclaimed . . . Perhaps you
think I am not very sincere. But if you have ever longed for
a thing, longed with your whole heart, with year after year
of your life, longed for it with all that is noblest in you and
worked for it with all that is most base and most calculating,
you would understand with what desolation of spirit one
beholds the dream made flesh.'

'I have never longed for anything like that.'

Nor ever shall, she added to herself.

'No?'

It was only courtesy, as Sophia knew, that tilted the in-
flexion of the monosyllable towards enquiry; and only
courtesy that turned the head, and directed that sleep-walk-
ing gaze; and yet, for all that, she felt a profound impulse to
unburden herself of the motive that had brought her to Paris,
to explain passionately and exactly all that she had felt, en-
dured, intended, telling all, from the expedition to the lime-
kiln to the conversation with the porter which had been like
eating a radish; as though the Jewess's impassive attention
had been a dark sleek-surfaced pool into which, as one is com-

pelled to cast a stone into those waters, she was compelled to cast her confidence.

All the while of her thought Minna's glance, sombre and attentive, waited upon her. The desperate riveted attention, thought Sophia, of the hostess who at the end of a too long protracted party dissembles with the last guest their mutual agony over a belated carriage, who stretches her eyes because to close them would open her jaws in a yawn, whose thoughts wander slowly in search of a subject for conversation.

' Why do you want this revolution ? What good do you think it will do ? '

The milk-coffee coloured shoulders tossed back the yellow satin scarf in a shrug.

' What good ? None, possibly. One does not await a revolution as one awaits the grocer's van, expecting to be handed packets of sugar and tapioca. My river in spring flood brought dead bodies, a hand or foot dismembered, a clot of entrails. So will this flood, maybe. But for all that it is the spring flood.'

The image that had been so fine in her narrative flagged in conversation to no more than gimcrack and rhodomontade ; and suppressing a feeling of disappointment—for why should she expect to be converted to revolutionary ideas by Frederick's Jewess ?—Sophia resorted to polite praises of Minna's eloquence, wishing with increased passion that Frederick would bring that cab.

For a moment it seemed that he had done so. Footsteps hastened up the stairs, Minna turned to the opened door with a look of recognition. But the head rising from the well of the stair was the head of a tempest-tossed poodle, and even on a night like this the news of a cab could not justify lips so dramatically parted, eyes so passionately beady.

'Gaston!'

'Minna!'

Had they been play-acting at conspirators, thought Sophia, their dramatic embrace could not have been more perfunctory.

'Has it begun? Has it really begun?'

'Begun! It is in full flow, nothing can stop it now. Paris is ours! No, not now,' he added petulantly, flinging away from the hand maternally patting his arm—'but by to-morrow night it will be, I can promise you that, I have seen to it. Listen, Minna! To-morrow night there will be bloodshed.'

'Not till then?'

The question was asked with melancholy irony.

'No! One must have the night,' he exclaimed, shaking back the poodle-locks from his bony countenance. 'One must have the effect of torchlight, the Rembrandtesque shadows, the solemnity and uncertainty of darkness. Besides, feelings run higher at night and there are more people at leisure to become spectators,' he added, suddenly assuming the tone of an organiser. 'What we have decided is this. There must be bloodshed, and it must come from them. It must be forced from them, they must be compelled to fire on the people, it must be decisive, a volley. This show of cottonwool benevolence must be torn away, this sham liberalism shown up. Very well, then. There must be a concentration of troops, and earlier in the day we have an attack on some public building—the Foreign Affairs probably

—sufficient to ensure that a detachment is told off to guard it. In the evening our procession forms—one can always manage a procession—a procession of the citizens with their children—children are essential for the right feeling, and I have arranged for the children. It is a peaceable procession, as it might be a picnic, it is full of patriotism and good feeling. Good! They listen to a speech from Marrast of the *National*, a speech of sympathy for their sufferings; they turn into the boulevard des Capucines, they come to the Foreign Affairs, they are confronted by the troops. They are shot down!'

'But if the troops do not fire? There have been orders——'

'They will fire. That will be seen to.'

'And then?'

To Sophia, standing unnoticed by the window, this conversation seemed repulsive and silly. People who arranged their revolutions standing on landings and gabbling at the tops of their voices . . . She listened with exasperation to the rapid dogmatic tones of the man greeted as Gaston, to the few interposed words from Minna, and the fact that they spoke in a foreign language seemed to set the whole affair farther off, to set it in some different time and place wherein she had no concern. The only words which could fall on her ears with relevance would be an announcement of that cab; and at this moment Gaston was babbling about a dray heaped with the bleeding forms of patriots.

Very well, then! She would walk back to the hotel. And with the same movement which turned her towards the door she sank down on a sofa, overborne by fatigue. There was a book by her hand and she took it up and opened it, and thought she was reading, until with a jolt she realised that she was falling asleep. In the ante-room the conversation continued, and from below came a dreary yowling, the songs of those manning the barricade, and finding it as hard as she did, she supposed, to watch through a night of such intolerable disjointedness and tedium. I must go, she told herself; and resolvedly keeping her eyes open with such sensations of pain that she might have been holding open two wounds, she stared round Minna's apartment, and could see nothing. The conversation and the singing continued, but she did not hear them. Sleep roared in her ears like the river roaring through Lithuania, and as her eyelids closed the landscape of France began to flash by, seen through the window of the railway carriage; but now, morassed in a wretched dream, the train was bearing her northwards, she was going home, empty, hopeless and undone. She had not even the child. But in her dream it was not for the loss of the child she mourned so desperately. Something else was lost, there was some other hope, some other promise, irretrievably mismanaged and irretrievably lost; and it was for this something, this unpossessed unknown, that she mourned in such desolation, having not even the comfort of knowing what was for ever left behind and forfeited—a speech unuttered or unheard, a book heavy with the black Hebrew characters, a bunch of tufted mimosa.

'Sleep, you must sleep, my beauty, my falcon,' a voice said. And scarcely knowing that she had for a moment awakened she lay passive under the hands that untied her bonnet-strings, and took off her shoes, and covered her with something warm and furry, stroking her, slowly, heavily, like the hands of sleep, stroking her hair and her brow.

It was full morning, the room was vividly alive and alight when she woke, hearing the sound of drums, and smelling coffee. A woodfire newly lit was crackling on the hearth, and with the first glance of her opening eyes she had seen an old woman of operatic ugliness vanishing from the room as though withdrawing in the fringe of a dream.

She was lying islanded in the middle of the room on a gilded sofa upholstered in pink brocade—the sofa, plebianly capacious, plebianly pink, of any provincial hotel's drawing-room, but so tarnished and tattered as to present a semblance of the aristocracy of a fallen fortune. Round her shoulders was the yellow ermine-lined scarf, and beyond a stretch of scarlet-dyed sheepskin her feet confronted her, wearing a pair of sky-blue woollen slippers, several sizes too large. It was like waking up in the bosom of a macaw.

With the benevolence of the well-slept she stared round the room. Over a basis of respectable furnished apartment was scattered what looked like the beginnings of a curiosity shop or the studio of a painter in genre. A mandoline leaned against a mounted suit of armour, a Gothic beaker, ecclesi-astically embossed with false gems, stood on a Louis-Seize trifle-table and propped an Indian doll with tinsel robes, beaded nose-ring, and black cotton features of a languishing cast. Dangling over a harp was a Moorish bridle. On the walls hung scimitars and bucklers, pieces of brilliant em-broidery, tapestries, and a quantity of pictures framed or un-framed. It was a room calculated to outrage Sophia's orderly sensibilities. Yet she looked round on it with tolerance; for however fantastic the effect, it was not with a studied fantasy. Profuse, eclectic, inconsequential, the room had a nomadic quality, as though an evening had spilt this extemporisation over the respectable furnished apartment and as though another evening might sweep it away.

She sat up, snuffing the aroma of coffee, her frame of mind light, complacent, exhilarated. To the lively drum-beats was added the sound of church bells, a noise that recalled to her the drive of yesternight, the domes she had seen bulging against the sky. She remembered that she was in Paris, that Paris was in a state of revolution. She jumped up, shook herself briskly, opened the window and leaned from the balcony. The shabby gaiety of the houses opposite charmed her. The colouring of the rue de la Carabine, the light-hearted pallor of the tall housefronts, was as reviving as a watercolour after the look of England, so solidly painted in oils.

At the clatter of the opening windows the men on the barricade glanced up, and one of them kissed his hand to her, shouting up a greeting in the name of the Revolution to her fair tumbled hair. Like cats who had been out and about all the night, they were sprucing themselves in the merry morning air. One was spluttering over a bucket of water, another was combing his hair with his fingers ; and as she watched she saw a third gravely disarray himself of one pair of trousers and put on a smarter pair which a young woman had brought out over her arm. Some tin coffee-pots, long wands of golden bread, a sausage in a paper chemise, gave a domesticated appearance to the barricade, as though the objects had arrived of their own good will in order to assure the beds and tables

that there was nothing, after all, so particularly odd or dis-
creditable in having spent a night in the street. But despite
the coffee-pots the barricade had taken on a more formidable
appearance than on the previous night, and paving-stones
were being methodically taken up, and earth heaped.

Round its defenders stood a small shifting crowd of
admirers and sympathisers—errand boys, shop-girls, work-
ing-men, students, women in shawl and slipper. There was a
babble of advice and encouragement, and presently from the
vine-painted wine-shop advanced a smiling man with a
number of bottles. Leaning against the barricade he un-
corked them with splendid gestures. 'To the Revolution,'
he said, and handed the first bottle to the young man who had
tossed up his greeting to Sophia's flaxen hair. 'To the
Revolution,' repeated he, and in turn handed the bottle to a
woman standing near by. As she raised it to her lips the tilt
of the unbonneted head revealed to Sophia that it was her
hostess who was drinking from a bottle in the street.

Now a group of men appeared, coming slowly down the
street. At every door they paused, and parleyed ; and at
almost every door they received a weapon of some sort—a
gun, or a pistol, or a rusty sabre. These were heaped upon
the following hand-cart, and the group moved on, the leader
scrawling in chalk upon the quitted door. As he came nearer
Sophia could read the inscription : *Armes données*.

The concierge who had overnight so fatalistically an-
nounced the building of the barricade was offering a large
household hammer and some lengths of iron dog-chain,
explaining that the label tied to them carried his name and
address, and that he would be glad of their return, ' after the

victory.' He was still expatiating on the various uses of a hammer, and the gladness with which he offered it to heroes, when Minna brushed past him. Sophia could hear her feet on the echoing stairs, a gait with a sort of lumbering lightness, and while she was still debating in her mind as to whether a bear who really enjoyed waltzing would not sound much the same, Minna entered.

'You slept?' she said; and holding Sophia's hand she gazed at her with a possessive earnest glance, a glance that instantly recalled the taste of the mulled wine offered overnight.

I cannot understand, thought Sophia, what Frederick could see in you. But *I* can see a great deal. Though it had never been her habit to drink mulled wine in the morning, it was impossible not to be gratified by the persuasive, rather melancholy warmth which flowed from the Jewess, and forgetting the improbability of the situation, forgetting, even, that she stood in a pair of blue woollen slippers several sizes too large for her, she spoke her thanks for the pink sofa.

The words were civil and correct, they were even genial; but at their close the Jewess sighed heavily, and turned away, gathering from the wall an assortment of rapiers and scimitars. Then, with the troubled air of a good housewife weighing out an unusual quantity of stores, she opened a drawer and took up a pair of fine duelling pistols.

Sophia had inherited from Papa a taste for firearms. It seemed to her that even a revolutionary might part from those pistols with regret, and she said so.

'They are by Watson,' sighed Minna. 'Well, they must go. But I have another pair.' Darkly swimming, her eyes rolled for a moment towards Sophia, ' A better pair.' And in a grand manner she called the old woman and bade her take down the offering, to the men below.

' Now——' she extended the word upon a skilful yawn. ' *Now* we can have our chocolate.'

For the last nine years of her life Sophia had seen in every human activity death as a factor. Water might drown, fire might burn. A wet stocking might lead to the grave, a raw fruit was a plummet that lowered the eater into that pit. In every tuft of warm grass lurked an adder, in every tuft of damp grass a consumption. Death's sting was in the wasp. Dogs bit, and were mad dogs. The cat might scratch a child's eye out, a pony shying might toss a child and break a neck. The sun had a heavy stroke on a child's head, and a morning fog wafted sickness into a nursery. In exchange for a kiss, or a penny dropped into a cottager's hand, fever and pestilence might be deposited. Rusty nails waited in sheds, falling slates hung patiently from roofs, in the hay a sickle lay craftily. A diet that was not heating was probably lowering, even the medicine bottle must be eyed as a deceiving enemy, and the best-warranted pill might bring on a fatal choking-fit, as easily as a random blue bead picked off the fire-screen. In every path death lay in wait: the death that after all had not had to wait for so very long since both Damian and Augusta lay dead.

Yet the day passed, and the February dusk had fallen, and Sophia had not once bethought her that death might wait upon a revolution. The superior pair of duelling pistols shown to her by Minna had roused but one thought only: a determination to visit a shooting-gallery and become a crack shot. That also was possible to her; she could do anything, go anywhere, if she could spend a day in such passionate amity with her husband's mistress. Hers was the liberty of a fallen woman now.

The cloaked man, propelling her up the staircase, had changed her life for her, with his polite gloved hand waving her into a new existence. It could not be of long duration, this new existence; another day even, in Minna's company (yet for no consideration possible would she forgo an hour of it), would madden her or kill her with excitement. No reason, no mortal frame, could long endure the ardour of this fantastic freedom from every inherited and practised restraint, nor the spur of that passionately sympathetic company. It was an air (however long and unknowingly she had panted for it) which must wear out breathing. Talking to Minna she supposed that she must talk herself to death as others bleed to death; and as a person with haemorrhage feels the blood beating and striving to escape, she felt the weight of her whole life throbbing to be recounted; and as a drowning man sees his whole life pass before him, and recognises as authentically his a hundred incidents and scenes which had lain forgotten in the un-death-awakened mind, her childhood, her youth, her womanhood rose up crowded and clear before her, and must be told—even to the day when she lay under the showering hawthorn watching the year's first scything of the lawn and eating, with such passionate appetite, the sweet grass-clippings, even to the old beggar-woman in Coblenz whose dry lips had grated in a kiss on her casual charitable hand.

Sitting on the pink sofa, her hair still falling about her shoulders, her feet still muffled in the blue slippers, her eyes blackened with excitement, her lips dry with fever, she continued her interminable, her dying speech.   At intervals, in some strange non-apparent way, there was food before her, and more wine in the glass, the fire built up or a lighted lamp carried into the room.   Sometimes a drum rattled somewhere through the echoing streets beating the *rappel*, or a burst of sudden voices rose from the barricade.   And with some outlying part of her brain she recognised that a revolution was going on outside.   News of it was brought by hurried visitors ; and as though a semi-awakening had blurred the superior reality of a dream, she listened drowsily to tidings of a fallen ministry, a stormed building, a palace in terror and disarray.   They went.   And instantly she began once more to talk and Minna, caressing her hand or with abstracted attention examining the fineness of her flaxen hair as though it were something marketable, to listen.   Neither woman, absorbed in this extraordinary colloquy, had expressed by word or sign the slightest consciousness that there was anything unusual about it.

' Well, Minna, well, Sophia.'

Frederick, arriving during the afternoon, seemed instantly felled into taking it for granted that his wife and his mistress should be seated together on the pink sofa, knit into this fathomless intimacy, and turning from it to entertain him with an identical patient politeness.   Stroking his hat as though it were a safe domestic animal he told them of Guizot's resignation, of the National Guards singing the Marseillaise in the Place de la Bastille, of the preparations for a universal illumination, and how the funeral of a young lady of the aristocracy had been interrupted and her coffin requisitioned for a barricade. Everything, he implied, was proceeding nicely though it was no affair of his; and now he would be going.

Pausing at the door, 'By the way, Sophia,' said he, 'if you are putting up at your respectable Meurice, you won't get much sleep to-night. There are troops all round the Tuileries, and there's sure to be a dust-up. I should stay here with Minna, if I were you.'

And with a bland glassy sweep of the eye over the blue slippers, he closed the door as on a sickroom.

Instantly forgetting his existence, save as a character in her narrative, Sophia went on talking. Minna's clasp tightened upon her hand.

A more effectual interruption came later when the concierge appeared, remarking sternly,

'Excuse me. But illuminations are obligatory.'

'Illuminations?' said Minna.

'To celebrate the fall of the tyrant. It is all one to me,' he added, 'but one cannot have the windows broken.'

'No, no, of course not. I will see to it. Natalia! Bring all the candles you can find. What news have you heard?'

'They have extinguished the gas in the outer boulevards.'

As the door closed behind him they laughed. It was the first laugh that had passed between them, and its occurrence momentarily remade them as strangers to each other. Minna averted her eyes, and began a rambling, unconvinced account of the absurdities of Égisippe Coton. Forgetting to answer, Sophia stared at her hostess. Under the scrutiny Minna began to wilt. Talking with nervous suppliant emphasis she had a harassed, a hunted expression.

They have extinguished the gas on the outer boulevards. The words were insultingly applicable to this wearied visage, jostled with speech. Using the cool patronage and consideration with which she would attend to the needs of something useful and inferior, order a bran-mash for a horse or send a servant to bed, she found herself thinking that for Minna, conscripted all day on this strange impulse to expound her heart, something must be done.

' I should like to take you out to dinner,' she said. ' Where can we get a good meal ? '

Hearing this loud British incivility proceeding so plumply from a good heart and a healthy appetite—and indeed, they had eaten nothing all day save hors-d'œuvres and pastries—her sense of shame was followed by an inward hysteria.

' That would be charming, there would be nothing I should like better. I am not sure if it can be managed, I expect everything is shut. Perhaps Natalia would know, she could go out and fetch something. No, that would not do, though, she shops abominably, she would bring us pickled herrings and lemonade. She has had such a sad life, poor Natalia, it seems to have turned her naturally towards brine. Has it ever struck you that unhappy women always crave for sour pickles ? '

Sophia said,

' But why should everything be shut ? '

' The Revolution——'

She had overlooked the Revolution again—an affair of foreign politics. But to Minna, of course, being a revolutionary, it must mean a great deal ; and she must be allowed to see something of it.

' If we went out we might see what's going on. But we must have a good dinner first, for I suppose we should have to walk.'

It was only when she had ordered the fillet-steak that Sophia realised that she had commandeered Minna's evening as high-handedly as she had taken her day. Never in my life, thought she, studying the wine list, have I acted quite like this. For though no doubt I have always been strong-minded, and lately seeing no one but my inferiors, may have got into a trick of domineering, nothing in my past, nothing in my upbringing, parallels this. For she is older than I am, and she is a woman of some eminence, and she is my husband's mistress—and here am I, taking her out to dinner and allow-ing her to see a little of her revolution as though she were a child to be given a treat—as though she were Caspar.

' A bottle of eighteen,' she said.

It had been an axiom of Papa's that under doubtful circum-stances it was best to order Beaujolais. These circumstances were admittedly doubtful, nor was this a place where one might hope much of the wine. Nothing in her past, nothing in her upbringing, would have prepared her to sit unescorted in a restaurant, or to walk at night through the streets of Paris. However, with the probable poorness of the wine went probable security from molestation. The restaurant was crowded, humble, and uninterested in the two women.

I wish I knew, thought Sophia, if I seem as odd to you as I do to myself.

As though overhearing the thought Minna remarked,

' How much I like being with English people! They manage everything so quietly and so well.'

' And am I as good as Frederick ? '

' You are much better.'

For an answer to an outrageous, to an unprovoked, insult, it was dexterous. It was more ; for the words were spoken with a composure and candour that seemed, in that stroke of speech, to dismiss for ever any need to insult or be insulted, and the smile that accompanied them, a smile of unalloyed pleasure at successful performance, was as absolving as any caper of triumph from a menaced and eluding animal.

She lives on her own applause, thought Sophia, watching Minna's revival into charm. This is what it is, I suppose, to be an artist, cheered and checked by the April of one's own mind. For she is an artist, though there is nothing to show for it but a collection of people going home from an evening party through the streets of a city in revolution, each one carrying with him the picture of a child standing beside a river in Lithuania. Yes, she is an artist, what they call a Bohemian. And I, in this strange holiday from my natural self, am being a Bohemian too, she thought with pride, staring about her at the walls painted with dashing views of Italy, at the worn red velvet of the benches, at the other diners, who expressed, all of them, a sort of shabby weariness countered by excitement, at the waiters, darting nimble as fish through the wreaths of tobacco smoke ; and yielding again to that wine-like sensation of ease and accomplished triumph which had been with her all day, she said,

' But Frederick would never bring you to a place like this.'

' No, indeed. He would bring a nice bunch of lilies of the valley, and dine with me.'

Damn him, was Sophia's instant thought.

'It is difficult,' continued Minna, 'for people like us not to misjudge people like Frederick. There is much that is admirable, much that is touching, in such gentleness and domesticity.'

'I have not had much opportunity to muse over Frederick's domesticity for the last three years,' said Sophia.

'No. And for part of that time I had perhaps rather too much. So you see we must both be biassed.'

'Poor Frederick!'

'Poor Frederick!'

Minna echoed the words but not the tone of irony.

'However,' she added, 'our faulty appreciation would not trouble him. Frederick completely despises all women. I think that is why he seems so dull and ineffectual.'

The artless analysis coming from lips on which rumour had heaped so many kisses distracted Sophia from the rage she naturally felt on hearing that Frederick despised all women. But the rage was there, and prompted the thought that she should not lag behind in comments of a kind and tolerant sort.

'However dull you found him, you did him an immense amount of good. I have never known him so pleasant, so rational, as he was on his last visit to England—his last visit to me, I mean. I do not know if he has visited England since then.'

'When was that?'

'When my children were dying.'

'Ah, no wonder! He would be at his best then, you see. For he felt an emotion that was perfectly genuine, and which he could express without any constraint, any *mauvaise honte*.

Men, who are so suspicious, so much ashamed, of any other emotion, have no shame in the feeling of fatherhood. It was his Volkslied he was singing then. It was no wonder he sang it well.

'I too,' she added, drooping her glance, holding tightly to the stem of her wine-glass, 'was very sorry.'

You are embarrassed, or you are making yourself feel so, thought Sophia. And that is a pity, for the moment you are embarrassed I lose my liking for you.

'This is horrible coffee,' she said. 'Coffee is a thing we manage much better in England, where we drink it strong. At this moment when I think of my children my chiefest regret is that their lives were so limited, so dreary. Nothing but restrictions and carefully prepared pap. When I was listening to you last night I thought with bitter reproach that they had never walked over a heath in their lives or seen the shedding of blood.'

But they were unreal to her at this moment, her children; and Augusta's remembered face, consuming in a rather stodgy resolute excitement as she begged to be allowed to watch the pig-killing, less actual than the sunburned shag-haired visage of the child in Lithuania chanting in her wild treble against the roaring voice of the bloodied river.

Later in the evening she had good bodily reason to re-member the Lithuanian childhood, the free wanderings over the heath. Minna still walked as though her foot were on a heath, and as though conducting her from one bird's-nest to another she led Sophia by innumerable short-cuts to various places where the Revolution might be expected to make a good showing. At least a dozen barricades were visited, and

over these they had been handed with great civility; falling
in with a procession they followed it to the Place de la
Bastille, where they waited for some time, listening to the
singing, and then in the wake of another procession they had
trudged to the Hôtel de Ville and listened to shouting. The
shouting was all, presumably, that revolutionary shouting
should be—loud, confident, and affable. Here and there,
bursting upwards from the level of the crowd, an orator
would emerge, twine like some short-lived flower to railings,
and sum up in a more polished and blossom-like fashion the
sentiments of the shouters.

But shaking her head in critical dissatisfaction, Minna said,
' There is more to see than this.'

' Shall we try the Champs-Élysées ? ' For there at any
rate, thought Sophia, there will be a chance to sit down. She
was intolerably footsore, and in the reality of that sensation
could feel nothing but despising for a revolution that was no
concern of hers.

' No.'

Minna turned northward again. As they went farther it
began to seem as though they were the only people walking
that way. Here there was little uproar, no illuminations, no
processions—but like leaves blown on some steady wind a
man, or three men, or six men, would come towards them and
pass them. They spoke very little, their faces wore no
particular expression except the look of wariness which comes
on the faces of all those who have to strive for a living. They
seemed in no great hurry, tramping on as though they were
going to their work. Among them, moving more swiftly as
though they were lighter leaves on the same steady wind,

came coveys of children, and groups of women, marching abreast with linked arms.   And while their following shadows still trailed on the pavement, on into the circle of lamplight would come one man, three men, six men.

'Do you see,' whispered Minna.   'It is the same yet, the old nursery of revolutions.'

'It frightens me,' said Sophia.   'And I believe that you, even, are a little afraid.'

'A little ?   I am horribly afraid.   How is it possible to have a good bed to sleep in, food in the larder, furs against the cold, books on one's shelves, money in one's purse, a taste for music, and not be afraid ?   It is ten years and more, thanks to my good fortune, since I could have looked at these without feeling afraid.'

'But you believe in revolution ? '

'With all my heart.'

They turned back, walking on the same wind as those others.   Sophia began to make conversation about Socialism, endeavouring to blame it as coolly as possible, pointing out that equality was a delusion, that the poor in office were the cruellest oppressors of the poor, etc.   By the time they struck into the boulevard des Capucines the changed character of the crowd had restored to her enough confidence to let the conversation drop.   For here they were back once more in the heartiest display of comic opera.   Earlier in the day the property rooms of the theatres had been raided by some enterprising collectors of arms, and under the light of the illuminations gilded spears and pasteboard helmets still wreathed with artificial flowers mingled their classical elegance with the morions and pikes which had last appeared in performances of *I Puritani*.

Moving slowly through the crowd were family groups of sight-seers, who had come out to enjoy the illuminations.

' That's nice, that one,' said a woman behind Sophia, pointing to a housefront garlanded with little coloured lamps, hanging on wires like festoons of fruit and centring in a large and miscellaneous trophy of flags.

' They should include the ground-floor,' her companion answered with a laugh of superior sarcasm ; and looking more attentively, Sophia saw that the ground-floor windows had been boarded up, and that a detachment of soldiers was on guard before the house.

Cheerfully, politely, as though the information would make amends for the partial embellishment only, the woman exclaimed,

' Look, Anatole ! Another procession, and this one with torches ! '

' They've been quadrilling outside the *National*,' replied the well-informed Anatole. ' Old Marrast has been letting off another of his speeches to them.'

' Children, too. The little darlings, how pleased they look ! I hope they won't set fire to anything with those torches. I'm glad now that we left Louise and Albertine at home. They would never be content until——'

The surging of the crowd carried them away from the words. Sophia tightened her hold on Minna's elbow, and stiffened herself protectively. Weary, footsore, sleepy, and bored, she still retained a core of carefulness for her companion, the last ember of emotion left waking from the earlier day.

' Did that fool jostle you ? ' she asked in a cross voice.

There was no answer. Minna, very pale, her mouth held stiffly open, was staring through the crowd at the approaching procession. It had neared the house with the boarded windows now, and while the children in shrill weary voices continued to sing the Marseillaise, its leader seemed to be haranguing the soldiers who stood before the boarded-up windows. 'Minions,' he exclaimed. And added something about tyranny.

'How bored those poor soldiers look,' said Sophia.

Every hair of the orator's head seemed to be standing on end, and the torchlight, wavering in the children's inattentive grasp, passed romantic shadows and revelations across his pale face, and the faces massed behind him. She recognised him as Minna's hairy friend of the previous evening, the man who had ranted so on the stairs, and had been greeted as Gaston. A wave of jealousy swept over her—of prim, disapproving, schoolmistressly jealousy. She bent a sharp glance upon Minna's countenance.

Minna shut her eyes.

At the same moment there was the crack of a pistol-shot. Upon it came the most extraordinary sound, a unanimous, multiplied gasping intake of breath, a sound like the recoil of a wave. Into this avid awaiting gasp from the crowd, plumped, as though compelled thither, a word of command, and a volley.

'Ah!'

Before the cries or the exclamations of the wounded could be heard the crowd had spoken, uttering its first word, not of rage or horror, but of profound physical satisfaction, a cry of relief. As though the shock of fulfilment had annihilated every lesser desire there was scarcely a movement around. The children with their torches, the knot of soldiers, the patriots and the sight-seers stood grouped as though for ever, staring at the only movement left—the jerks and writhings of the wounded and dying. Into this silence and immobility Gaston began to launch another oration. On his words followed a rising hubbub of anger and sympathy and denunciation; but as it increased Sophia saw the soldiers relax, as it were, from their official inhumanity, and into their abashed and embarrassed looks there came a growing tincture of relief. Only their officer continued to stare before him with an expression of unmitigated dismay.

The crowd began to break up, swinging this way and that; some to escape homewards, others to gather round the bodies on the pavement. Sighing profoundly Minna disentangled herself from Sophia's clutch, ran forward, and joined herself to those who were attending to the wounded. Gaston swooped downward from his harangue to say something to her as she knelt on the pavement, but it was not possible to see how she answered him, for the crowd thickened, and swallowed them up.

'Here, take these,' said Sophia, thrusting her smelling-salts, a handkerchief, and a long ribbon ripped from her dress into the hands of a shop-girl who was holding out bloodied hands and demanding bandages for the wounded. And when, soon after, a hat was passed round, she put money into it, wishing that at the same time she could offer drinks to the soldiers.

For she found herself entirely impartial, even able to relish the smell of gunpowder as though this were a Blandamer

shooting-party, and her natural instinct to take charge of any
catastrophe was frozen in her. More accurately than she had
known, it seemed, her mind had listened to that conversation
overnight. So far, everything had fallen out according to
plan. Here were the children, and the Rembrandtesque
shadows, the peaceable procession, as it were a picnic, and
the provoked volley from the soldiers. Even the building—
she recognised it now—was the Ministry of Foreign Affairs.
I will wait, she said to herself, for the dray.

The sediment of peaceful-minded had fallen out of the
crowd and it seemed that she was the only person there who
was not armed, who was not angry, and who had not a great
deal to say. An uncomfortable neutrality. Pinned against
the wall she could not but be aware that each glance that fell
on her was more disapproving, more antagonistic, than the
last. As though challenging her silence a dishevelled young
man, glaring under an operatic helmet, enquired of her if it
had not been vilely done, this attack on peaceful citizens;
and getting no answer, he drove his elbow into her breast as
he shoved himself onward. But already his gilded crest was
out of sight, and her look of rage now lit upon a countenance
so pale with hunger, so wasted with intellectual melancholy,
so burning with indignant idealism that she had to catch back
an apology. If he had seen her, though, he had not noticed
her; and in a moment he was gone, carrying his strange
flame with him, as much a solitary in that crowd as I, she
thought, her imagination diving after the image which had
sunk so deeply and instantaneously into her consciousness.
But one cannot meditate in a crowd; and pinned under the
light, her conspicuousness of stature and complexion and

expensive mourning apparel placarded by her immobility and non-currence, she became aware with annoyance that her position was becoming increasingly dangerous.

If I am not torn in pieces, she reflected, I suppose I shall be shot by accident. For now shots were being exchanged as well as shouts ; and it was strange to hear in this earnest and with these town-bred echoes, the sound so reminiscent of peaceful autumn mornings, of the motionless tawny bulk of the woodlands, of all the virgilian romance and dignity of the landscape in which the English landed gentry go out to shoot pheasants. A life rooted in that life, nourished in the pure leaf-mould of land-owning and fenced round with the Game Laws, does not easily let go its hold. In her worst frustration and weariness of soul Sophia had never contemplated death as a consolation ; and to have travelled to Paris and taken her room at the Meurice in order to be killed in the boulevard des Capucines was a turn of Fate which had nothing to commend it. With all of her reason and with half of her heart she would have given away the other half in order to do what was the obvious and sensible thing—to extract herself from this unpleasant and dangerous turmoil, walk off to the hotel and go to bed. But the other half of her heart, the half which had landed her in this situation, held firm, and kept her there.

A sudden acclaiming clamour of rage and emotion swelled out, and like the chord in a progression of music which with its strong gesture tilts the melody from one key into another, turned the weight of mob-feeling into a new and deeper channel. What it was that had called out this cry Sophia could not see, nor could those immediately around her ; but for all that their exclamations tuned in with that other, so that it seemed natural and ordained that presently the mob should divide, pressing itself into mournful hedgerows, leaving, as for a procession of something royal or holy, a space down which the raw-boned cart-horse, its white blaze showy in the gas-light, could be led. The dray it drew forward was heaped with bodies, dead or subsiding into death, and marching beside it, and after it, in silence, with solemn, showmanly looks, were children carrying torches, were the patriots, grimed and bloodied, and women over whose furious faces the tears ran down.

The blood, the tears, the dead and dying bodies were real, as real as the dramatic talent which had organised this clinch-ing raree-show. Real too, though by a momentary inatten-tion compromising the dramatic effect, was Gaston, walking arm in arm with Minna among the mourners, deep in conversation.

To see the pair of them so ridiculously trivial, gabbling with their noses together like a couple of schoolgirls, was the last straw to Sophia's patience. Empowered by rage she wrenched herself out of the crowd, darted upon Minna, and catching her by the shoulder tweaked her away from her companion and out of the procession, and hauled her into a doorway.

' The whole thing has been engineered ! It is nothing but a cold-blooded farce, it is beyond my comprehension how you can lend yourself to such . . . to such goings-on,' she concluded, lamely and violently, and in English. ' Can you deny it, dare you deny it ? '

Because in Minna's fixed and mournful stare she seemed

to detect a look of pity her rage became even more arrogant.

'Fortunately it is no affair of mine how you manage your glorious triumphs of liberty.

'How will you get back to the rue de la Carabine? Will one of your friends see you home?'

It was the last blow that landed. Wincing from it, putting up her hand to her cheek as though a real blow had struck her, Minna said,

'I can go home alone, Sophia.'

'Good!'

But still the crowd kept them where they stood; and if moral loss of temper and the deeper rage of disillusionment could have allowed Sophia to feel any pity she must have felt it then, if only for that pilloried embarrassment. Her hand, like a policeman's, still gripped Minna's shoulder, having left it so long she must keep it there still, for so unnaturally vital was the tension between them that a movement towards convention would only make things worse. Under that grip Minna stood passive and resigned, as though to be held in custody, bullied and abused, were nothing out of the way to her. She made no attempt to speak, her glance, suppliant and patient, wandered to Sophia's face and wandered off again, watching the crowd that surged past them. These fawning, persecuted Israelites, thought Sophia, whetting her resentment on that sure stone.

On the twenty-fourth of February Louis Philippe abdicated, hastening through the gardens of the Tuileries on foot and under an umbrella, for it was raining pretty smartly. His wife, weeping and indignant, hung on his arm, and at the little gate of the Pont Tournant he was glad to climb into the cab which was in waiting there. The cab took the route towards Neuilly. There was no attempt to follow it.

A little later his daughter-in-law made her way to the Chamber of Deputies, taking her child with her. She was given a chair, and sat on it for some hours, unnoticed. A few polite voices had mentioned a regency, but no one had time or inclination to attend to her, though it was generally admitted that she had shown great courage and female dignity, besides being a mother, which is always venerable. At length, compelled by the calls of nature, she retired as inconspicuously as possible to the Invalides.

Meanwhile a provisional government of the left was proposed and agreed on; and other provisional governments were agreed upon with equal enthusiasm and unanimity at the offices of two newspapers, the *National* and the *Réforme*. The adherents of each government, everything being settled so satisfactorily, joined their triumphal processions before the Hôtel de Ville, where there was a vast scene of rejoicing and fraternity.

All this Sophia heard from the valet who brought dinner to her room. He was a young man, and he admitted himself to be moved, saying that the slaughter had been frightful, and would have been worse if it had not been for the refusal of the National Guards to take any part in it, sticking nosegays in the muzzles of their guns to show the harmlessness of their intentions. To-morrow, he said, a new era would begin.

She listened with exasperation. And yet when he had left the room she could have wished him and his babble back again; for to spend a whole day alone in a hotel bedroom,

with the noise of a revolution sounding beneath one's
window, is an ordeal which will fray the most resolute nerves.
She would receive no one, she had said. No one had come.
She was still in the vilest of tempers, footsore, and sour with
sleeplessness, for the noise which had gone on all night made
sleep impossible, and the slumber on the pink sofa seemed to
have taken place in another world, so far removed was it.
The day of confidences on that same sofa seemed as unreal, as
far forgotten. Had there been any life left in the recollection
it must have perished under her will's heel.

To-morrow a new era would begin, and she would leave
Paris. No, she would not. She would stay, order new
clothes at the dressmakers, and visit great-aunt Léocadie.
There she would find reason, dignity, and routine—every-
thing that is dear to a woman of good sense who has dis-
missed her husband, lost her children, discarded the senti-
mental enthusiasms of youth which sit so ill on a woman of
twenty-eight. It would be interesting and consoling to hear
what Léocadie had to say about the Revolution. This was
her third.

Curious how affinity of character could abolish differences
of age, race, and tradition! Though Sophia had been a child,
and great-aunt Léocadie installed in old age, taking as her due
an arm to lean on, hot rum, and a chair with ears; though she
had insisted on being spoken to in French and revised every
faltering sentence, in her company Sophia had enjoyed an
intimacy of confidence never known before, an intimacy lift-
ing her from the discomforts of childhood, setting her among
the ranks of women grown. How much pleasanter to be
great-aunt Léocadie's Sophie than Mamma's Sophia, what

satisfaction in those interminable games of picquet! Mamma's
Sophia was praised with faint condolence upon being such a
good little girl with the old lady. The praises were accepted,
and spat out privately, as one spat out a mawkish lozenge; it
would not do to disclose to the one woman that one liked the
other quite as well. Better, indeed. Sophia much preferred
Léocadie, enjoying her smell, so richly ambered, her cold dry
hands, her rather flat voice, loftily unmodulated, and admir-
ing with relief a head which never ached, a back which never
tired, an imperious digestion which, for all that extravagant
greed and extravagant palate, had never met its match.

I must certainly improve on my bonnet, thought Sophia,
stalking about the room in long-limbed nakedness, the
London bonnet held out at arm's length. Great-aunt
Léocadie had attained her third revolution, the least tribute
one could pay would be a bonnet in the highest and latest
fashion. Warming herself before the hearth Sophia re-
collected how great-aunt Léocadie had praised her for those
long legs; how, coming into the nursery, she had insisted
upon viewing them naked, to make sure that there was no
trace of rickets. In the nursery also there had been a blaze of
logs, and the child had strutted to and fro, holding up her
shift, pleased to be shocking the nursemaids, proud of her
legs, so long and fine, and the narrow knee-joints which
would be in time, so great-aunt Léocadie said, one of her
beauties. Léocadie had spoken praises in her flat voice, the
nursemaids had clucked like hens, and the child had strutted
up and down, lording it over that poultry-yard. Now once
more it was a pleasure to warm her legs at the fire, to be free
and naked, and to hold that expensive bonnet in her hand,

deciding that it would not do. Since she had freed herself of
Frederick nakedness was again a pleasure. Mrs Frederick
Willoughby, sharing a great bed with Mr Frederick Wil-
loughby, or hearing him splashing and crashing in his
dressing-room, had been as shy as a nymph, as disobliging as
a virgin martyr, armouring herself in great starched dressing-
gowns voluminous as clouds.

She tossed the bonnet across the room, and looked at the
bed. Abruptly and absolutely, as though a strain of music
had been broken off, her mood of excited self-satisfaction was
snapped through. A bonnet, a she-septuagenarian . . . it
was not for these that she had come to Paris. Everything,
everything was over, henceforth she would have nothing
better to do than to toss over such trivialities. There was no
purpose, no savour in her life, and yesterday she had made
a fool of herself.

Another procession was approaching, a procession with
drums and singing and a brass band. To those thumps and
brazen pantings she despatched herself to bed, settling rigidly
between the cold sheets, forcing down her eyelids.

Yet however trivial these trivialities, she must keep to
them, or go altogether to pieces ; and hunting a new bonnet
presented difficulties enough for the overcoming of them to
raise her spirits a little. Every shop was shut, it was not
until after midday that she had at last contrived to get herself
admitted to a milliner's by a side door. There, in semi-
darkness behind the shuttered windows, a trembling hand
pinned bows and snatched at the English gold. ' Gold is
always gold, is it not ? ' With that voice, mingled of hope
and doubt, in her ears Sophia remembered an aspect of the

Revolution which might well concern her, and went to Daly's Bank.   The bank was shut.

Gold is always gold.   It was extraordinary to see how already a pious respect for property had manifested itself, as though Paris had said, ' It is true that yesterday we sacked two palaces, havocked every nest where golden eggs are laid, broke, burned, and plundered.   But see how scrupulously we are preserving the ruins.'   Wherever she turned Sophia saw pickets and sentinels, cockaded or badged with red, armed and accoutred like comic-opera bandits, but behaving with the utmost decorum.   Outside the Tuileries stood several furniture vans, and into these the Polytechnic students were packing pictures, ornaments, chandeliers, wine, and kitchen utensils.   On the felled and mangled trees along the boulevards an official hand had scrawled in chalk, *Property of the Republic.   Citizens, respect it!*   And when a small handcart passed her, conveying a harmonium, Sophia was not astonished to see that its bearers were accompanied by an escort of two gentlemen, their substantial overcoats girded by sword-belts, red cockades in their top-hats.   Indeed, it needed a certain adroitness to avoid incurring an escort for herself, so universal was the helpfulness and good feeling through which she picked her way as she scrambled over barricades or waded through the mud where pavements had been.

All this behaviour was most sensible, most praiseworthy. Every countenance beamed with good-will, every official placard breathed peace and respect for property, never in her life had she read such a quantity of elevated adjectives.   Nor could there be any doubt but that this smugness was, for the

moment at any rate, perfectly sincere. It was a shock to
encounter amidst this respectable hubbub the unchanged
indifferent countenance of the river, as though amidst the
fuss and clatter of a philanthropic meeting one were to meet
a large snake threading its way among the boots and petti-
coats. However much blood might flow into that river, no
tincture, no composition, could possibly result. Blood would
not mix with that cold vein of Nature. And leaning on the
balustrade, Sophia thought how, through every city, some
river flows, bearing its witness against the human delusion,
discouraging as the sight of a snake. Only a romantic
charlatan, speaking for effect, could pretend, as Minna had
done, that the sight of a river could bolster up ideas of liberty.
Turn our captivity, O Lord, as the rivers in the South! Turn
our metaphors, O Lord, refresh our perorations! And in
her fancy Sophia took firm hold of Madame Lemuel, holding
her down under that cold tide, keeping her there until, soused
and breathless, she had revised her notions about rivers. A
silly and dangerous woman. Yes, dangerous, as this moment
could prove. For even now, leaning against the balustrade,
watching the river which she must presently cross, Sophia
found herself thinking how, in setting foot on the Left Bank,
she would be entering Minna's territory. What patent non-
sense! The Left Bank was as much great-aunt Léocadie's
territory as Minna's. But the thought of great-aunt Léocadie
would not spread this sensation of excitement through one's
limbs, call out this faint cold sweat of anticipation, knock so
heavily on one's heart.

The dangerous woman must indeed have endangered her
wits, laid some spell on her common sense. Only now did

it occur to her that to arrive, without a word of warning, in great-aunt Léocadie's drawing-room, on the heels of a revolution, would demand rather more pretext than a new bonnet could supply. *I came to Paris to extort a child from my husband.* That would hardly do ; though great-aunt Léocadie would see the force of it, might even approve of the expediency, she could never tolerate the statement. *I came to Paris to buy a bonnet.* That, on the other hand, was too feeble an excuse. Bonnet-buying, however necessary, would be preceded by a letter, one did not pounce after bonnets like a hawk or cattle-raider. Some good reasonable reason must be invented, for at all costs Léocadie must be preserved from supposing that the real reason was, *I heard that there was a revolution and came to look after you.* That unmerited insult must never be suggested, could never be forgiven.

Sophia was still framing the pretext which might decently wrap her appearance when the thought came that great-aunt Léocadie, so capable of looking after herself in any difficulties, might have treated this revolution as she had done others, turning her back upon it. Perhaps even now she was arriving at Blandamer. That was why she had come in 1830. Mamma had said, ' Your poor Aunt Clotilde's mother is coming to live with us for a little while. We must all be very kind to her, poor old lady. She has had so many sorrows.' And Papa, adding that respect would be quite as much called for as kindness, explained that there had been another deplorable revolution. The King of France had been obliged to fly to England. England was, etc.

Not even the shades of the guillotine could do much to ennoble the coming shadow of Madame de Saint Gonval.

Aunt Clotilde had been a very washy character; she had had a baby, and died, the baby had died too, and Uncle Julius Rathbone had become a disconsolate widower and married again. The mother of a dull dead aunt promised little to the ten-year-old Sophia. She came, and remained for a year. Sophia learned to play picquet, learned to speak French, learned to admire her long legs, learned what it was to love some one of her own sex. Till then she had loved only Papa and animals. To love great-aunt Léocadie demanded the same respectful application as the performance of a difficult piece of piano-music. There must be the same agility, the same watchfulness, the same attention to phrasing and expression-marks, and simultaneously one must sit well upright, keeping the shoulders down, the elbows in, the wrists arched, the knuckles depressed. Moreover, even in the most taxing passages, one must breathe through the nose and preserve a pleasing and unaffected smile. Exercised daily in loving great-aunt Léocadie, Sophia, by the year's end, loved almost without a flaw in execution and deportment. Never since then had she loved so well; and though with course of time her love for great-aunt Léocadie had been put aside, as one puts aside a piece of piano-music, the well-learned was still with her, she could still play it by heart.

The metaphor held good. In the instant of hearing that flat familiar voice, of smelling that richly ambered scent, the former amity renewed itself, carrying her smoothly over what she had foreboded as the difficulties of arrival. But in this foreboding Sophia had forgotten one trait of great-aunt Léocadie's; that in any circumstances, however odd or unforeseen, Léocadie's chief concern was Léocadie. Sophia, the

Revolution, the bonnet, all fell back into their place before the fact that great-aunt Léocadie had taken to spinning.

'The only tolerable occupation, my dear, for an old woman. Listen!' She gave the wheel a turn. 'That garrulous gentle doting voice. All the satisfaction of listening to a gossip and none of the trouble of saying *Yes*, or *Well*, or *And what happened then?* It is traditional, too, it is Gothic. And that makes it tolerably fashionable. It was an inspiration, that I should spin. You look very well in black, my child. Most women do, and it is providential since life compels us to mourn so often.'

She raised her head and glanced at the portraits of her son Anne-Victor, who was killed in a duel, of her daughter Clotilde, who died in childbirth. The glance travelled from the one portrait to the other, deft and sure as the toe of a ballet-dancer. With those words and that glance she established her precedence of sorrow. There was no more contestation about it than there would have been over any other uncontestable social precedence.

'I heard it said the other day, that women all like vinegar for the same reason.'

'Nonsense! Women recruit themselves with vinegar after love. It is astringent to the nerves. And so you are not living with Frederick?'

'No.'

'No. But how do you manage that in England? Don't your acquaintances pretend to be shocked?'

'I have not consulted them.'

'That will scarcely prevent them cold-shouldering you. I do not pretend to be shocked myself, still, I should be glad to see you reconciled. While the children were alive it was quite reasonable, I dare say. But now I recommend you to patch things up. There should be an heir to the property.'

How far-off, now, the lime-kiln's winking signal, the tumult of spirit in which she had conceived the expedient that came so naturally to great-aunt Léocadie's practical mind! However, she thought, I was being practical, though failing to recognise it.

' I think I shall take to spinning,' she said.

' At your age it would be thriftless. Thirty years hence you may certainly spin, meanwhile . . . Hand me that bag,, if you please. I need more wool. Meanwhile, Sophie, you should make up your mind to one of three things—religion, love, or family life. Religion would never suit you, your temperament is too cold. Love is out of the question, too, I hope ?——'

' Quite.'

' So you see, there is nothing for it but family life. You will find Frederick considerably improved.'

' Do you see Frederick ? '

Great-aunt Léocadie looked up from the bag in which she was searching.

' Delighted as I am to see the last of the Orléans pack, I could wish the dynasty had endured until I had received a fresh supply of wool. Never mind! *À brebis tondue Dieu mesure le vent.* When my wool falls short you arrive on a visit. You will stay here, of course. I can assure you I shall be very glad of a little protection.'

And see Frederick, and be patched up. Not if I know it, thought Sophia.

'A more despicable family! . . . I hear that the great ambition of the rabble at the Tuileries is to wear the late Adélaïde's bonnets. I wish them joy of her bonnets, they would have been welcome to the head for all I care. Have you noticed, my child, that Liberal families are always run by their old women? And the Queen, did you hear of her great speech? It appears that they were all in tears, packing for their lives, and falling over each other to hand Papa the pen and the ink-pot that he might sign the abdication. All but she. She took up a nobler attitude, and told him that he should go out into the Carrousel, confront the mob, and die fighting. "*Je vous bénirai du haut du balcon*," she said. What an inducement!'

Delicately licking her lips she listened unsmiling to Sophia's laughter.

'And who do you think told me that? Your husband! I assure you, he is improved beyond recognition.'

'I have no doubt that Madame Lemuel has done him a great deal of good.'

'Incontestably. You were far too delicate a file for him. I saw that at a glance, when you brought him here in '39. Besides, my dear, you are too proud and too indolent—too British, in fact—to shape an unsatisfactory husband. Now that little Jewess, she was exactly what he needed. She is supple, she has immense application, she flattered away and filed away. She has been the making of him.'

'These Jewish tailoresses,' said Sophia, 'turn out their wares quite marvellously, I understand. Still, I am not convinced that I want to array myself in a slop-suit.'

'You underestimate the woman. Really, she is quite

worthy of your jealousy. For one thing, she is certainly an artist. I have been to some of her recitals myself, and her diction gave me real pleasure.'

' But how is she an artist ? What does she do ? '

' She tells fairy-stories and fables. It is something quite particular, a narrow talent, but perfectly cultivated.'

' Well ? '

' My dear Sophie, for a woman of that sort a perfectly cultivated talent is already a great deal.'

' You cannot make me believe that Madame Lemuel has held Frederick spell-bound by telling him fairy-stories.'

' I should not attempt to believe it myself.'

She turned her wheel, letting it laugh for her, a smooth delighted murmur.

' I see that I can do nothing, you will not condescend to poor fairy-story-telling Jewesses, so I say no more. But it is very unselfish of me, for she is really a most extraordinary person, and has had the most interesting career, and I should have enjoyed telling you about her. You see, I am infected myself. I also want to tell stories.'

And Frederick had purveyed those stories, no doubt, the pogroms and the lovers, and all the other details of that interesting career, of that narrow talent extensively cultivated. For an instant Sophia experienced a passionate curiosity to hear all that Léocadie had to tell about Minna—O God, as passionate a curiosity as Minna, two days ago, had seemed to feel, hearing Sophia tell all about Sophia !

That was the flea she had caught, sleeping on the pink sofa, a flea that was still lodged somewhere about her, and bit on. And even when the fresh arrivals, an old lady, and a middle-aged lady, and an old gentleman, and Père Hyacinthe, great-aunt Léocadie's spiritual director, had come in, each one arriving triumphantly endangered and out of breath, and bearing, like doves returning with particularly ample olive-branches, each some new story, discreditably ludicrous, of the fall of the dynasty, Sophia found that she was expecting them to speak of Madame Lemuel.

In this Legitimist drawing-room a new era, it seemed, had begun also. The blessing from the balcony was recounted, the Duc de Nemours fainted repeatedly, each time that the clattering tongues hoisted Louis Philippe into his cab he was damper, more trembling, more abject than before. Sophia was applied to for assurances that only the most ignominious charity awaited the Orléans family on the farther side of the Channel, should they get so far. It seemed taken for granted that the Younger Branch had only to go out for the Elder Branch to come in, like the man and the woman in the weathercock. Amidst these carollings the fact of the Revolution passed almost unmentioned. The mob's heart was in the right place, it was only wearing a red cockade as a preparatory emphasis to the white ribbon which would come after. And if corroboration were needed, some one remembered to point out that M. de Lamartine was infinitely more elegant than M. Guizot; alternatively that a week of the provisional government would entail starvation and stoppage, and what could be more rallying than that?

In the trees of the Place Bellechasse a thrush was trying its song in the gusty evening, and against the large pale clouds that moved with a slackening pace across the eastern sky the scaffolding of the unfinished church of Ste. Clotilde asserted its cocksure right-angles. It is a view that I shall get to know by heart, she thought. But any port in a storm, and still more any port in a calm so leaden, so dispiriting, as that into which her life had fallen. Père Hyacinthe, levitating slightly above the things of this world, began to speak of the beauties of architecture, the religious sensations aroused by cusps and flying buttresses, questioning her with an inflection of congratulation upon the purifying influence of Pugin and Barry. And as she answered him, concealing her ignorance, she looked forward through metaphors of furs laid by with camphor, silver wrapped in green baize, fruit trees released of their fruit and nailed back against the wall, to the moment when all these people would go and she would begin to play picquet with great-aunt Léocadie.

Any port in a calm. She could stagnate here as well as anywhere else, better, indeed, for she would be living in accordance with every canon of reputable behaviour, and pleasing an old woman who had been kind to her and must soon die. As for Frederick, he could be kept at arm's length ; and the stories about Minna need never be told, she would not knock on the door of that Bluebeard's cupboard.

The wool from Berri came, though the triumph of the Legitimists tarried. The spinning-wheel turned, every day there came a stock of new scandals, new doves flying to the vast dovecot of great-aunt Léocadie's memory, and Père Hyacinthe came daily too, applying himself like a cold-cream to the upkeep of great-aunt Léocadie's spiritual complexion. Sophia observed that in great-aunt Léocadie a change had taken place, a susceptibility to the spirit of the age manifesting itself in her, just as it had manifested itself in Mamma.

Léocadie now respected the Church. She went regularly to mass, and distinguished among the different physiognomies of the Virgin, finding Our Lady of Carmel, for instance, more sympathetic than she of Victories. So Père Hyacinthe came daily, to be applied like the *Secret de Bonne Femme.* He never spoke of religion, but doubtless he breathed it ; and in the minute formalities attending his arrival and his departure, his ambassadorial airs and accolade of benediction, there seemed to be a rehearsal of the superior ceremonials which would be restored with the restoration of the House of Bourbon.

'I do not wish to meet Frederick yet,' she had said, knowing that great-aunt Léocadie's tactical feelings, if nothing else, would ensure the wish attention. There had been no need to say, 'I do not wish to hear about Madame Lemuel'; and it was with a strangely cool heart that she found herself reading the placard of a concert to be given to raise funds for the wounded of the Revolution. Mademoiselle Louise Bertin would play a nocturne of her own composition, a bass from the opera would sing, Madame Lemuel would recount a legend.

It was a shabby enough list, second-rate celebrities padded out with pupils of the Conservatory ; and the narrow talent, the diction which had won great-aunt Léocadie's approval, was not, it seemed, sufficiently admitted to be granted any emphasis of lettering. The street was empty and lifeless, the placard, cheaply printed, crumpled, and stuck up askew, gave the impression that it never had been read, and never would be. Sophia foresaw the dreariness of a charity concert, the empty seats, the mumping airs of the programme sellers, enraged at having to attend a performance with such poor promise of tips. Every possible expense would be spared, the floor would be dirty, the platform encumbered with the relics of a previous recital, a harp in a bag perhaps, or a bower of paper roses ; a barrel-organ would play outside, and only half the lights would be turned on.

Under such conditions the tedium of listening to a quartet by Habeneck, the Overture to *La Vestale* played as a duet, a series of variations on *Là ci darem* for the flute would be immeasurable ; and yet it seemed to Sophia that she would be there, and already she felt the draught playing upon her shoulders and saw the glove buttons which she would sum and study.

It seemed to her that she would be alone. Yet when the day of the concert came great-aunt Léocadie sat on one side of her, Frederick on the other, and beyond great-aunt Léocadie sat Père Hyacinthe, and beyond Frederick sat two elderly Legitimist ladies. ' Six tickets,' great-aunt Léocadie had said with decision. ' It is one's duty to help these poor wounded creatures. Whatever their opinions, they bled to free us of a tyrant. And a quantity of them were wounded by accident.'

' Suffering,' added Père Hyacinthe, ' appeals in an universal language.'

' We, in particular,' continued Madame de Saint Gonval, ' must not hold back, now that once more we have a duty towards the people.'

' They will recognise it,' said Père Hyacinthe, ' presently. In their hearts they recognise it already. France is as essentially feudal as it is essentially catholic. In the last few days I have noticed some quite remarkable movements of piety.'

Holding a lozenge between his finger and thumb, he spoke of the religious demeanour of the crowd who watched the funeral celebrations on the fourth of March, of the black cloth hangings which covered the Madeleine, of the pompous moment when, to the strains of the organ, the clergy came forward to receive the dead. Even the orations, he said, had been free from offence, and in all that vast crowd there had not been a single accident.

'Except to the Statue of Liberty,' said great-aunt Léocadie. 'Didn't it fall off the triumphal car?'

'It might perhaps have been a little more securely fastened.' And in popped the lozenge like a reward.

All things wrought together for those who loved Henry V. The Statue of Liberty toppled, and six Legitimists in a row would be an oriflamme. Sophia said,

'I am afraid it will be a very dull programme.'

'Not to me,' answered great-aunt Léocadie. 'Is there not a nocturne by the celebrated Mademoiselle Bertin? For ten years at least I have been watching her talents unclose. It is a unique spectacle, imperceptible almost, gradual as the coming of the dawn. She advances on fame with the majestic pace of a planet.'

'Is she very celebrated?'

'Her brother, my dear, is the director of the *Journal des Débats*. A little more wool, if you please.'

She had decided to go. Should she find her disorderly feelings for Madame Lemuel threatening to be too much for her, no doubt it would be better to be one of a party; nor was it possible to put up much opposition to Frederick being among those who would, if need arose, stuff handkerchiefs into her mouth and sit on her head. For she was Léocadie's guest, and Frederick Léocadie's visitor. Civility—even a sense of the ridiculous—made it scarcely possible to refuse to encounter him. 'I can promise,' the old lady had said, 'that he will come only when others visit me. There can be nothing awkward. And really, my child, it will be less scandalous to meet him on such a footing than be overwhelmed with sudden sick headache whenever he is announced.'

With great-aunt Léocadie Sophia had found everything that she as a woman of good sense had sought there—reason, routine, dignity. Even in another one must admire the qualities one admires in oneself. Sophia, listening to the clock bestridden by a dimpled and gilded Time, lying awake on an impeccable mattress, owned freely that the old lady wielded reason, routine, and dignity far better than she did. As wary singers and dancers go back to their masters for an overhaul of technique she might consider herself returned to the Academy of Madame de Saint Gonval; and with the humble admiration that tyros cannot feel she admired the precision and deftness of her schoolmistress. She can even manage Frederick, she thought, prostrating herself in a fit of technical admiration. For the promise had held good, there was nothing awkward in the meetings to which she was now growing accustomed. Frederick came only at visiting hours, did not fidget, did not stare, talked, and did not talk too much. His approach was neither stiff nor familiar, he posed neither as husband nor suitor; and if, as she sometimes admitted to herself, great-aunt Léocadie, and under her guidance Frederick, was slowly, delicately, manœuvring her from the position of an offended wife into the position of a misguided one, the pressure was so tactful, the strategy so benevolent, she must feel that only magnanimity had prompted the manœuvre, and that she was being insinuated into the wrong only that she might step with more dignity into the right. How much more dignified a reconciliation based on reason, brought about by routine, than the climbing-down from a fit of bad temper implicit in a mere vulgar forgiveness, or an equally vulgar continued resentment!

All this she knew, with little more emotional independence than the oyster may be supposed to have, feeling the change of tide under which it will open. A moment would come, she admitted that now, when she would open, when a reunited Mr and Mrs Willoughby would return to Blandamer, when all the past would be forgiven or forgotten, one process cancelling out the other. Meanwhile Frederick came, stayed a little, conversed, handed a tumbler or picked up a shawl, and went again. And as though he had been met and made up by great-aunt Léocadie in the ante-room, with each appearance he increased a delicate fard of melancholy. 'I bear no resentment,' that demeanour said. 'I am a little pained. It is sad. My wife will not admit me, my children are dead, I am living in a hotel and eat at a restaurant. Exiled from the joys of the hearth and having abandoned the flashy consolations of my mistress, I am naturally dejected. But I accuse no one, I do not murmur, and you must see how grief has refined my manners.' If he turned anywhere for consolation, it was to Père Hyacinthe, as though delicacy forbade that his sexual plaint should be confided to any bosom save one which could not feel as a woman's and had renounced to feel as a man's. Even then the plaint was intimated with scrupulous reserve, voicing itself as a gently growing interest in ecclesiology. Together they would look out of the window at the unfinished Ste. Clotilde, and an artistic conversation would take place, Père Hyacinthe with roulades of language expatiating on the beauties of Gothic, Frederick supplying cadences of agreement, till the two voices joined, as it were, in a duet, aspiring in thirds and sixths towards the day when the scaffolding would be removed, and the edifice completed.

Then, when the tenor had taken his hat and departed, the basso allowed himself to observe that Mr Willoughby had a great deal of heart.

The two carriages which conveyed the oriflamme had their armorial bearings obliterated from the panels . . . a tactful concession to the people whose heart was in the right place though their king, as yet, was not. The concert-room was quite as half-baked as Sophia had guessed it would be, and emptier beyond her most cynical guess. Another sign of the times, observed Père Hyacinthe. The arts could never flourish in a soil undermined by social disquiet, unwarmed, if he might say so, by the sun of majesty. The elderly lady beyond him added that no one could buy concert tickets when the country was on the verge of bankruptcy. On this followed an animated lamentation on bank failures, the ruin of those who held railway shares, the price of gold and the demented theories of Louis Blanc, Frederick adding that Louis Blanc was the illegitimate son of Pozzo di Borgo, deriving his surname from the blank space in the baptismal register. The burst of applause following this statement applied, however, to the appearance of the duettists who were to perform the Overture to *La Vestale*.

It was an archipelago of a concert, quantities of short items isled in long pauses. Long as the pauses were, the financial situation filled them, and Sophia, who had at first felt somewhat hypocritical in her agreement to be alarmed, knowing of the solid English gold which she had ordered to be conveyed to her agent, fell later to pondering what would happen if by some stroke of Communism that gold were laid hands on. She had an independent spirit, and had never lacked for money. The idea of finding herself penniless (even artificially and temporarily penniless) was repulsive and bewildering, and with growing exasperation she turned over such expedients as selling her diamond brooch, giving lessons in English, or journeying to Calais on foot. The knowledge that her panic was unreasonable did not make it less, and the act of thinking to music heightened her disquiet, the quartet by Habeneck dragging her thoughts at its steadily grinding chariot wheels. It was all very well for the others, she assured herself. For them this chaos which they canvassed so freely was like every other development of the Revolution : another proof of the incompetency of the late government, another argument against liberalism, another preliminary darkness on which the restoration must certainly lighten. They could have it their own way ; but neither buffet to one regime nor wind to the sails of another would be of the least consolation to Sophia stranded in Paris with an empty purse. Hearing Frederick murmur confidentially, ' They're laying it on a bit thick,' she glanced at him with real gratitude for the English phrase and the English phlegm.

And he—with what sensations was he waiting for Madame Lemuel's part in the programme ? Whatever they were, he gave no indication, listening to the flute variations on *Là ci darem* with such gentlemanly melancholy that he did not even appear to be numbering them.

Nevertheless, thought Sophia, it is a situation. Man and wife cannot sit side by side waiting for the man's mistress to come forward bowing and public-figured without it being a situation. I hate situations. I loathe drama, and I wish I had never come. Frantically, intently, conscience-strickenly aware how little time remained for the process, she began to freeze herself, while the remaining variations, each more hurried, squeaking, and breathless than the last, scampered to the final trill and the final arpeggio. Now there would be applause, and then another of those intervals.

She must have frozen better than she knew. When the crimson curtains parted and Minna came forward, bowing and public-figured, it was as though she had never seen the woman before. Gravely, carefully, almost as though she were telling the story on oath, Minna told the story of Puss in Boots. Like everything else in the programme, her performance fell flat, and the vigour of a few applauding hands only emphasised the inattention of the other applauders. All the way back great-aunt Léocadie spoke with delight of Madame Lemuel's narrative. It was perfect, she said; the very spirit of old France. In her satisfaction she even forgot to mention the nocturne by Mademoiselle Bertin.

I feel, thought Sophia, as though I had visited a church-yard, and it had been the wrong churchyard. She had caught a cold, as people who visit churchyards often do. Dull with fever, she consented willingly enough to Léocadie's diagnosis of *grippe*, and to the prescription of bed and tisane. She was

pleased to lie in bed, and had not enough enterprise of spirit
left to wish to die.

When she got up again it was as she expected. The
negotiations in which her part had been so passive had gone
on perfectly without her. Frederick had brought flowers,
and the reconciliation was completed. However, her money
had arrived safely, that was one comfort—now, presumably,
she would need to buy another trousseau. Only the for-
malities remained, and those were well in hand. 'I have a
whim,' said great-aunt Léocadie, 'an old woman's whim,
that must be indulged. Seeing you here together, hearing
your English accents, has given me the idea how delightful
it would be to have a high tea together, an English nursery
high tea, all by ourselves. Just such a feast, my Sophie, as I
learned to enjoy at Blandamer, when you were a little girl in
a tippet. We will get the buns from Columbin. Shall we
say, Saturday ? '

Buns on Saturday, thought Sophia. Te Deum on Sunday.

Only now did the slow-witted creature realise how patently,
appearing without warning and without pretext, she must
have seemed to great-aunt Léocadie to be throwing herself
upon those managing mercies, mutely holding out a rended
matrimony as a child holds a broken toy or a torn pinafore.
Her first refusal to meet Frederick, how affected and mawkish
that must have appeared !—her yielding, how natural ! Tying
on her bonnet before the glass, contemplating her face,
blankly handsome, Sophia assured herself that for the last
month she had indeed been exactly like the fairy-tale goose
that ran about ready-roasted with a knife and fork in its
back. It was too late to do anything about it now. Casting

back her mind she could not discern a moment since her coming to the Place Bellechasse when it had not been too late, so completely had she pulled the net about her. Really, if one were such a fool when left to one's own devices, it might be as well to resume a husband as soon as possible.

Soon it would be. This was Saturday and she was going out to choose the buns. Having left matters so late, this was all she could do as a show of interest in the reconciliation so kindly arranged for her. And like every one who asserts himself too late she had asserted herself too violently, saying 'I will go to Columbin's for the buns,' as though she were volunteering to go through fire and water for them.

'Pray do, my child. Choose them yourself. Madeleine will go with you to carry them.'

Columbin, the English pastrycook, had his shop in the rue de Luxembourg; before going there Sophia went to the agent and picked up the money which awaited her. Twenty-five good golden English pounds—a reassuring weight, a comfortable gravity.

'I love money,' she told herself, walking obliviously past shop-windows. 'There, perhaps, the true unexplored passion of my life awaits me.' And remembering how Byron had written,

> So for a good old-gentlemanly vice
> I think I must take up with avarice,

she took pleasure in imagining herself back again at Blanda-mer, sitting by the library fire, reading *Don Juan*, and letting her thoughts stray with the turning of a page to rent-roll and consolidated bonds. True, Frederick would be lounging near by : Frederick who was no buttress to the pleasures of avarice. But it was ill-advised to think of that, better to look on the other side of the penny, better to remember that the honourable estate of matrimony allowed one to read *Don Juan* in honour and ease, rather than by snatches in a cold bedroom.

The pleasures of avarice were emphasised by the surroundings. It was difficult to believe that this was Paris, so nipped and dingy did it look, so down-hearted and down-at-heel. A shrewish wind was blowing, and if the sun had tempted out the café tables and chairs, it had tempted out nothing else; for the few drinkers sat within the glass doors, and seemed to have wrapped newspapers round them for further protection. Certainly they had no mind for the stumpy young man who had been playing his guitar to a set of tables and chairs, and had now gone in to make his collection. As she passed, idly surveying, he came out again, pausing at the door for one more bow and one more soliciting glance around. A voice, protesting against the draught, cut short the poor hope. They met face to face and Sophia supposed he was about to hold out his hat to her, when he put it on in order to take it off, bowing with stiff politeness. Only then, seeing herself recognised, did she recognise him. It was the hump-backed little Jew who had offered her a chair at the rue de la Carabine, and to whom Minna had spoken of his symphony.

Poor child!—she thought. How cold he looks, what agony to press wire strings with such chilblained hands! Pity softened her blank good looks into beauty. Encouraged and romantic, he stood beside her, with his hat in one hand and his instrument in the other, asking if she were alone, if he might have the honour of escorting her. The Revolution, he said, had made Paris less agreeable than of old.

'You can go home, Madeleine,' she said, beckoning to
the lady's-maid, who had withdrawn herself from the spec-
tacle of Mrs Willoughby conversing with a street-musician
—and on the very eve, too, of her reconciliation with Mr
Willoughby.   'I will bring the buns.'

'I have been staying,' she said, 'with an elderly relation
in the Faubourg St Germain. We play picquet and lament
for Charles X. This revolution seems hardly real to me. I
wish you would tell me about it, I am as ignorant as the
carp at Chantilly.'

If I can get you to Columbin's, her thoughts added, I will
feed you. A good square meal is what you need, hopping
beside me like a famished sparrow.

'It is magnificent. It is not like any other revolution.
It is purer, more noble, more idealistic.'

She managed to convert an English *humph* into a more
sympathetic noise of assent.

'It is a marvellous experience,' he continued, 'to live
under a republic. One breathes a different air. Freedom of
thought, freedom of speech, no more suspicion or hypocrisy,
no more . . .'

A violent fit of coughing interrupted him.

'I fear that the air of a republic has not been very good
for your chest.'

Protests and coughs brought them to Columbin's door.
Would he jib, recollecting his guitar, his shabbiness ? Not
at all. Hunger, that brings the wolf out of the wood, carried
him into the pastrycook's. The hunger, though, was not
for the hot chocolate and sandwiches she ordered. Loneli-
ness was the famine which had tamed him ; and in the release

of having some one to talk to he forgot the where and the when, forgot the unintimacy between them, forgot even the lack of credence which she could not conceal as she listened to his rhodomontades. But by degrees his sincerity gained on her, and she began to listen and question in earnest.

' But surely no state can afford to be completely altruistic. Even granting that France has become a good example to the rest of Europe, that is not a national industry. Revenues must be collected, wages earned and paid. I must seem to you very grovelling—but I fear that Europe, instead of looking on France as an example, will be quite as likely to look on her as a warning.'

' They should change their spectacles, then, if they are so old that they cannot see beyond their noses. The spirit of a people is more than material prosperity. Besides, the republic is prosperous. It is only a few luxuries that have been lopped off. That is nothing.'

' It has been my experience,' she answered, ' that soon after people pawn the clock and the tea-set they pawn their tools and their bedding. A nation does not lop off luxuries unless it feels a threat to essentials.'

' Even if we have pawned the clock, even if our house seems bare, I would rather live in it so. Never before has there been so much room for hope.'

At this moment a waiter walked past, ostentatiously skirting the guitar and then returning for another look at it. In a cold angry voice Sophia began to give him her order for buns.

' Poor guitar ! I should not have brought it. It offends a waiter and I am afraid it has done worse. Tell me, has not that unfortunate instrument prejudiced you a little against the republic ? '

' Tell me, when did you exchange composing symphonies for playing the guitar ? '

' I compose still. Better than before.'

' I beg your pardon,' she said abashed.

' But I admit it,' he continued. ' You are quite right. I am one of the luxuries that have been lopped off. And sometimes I tremble for the threat to the essentials . . . to the greatest of essentials, to art.'

Candour gave a quality almost like blitheness to the story, as he told how surely and swiftly the prophecy of the man in the shawl had been fulfilled. His allowance had ceased, for his father, a jeweller, did no more business. The orchestras were disbanded, no one wished for music-lessons, there was no copying to be had. Revolutions had no need for symphonies, and it was hard enough to pick up a living by playing his guitar. And there were a hundred others, he added, the blitheness falling from his tune, in the same case—others better than he.

' But your friends,' said Sophia slowly. ' Surely there must be some people who can help you. Madame Lemuel. . . .'

' Minna ! ' For the first time his face, so pinched and pale, lost its bird's look of confidence. And yet, she thought, I have always heard that Jews help Jews. However meanly she had come to think of Minna, it had not occurred to her that Minna would practise the good old-gentlemanly vice.

' Minna ! ' he repeated. ' You have hit on the only thing that can make me doubt of the Revolution. Minna should not be left to starve.'

' To starve ? ' she said, unbelieving.

' To starve twice over. To be so poor that she cannot help others—that is a double starvation to a heart like hers. I would give my right hand,' he said, striking the table, ' if I could save her from that.'

' But—things cannot be so bad with her. How long is it since we met at her apartment ? Five weeks ? '

' She could beggar herself in a day,' he said with pride.

' But what has happened ? '

' She is an artist, and there is no time now for art. And because she had a position her plight is the worse, since the younger, the poorer, have gone to her for help. I did myself, more blame to me. She was not in, but five people were waiting to see her. Two of them were duns, three of them beggars like myself. The concierge told me this, licking his vile lips with malice.'

' Did you see her ? '

' Yes. She came back at last. Back from a charity concert, unpaid, of course. She had done abominably, she said so. And no wonder, for how can one hold an audience like that, an audience of well-fed idlers, on a little salad ? '

' I met people who were at that very concert. They were enthusiastic about her. Her talent is so much admired, she is so well known. . . . Would it not be possible . . .' She paused, thinking it must be delicately phrased, and some mocker in her mind repeating the rhyme about the big fleas and the little fleas.

' Not they ! ' said he.

While she was staring at the pattern of the table-cloth he broke out again.

' But that is not the worst of it, she is starving for more

than food and drink. The worst of it is, that as a re-
volutionary she is out of fashion. Before, she was an inspira-
tion. But inspiration is not wanted now, it seems. One must
be practical, one must be administrative, one must understand
economics and systems. She pines. She said to me, that very
evening, " Our Moses was luckier than he knew, to die before
he went into the promised land." '

He stopped. It seemed to him she was no longer listening.
And after a moment's silence he saw her making ready to go.

Aware that he had outstayed his welcome, more aware of it
than she, he picked up the guitar and followed her to the door.
Frowning abstractedly she listened to his thanks, availing herself
of a tact which smoothed the finish of their meeting. Not till the
river was crossed did she think, fleetingly, that she should have
offered—since he could not be tipped—to take singing-lessons.

She was even later than she had expected, but for all that
she spent some time arranging herself for the peace-treaty tea,
smoothing her hair and polishing her nails. It was as though
she must not allow herself to be hurried, as though some
heavenly mamma had admonished, ' My dear, in your con-
dition it is imperative to avoid the slightest flurry. Above all,
do not trip on the stairs.'

Obediently tranquil, she entered the salon, and saw with-
out the least emotion of apology great-aunt Léocadie and
Frederick sitting poised above their boiled eggs, and the
table spread with cakes and bread-and-butter, and the bouquet
of camellias beside her plate. She seated herself in silence.
To Léocadie's polite fears that the buns had given her a great
deal of trouble she replied politely that they had given her no
trouble whatever ; and like a good child, seen and not heard,

she crumbled bread-and-butter, and listened to the other two conversing. At intervals, as kind elders do, they made an opening for her in the conversation, pausing, casting encouraging glances; but they got nothing beyond *Yes* or *No* for their pains.

Meanwhile their talk became increasingly animated, increasingly a performance in which great-aunt Léocadie was the ballerina and Frederick the suave athletic partner, respectfully leading her round by one leg as she quivered on the tip-toe of the other.

Now Frederick was doing a little *pas de fascination* on his own, recounting how he had become involved in the planting of a Tree of Liberty. With humour he described the dejected sapling, tied up in the tricolour, the band of squalling school-children, the mayor of the arrondissement who blew his nose continually, the two gentlemen with their rival speeches on fraternity. When the speeches were concluded, and the tree set toppling in its little pit it was discovered that the gardener had gone away, taking his spade with him; but undeterred by this, said Frederick, they began to pass round a hat for contributions. Abstractedly he had put his hand into his pocket, drawn out his case, and dropped a cigar into the hat.

'Ridiculous wool-gatherer!' commented Léocadie tenderly, 'you are not fit to look after yourself. Is he, Sophie?'

She still kept silence. Frederick remarked that he could not help being absent-minded. It was a quality that accompanied untidiness, he was untidy too.

'Am I not, Sophia?' he added, with malice.

'Yes, you are untidy.'

'You see, Frederick. Even our Sophie condemns you.'

'All the same,' Sophia continued, and it seemed to her that she must be shouting at the top of her voice, 'however casual and ineffable you are, I think you might take the trouble to tidy up your liaisons. You might at least pension off your mistresses before you start dog's-earing your new leaf——'

'Sophia!'

'Sophie, my child!'

'Instead of leaving them to starve.'

'Sophie, one does not make accusations in such a tone of voice.'

'I beg your pardon, great-aunt Léocadie. I should not have shouted. But I hold to the accusation. To-day I heard that Madame Lemuel is destitute and starving. And I mean to have this remedied.'

'Starving! Poor creature, how terribly sad!'

'Destitute? That's unexpected! Sophia, who did you hear this from?'

'From a friend of hers. A young man, a hump-back. He composes music.'

'Guitermann!' Frederick gave a spurt of laughter. 'How these Jews cling together. They're all penniless, aren't they, each worse than the last? My poor innocent, he was touting for her. How much did he get out of you?'

'It is dreadful, it is tragic,' interposed great-aunt Léocadie. 'Such an admirable artist, such a rare talent! But these are cruel days for artists, I have heard the most heart-rending stories of their plight, poor things! Sophie is right, Frederick, this must be remedied. It can easily be done, she has so many—so many people who appreciate her talent. A commission or two, one might get up a recital, or find her pupils.

Perhaps, since she is in such straits, a little purse. It could be given delicately. One would not wish to wound her.'

' Perhaps young Guitermann would like a little purse too. His father is a jeweller, and rolling, but for all that I dare say young Guitermann wouldn't be above a little purse, provided it was given delicately enough.'

'I don't think I have heard anything by this Monsieur Guitermann. What a musical race they are! Meyerbeer, and Bellini, and . . . Paganini, and . . .'

'Whether it be given delicately or indelicately,' said Sophia, ' Minna Lemuel cannot be left to starve. And since Frederick can do nothing about his obligations but snigger out of them like a schoolboy, I shall see to it myself.

' Now,' she added, rising to her feet.

Presumably they spoke, but no words remained in her memory. When she was out of doors her rage thinned away like the smoke from an explosion, and hurrying through the limpid spring evening she felt as though in the relief of speaking and acting out her rage she had become almost disembodied. But the weight of that good English gold she carried was real, and her heart-beats were real—heavy and full, thudding like coins let fall one after another.

Acts of impulse are of two kinds. Those performed by people of a naturally impulsive character come with the suavity of habit, they are put forth like the tendrils of a vine, and there is time to meditate them a little, to dispose their curvings with grace. However spontaneous, the mind which generates them has done the same sort of thing before, and in the instant between thought and deed there is an unflurried leisure, in which habit and cunning can contrive their adjustments. But when people of a slow or cautious disposition act upon impulse, the impulse surprises them even more than it surprises those upon whom it is directed. Such astonishment leaves no room for thoughts of contrivance, the assent of the will has been so overwhelming that diplomacy and manœuvring seem not so much impossible as out of the question.

Leaving the pastrycook's, Sophia had no project whatever, feeling only a sullen fury, an emotion so pure and absorbing that it had given her a sensation almost like complacence. With this to nurse in her lap she had sat blandly through the first stages of the peace-treaty tea, impregnable in bad behaviour, and when Frederick's brag of untidiness had tossed her the cue for her outburst, the sight of the intention leaping out of her rage had staggered her like a flash of lightning dazzling between her and the tea-pot. Blinded to everything but that suddenly scribbled zig-zag of purpose, the time it must take to reach the rue de la Carabine was no time at all. It was a hiatus, a darkness through which her purpose must travel to its expression as the rocket arches its dark journey between the moments of being touched off and of exploding its fires. The red winking eye of the lime-kiln had let her off on just such another journey. But her mind, for all its natural bent towards the sardonic and belittling, did not remind her now of the ignominious splutter with which that other rocket had turned itself into a squib, nor of all those misfiring impulses, inappropriate and unavailing, which had defaced her career.

Incapable of considering the how, she had not considered the where either. She was going to Minna; and as her imagination showed Minna, so doubtless she would find her—

in the house in the rue de la Carabine, standing by the pink sofa, the ermine scarf drooping lopsidedly from her shoulders. With this meeting so clear in mind, her impetus towards it carried her past Minna encountered in the street. The recognition that halted her, stock-still on the pavement, was only at second-sight realised as a recognition of the woman she sought. For the instantaneous, the overwhelming impression was, that for the first time in her life she had seen despair.

Standing open-mouthed on the pavement, holding her burden of English gold, twenty-five pounds, seven hundred and fifty francs, purpose and pity alike were obliterated by an astonishment that was almost like triumph. She had seen what is seen by perhaps one person in a thousand : the unmitigated aspect of a human emotion. And she had seen it in the street, as one sees a lamp-post, a brown horse, an umbrella, a funeral. The shock was a challenge to her whole previous existence, to her outlook on life. Life would never be the same again, she would be henceforth always the woman who had seen the authentic look of despair.

It was not until she turned and walked in pursuit of Minna that astonishment fell away and pity took its place. Pity seemed a vague thing, wavering from one speculation to another, and all the energy of her purpose was gone, for why should she be following, with her twenty-five pounds, a person whose air proclaimed a zero that could quell any other cyphers, a not-having beyond the dreams of avarice ?— and she began to walk more slowly, putting off the moment when she must overtake her quarry. Yet flesh and blood must live, and the money be given. Wherever Minna Lemuel was going she was not going to her death. One does

not saunter to suicide, thought Sophia, studying that rather
stocky figure, large-headed and broad-shouldered, a build
oddly at variance with a singularly graceful gait and carriage.
And since wherever Minna Lemuel was taking her despair
through the limpid spring evening, it was not to death, flesh
and blood must be succoured, and the money given.

But how ? As alms, as recompense, as hush-money ?
Let that alone, thought Sophia, mastering a swoon of panic.
Given it must be.

Like following an animal, she said to herself. If a hind
were to be walking in the rue de l'Abbé de l'Épée it could not
be more alien, more unmixing than such despair as I saw in her
looks. And with the idea of Minna being like an animal her
wavering ineffectual pity was abruptly changed into a deep
concern, as though it had taken on flesh and blood. A hind
would not pass unremarked, it would be admired, stones
would be thrown at it or it would be taken to the police-
station. So far, no stone had been thrown at Minna. Could
it be, suggested concern, quick to snatch at any hope, that she
had been mistaken, that Minna's look had not been despairing
after all, or that the look had been of the moment only ? Care,
illness, hunger—these on that mobile and dramatic visage
might mimic the other look : but presently she saw a man,
passing Minna, turn back and stare at her ; and in that second
glance there was a greedy astonishment which might well be
followed by stone-throwing, for it was clear that he had never
seen anything like that before and had a natural mind to assault
the wonder. The stone was only a laugh ; but it was aimed
well enough to make Sophia hasten forward to glare him down.

She was within a hand's touch of Minna as Minna entered

the Luxembourg garden. The fountain, thought Sophia, and wondered why she should be so sure of it ; for unless water were deep enough to drown in, her imagination had not so far admitted the affinity between water and woe.

Though the trees were so scantly leaved, there was dusk under their branches, and the look of the water in the tank, sifting the reflections of shadow and sky, was profound enough to beckon down any grief. Here, then, she would wait until Minna raised her eyes and saw her. Yet it was anguish to stand in patience, hearing the condoling voice of water, feeling the melancholy chill of evening, while feet scratched by on the gravel and children bowled their hoops, while the stress of her concern grew to a burden heavier than the weight of the gold she carried. She looks worse than desperate, said that concern. She looks dead. Only the dead look so bitterly resigned.

Without raising her eyes Minna moved slowly away.

Yet perhaps to accost her under those trees, and within the spell of the fountain's melancholy voice, would have been too elegiac. For this was real life, and the accompaniments of real life are not water and trees, but clerks hurrying with papers under their arms, children bowling hoops, gentlemen enjoying the spring evening with their hats off. In any case —Sophia shook up her decision—before Minna was out of the gardens of the Luxembourg speak she would.

' Minna.'

She has recognised me, she thought, seeing the flicker of those heavy eyelids. Just so one might speak to the dying, and know oneself recognised, though no answer came.

' You look ill. What has happened to you ? '

She answered now, speaking slowly after a long examining pause.

'You have got a good memory—to recognise me.'

'I have been following you for a long time. I was coming to see you when I recognised you in the rue de l'Abbé de l'Épée.'

'You were coming to see me? Why did you follow me for so long?'

'I wanted to watch you, to see for myself if what I heard was true, that you were ill and unhappy.'

'And am I?'

'Yes.'

People went by them, and giving to the tide of movement they began to walk, arm in arm.

'But have you never felt unhappy in spring? I have, many times.'

'I cannot believe that you have often been as unhappy as you looked when I met you. You could not, and survive it.'

'I expect I shall survive it. We Jews are very tough.'

There was a sombre pride in her tone, and a little malice. You are coming to life, thought Sophia; under your guise of death-bed your cunning has awakened and you have begun to watch me. So you shall be the next to speak.

'Why were you coming to see me?'

'Various reasons. Some good, some bad. One disgraceful.'

'Oh! Was that all?'

On her arm she felt Minna's fingers touching out a small ruminative rhythm. Clerks and deputations were going to and from the Palace, to be walking through this businesslike brisk throng was a better privacy than trees and the fountain could have given.

'And this meeting?—Has it fulfilled all your various reasons for coming to see me—some good, some bad, and one disgraceful?'

'Not the disgraceful one.   Yet.'

But it shall, she thought, swinging her muff, heavy with its golden lining. The woman beside her, so venal, so unaccountably dear, should live as long as twenty-five pounds might warrant, and exercise that unjustifiable enchantment, though others only should feel it. For the money once given, the giver must go.

'And then you will disappear again? Climb into your cloud, and disappear?'

'Then I shall disappear.'

On her arm the fingered rhythm began again, soft and pondering, imperturbably patient. As though respecting those private calculations, she kept silence.

'Ah! Madame Lemuel!'

The pondering fingertips closed upon her arm, an impact so sharp, so unexpectedly actual that it was like a wasp-sting. The man who had uttered the greeting spoke in tones of false cordiality, was undersized and overdressed, and carried a large portfolio. And instantly he began to explain with importance that he was about to present to the Executive Committee sitting in the Palace a petition on behalf of the bakers. Their cause—he made this clear—was as good as won since he was forwarding it.

After the bakers, he added, and the night-soil men, and the fish-porters, he proposed to busy himself in the matter of distressed artists.

'And then, dear lady, I shall avail myself of your advice.

I shall find it invaluable,' he added, with confidence; and bounded forward, leaving them where his eloquence had convoyed them, in the hall of the Palace.

'My God, what an intolerable upstart!' exclaimed Sophia, gazing round with fury at surroundings which seemed part and parcel of the upstart's complacent industry. For on every hand were run-up partitions, desks, notices, waste-paper baskets, ink-pots and coloured forms, clerks and officials. There was also a variety of collecting-boxes, no church could display more, labelled For the Veterans of the Republic, For the Polish Patriots, For the Belgians, For the Wounded, For the Orphans, and so forth.

Here, in this den of bureaucracy, the speech should be spoken, the gift should be given, the oddest encounter of her life wound up and ended.

'Before I climb into my cloud,' she began in a pedestrian voice . . .

'I beg your pardon?'

'Before I go,' said Sophia, steadily glaring down that smile of melancholy amusement, the grimace of an affectionate and misunderstood ape, 'I want, for my own peace of mind, to give you this. Minna, you must take it.'

At the weight of the chamois-leather bag, coming so warm from Sophia's muff, Minna's eyebrows flicked upward.

'Gold,' she said, and counted the pieces. 'Twenty-five English pounds. Well?'

Under her play-acting of Shylock she was trembling violently, as people tremble with famine, with excitement, with intolerable strain of anxiety.

'Well, Sophia?'

' This mangy republic,' said Sophia, ' that prancing little cur with the portfolio—You'll perish among them, I know it.'

' I like English gold,' said Minna. ' It's so wonderfully sturdy. Thirty francs at the present exchange for each of these. Thirty mangy republican francs.'

' I told you,' retorted Sophia, ' that one of my reasons was a disgraceful one. It is always disgraceful to offer money, and grand to refuse it. But out of my disgrace, Minna, I beg of you not to refuse.'

' I haven't refused yet. I might, you know, be holding out for more. For though twenty-five pounds is a handsome alms . . .

' Why do we quarrel like this ? ' she exclaimed. ' It is ignoble, it is untrue. I will take the money and be grateful.'

' Take the truth with it, then. It is not as you think, as you have every right to think. I am not trying to pay off Frederick's arrears of honour. When I set out to find you, an hour ago, I thought I was. I was in a rage, I had one of my impulses, I set off at once with all I had. It ought to convince you,' she said wryly, ' that this is not a meditated insult, since I bring so little. But now it seems to me that if any one has treated you shabbily, it is I. So it is only fit that the amends should be shabby too.'

She had spoken, staring at the floor, at the hem of Minna's dress. Now, seeing it stirred, she looked up to say farewell. With the carriage of some one moving proudly through a dance Minna walked towards a collecting box labelled For the Polish Patriots. When the last coin had fallen through the slit she turned on Sophia with a look of brilliant happiness.

' It was all that you had,' she said, her voice smoothly

quivering like water under the sun, ' and there it goes. *Vive la liberté !* '

' *Vive la liberté !* ' answered Sophia.

For she was released, God knows how, and could praise liberty with a free mind. Somehow, by that action, so inexplicable, unreasonable, and showy, Minna had revealed a new world ; and it was as though from the floor of the Luxembourg Palace Sophia had seen a fountain spring up, a moment before unsuspected and now to play for ever, prancing upwards, glittering and incorruptible, with the first splash washing off all her care and careful indifference to joy.

' Yes, Sophia, I have beggared you. Till Monday morning, at any rate, you are as poor as I. I dare say you have not enough money, even, to pay for a cab to take you back to the Meurice.'

' My uncle's first wife's mother in the Place Bellechasse, Minna.'

' Your uncle's first wife's mother in the Place Bellechasse would not like to see you destitute, and in rags. You had better come to the rue de la Carabine. It is nearer than the Place Bellechasse. We will collect our supper on the way.'

' How can we pay for it ? '

' We need not pay for it. If you come into the shop with me your bonnet alone will be as good as a fortnight's credit.'

Their words, light and taunting, rose up like bubbles delicately exploding from a wine they were to drink together. People whom they encountered turned round to stare after them. It was not common, in those lean days, to see two faces so carelessly joyful.

III

'Well, Sophia?'

'I was thinking,' answered Sophia, turning back from the window, 'how odd it is to see houses, and be on land. For I feel exactly as though I had run away and gone to sea, like a bad youth in a Sunday School story-book.'

'You have run away,' said Minna placidly. 'You'll never go back now, you know. I've encouraged a quantity of people to run away, but I have never seen any one so decisively escaped as you.'

And with dusters tied on her feet she made another glide across the polished floor, moving with the rounded nonchalant swoop of some heavy water bird. Her sleeves were rolled up, she wore a large check apron, she had all the majestic unconvincingness of a gifted tragedy actress playing the part of a servant—a part which would flare into splendour in the last act.

'But what have I run away from?'

'From sitting bored among the tyrants. From Sunday Schools, and cold-hearted respectability, and hypocrisy, and prison.

'And domesticity,' she added, stepping out of the dusters. 'This floor's quite polished enough. You would never believe, Sophia, how filthily that Natalia kept everything. My beautiful dish-cloths all rolled up in dirty balls, my china broken, verdigris on the coffee-pot . . . she would have poisoned me if I had kept her a day longer.'

'Was that the servant who ate pickles because she had known so many sorrows?'

'Ate pickles? She engulfed them. She drank the brandy, she stole the linen, she was in league with the concierge, she lowered down bottles of wine to him from the balcony, she had the soul of a snake, the greed of a wolf, the shamelessness of a lawyer. Go! I said to her. March off this instant! You have deceived me, you must go. And even as I spoke, Sophia, such was her malice, she dropped a trayful of wine-glasses and broke every one of them.'

With eyes blazing in a face pale with austere horror she leant forward and whispered,

'And after she had gone I found a monkey's tail in the rubbish-bin.'

'A monkey's tail?'

'A monkey's tail. Judge for yourself if she was depraved or no.'

From sitting bored among the tyrants. . . . The she-party of those tyrants from whom she was now delivered had talked, Sophia recalled, at endless length about their servants. The cook had pilfered the sugar, the laundry-maid had scorched a pillow-case, the under-housemaid had exhibited herself with a coloured ribbon. Now she was listening to talk about servants once again. But search her sensations as she would, sharply as any good housewife examining after dust, she could not find a shred of the former boredom or disdain.

'I suppose,' she said, thoughtlessly voicing her thought, 'it's because you're so patently a liar.'

'A liar? I a liar, my lovely one? Alas, I am incapable of

lies. I am a poor recounter of stories only, I cannot make them up.'

And she flipped the dusters out of the window, watching the dust scatter down on Madame Coton's ferns, exposed for an airing on the pavement below, murmuring to herself, ' Really, those unfortunate Cotons ! . . . They have no luck with their horticulture.'

' Was it from this balcony,' enquired Sophia, ' that the wine was lowered ? '

Minna feigned inattention to this lure.

' I would lay down my life for the truth,' she added serenely.

The last fleck of dust drifted downwards to the Cotons' ferns, the April morning air pushed, gentle and infantine, against their faces. Sighing with appreciation Minna stepped out on to her balcony, tilting her face to the sunlight, staring upwards with the gaze, blank and transfigured, of a cat who with a bird in her belly sits watching the birds. Her head, with the black hair fitting so purely to the curve of her brow, seemed, outlined against the sky, another of the domes of Paris, and it was part of her outrageous freedom from anything like conscience that a visage so inharmonious, so frayed with former passions and disfigured with recent want should appear in that very trying full light exaltedly beautiful as the face of an angel.

' How blue ! how vast ! ' she breathed, and it was as though she had stretched the heavens like a canvas, and painted them with one sweep of a calm brush. ' And look, Sophia. In all that firmament, so large, so clear, so open to our inspection, I do not see one little cherub, even, getting ready to go to mass.

'No!' She shook her head. 'Only sparrows.'

Her glance, following the flirting couple, descended towards the street. And with noiseless alacrity she stepped back from the balcony.

'Oh the devil! Here come Wlodomir Macgusty, poor soul! But I don't think he's seen me. He's certainly coming here, and he'll stay for the day, and I don't want him.'

'Is Wlodomir Macgusty a patriot?'

'He's two patriots. His great-grandfather was an exiled Highlander, and all his other relations were injured Poles. He is really a very noble creature,' she added, arranging herself under Sophia's scrutiny, 'and has suffered intensely—wait a minute, let me make sure that the door is locked—and has the most interesting scheme for the redistribution of Europe, and altogether, dear Sophia, I could not have given your twenty-five pounds to a worthier object. But not just now, I feel.'

'Wouldn't it broaden my mind to meet this fellow free spirit?'

'No, not at all. It would narrow it, for you'd certainly think poorly of him. Besides, you have met him. He was at my party. You must have noticed him. He sobbed. Hush!'

The double patriot was apparently footed to correspond, for two sets of footsteps trod the stairs.

'Minna!' exclaimed a high-pitched voice, and the door-handle was rattled. 'Minna! We've brought you a little cheese. Won't you let us in?'

'Who's the other one?'

'I don't know. I didn't notice.'

'A little cheese, Minna.'

' Minna ! '

The second voice called more imperiously. It was a rasping voice, a voice of a quality which once heard is scarcely forgotten. Nor had Sophia forgotten it.

' I think it must be your friend Monsieur Gaston,' she said, not troubling to lower her voice. But the descent of her reproach was turned aside by the sight of Minna's embarrassment—the spaniel-like rolling of eyes, the mouth twitched this way and that between distress and an urchin's amusement. And continuing to look severely at Minna she experienced an exquisite sense of flattery.

Meanwhile the two voices were mingling invocation with argument.

' Of course she's in. I heard a voice quite clearly.'

' No, no, Gaston ! She's not there, I'm sure. Minna ! You would not bar your door to me, would you ? There ! She doesn't answer, you see. She's not there.'

' She is there. Min-na ! '

' Hush ! Perhaps she's asleep. She may talk in her sleep, you know.'

' Pooh ! She's awake, confound her, but she won't let you in.'

' What ? Not let me in ? Do you really think so ? Oh ! Oh ! Oh ! '

' In heaven's name, Macgusty, don't start crying.'

' Oh ! Oh ! Minna ! '

And the door was shaken as though by a tempest.

' Let go my dress, Minna. I intend to put a stop to this.'

Though she was shaking with laughter, Minna held firm.

' Nor do I think you should laugh at that misery outside.'

'Dear Sophia, I wouldn't laugh at him for worlds. It's you I'm laughing at. There you stand, looking so like an English Prime Minister, and all the time I've got hold of your skirt.'

'It is extraordinary to me,' said Sophia, seating herself with rigidity and emphasis, 'why more people who can see jokes are not strangled.'

With a hitch of the head and a gesture of the eyebrows Minna assented, laying a finger to her lips. But on the farther side of the door Gaston's voice had reached such a hearty pitch of exasperation that Wlodomir Macgusty's laments were well-nigh smothered, and the two women could have talked as they pleased and remained unheard.

'As for me,' repeated Gaston, 'I'm going.'

And his footsteps tramped towards the stairs, Wlodomir's pattering after them.

'But my cheese, my little cheese! If I leave it there, the concierge will eat it.'

'Let him eat it.'

'Yes. . . . Yes, I suppose that would be best.'

There was a sniff and a sigh. The pattering footsteps paused, breaking from their allegiance to the trampling footsteps. Then they returned, and with a rustle of paper made off down the stairs.

Smoothing her hair as though all this had dishevelled it, Sophia rose with dignity.

'His little cheese!' said Minna in a tone of profound tenderness.

Exasperation compelled Sophia to gasp for breath, and with her hands still clawing her brow she remained, consciously

gaping, but for the moment past any redressing of counten-
ance. I am fascinated, she thought. I have never known such
freedom, such exhilaration, as I taste in her presence. But she
is indubitably out of her wits, and I suppose I shall be out of
mine too, shortly. At the end of this thought, which passed
through her mind, complete and glib and unconvincing as a
lesson repeated, she was able to lower her hands, fold them
resignedly, and clear her throat.

' You should not scorn him, Sophia, poor little Wlodomir
and his cheese. You should not scorn him, even though he
is ludicrous, and cries through the keyhole, and is abominably
treated by all his friends. Do you not see,' she went on
earnestly, ' that there is something noble in being so com-
pletely, so inflexibly vulnerable. When I think of Wlodomir
I feel with shame how traitorously I have dealt with my own
heart.'

' But a little self-control . . . ! '

' Why, if one has the courage to do without it ? Never
have I known Wlodomir feign or conceal. What he feels he
expresses, when he is hurt he cries out, he is incapable of
duplicity, of keeping himself locked up like a mean housewife
with a larder. When I am with him I feel like a mousetrap
beside a flower. I feel myself unworthy, yes, Sophia, un-
worthy, to be in his company. Why are you smiling ?—
Because I did not let him in, him and his cheese ? That proves
exactly what I say. I am unworthy.'

And turning her irrevocably mournful gaze to the window,
she smiled a false sleek demonstrator's smile.

' Such a beautiful day. It would be a pity to stay indoors
fobbing off bores, you know. I feel more inclined for some-

thing noble and silent—a lion, perhaps. Shall we go to the
Jardin des Plantes ? '

Turning from the uproar of the lions and the gabble of
the crowd assembled to watch them fed, they left the cages,
the bear-pit, the artists with their easels, the family parties
and the other parties whose demeanour proclaimed a freedom
from any shadow of being a family.

' Do you come here often ? '

' Constantly. To study the animals—I am working now
on the fairy-stories of Grimm, and in order to tell them one
may have to become a fox or a bear—but more often to walk
and meditate, and to be peaceful and solitary. I am an expert
in the unfrequented alleys, the corners where no one pene-
trates——'

' You cannot go down there. *Messieurs.*'

' No, no, of course not. You are very observant. The
English are, I believe, they are great naturalists, authorities
on migration and the rainfall. No Jew would care a tittle for
migration, he is always a migrant himself, a swallow means
nothing to him. And rain does not mean much to us, either,
we are a hardy patient people. Now here, Sophia, is a place
that I am particularly attached to.'

They halted before a hillock, on which grew a few common
wild-flowers and some untidy natural grass. Children were
swarming up it and rolling down, there was a great din and
a smell of bruised herbage.

' It's like being in the country, isn't it ? ' she said, raising
her face, where rested for the moment a look of perfect
sincerity.

It was a hardy and patient little hillock, preserving its

natural tough grasses, its colt's-foot and dandelion, speaking its dialect in the midst of the city.

' It reminds me of a donkey,' said Sophia.

' Exactly! So uncouth and thistly. Shall we sit here? It's nicer. There's nothing to pay.

' Such a heavenly silence,' she said; and added, with the appreciation one artist gives to another artist, ' How well those parrots place their voice. One can hear them even here.'

In the foreground of sound were the children playing, and in sound's distance the noise of the city—a brass band playing, the hooting of tugs on the river, the steady melancholy thrumming of life lived against a sounding-board of stone. It was odd to hear floating among these the roaring of lions, the screaming of tropical birds, noises so romantically desolate and unassimilated, and not to feel it odder. For now, thought Sophia, I seem able to take everything as a matter of course, as one does in a dream; though no doubt my knowledge that they are in cages must count for a good deal. The hillock was far from comfortable, she had never had much knack for sitting on the ground, and the children were smelly and insistent. Yet it seemed to her that she had never felt a more ample peace of spirit, a securer leisure. Sitting here, and thus, she had attained to a state which she could never have desired, not even conceived. And being so unforeseen, so alien to her character and upbringing, her felicity had an absolute perfection; no comparison between the desired and the actual could tear holes in it, no ambition whisper, But this is not quite what you wanted, is it?—no busybody ideal suggest improvements. Her black moire flounces seemed

settled into an endless repose on the dirty grass, her glove-
buttons winked tranquilly in the sun, she saw herself simul-
taneously as a figure ludicrously inappropriate, and as some-
thing exactly fitted into its right station on the face of the
globe.

In this amplitude of mind it was a pleasure to meditate
upon practical considerations; and as some people, being
idle, crown their contentment by taking a piece of knotted
string to unravel, she turned herself to the solution of a
problem which had first presented itself as they left the
Luxembourg, which had since roamed vaguely through her
mind as a piece of sea-weed appears and sinks again in the
wave, which Minna's words 'It's nicer, there's nothing to
pay,' and her subsequent silence had cast to shore and left
high and dry.

How was she to intimate to Minna that the twenty-five
pounds devoted to the Patriots of Poland was not the ending
of her resources? On that triumphant outcry of ' I have
beggared you now ! ' it would have been tactless to mention
the margin between herself and beggary; and even when
the sudden squall of rain overtook them on the way to the
wine-shop she had not undermined the assumption of a
heaven-bestowed destitution by mentioning that she had
quite enough petty cash to pay for both the wine and a cab,
thinking, as they hurried under the sharp pellets of rain, the
sudden wrath of cold and darkness, that the woman beside
her, so ugly and so entrancing, so streaked and freaked with
moods, so incandescent with candour and so tunnelled with
deceitfulness, was like a demonstration by earth that working
in clay she could contrive a match for any atmospheric April.

Yet Minna, however capable of staring facts in the face and denying their existence (and Sophia could see that she was capable of great feats in that kind), could scarcely have been Frederick's mistress and yet suppose that twenty-five pounds was all that stood between Mrs Frederick Willoughby and indigence. Besides, she was a Jewess, one of a race who can divine gold even in the rock; she should be able to divine it in a bank too. Ridiculous, thought Sophia, still turning and twiddling the problem; ridiculous that one should feel obliged to break it gently to her that one is blessed with comfortable means. Of all people, she should digest such information most naturally; for she is a Jewess, with a proper esteem for money, and she is an artist, with no hoity-toity scruples about taking it. Most certainly, money must by some means or other be injected into Minna's way of living; she could not be allowed to go on drinking bad wine and eating messes of sour cabbage spiced with carroway, paddling through the wet streets in broken slippers, and over her own parquet in dusters, ogling jellied eels as though they were quails, and fencing her heavy quaking shoulders against the cold with a wrap that should be at the cleaners.

Even allowing for dramatic instinct, a terrific virtuosity of rhetorical effect, Minna must be painfully poor. All the curiosity-shop trimmings of her apartment, the old masters and the embroideries, the Gothic beaker and the damascened andirons were gone—gone too, most probably, most regrettably, those superior duelling pistols. Natalia also was gone—a good riddance, maybe, but, since she had no replacer, a bad sign; and despite the curtain-fire of Sophia's bonnet, and sealskin muff and pelerine, and well-funded

demeanour, Madame Coton's glance was superciliously in-
quisitive, and the man in the wine-shop far too affable.

And only some one, thought Sophia with a flash of in-
tuition, only some one who has felt authentic destitution
could throw away twenty-five good pounds as soon as look
at it.

You must be fed, properly fed, clothed and warmed, she
resolved, glancing under her eyelashes at Minna. Her mind
almost added, cleaned ; for poverty had laid a tarnish on that
skin, turned its warm milk-coffee colour towards sallowness,
dulled those jet-black locks to the black of a cheap coffin. In
that glance love reabsorbed her, and the knot, turning
suddenly in her exploring fingers, presented its aspect of
how at all costs she must not let a Midas-touch strike stiff,
strike cold and dead, the happiness which that exulting 'I
have beggared you, Sophia,' had brought to life. Poverty
in some way warded their relationship, was the battered
Aladdin's lamp which had unlocked the undreamed-of
riches.

So on the whole the best plan would be to pawn her
diamonds, the ring on her hand, the brooch on the dressing-
table in the Place Bellechasse. The money resulting from a
visit to the Mont de Piété would be, in some mystical way,
cleansed from the sin original of wealth ; it would not offend
Minna, or flaw the illusion of poverty on which, she supposed,
everything depended ; and it would be quite enough for her
present purpose.

Pleased to have arranged everything so well, she stretched
herself and turned with a smile to her companion.

' Tell me, Sophia. Have you ever stolen anything ? '

' Never.   Why ? '

' Because at this moment you look exactly as though you had been robbing an orchard.   Your expression is sly and self-satisfied.   Would you thieve, Sophia ? '

' Yes, I expect so.'

' So would I.   When I was in the priest's house I stole like an angel—cigars, money, his bandannas, the wine for the sacrament, everything I could lay hands on.   If I had not discovered my talent for thieving I could never have kept my self-respect.   But when I looked at the things I had stolen it re-established me.   *Le vol, c'est la propriété.*'

' What did you do with the things you stole ? '

' Oh, threw them away—except the wine and the cigars. Or put them back again when they were missed.   It was the sensation I wanted, I could not hazard that by being found out.'

' And the priest ? '

' Exorcised the house against the Poltergeist.   He was a fat man, full of gas, he rumbled like a goat.   He drew in coloured chalks, pictures of hell, and showed me a new one every day, saying that there was a special hell for the Jews. At night I was locked into a cupboard, and sometimes he would come in with a candle and another picture.   Then he would pray, and weep, and enjoy himself.   He drew like a schoolboy, his devils and his damned had hay-fork fingers and bodies like turnips, his chalks were the brightest colours, yellow, and purple . . .'

Caught by her voice, one of the children playing on the hillock approached, and stood listening open-mouthed.   His playmate called to him, and finding that of no avail, came up,

and tugged him by the arm. The first child shook his head.
The second child stayed.

'The priest's housekeeper was a very old woman called
Rosa. She had a long plait of grey hair, and into it she
twined leaves of mountain ash and elder, as charms to keep
away the wood-spirits. She had charms in her pockets,
charms round her neck, charms sewn into her slippers to
prevent her falling into the well. In one eye she had a cataract,
that eye seemed to me to be made of snow, dirty snow pressed
into a pellet and beginning to thaw.'

One after another the children left their play and came
nearer, the bolder shoving forward the timid. Two women
went by, and Sophia heard the one say to the other, ' Look,
the pretty dears ! How children love a fairy-story.'

'She was pious and cruel, that old woman. Before she
thrashed me she made the sign of the cross over my back.
But I got even with her. One day . . .'

The story was animated and indecent. The children
pressed closer, giggling, nudging each other in delight.
Passers-by stopped. Arrested by curiosity, they stayed for
entertainment, and at the end of the anecdote the shrill titters
of the children were reinforced by several adult guffaws.

'Yes, I avenged myself. But even victory is a poor thing
when one is alone, with one's back to the wall. Good God,
how unhappy I was ! How endless the winters were, how
agonising the nights when I lay shivering, thinking the
night as long as a winter. And I no older than these children
here,' she said, turning to Sophia, her voice lowering its
lights, trailing under a weight of woe. ' No, I should have
gone under, I should have died of misery if it had not been

for Corporal Lecoq. A little old fellow, Sophia, limping with
a quick step, holding himself upright, his chin always well-
shaved, his moustaches curled like ram's horns, his eyes
bulging wrathfully from his scarred face. The ice had
scarcely melted when he came to the village, limping through
the slush, beating a quick-step on his drum, his two dogs
following him, wearing coats of red velvet trimmed with gold
braid, tarnished but splendid. Outside the church he came to
a stop. He unfolded a piece of carpet and laid it down on the
slush, and immediately the two dogs sat up to attention. He
beat a flourish on his drum and cried out, with a loud voice,
with a strange accent, " Ladies and Gentlemen, good people
all, you shall see something worth seeing. These are my two
celebrated dogs, Bastien and Bastienne. And before your
delighted eyes they will dance the minuet, as it is danced in all
the politest courts of Europe."

' He drummed out the rhythm of a minuet, *Tra, la-la-la-la,
Tra, la,* and the dogs stood up and danced, their haunches
trembling, their front paws dangling with affectation from
the cuffs of their red velvet coats. At the end of the dance
they dropped on their four legs, became dogs again, running
round him and barking with excitement, rousing every watch-
dog in the village. At the noise of the drumming every one
ran out, the women and children, the men from the tavern.
They chattered and screamed, and said that it was witch-
craft ; and the village idiot, a woman of fifty with the face of
an infant, declared that just so was the minuet danced in the
courts of Europe. I only dared not go near. But I hung
over the paling of the priest's yard, knocking my hatchet
against the wood so that Rosa might think I was still at work.

Corporal Lecoq said, " I see a young lady yonder who has
a fine ear for music. Bastien, go and make your bow to the
young lady," and he pointed with his finger, and the dog ran
to the priest's palings, rose on its hind-legs and made me a
bow. Alas, it did me no good! There was an uproar of
voices, saying that I was a Jewess, a scapegrace, a good-for-
nothing; and Rosa took hold of my arm and sent me whirl-
ing into the house.

' Outside the drumming went on, marches and mazourkas,
and the villagers laughed and exclaimed. And then I heard
the quick-step, the dogs barking, his voice hallooing to them,
friendly and imperious; and they were gone.

' For ever, so I thought. Music, red velvet, a dog that
bowed, a human being that spoke me kindly—such things
were not likely to come my way again. But a few evenings
later I felt something touch my leg, and turning, there was
the dog Bastien, standing beside me, striking me gently with
his paw. " Good evening," said a voice, soft and rough
like the touch of moss. Corporal Lecoq was leaning on
the palings, his curling moustaches silhouetted against the
sky. " Is the priest in ? " said he. " I want to make my
confession."

' Ah, thought I, you are no friend after all. You are
another Catholic, another of those leagued against me. And
when he and the priest came out of the church later, roaring
with laughter, arm in arm, I hated them alike—no, I hated
the corporal worse of the two, for of the priest I had never
expected anything but ill. He came often, boasting himself
a good Catholic, he and the priest used to sit together, telling
stories and drinking sloe gin, and to Rosa he gave a miraculous

plaster statue so that after that she fed his dogs when they came into the kitchen. But he never spoke to me, nor I to him, until one hot summer afternoon when I was ironing the church linen, alone for once. " Hot work ? " said he. For answer I spat on the surplice. " So you are still a Jewess ? " " Always a Jewess," said I. " Foolish child," said he. " *Paris vaut bien une messe*." And he told me the story of Henry IV, and how, if I would seem to yield a little, Rosa might allow me to talk with him, since he was such a good Catholic, and that he would tell me about Paris, and teach me to speak French. My tears fell on the linen, but I went on ironing, I gave no answer.

' Later again he brought Rosa the two red velvet coats, asking her to mend them. " I mend for your filthy animals ? " cried she. " Never ! Give the coats to the Jewess. Dogs defile Jews, let her mend the coats." " I have mended the cassock," I said. " I will mend the dogs' coats too."

' There was this to be done, that to be done, holes darned, the gilt braid re-stitched, new linings ; and he seemed to make a great fuss, and however I worked was not satisfied, I must do it over again to his liking, and at last he must oversee it all, since I worked so doltishly. That day he sat by me as I sewed, talking of Napoleon, whose soldier he had been, of the retreat from Moscow, and how he was left behind, frost-bitten, as good as dead. But he had been sheltered, and had picked up a living since, tramping from fair to fair with his dogs and his drum, or singing in taverns, or in choirs. For he had a great bass voice, Greek chants, or Roman, or Lutheran psalms were all alike to him. And he could shave too, and dress hair ; for in his youth he had been apprenticed to a hair-dresser in Paris, leaving that profession to become a strolling actor. And then he talked to me of the theatre, of the lamps and the dresses, the tragedies of Voltaire and Grétry's operas.

' " I have finished the coats," said I.

' " Rip them up," said he. " And then I will bring them again, and teach you a speech from a tragedy."

' All that summer he came to the priest's house. We had a language of signals ; for I had a quick ear, he had only to tap out the rhythm of some tune we had agreed upon and I would know what he meant, and answer it, banging my hatchet on the wood, or clattering one dish against another at the sink. I stole comfits for his dogs, and cigars for him, I began to be a little happy, for I had a friend. One day he said to Rosa, " My dogs have fleas, come with me to the sheep-washing trough and hold them while I wash them." " Let the Jewess do that," said she, " and be defiled." I put on a sulky face and went with him.

' " Now we will fall to work," he said, when we got to the sheep-washing trough. And on the grass he laid out soap, and a towel, and a comb, pomade in a china box, and a pair of curling-tongs. " What, do you curl the dog's hair ? " said I. " No," he answered. " But I curl young ladies." And taking me by the scruff of the neck he pushed my head into the cool running water and lathered my hair, scolding at the lice, and the dirt, and the tangles. For a long while he soaped, and rinsed, and soaped and rinsed again, and I, forgetting my first fear, gave myself up to the pleasure of feeling myself so well handled, shivering with voluptuousness when he rubbed the nape of my neck, arching my head

back against his strong hand. Then he rubbed it dry with a
towel, combed it, and smeared on the pomade that smelled
of violets. Last of all he kindled a little fire of sticks, heated
the tongs, and curled my hair into ringlets.

'"There," said he, standing back to look at me well.
"Those ringlets are called *Anglaises*. And now for the
finishing touch." Out of his pocket he pulled an artificial
rose, frayed and crumpled, and stuck it behind my ear.

'When I looked in the sheep-trough, I did not know
myself. He too seemed changed, singing a song in French,
pretending to pluck the strings of a guitar which was not
there. Then he picked up the soap, what was left of it, the
towel, and the rest of his gear, and marched off, still singing,
waving his arms and staggering. I guessed then that he was
a little drunk.

'I, poor little fool, went dreaming back to the priest's
house with my ringlets and my false rose, and my odour of
violets which surrounded me like a cloud. "Harlot!" cried
Rosa, "bedizened little infidel, stinking trumpery, you are
not fit to be clean!" And slobbering with rage she tore the
rose out of my hair, and a handful of my hair with it, and
began to daub my face with dirty pig's lard from the
frying-pan.'

'No!' exclaimed a solemn voice from the crowd.
'That was too much, that was infamous.' 'Old hag,'
said another voice.

'But this time I did not submit. I kicked her shins, I hit
her in the breast with my bony knuckles till she howled
with anger and astonishment. Her howls fetched the priest
into the kitchen, puffing and snorting. Out of my face,

daubed with pig's lard, through my dishevelled heroine's ringlets, I glared at him. " Tremble, tyrant ! " I cried. And as though it were a charm, an exorcism, I began to repeat a French tragedy speech which I had learned from Corporal Lecoq. I remembered the gestures he had taught me, the raising of the arm, the tossing back of the hair, the furling of the imaginary mantle, the hand laid on the heart. I swelled my voice to the clang of an organ, I made it cold with scorn, exact and small with menace as a dagger's point. And while I spoke, my glance resting upon them as though they were a long way off, I saw them begin to shrink, and draw back, and cross themselves.

' Coming to the end of my speech, I went through it again. Still reciting, still making the right gestures, rolling out my Alexandrines, dwelling terribly upon the caesuras, I began to step backwards, haughtily, towards the door. And on the threshold I finished my tirade, and rolled my eyes over them once more. And so I walked off, free and unimpeded, to find Corporal Lecoq at the inn.'

She rose to her feet, shaking out her crumpled skirts, rising as though from the ocean of a curtsey. And holding her bonnet before her she moved among the crowd, graciously accepting their congratulations and their contributions, her face pale and noble, her demeanour stately as a sleep-walker's.

To Sophia she returned more briskly, holding out the bonnet as though she were a retriever and the bonnet a pheasant.

' For the Patriots of Poland, Minna ? '

' Oh, no ! For our supper. I have always allowed my talent to support me.'

' I had been thinking of pawning my diamond brooch for our supper.'

' Don't, I beg of you !   Keep it till we really need it, keep it '—she said earnestly—' till I break my leg.'

Enraptured with her own performance, floating on the goodwill of the self-approved, she insisted upon visiting and feeding the bears, the monkeys, the camels, the vultures, the crocodile, the buffaloes and the sloth; and infected, as captive animals will be, by the mood of their visitor, the gentry behind the bars greeted her with congratulating interest, even the crocodile, it seemed to Sophia, coming leering up from its muddy tank like an approving impresario.

The funds in the bonnet allowed them to take a cab, a proceeding that seemed ordinary enough until Sophia noticed the driver's face assume an expression of dreamlike bewilderment.   Minna, it seemed, had again been studying for Grimm's Fairy Tales, and had chosen the moment of directing the driver to transform herself into a bear.

' All I ask, Minna, is that you should not be a wolf when it comes to paying him.'

' No, no !   Then I will be a princess.'

Emerging from his onion-scented den Égisippe Coton handed each lady a large formal bouquet.   The gentleman had expressed his regrets at not finding the ladies at home.

Dangling from each bouquet was Frederick's card, each card inscribed in his large easy handwriting, ' With Kind Enquiries.'   Another of his lucky cannons, thought Sophia ; and a sort of affable appreciation spread itself over her first annoyance.   She had always preferred Frederick when some

waft of rogue's luck puffed out his sails—any development of
impertinence, of brag, of manly floridity, was an improvement
on his usual tedious good manners. Accepting her own roses
and lilies in this spirit, it was disturbing to see Minna flinch as
though she had been smacked in the face.

' Ridiculous nosegays,' she said soothingly.

' What is so frightful to me, Sophia, what upsets me, is to
think of the cost of these flowers. What cynicism to spend
all this on flowers at a time when people round us lack fire,
lack bread! Only a hard heart, only a character stupefied by
a false arrangement of society, could throw away money like
this. Twenty francs, I dare say, or more.'

' Besides the tip to Coton. That must have been
considerable.'

' My God, yes! That Coton! At our very doors we
have these individuals, these parasites. We must pass them
whenever we go in or out, as peasants stump past their
dunghills.'

As she spoke her hands, moving with Jewish nimbleness,
tweaked out the wires from the bouquet, snipped the rose
stalks, arranged the blossoms to show at their best.

' I am wondering, Minna, if we could do anything to
redress the state of society by making up these flowers into
buttonholes, and selling them in the street.'

Minna turned, her mouth twitching with laughter, her
eyes angry with tears.

' I am sincere, I am far more sincere than you think. It
does truly shock me, this waste of money on flowers. But
how can you expect me to be truthful while you are so calm.
We were so happy, so simple, on our hillock like a donkey.

And then to come back and find this sophisticated sneer, this crack of the whip.'

' Infuriating,' agreed Sophia, herself infuriated by those last words. ' But quite insignificant. Frederick has these happy thoughts occasionally, but he can never follow them up. This is just another of his runaway knocks.'

For there are some circumstances in which it is useless to attempt tact ; and since Frederick's runaway knocks had been bestowed on either of them as impartially as his nosegays, wife and mistress might as well avail themselves of the enfranchisement warranted by this. Nor had the words carried any scathe with them. Minna's sigh was for the wire's stranglehold on the best rose of Sophia's bouquet—for having arranged her own she was now briskly at work on the other.

Leaning against the mantelpiece, staring at Minna's hands, Sophia mentored herself against anger. For what could be sillier than to waste a moment of her consciousness in the stale occupation of feeling angry with Frederick when she stood here, centred in this exciting existence of being happy, free, and passionately entertained ? From the time when they left the Luxembourg Palace she had breathed this intoxication of being mentally at ease, free to speak without constraint, listen without reservation. She would be a triple fool to stoop out of this air to that old lure of being annoyed by Frederick, even though the old lure had been smeared over to seem a new one —for with all the force of her temper she could imagine what it would be like to hate Frederick on Minna's behalf.

' In a way I am sorry we missed him. He could have carried my note to my great-aunt Léocadie—the note I have not yet written.'

'Your great-aunt Léocadie ? '

'Madame de Saint Gonval. I was living with her, you know, when I broke out and came to you. I must write to her. Though Frederick by now will have allayed any alarms she may have felt.'

'Madame de Saint Gonval ? Yes, indeed you must write.'

'I doubt if she has lost a wink of sleep through not knowing my whereabouts.'

'Perhaps not. I dare say she has not much heart. But what polish, what discrimination ! I have spoken to her once or twice—she introduced herself to me at one of my recitals—and I thought her charming, charming and intelligent.'

'She's shrewd. But do you really consider her intelligent?'

'Indeed I do. Her taste is so pure. Narrow, of course—what would you expect ?—but exquisitely cultivated.'

'Yes, I think her taste is good.'

'Sophia, I assure you that a cultivated taste is already a great deal, especially in that class of society. Sophia, why are you laughing ? '

'Because you talk about my great-aunt Léocadie exactly as my great-aunt Léocadie talks about you.'

'And you laugh at us both. There ! '

The two flower vases were completed and set, formal splendours, on either side of the mantelshelf. In her admiring voice, in her admiring survey, there was no overtone of rancour or ironical forgiveness. The flowers were beautiful and she had arranged them beautifully, and now she stood admiring them, delighted as a child.

'I could bow down before you,' said Sophia. 'You are genuinely good, good as bread.'

' One ought to be, you know,' replied the other, seriously. And putting up her large hand she pulled away the last noosing wire.

Into the pause that followed, her words came with a rustic earnestness and urgency.

' For how else can one nourish others ? '

The letter to great-aunt Léocadie was not written. Wlodomir Macgusty came in, and on his heels came the bald-headed man still wearing the Scotch shawl, the man who had told Minna that revolutions have no second flute-players to spare. As the room filled up Sophia recognised many faces which she had seen on her first visit; but the general aspect of the company was changed, there were no ball-dresses now, no elegant escorting young gentlemen. A change for the better, she thought. Though she had yet no sympathy for republican opinions, she preferred any opinion grave and ungarnished. She was impressed by the way these strangers accepted her, feeling apparently none of the awkward hostility which she could not but feel towards them. They were cordial, sincere, dispassionate; discovering that she was English they began to question her about the Chartists, the poor-law, the franchise, the Fenians, the amount of bacon eaten by English peasants, the experiments of the Co-Operatives. With surprise she discovered that they thought highly of the British Constitution and with embarrassment she realised that she knew rather less about it than they did. She found herself ignorant on other counts, too, forced to admit to one young man, whose broad forehead, slow eyes, and cockade of heavy close-cropped curls gave him a singular resemblance to a young bull, that she knew nothing of the work of an artist called Blake. ' You should,' he said, gravely and sadly. ' He is formidable.' As one young bull might speak of another, she thought.

Though without any particular concurrence, she was enjoying herself when Égisippe Coton, his countenance bleak of all personal opinion, breathed in her ear that a footman from the Place Bellechasse had brought her luggage, and a note from Mr Willoughby. Letting the conversation drift away from her, she opened it.

> *Dear Sophia,*
>
> *I was sorry not to see you this afternoon as I had hoped to gather from you some information about your plans for the future, and possibly some message of common politeness to your great-aunt. We suppose that you are not likely to return to the Place Bellechasse, at any rate for the present, so your belongings are being packed and sent to you.*
>
> *I have told Madeleine, by the way, not to send your jewel-case, or any of your valuables. While Minna continues to keep ' open-house,' the risk of losing them would be too great. So you must depend on your beauty unadorned—more than adequate—to enchant the revolutionary bobtail.*
>
> *Your affectionate husband, Frederick.*
>
> *P.S.—Homage to Minna, of course.*

' Well, I'm blowed,' she murmured.
Nothing pained Frederick more than to hear vulgarity on a woman's lips, the phrase came naturally, and was comforting. With a deepened conviction she repeated it.

Wlodomir Macgusty, sitting patiently at her side, remarked on the beautiful sounds of the English language, a tongue at once so expressive and sonorous. Nothing, he said, could equal the pleasure with which he listened to readings from Moore and Shakespeare, a pleasure which was not impaired by ignorance of the sense, for it was possible, was it not, to listen with the soul? What she had said just then, for instance, he had not understood; but it had been perfectly clear to him that the ejaculation expressed wonder and reverence, a deep but tranquil movement of the spirit such as one experiences, for example, in looking at the ocean, or the Alps.

Did he listen much to Shakespeare, she asked?

In his youth, often. In his youth he had been employed as a secretary in the household of a Russian nobleman, and an English governess had also been one of the Count's household. They met frequently in the garden, two exiles meeting to mix their sighs, she nostalgic for her England, he for the Poland of his ideals. In her walks she carried a book in her hand, and when conversation failed them she would read aloud; for hours, sometimes, readings only broken by his cries of appreciation and her coughing fits. For she coughed, daily she grew thinner, daily her pink and white complexion grew more alarmingly vivid. After her death he had composed an elegy. ' *Elle était jeune,*' it began, ' *elle était belle, elle s'appelait Miss Robinson.*'

The remainder of the elegy did not live up to this arresting beginning, and while it lasted she could look through the letter again. Wlodomir Macgusty had shown discernment: as a specimen of insolence the letter was indeed an Alp. So long accustomed to despising Frederick, even now she could not pay him the tribute of an unmixed anger. Astonishment, an almost congratulating astonishment, qualified her rage. As a specimen of firm and blackguardly advantage-taking, this was beyond what she would have given him credit for. Yet it must certainly be all his own; Léocadie had no more hamper of scruples than he, but her unscrupulousness would have gone otherwise to work.

Strategic sense granted that the advantage Frederick had taken she had given; nothing could have been more uncivil or more unwise than her behaviour towards the Place Belle-chasse, nothing could have given him a better-justified stick to beat her with. But that the stick should have been raised, should, indeed have fallen—for the jewel-case had been kept back, the husbandly thump administered—surpassed her theory of Frederick.

The elegy had concluded with vows of testifying celibacy.

'You have never married, Monsieur Macgusty?'

'Twice,' said he. 'One angel after another. They stayed with me no longer than angels would. One died. The other spread her wings. She died too, after a while; but not in my arms.'

'Which do you consider the most essential quality in a husband—firmness, or sensibility?'

'Firmness, Madame. Woman demands it. Without it, she pines.'

Without it she—spreads her wings. 'For I do not see myself flying back to Frederick,' she said to herself. 'He has put out his arresting firmness a little too late.' Her anger, like a rapid wine, had flown to her head; she felt herself mettled, sleek as the oiled wrestler, affable as only the powerful may be. She looked round on the assembly with bonhommie, she found herself rising, like any triumphant tippler, to make a speech.

'Minna! I have a proposal to make. Will you not allow me to offer your guests some supper?'

The candid pleasure at this proposal made her feel even more warmly towards the guests.

'Unfortunately, as you know, I have no money. But I have this ring, it must be worth something. Perhaps one of these gentlemen would take it to the pawn-shop for me. It is not too late for that, I hope?'

As with one voice her guests could assure her as to the closing hour of the offices of the Mont de Piété, as with one pair of legs they were ready to go on her errand. Pleasant creatures, she thought, kindly and unaffected. It was a pity that they were all so crazy, so improvident, so surely doomed to end in the jail or the gutter.

'I suppose you know, young lady,' said the bald shawled one, speaking with fatherly gruffness, 'that you will make a very bad bargain over this? Diamonds are not what they were. Socially speaking, this is excellent. But for you it is unfortunate.'

Meanwhile it was being canvassed with great earnestness whose pawn-shop technique best equipped him for the errand. Strange that in a company where so many were Jews no Jewish candidate was proposed. The choice lay, it seemed, between a mouse-mannered student of engineering and the bull-fronted young man who had spoken about an artist called Blake.

The choice fell on the latter. Tying the ring into a corner of his handkerchief, and pressing the handkerchief down his boot, he remarked, 'You see in me, Madame, the triumph of the Latin over the Semite. And if I may say so,'—here he bowed courteously to the mouse—' of the peasant over the Parisian.'

The writing on the wall, she supposed, had been there long enough for these affable gentry to be able to revel without as much as a glance at it; practically delighting in an unexpectedly good supper they discussed the progress of a republic which had from poverty made them poorer yet, and the only acrimonious note was struck by the bald man of the shawl (whose name, it seemed was Ingelbrecht) when the mouse disputed his prophecy that except in Paris the elections would go flat against the republic. For while the peasant, said he, thinks the best thing he can do is to work like a beast, while he would rather skulk in virtuous industry than expose himself to the danger of thinking, any republic will be of the town only and in a state of siege. Even Dury, there, was as bad a peasant as the rest of them. He laboured his canvases as though they were his fields, he asked nothing better than to paint from dawn to sundown.

' I am not ashamed of being a peasant,' said Dury pleasantly. ' He is an astute animal, the peasant, and art demands a great deal of low cunning.'

Marching over the protests which this statement roused from Macgusty, Ingelbrecht turned to Sophia, ' And what do you think of the peasant? You have some of your own, I understand.'

' I find them almost intolerable,' she replied.

' There, you see. She finds them almost intolerable. And so you let them die of starvation, eh, harness them in carts and send them to the poorhouse?'

In his grumpy voice with its snarling Belgian accent, in his staring angry eyes, there was considerable kindliness.

'She does nothing of the sort, I'll swear,' interposed Minna. 'She has a heart and can feel pity, she is not like you, you old humgruffin.'

'It seems to me,' said Sophia, 'that if you wish to help these peasants it is fatal to pity them. Once show compassion for their misfortunes and they will persist in them to get whatever almsgiving your compassion throws. When a horse is down you beat it to get it up again, pity will never raise it.'

'Excellent, excellent!' shouted Ingelbrecht. 'I wish more republicans thought like this aristocrat. But your brains are in the wrong place. They should be under a red cap instead of a fashionable bonnet. Why were you not born one of your own poachers, Mrs Willoughby?'

'I have wished it myself.'

He continued to stare at her, growling under his breath. Though the allusion to the bonnet rankled, she liked him. Frederick had left her with her beauty unadorned to enchant the revolutionary bobtail; she would have been glad to discard that also, the bonnet and the sleek hood of flaxen hair beneath it, she would have pawned her pink fingernails along with the diamond ring. It irked her to find that even in this circle her petticoats beringed her first and foremost.

'Should there be no brains under bonnets?'

'Yes, if you please. But the woman of the future will demand to own not brains but vigour. Yes, yes, I dare say you are vigorous too. But unless you are careful your brains will step in first and tell you that it is more dignified and reasonable to remain passive.'

'I see. I will be on my guard, then.'

She was sorry when with another twinkling glare he
walked off. She found him the most congenial of all her
diamond's guests; and afterwards with a certain sleeking of
pride she listened to Minna's congratulations, learning that
even among revolutionaries Ingelbrecht was considered to go
too far.

'He would destroy you without a moment's compunction
if you did not accept his ideas. Me too,' she added as an
afterthought.

'And do you?'

'Do I? Oh, accept his ideas. I do not understand them,
they are harsh and abstruse and I—alas!—can grasp only the
first quality. But I know'—and her expression was one of
piety—' that he has been obliged to fly from twelve European
countries, and that is enough for me.'

They were standing in the middle of the room, a room
made cold and oppressive by the departure of so many people.
Minna took her hand and caressed it.

'Beautiful hand, so smooth and reckless. I love it better
without the ring. How much did Dury bring you?'

'Enough to take me back to the Meurice. What time is it,
Minna?'

Even before she heard her voice so flatly speaking them,
she had known the craven falsity of those words, words only
spoken because to act on them would spare her the humilia-
tion of admitting herself compromised by Frederick's malice.
To Mrs Frederick Willoughby of Blandamer it was one thing
to stay under Madame Lemuel's roof as a benefactress, quite
another to remain there as a possible benefitee.

It was as though, shooting off what she knew to be a pop-gun, she had seen the spurting authentic answer of blood. In an instant Minna had become the desolate ghost of the Medici fountain, the resigned outcast she had bullied on that night of February; and the hand, still holding hers, became cold as death in the moment before it loosed its hold.

'You wound me,' she murmured, and fell insensible.

Even more than in sleep her face in unconsciousness became unmistakably ugly, unmistakably noble. The look of life receding from those features left the hooked nose, the florid melancholy lips, the grandiloquent sweep of the jaw from ear to chin, as time leaves the fragmentary grandeur of a forsaken temple, still rearing its gesture of arch and colonnade from drifting sand, from slowly-heaping mould. It was un-believable that those features could ever have worn cajoling looks.

Equally baffling was Minna's behaviour when she had been brought to. Shaking in every limb, passionately complaining of cold, she sat humped on the pink sofa, talking with de-riding eloquence on any and every subject save subjects which Sophia would have discussed. She would not eat nor drink, nor go to bed, nor move nearer the fire. She would do nothing but smoke and talk.

After the second cigar, she rose to her feet, sallow and shaking.

'I see I bore you,' she said furiously.

'You do not bore me, you exasperate me. How can I attend to what you are saying when I am thinking all the time what should be done with you?'

'I have never met an English person yet,' cried Minna,

'man or woman, who was not heartless. And who did not mask that heartlessness with an appearance of practical philanthropy.'

With the aim of a savage or a schoolboy she threw Sophia's vinaigrette at Frederick's flowers, burst into a fit of weeping, and rushed from the room. An instant after Sophia heard her being violently sick.

'Oh, how the devil,' said Sophia, speaking loudly to the echoing unhearing walls, 'am I to save you now?'

A groan like a mortally stricken animal's answered her; and kneeling on the floor, holding Minna's body across her lap, she remembered the grotesque couples she had watched at sheep-shearings: the man crouched over his victim, working with the brutal fury of skill, the sheep sullen with terror, lying lumpish and inert under that heavy grasp, that travelling bite of steel.

The sheep lay still out of cunning. Let the grasp slacken ever so little, and it would leap away, trailing its flounce of half-severed fleece; and searching Minna's countenance her imagination watched for some kindred sign of animal strategy, while ruthless and methodical she continued to dribble brandy over those clenched teeth, or slap those icy hands.

'If I could only warm you,' she exclaimed, measuring Minna's weight against her own, measuring the distance from floor to bed. It was too far; but fetching the blankets and eiderdowns she padded Minna round with them, and then laid herself down alongside her in a desperate calculated caress.

It was shocking to smell on that deathly body the scent of the living Minna—the smoky perfume of her black hair, the concocted exhalation of irises lingering on the cold neck as though the real flowers were there, trapped in a sudden frost. It was spring, she remembered. In another month the irises would be coming into flower. But now it was April, the cheat month, when the deadliest frosts might fall, when snow might cover the earth, lying hard and authentic on the English acres as it lay over the wastes of Lithuania. There, in one direction, was Blandamer, familiar as a bed; and there, in another, was Lithuania, the unknown, where a Jewish child had watched the cranes fly over, had stood beside the breaking river. And here, in Paris, lay Sophia Willoughby, lying on the floor in the draughty passage-way between bedroom and dressing-closet, her body pressed against the body of her husband's mistress.

'But is it I, *I*, who will save her,' she murmured. After a while, like a leisurely answer to those words, came the cold chiming of a church clock. Save her wherefore, save her for what?

It was three o'clock, the hour of Napoleon's courage, the hour when people die. How much longer could she hold out? Cautiously she slid her cheek against her shoulder. There was still warmth there, she still had warmth to give. But opposing it, quite as positive, was this deadly cold she embraced, a body of ice in which, like some device at the fishmongers, a clock-heart beat, a muted tick-tock of breath stirred.

The quarter chimed, continuing the conversation between them. *Where-for?* it said on an interval of a major third. Why, indeed? Immediately, the answer was simple enough. When one finds oneself with some one at the point of death one naturally does what one can to help them. Not from liking, necessarily; not from Christian compassion, not from training, even. A more secret tie compels one in the presence of death, one falls into rank against the common enemy, exerting oneself maybe for the life of one's worst foe in order to demonstrate a victory over that adversary. . . . One's worst foe. In the eyes of the world Minna might be exactly that; and to preserve her now, if she could preserve her, an act of idiocy, magnanimity, and destiny.

The candle was on the point of going out, shooting up a flapping flame. Cautiously she raised herself on her elbow, as though in this last allowance of sight she might surprise the answer to the church clock's enquiry. As though she had never noticed them before she found herself absorbed in admiring Minna's eyelashes, the only detail in her face that corroborated the suavity of her voice. From the moment I got wind of your voice, she thought, from the moment that Frederick, standing by Augusta's death-bed, echoed those melancholy harp-notes, I have been under some extraordinary enchantment; I have hastened on, troubled, uncomprehending, and resolute from one piece of madness to another. I have thought I could have a child by the lime-kiln man, more demented still I have proposed to have a child by Frederick. I have sketched myself sailing among the islands of the South Seas with Caspar and his guitar, voyaging on the Rhine with Mrs Hervey, disguising myself as a poacher and foraying among my own woods, dwelling meekly at the Academy Saint Gonval. I have left Blandamer as though I should never return, I have been in a street battle, I have pawned my diamond ring in order to entertain a collection of revolutionary ragamuffins. From sheer inattention I have been on the brink of a reconciliation with my husband, and as inattentively I have got myself into a position in which he seems able to cast me off. And now I am lying on the floor beside you, renewing the contact which, whenever I make it, shoots me off into some fresh fit of impassioned wool-gathering.

The candle had gone out. In the darkness Minna stirred and sighed, a rational deploring sigh of one in pain.

' What is it ? '

' My head—aches.'

Now we are off again, thought Sophia, the thought exploding within her like triumph; and it was with only rather more pity than impatience for life to recommence that she asked,

' But how do you feel ? Do you feel better ? Let me light a candle.'

' No ! '

' But, Minna, you can't lie here on the floor.'

' I can.'

The tone was at once meek and grim. So might an animal have spoken, lying limp and leaden in its burrow.

' Well then, let me arrange you more comfortably. Let me make you a cup of tea.'

' On a spirit-lamp, like an Englishwoman in the desert.' Her teeth chattered as she spoke, her attempted laugh was broken off sharp by pain.

' Lie beside me, Sophia.'

Obediently, and with an embarrassment bred of finding herself obedient, she laid herself down, the pain in her limbs teaching her how to lie as she had lain before, finding again the scent of the irises, the smoky perfume of the loosened hair. Her mind was at war with her reposing attitude, she listened suspiciously to Minna's breathing, and laid a caressing hand upon her wrist in order to measure the pulse-beats.

Battened down, her triumph and impatience still raged inside her, sharpening her thoughts to a feverish practicality. This must be done, the other must be done, done by her, for the time had come for her to assert herself, she must be no longer jerked hither and thither by the electrical propulsion of contact with Minna. Somehow this wildfire force must be appeased, must be granted a *raison d'être* which would release it from accident into purpose. Scurrying thus briskly, her thought suddenly lighted upon the vision of her trunk and her dressing-case, standing in the entry where Égisippe Coton had set them down. Frederick must be dealt with too.

No. On second thoughts, that obligation was over. She could see no reason why she need ever deal with Frederick again. The necessary treaty for her jewels and valuables could be carried on by some third party. That would be the more dignified method. Most dignified of all would be to relinquish to him all that he thought so compelling: the pearl bracelets, the amethyst parure, the gold net reticule, the brooch. But the original Aspen in her would not give so far. Frederick had leeched quite enough during the years of their marriage, she would not trouble to climb to the apex of dignity in order to gratify him with a pair of pearl bracelets.

No burden more fidgeting than an impecunious husband. Her pride had always snarled at seeing him spend what was in truth her money, and her prudence had snarled to see him

spending it so lavishly. He was as wasteful as a servant.
She remembered the blank sniffing look on her father's face,
his voice saying coldly and hastily, ' Certainly, Frederick, by
all means ' ; as though he would deny like an ill odour the
spectacle of an insolvent son-in-law ; and with the same
distaste and embarrassment he had whisked over the question
of the marriage settlements, depositing me, she thought, with
the same haughty embarrassment as he might drop a shilling
into the hand of an importunate widow, come over from
Ireland with her brats for the hay-making. Why ever had
Papa countenanced the marriage ?—what could have softened
him towards that dowerless beauty, that lad with a long
pedigree ? Not her own vehemence, that sudden imperious
curiosity to know what the love of man and woman might be,
which at the first learning had shrivelled away and left her cold
and unamorous. Mamma. Her breath had fanned the match,
her steadfast gentle talk, like a woollen web, so meek, so
muffling, had trawled them all towards that altar where Papa
had given this woman to be married to this man. Clear out
of the past leapt the recollection of those overheard words,
' My dear, for Sophia an early match is the safest match ' ; and
Papa's face, his look of incredulity traversed with alarm.
And so, for Sophia's safety, he had given that woman to be
married to that man, overlooking even the whiskers. For to
Papa, socketed in a smooth-cheeked era, those whiskers had
been perhaps what went down his gullet with the greatest
difficulty.

  Papa, Mamma . . . She looked back at them now with
the peculiar tenderness which ripens only on the farther side
of an irreparable estrangement. There they were in her

memory, far off, so far off that they were almost blue, walk-
ing beside the lake at Blandamer as the gentleman and the lady
walked beside the lake on the blue transfer breakfast service.
Henceforth she could think of them only with this particular
secreted tenderness, seeing them away on their side of the
water, they on their side, she on hers. Their departure into
death seemed almost immaterial, so greatly was it transcended
by her living departure. They at Blandamer, resuming their
rightful ownership from their double-bedded grave, where
Mama's willow murmured and dripped; she here, lying on
the floor of an apartment in the rue de la Carabine, her body
fostering this enigmatical sleeper, her mind wandering excited
and tentative through this newly begun riff-raff existence,
as one wanders through a new house, where everything is still
uncertain or unknown, where none of the furniture has been
unpacked.

It was almost midday before she examined the trunk and
the dressing-case. They had been most carefully dealt with,
the dressing-case in particular. Even the gold tops had been
removed from the flasks and pomade-pots, and corks of
assorted sizes rammed down in their stead. Hidden under a
silk band—pious observance of Papa's axiom that one should
always keep five pounds against emergency—had been a
Bank of England note. This also had been removed.
Frederick had been indeed a most thorough and conscientious
steward of her goods.

But her anger was insubstantial, muted by the fatigue of
the night, bleached by the reality of her relief at Minna's re-
emergence to life.

'One of my migraines,' she had said. Her voice was

tinged with regretful pride, as though, mauled and bloodied, she had said, ' One of my tigers.' And languid and compliant she had allowed herself to be put to bed, murmuring in her most plaintive stockdove note, ' Ah, Sophia! How unfortunate that I broke your vinaigrette ! '

No other allusion was made to the night before. It was a morning for practical dealings—Minna in bed, the apartment dishevelled with the party of overnight, her own crumpled estate to be remedied, and as usual, no food in the house.

She was in the porter's lodge, a shopping list in hand, impelling Madame Coton to trudge on her errands, when she heard herself saluted, and turned to meet the man called Ingelbrecht.

' *Visite de digestion*,' he said, and bowed with formality.

This old man who had been driven from so many capital cities came welcome to her eyes, his cosmopolitan exile seemed to have given him something of the godlike quality of a head waiter.

' Minna is ill.'

' Ah! I am sorry. I will postpone the visit then, and do your shopping for you instead.'

Madame Coton protested that for nothing could she relinquish the privilege of shopping for Madame Lemuel, so endeared and so stricken. But defrauding her of the unconcluded tip he took the list from her hands and walked off.

There on the landing stood the trunk and the dressing-case, unpleasing reminders of obligations unfulfilled. Sooner or later the apology must be made to great-aunt Léocadie, sooner or later the affair of her valuables must be settled. Ingelbrecht, indeed, gave such promise of imperturbable reliability that he might well be the third party empowered to treat for them ; but on the whole it would be simpler to ask him to take her place within earshot of Minna's interminable drowsiness while she went to the Place Bellechasse, did the civil to Léocadie and at the same time removed her goods.

But seeing his unmoved agreement, she felt a compunction at so commandeering him.

' No,' said he. ' I shall be quite happy here. I shall go on with my writing.' And from his pocket he drew a large note-book and a pencil.

' You are writing a book ? '

' A treatise on the proper management of revolutions.'

As she went on her way the image remained with her of Ingelbrecht, his shawl wrapped about his knees, his wrinkled face intent and unmoved, writing smoothly in his child's exercise book.

Thinking of Minna, of Ingelbrecht, and of herself, she had forgotten to expect the former things of the Place Bellechasse ; but entering she saw with no surprise save that she should have forgotten that he would be there, Père Hyacinthe, visiting at his customary hour, his feet, prudently paired like begging friars, resting on the customary flourish of the Aubusson carpet. There, too, in its place, was the spinning-wheel, gently whirling, and there was Frederick, still handing great-aunt Léocadie another tod of wool. It was as though they had been sitting there like that ever since her departure, sitting up for her as people sit up for the event of a death-bed, having called in the consolation of the Church in case it might be necessary. There they had sat, through daylight and lamplight, whiling away the time with subdued conversation. One of them, however, had absented himself long enough from the vigil to pack her trunk and pillage her dressing-case.

No professional *croque-morts* could have received her more calmly, manipulated her more suavely. No word was said of her absence, such was their tact that only a nominal reference was made to her presence. Taking a little turn towards the weather the conversation picked her up, as it were, and brought her back, through rain in England, to the discussion of the status of Claremont among the English country houses.

'It has always been used for oddities,' said Frederick. 'The Prince Consort lived there. The old one.'

'With his dowdy Louise's predecessor. Poor creature! Of course one cannot always draw the winning number, but still it must be painful to sink from the only daughter of England to one of the corps-de-ballet of Orléans.'

'She is truly religious, I believe. One can but pity her.'

'Not his first experience among *les rats*,' said Frederick. 'Do you remember the stories about that German barn-stormer of his—Caroline something or other—and how she blackmailed him?'

'I suppose she needed the money,' remarked Frederick's wife.

She had not been in the room for a couple of minutes before she became aware that her skirts were creased, her gloves dirty, her face flushed, and that she had a stain on her cuff. Even her voice, it seemed to her, had lost its gloss.

Frederick came forward with a footstool. Resting her feet on it she noticed that the tips of her shoes were rubbed.

As well be hanged for a sheep as a lamb. She would be as vulgar as a washerwoman, she would take off her gloves. Off they came, and there were her hands, unmistakably the worse for wear, the hands that had that morning washed glass and china, burned themselves on the charcoal stove, swept up cigar ash and emptied slops. Such hands would signal the retire to any delicate intelligence. Quite shortly—she knew it—Frederick and Père Hyacinthe would again be aspiring towards the completion of Ste. Clotilde.

They were. The duet proceeded to its cadence. But this time it was the basso who bowed himself away, casting a sprig or two from his bouquet of blessings on those remaining. And this time it was the tenor who eulogised the nice feeling of the basso, remarking,

'Well, he has tact, has Père Hyacinthe. Knows when to take himself off.'

'More tact than you, perhaps, my good Frederick. Still, Frederick is right. Let us be open, and admit that we are glad to be alone, and able to express ourselves. My dearest Sophie, how consoling it is to see you again ! I was becoming a little anxious, a little impatient. But seeing you returned, I forget all my reproaches.'

Though after the first sentence she had duly turned to Sophia, it was upon Frederick that her glance still rested.

'I quite agree, said Frederick. 'Least said, soonest mended.'

'I was relieved, too,' said Sophia, 'when Père Hyacinthe went. I have something to say to Frederick which I should prefer to say in private. But before anything else, great-aunt

Léocadie, I must beg your pardon for my bad manners. I should not have flounced off as I did.'

'My child, say no more of that. At my age, when one has outlived for so long one's own impetuosity, one is touched to see an act of impulse. It reassures one, it convinces one that there is still youth in the world that one is about to quit. Think no more of it, distress yourself no longer, my little Sophie.'

'I must ask pardon for more than that. Impetuosity cannot be the excuse for letting two days go by without writing to you.'

'No, my child. Frankly, that was badly done. But do not let us niggle over details. The essential thing is that you are here again ; and if you have black lines under your eyes, no doubt they are little black marks placed there by your poor guardian angel. So the heavenly honour is satisfied, and we mortals will be satisfied too.'

How to fell this old indomitable, wiry-legged, wiry-hearted ballerina ? I cannot, thought Sophia. There is Frederick to settle with, on the way back I want to buy more smelling-salts and some oysters, I cannot leave Ingel-brecht waiting indefinitely. Smashing down on these con-siderations came, *Suppose Minna is really ill?* Abstractedly she leaned down her cheek to the old woman's kiss.

When Frederick had ushered her into the dining-room and closed the door behind them her consciousness, bent on what was to come next, became slowly and embarrassingly aware that what was to come next threatened to be something compromising and bawdy. Looking round with an enquiring frown she saw the whiskered cheek a few inches from her eye, and understood that Frederick also was about to impose a kiss of pardon and peace.

She gave an alert cough, and spoke.

'Frederick! I should like my jewellery. I will take it with me now. And I will take the remaining fittings of my dressing-case too. I find the corks which you supplied very inconvenient.'

'And where do you propose to take them, Sophia?'

'To Madame Lemuel's.'

'Ah!' said Frederick, and seated himself. Thoughtfully he took out his cigar-case and pondered it—then, with a glance round, appeared to bethink himself of Madame de Saint Gonval's dining-room, and put it back again.

If there had been time she would have opposed her silence to his, frozen him, as she had done so often before, out of his impudence. But Ingelbrecht could not be left to finish out his exercise book, Minna might be worse. She must despatch.

'If you are thinking out a speech, Frederick, you can spare yourself the trouble. I had your letter. You made yourself sufficiently clear in that.'

'Did I, though?'

'Perfectly, I should say.'

'Then what the devil are you here for?'

He is going to fight over this trumpery, she thought. What a fool I was to come for it.

'*Visite de digestion*,' she said.

He opened his mouth like an angry fish. How often in times past his gapings at Blandamer had revealed to her those large regular tedious teeth, that healthy pink maw!

'Let us consider it paid, shall we? I will get my things

from Madeleine on my way out. You need not trouble to come with me.'

' Still after your gimcracks, eh ?   Let the bride forget her ornaments. . . . Well, Madeleine hasn't got them. *I've got them !* '

Those three words were spoken in a voice so gross, so heavy with plebeian malice, that she turned on him in astonishment. She could not recover her senses as promptly as he recovered his usual manner ; and he had been speaking for some time before she brought herself to attend to what he was saying.

' And you must not run away with the idea that I am doing this without consideration, out of spite or anything of that sort. I have discussed it thoroughly with your great-aunt Léocadie, and she quite agrees with me. You will admit *her* knowledge of the world at any rate, whatever your low opinion of mine. I only wish that she was doing the talking, it would come much better from her. This is an awkward sort of thing to discuss with one's wife.'

' I'm sorry, Frederick. I'm afraid I've not been attending. What exactly is that that you have discussed with Léocadie and find so awkward to discuss with me ? '

' Don't quibble, Sophia. You are not a child, you know perfectly well what people will say of this. Minna Lemuel is not a fit person for you to associate with.'

' As you know yourself from personal experience ? '

' As I know myself from personal experience.'

Trapped by her intonation an appeasing boon-companion's grin spread over his face. The crease was still on his flat cheek when she struck with the whole force of her fist.

'God damn you, Sophia!'

'God damn you, Frederick!'

So long-nursed, so well-established the hatred between them that this declaration of it scarcely interrupted their conversation. The mark of her knuckles was still white on his flushed cheek, and an involuntary tear only halfway down it, when he resumed his exposition of himself and great-aunt Léocadie.

'I must suppose that, at present at any rate, it is useless to appeal to your better feelings, to your feeling as a wife and mother—though when I see you, Sophia, still wearing black for those two poor little babies of ours, I should have thought——'

Taking advantage of the pause he wiped off the involuntary tear.

'However, I see that any such appeal would be useless. And as that is so I intend to assert one right, at least, as your husband. Go with Minna Lemuel if you please. But you go without what you please to call your property.'

'Do you mean to say, Frederick, that you have really been making all these speeches, holding all these confabulations with Léocadie, about my jewel-case and the tops of my scent-bottles?'

'I mean what I say. I mean that until you mend your manners you can whistle for your jewels and your scent-bottles, and everything else you like to think yours. Not a penny do you get from me. It's mine, do you understand? By the law, it's mine. When you married me it became mine, and now after ten years it's high time you understood it. You don't seem to grasp that very easily, do you? You'd

better talk it over with Minna. She's a Jew, she understands
money, she'll be able to explain to you which side a wife's
bread is buttered. Meanwhile, as I don't want to expose you
to any humiliation, let me tell you that it will be useless to
write your Sophia Willoughby on any draft. I've written
to the bank already and given orders that your signature is
not to be honoured.'

'Thank you, Frederick. That is very obliging.'

She walked to the door and stood waiting.

Holding it open for her to pass through, as though the
action constrained him to a resumption of civility, he said in
his pleasantest, most affable tones,

'Look here, Sophia, can't we patch it up? Lord knows,
I don't want to do the heavy husband. But really, what else
am I to do? I must be responsible for you, I can't let you
compromise yourself without asserting myself in some way.
Your great-aunt Léocadie . . .'

In the ante-room was a little table with a salver on it for
visiting cards. Taking out her card and a pencil she dog's-
eared the card and wrote on it, *p.p.c.*

'*Pour prendre congé*,' she explained. 'The usual
etiquette.'

Stronger than rage, astonishment, contempt, the pleasur-
able sense that at last she had slapped Frederick's face, the
less pleasurable surmise that his slap back would be longer-
lasting; stronger even than the desire to see Minna was her
feeling that of all things, all people, she most at this moment
wished to see Ingelbrecht, and the sturdy assurance that she
would find in him everything that she expected. If she had
gone up the stairs in the rue de la Carabine on her knees, she

could not have ascended with a more zealotical faith that there would be healing at the top; and when he opened the door to her, enquiring politely if her errands had gone well she replied with enthusiasm, ' Perfectly. My husband—it was he I went to see—has just threatened to cut me off with a penny.'

' A lock-out,' said Ingelbrecht. ' Very natural. It is a symptom of capitalistic anxiety. I suppose he has always been afraid of you.'

She nodded, and her lips curved in a grin of satisfaction.

' How is Minna ? '

' Still asleep. In that matter, Minna is superb. Her physical aplomb is infallible, when any one else would go to pieces, she develops a migraine and goes to sleep. If only— but it is a gift, and it is idle to envy gifts. The rest of us must do what we can. . . . You had better have some coffee.'

There, on the table beside the closed exercise book was the coffee-tray, neatly arranged.

He is everything, she thought, that I expected, everything that I desired; grim and flat, positive without any flavour, a man like plain cold water.

' And can your husband cut off with a penny ? '

' I suppose so.'

' You do not know for certain ? '

' No.'

' Then you must find out. He may be bluffing you. You had better write to your man of business and enquire exactly how you stand.'

She looked at him abashed but contented.

' You take the wind out of my sails.'

'No, I don't,' he replied. 'But I think you may be leaving the harbour with too much canvas.'

'I should like some coffee, too.'

It was the voice of the convalescent, velveted with sleep. A yawn followed it, a rustle; and Minna strolled into the room, wearing the sleek shriven look of the healthily awakened. Her brown ankles emerged from the blue woollen slippers with an astonishing authenticity of colour, they seemed still tanned and supple from her barefoot childhood. Over her nightgown she wore a purple velvet pelisse, through her hair, hanging in elf-locks, glittered the shallower black of her jet ear-rings.

'He has watched over me like a guardian angel. But more peaceably.'

Sophia glanced at the book and the pencil.

'Perhaps more like a recording angel.'

'More like a recording angel than she knows.'

'Why, Ingelbrecht, am *I* in your book?'

Flowers for me? asked the prima-donna. Only a natural aptitude for domination polished by years of practice could have achieved that note of candid gratification. Only an aptitude quite as pronounced and the imperturbable unaffectedness of a long vocation could have replied with such simplicity.

'Not your name, Minna. Your defects, in so far as they are typical and instructive.'

Answering a look of genuine grief, he added,

'You will be of great value to future insurgents, my dear.'

What I feel, thought Sophia, is what I have seen painted sometimes on the faces of people listening to Beethoven;

the look of those listening to a discourse, to an argument carried on in entire sincerity, an argument in which nothing is impassioned, or persuasive, or reasonable, except by force of sincerity; and there they sit in a heavenly thraldom, as blind people sit in the sun making a purer acknowledgment with their skin than sight, running after this or that flashing tinsel, can ever make. I cannot for the life of me see what Minna and Ingelbrecht are after; to me a revolution means that there is a turmoil and after it people are worse off than they were before; and yet as I see them there, Minna looking like some one in a charade and Ingelbrecht like a respectable Unitarian artisan, it is as though I were listening to music, able to feel and follow the workings of a different world. For it is there, that irrefutable force and logic of a different existence. In Ingelbrecht's every word and gesture it is manifested, and in this instant I have seen it touch Minna and change her from the world's wiliest baggage to some one completely humble and sincere.

'What have you written about Minna?' she asked. 'I should like to hear it.'

Watching Ingelbrecht turn over the pages of his book, and Minna settling herself to attend, it seemed incredible to her that human beings should ever mince, belittle themselves, or expostulate.

'*There are some revolutionaries, on the other hand, who seem incapable of feeling a durable anger against the conditions which they seek to overthrow. In these characters the imagination is too rich, the emotional force too turbulent. The anger which they undoubtedly feel is neutralised by the pleasure they experience in expressing it. They are speech-makers, they are frequently assassins; but when they have finished their speech, or poignarded their tyrant, they are in such a mood of satisfied excitement that they are almost ready to forgive the state of society which allows them such abuses on which to avenge themselves. And this they themselves commonly admit in such remarks as, " It is enough," or, " I have achieved my destiny."*

' *In using that antiquated and romantic expression, "poignarded the tyrant," I use it with intention. These revolutionaries are penetrated with artistic and historical feeling, they turn naturally to the weapons of the past, and to methods which, by being outmoded, appear to be chivalrous. (I point out that there must be an element of the gothic in all chivalry. No perfectly contemporary action can be described as chivalrous.) This tendency, which is natural in any such character, and therefore ineradicable by any application of reason or analysis, is abetted by another characteristic proper to persons of this temperament—great technical facility. The argument that it is easier to kill a man with a gun than with a rapier carries little force with them, because they are already so skilful with a rapier; the ancestors of these revolutionaries were such good archers that the invention of gunpowder only bored them, so skilful with the flint bolt that no demonstration of the feathered arrow could have persuaded them to a change of weapon. In consequence of this, these skilful assassins seldom despatch more than one tyrant; like the bee they sting once, and lose with that injury their power to inflict another.*'

' If I could kill one tyrant,' murmured Minna, ' I would die happy.'

'Exactly.' He turned a page. '*The assassination of Galeazzo Maria Szorza in 1476 is a typical piece of work in this kind—classical republican sentiments, the choice of a showy moment for the deed itself and, the deed ended, no plan of subsequent action. Even more typical is the enthusiasm which this assassination aroused in Italy, despite the fact that as a political* coup *it was an utter failure; it was sufficient for the enthusiasm of society that the assassination had been conceived and carried out on classical lines, and the fact that all three perpetrators died on the scaffold only added sublimity to the spectacle.*

'*For the greatest danger to revolutionary work of this class of revolutionaries is not their personal improvidence (the consequences of that as a rule affect only themselves), not their tendency to exhaust themselves in gusts of eloquence and* coups de théâtre, *not even their lack of discipline; but in their appeal to bourgeois sympathies. One such revolutionary may attract ten undesirable recruits from the bourgeoisie, sentimentalists, sensation-seekers, idealists, etc. These miserable camp-followers clog action, talk incessantly, make the movement ridiculous, and, parasites themselves, harbour further parasites of spies and* agents provocateurs. *Moreover, they are extremely difficult to dislodge.*'

He read without any appearance of authorship, his little grey eyes like shot rolling swiftly back and forth as though they were the only visibly moving part of the machine which was the man. And when the reading was finished and the book closed the eyes rested upon Minna in a steadfastness that betokened trust and goodwill.

'I feel really proud, Ingelbrecht, that any part of your

book should have been written under my roof. In a hundred years' time people will be reading your book and thinking, It is universal, as true now as when it was written. . . . No, no! What am I saying? In a hundred years' time, thanks to your book, it will all be different, in 1948 the Revolution will be too strong to be endangered any longer by people like me.'

'Or by the despicable characters you attract,' added Sophia.

'There, you see, Ingelbrecht. You are always right, I have done it again. I have converted Sophia now. She admits it.'

Under the easy mischief of her voice was a note of excitement, and the glance she cast on Sophia was at once fostering and predatory.

'I forgot to read you a foot-note,' said Ingelbrecht. '*It must be stated, however, that these bourgeois disciples are often both wealthy and generous. Since the character of the party is at all times more important than its finances, this should never be thought a reason for welcoming such recruits. If the party be sufficiently strong it does render their introduction less undesirable, but a weak party should arm itself against them as against a pestilence.*'

It seemed unbelievable that such an eye should wink. Wink, however, it did. Untying her bonnet-strings, staring Ingelbrecht resolutely in the face, Sophia said with gravity,

'I will write to my man of business to-morrow.'

'Pray do,' said he. And having advised Minna to eat more and smoke less, he gathered up the book and the rug, bowed like a benevolent gnome and went away.

From the balcony she watched him go down the street, and as, watching Minna in the rue de l'Abbé de l'Épée she had thought of an animal, Ingelbrecht reminded her of an animal too, so swiftly and circumspectly he made his way, seeming to trot on some intent personal errand, true to his own laws and oblivious of all else.

'Does he always wear that shawl?'

'Yes, almost always. He was imprisoned in the Spielberg, you know. And he was so cold there, so wretchedly cold, that it got into his bones, and he has felt chilly ever since.'

'Have you ever been in a prison, Minna?'

'Yes, once or twice. But never for anything creditable. Vagrancy and theft and so forth, wretched little poverty offences. When I was a girl, going about with Lecoq and his dogs. But once in Vienna I was nearly had for the real thing. I was being very harmless, I was telling my fairy-stories. I described an ogre, a sleek grey ogre, sleek as ice. Wherever he went, I said, it was like a black frost. Whatever he touched stiffened, birds fell dead, the young fruit dropped off the trees. The name of this ogre, I said, was Mitternacht— you know what they call Metternich. There were some students in the audience, and in an instant they were up, shouting and applauding. A riot!

'It was marvellous,' she said, swooping forward like some purple-plumaged bird of prey, her hooked nose impending— 'Marvellous! To have such power, to have them up at a word. . . . Just what Ingelbrecht would disapprove of, too.'

In the silence that followed both women turned and looked at the empty chair, the table, the inkpot.

'I do, I do appreciate him!' exclaimed Minna. 'I

appreciate him implicitly. If he were to say to me, Minna,
never another word, no more stories of the oppressed, no
more of your sorceries with fairy-tales, I would sew up my
mouth. But this afternoon how could I help feeling a little
dulled ? All the time he was here, the pen whispering on, the
shadow of the curtain moving over the bald head, I was say-
ing to myself—That Sophia. . . . Will she ever come back ? '

Into this opening she must dive.

' Minna ! Do you feel equal to a piece of tiresome news ? '

' One is always equal to that.'

' I went to see Frederick. I had to. And Frederick has
been asserting himself.'

At a nod, wise and parrot-like, the jet ear-rings began to
swing slowly in and out of the black hair.

' He dislikes me being with you——'

' He is jealous of you ? '

' Yes. I suppose that is what it is. He is jealous.'

' And no wonder.' The blue slippers moved into a more
dignified position, a deft hand tweaked the purple pelisse into
nobler folds. Holding her head aloft she said grandly, ' If he
were to strive for a lifetime, that poor Frederick, he could not
appreciate me as you did in our first five minutes. And no
doubt that in his darkened way he knows this.'

' No doubt. And so, on the best military models, he has
cut off my supplies.'

There was a swift gesture, called back. Locking her hands
together, staring down on them as though to ward them from
further movement, Minna was silent.

' He has cut off my supplies. As he is entitled to do, being
my husband. He has told the bank not to honour my

signature, he has removed the gold fittings from my dressing-case. So you see, Minna, I am penniless, or soon shall be. I have what is left over from my ring, that will last a while. I have my clothes, for what they are worth. And my hair. I believe one can always sell one's hair. After that, unless I comply with Frederick's wishes, nothing.'

'You will stay? You must, if only to gall him.'

'I don't think that much of a reason.'

'But you will stay?'

'I will stay if you wish it.'

It seemed to her that the words fell cold and glum as ice-pellets. Only beneath the crust of thought did her being assent as by right to that flush of pleasure, that triumphant cry.

'But of course,' said Minna a few hours later, thoughtfully licking the last oyster shell, 'we must be practical.'

This remark she had already made repeatedly, speaking with the excitement of an adventurous mind contemplating a new and hazardous experience. Each time the remark had led to some fresh attempt at practicality, attempts that never got beyond a beginning. On the sofa lay Sophia's dresses, three of them valued with the adeptness of an old-clothes woman, the rest only admired and exclaimed over. On the table were strewn several manuscript poems and a novel which only needed finishing and a publisher to make their fortune. Mixed in with these and, like these, read aloud in their more striking passages, were various letters, any one of which, she said, would be a gold-mine if properly negotiated. And why, she added, this prejudice against blackmail, if the results were to be applied to a good end? Why indeed, had answered

Sophia, brooding upon the vileness of those who wrote such letters.

'Yes, we must be practical. No more oysters, no more supper-parties. Ah, how I reproach myself that you sold your ring. I don't suppose Dury got half its value, rushing off like that to a Mont de Piété. If we could raise the money to buy it back, then we could sell it again.'

'I regretted that ring this afternoon. You see, I lost my temper and hit him in the face. And the moment I had done it I remembered my ring and thought how much more it would have hurt if I had been wearing it.'

'Yes. A knuckle-duster. Rings are invaluable, I know, and diamonds most painful of all. Still, I expect you didn't do too badly. You must be very strong. I suppose you wouldn't . . . No. That would be out of the question, I'm afraid.'

'What ? '

'Appear—under good auspices, you know—as a female pugilist. With your figure and height it would be marvellous. But I see that it wouldn't really do, it is just my natural tendency to turn to circuses. You might not believe it, Sophia, to look at me now, but when I was young and slender as a reed I could go right round the ring in a series of somersaults. And the applause would be like thunder. But now, even if I were to thin, I don't suppose I should be good for much.'

'I wonder what Ingelbrecht would suggest ? '

'He would tell us to move to a cheaper apartment and work as laundresses.'

'In England that is what we prescribe for fallen women.

They are all set to laundry work, in institutions. In fact, now that I come to think of it, I am among the patronesses of such an institution myself. But if I am to keep that splendid position, Frederick will have to pay my next subscription for me.'

They looked at each other with eyes brilliant with laughter and complicity. Too much excited to finish the meal they began to pace up and down the room arm in arm. Through the long window came the smell of the spring night and the smell of the city. In the windows of the house opposite they could see the life of half a dozen families, a woman in petticoat and camisole washing a pair of stockings in a basin, a young man reading while a girl rubbed her face against the back of his neck, another man yawning and fastening on a night-cap, an elderly couple leaning over the sill with a coffee-pot between them. A newspaper was being cried down the street, from the café where the local club held its sitting came the long vague rumour of declamation and bursts of applause, further away some children marched and sang, and a drum beat fitfully. But drum beats and processions were common noises now. And though they heard, immediately below, a door open, the foot of the cautious Égisippe Coton shuffle on the pavement, nothing followed but his flat voice remarking, 'It's nothing. It's only a drum.'

During the days that followed Minna continued to rejoice in the prospect of being severely practical, and to the many visitors who came to her apartment and were fed there she explained Sophia's position and the value which would be set upon any advice they could give. To Sophia it was at first slightly embarrassing to be assured of the nobility of her conduct.

'For it is not true, Minna, that I have left Frederick and renounced my income because my sympathies are with the Revolution. I am here as I am because I saw a chance of being happy and took it. As for the Revolution, when I smacked my husband's face and sent him to the devil, I never gave it a thought.

'Anyhow,' she added, countering a look of triumph on Minna's face, 'I had done with Frederick long before. The smack was only a postscript.'

'You had done with Frederick, yes. But what is that? So had I. So had dozens of other women. To give up a thing or a person, that is of no significance. It is when you put out your hand for something else, something better, that you declare yourself. And though you may think you have chosen me, Sophia, or chosen happiness, it is the Revolution you have chosen.'

'As for the money,' Sophia persevered, 'I regret it most sincerely. Nothing would please me better than to have it back.'

'Exactly what Ingelbrecht says. He considers it most unfortunate. I was talking to him about it yesterday evening.'

' " These bourgeois disciples are often both wealthy and generous," ' said Sophia reminiscently.

Minna continued,

'I asked him if he thought it better if you should recover your money by a little compliance to Frederick, if I should try to persuade you to that.'

'If he had advised it, would you have tried?'

'Caught! You take it for granted that he did not advise

such tactics. A week ago even, you would not have been sure of that.'

' Would you have tried ? '

' No.'

In the matter of being severely practical, it was the young man called Dury who gave it the greatest consideration. Priding himself, he said, upon being a peasant and with a peasant's astuteness, he promised to bend his mind upon the problem, and return in a day or two with a solution.

Returning, he happened to find Sophia alone. His glance rested upon her with extraordinary satisfaction, as though, for the purpose he had in mind, she were even better suited than he had supposed.

' It is nothing showy, my project,' said he. ' But it is better to begin in a small way, with no outlay, with a certainty of gains, however small. And this expedient is perfectly reliable, a sitting bird. Doubtless you can sing the hymns of England ? '

' Rule Britannia ? '

' No, no. The ecclesiastical hymns. A friend of mine, a sculptor, a young man of real talent, is looking for a fair-haired lady who can sing English hymns.'

' I would certainly try, but I doubt if I should be of any use to your friend. I am not much practised in singing hymns, and when I sat for my portrait I found it very difficult to sit still. If I had to sing as well . . .'

' Oh, there is no question of sitting. Actually, at this moment, sculpture presents certain difficulties. Unless one tears up a paving-stone, it is difficult to procure the material for any large work. Buyers, too, are hard to come by. But

Raoul can also play the accordion, and talk like a cheap-jack, and it is on these talents that he is relying. He wishes to make speeches in the streets against the Church—our Church—and especially against this abominable celibacy. It is his idea that you should accompany him, as an escaped nun, thrust into a convent against her will, suffering untold atrocities—you know the sort of thing. And it occurred to us that if you were to be an English Protestant, an heiress, taken and held by force, it would be even more affecting. He would ask nothing more of you than you should sing a hymn or two, and wear your hair in long plaits. Everything else he would be responsible for. There is always a little collection, you know, and this he would share with you. The profits are steady, and as you see, there is no outlay whatsoever. He made quite a success of it during March with a young woman (also escaped from a convent, this time a Spanish one) who danced and played a tambourine. Unfortunately for him one of their sympathising listeners took such a fancy to her that he took her into keeping. It was a blow to Raoul. Just when they were doing so well. But of course he could not stand in the girl's way. It was a great chance for her.'

'But I understood that nuns always have their hair cut short. Surely those long plaits . . .'

'In point of fact, yes. In point of effect, no. It is to the sympathies of the crowd that one appeals rather than to their sense of accuracy. And long tresses are undoubtedly moving. You cannot, for instance, imagine a short-haired Magdalen repenting to any purpose. It is the descent, the long line, the weeping-willow quality. . . .'

With his squat peasant's paws he demonstrated the curves of a willow.

' Then should I not wear my hair unbound ? '

' No, Madame.   For a Protestant, plaits.'

Minna found her standing in the middle of the room, attentively rehearsing hymns in a Sunday School squall.   For a while affection and ear strove together.   Ear won.

' My dearest, what a very dismal tumult ! '

' Frightful, isn't it ?   It is an English hymn.   That obliging young man who pawned my ring . . .'

She explained the project.   Minna's listening looks became slowly overcast.   Doubt deepened to a noble desolation, to a grief magnanimously borne.

' I'm afraid you do not approve, Minna.   You think, perhaps, I should not sing in the street.   Of course it is a most outrageous cheat.'

' Cheat !   Am I one to discountenance cheating ?   No, no, Sophia !   It is envy that gnaws me.   It seems to me that Dury might have cast me also for a little part in this comedy.   However . . . Well, at any rate, my past can enrich your future.   You don't pitch your voice right for the street.'

The more Sophia considered the society in which she found herself, the more puzzled she became.   What at first had made them easy to settle among—their inconsequentiality, their rather slipshod affability, the intimacy amongst themselves so easily extended to her, the general impression which they gave of being somehow perched temporarily, like a large family stranded for a night in a waiting-room, made them as time went on, very unsettling company.

They were idle, or unoccupied; but that was nothing new; the greater part of her life had been spent among the idle, the society of honest shopkeepers would have been much more alien to her than this.

In their assumption of simplicity they were arrogant: listening to their chatter, their easy turnings upside down of all accepted judgments, she felt herself like a shy governess imported from a foreign land; but this again was nothing new to her, all her life she had been listening to people who could talk more cleverly than she, and despising them.

They were idle and they were arrogant. Often, half-closing her senses, she might have fancied herself again in Adelaide Willoughby's drawing-room among Adelaide Willoughby's friends. There too, people had strayed in and out, too intimate for greetings, hurrying in, it seemed, in order to express an urgent admiration for a new opera singer or a new-moded abhorrence for an established one. And then, having made their little somersault, they would whisk off again, just delaying for a moment of patronage towards the country relation. Pausing at the door they would chatter interminably.

Minna's society was politer, and was more entertaining than Adelaide's. But that was not all. Had it been all, she would not have known, as she did increasingly, this curious anxiety on their behalf. She felt in herself the stirrings of an impulse, half maternal, half missionary, to rally this odd troop, to warn them of danger, call them back from some impending destruction. As for the nature of the destruction, that need not be far to seek. It was obvious to her that if they persevered in this manner of life they would all be dead of starvation in six months' time. As it was, they appeared to be living on air, on credit, on taking in each other's washing, only supplementing these means by occasional more solid mouthfuls of living on Minna. For that matter, how did Minna live ? On air, on credit, on what she called ' another of my windfalls,' on Sophia's sealskin and the remains of her ring. And with these mayflies, she thought, standing blandly in the May sunshine, admiring the new spikes of blossom on the horse-chestnut trees, listening inattentively to Raoul's invectives against celibacy and waiting for her cue to intone another Sunday School hymn, with these mayflies I, too, shall go down ; for certainly I cannot support myself by singing long-haired hymns on the boulevards, and equally certainly I will never go back to Frederick.

Whoever else might hope to survive a year of the republic, its revolutionaries certainly could not. In this half-baked republic they perched temporarily like a large family stranded for the night in a waiting-room ; but the morning would never come, no train would ever take them on to their destination. Here they would remain, arguing passionately about the National Workshops and declaring the inalienable right of man to live by his earnings, without attempt or hope, apparently, of earning a livelihood for themselves. And one cold winter's morning the cold would attract their attention and they would all drop down dead.

> ' In works of Labour or of Skill,
>   I would be busy too ;
>   For Satan finds some mischief still . . .'

Undoubtedly Satan, that old friend of the family, would be surprised, if he came this way, to discover the present

occupation of little Sophia Aspen ; though whether my sing-
ing, she thought, could be considered either skilful or
laborious enough to keep him at bay is questionable. Lord,
how that tasking-master of a Satan would be delighted with
the Paris of May 1848 ! And remembering Minna's technical
advice she concluded on a heart-rending howl that fetched
applause from the crowd—the idle shabby sauntering crowd,
workmen out of work, housewives away from their houses,
students truant from their lectures, Civil Guards straying
from their round-houses.

Loftily, pensively, for she was supposed to have a soul
above lucre, she gazed at the chestnut blossom while Raoul
went round with the hat. Already her ears had learned to
distinguish between the noise of a giving and ungiving
assembly. A year ago, a little less than a year ago, for chest-
nuts flower rather later in England, she must have been look-
ing at the chestnuts by the gate of Blandamer, those same trees
which, their blossom discarded, had pleased her better so, that
morning when she had taken the children to the lime-kiln.

So deeply rooted then, and now so fugitive, it was small
wonder that she could say to herself with comparative calm,
' In six months' time I, with all these other people, shall be
dead of starvation and incompetence.'

Arm in arm with the sculptor she walked off to their next
station, while he in his intellectual-cum-gutter-snipe voice
explained why the spirit of France must for choice express
itself in the round rather than linearly.

' Boucher's bottoms,' she said, acquiescing. Glancing
down she saw his eyelashes collide as he blinked away the
unwomanly comment.

But it is not desperation, she continued in her thoughts, that makes me so casual. I am undoubtedly enjoying myself. I am happier than I have ever been before. I suppose we are really all going mad, and I have caught the madness and whirl on with the rest as carelessly as they. But I am happier. These people in whose extraordinary company I find such happiness are not happy at all. Their revolution has been no real pleasure to them ; their republic, now they have got it, brings them no contentment. Apart from being threatened with starvation, they are not at ease in it. Their idleness is more like some sort of deliberate idling, a killing of time, and their arrogance the jauntiness of children who won't admit a fault, who are waiting to be found out. It is not just peril of starvation that frets them, it is some moral worm, some malaise of the spirit. They are like—the thought jumped up, exact and clinching—they are like people sickening for a fever ; excited, restless, listless, blown this way and that like windlestraws in the gusts that stir before a thunderstorm.

Idle and arrogant . . . there were only two people in whom the taint, the preliminary sickening, displayed itself in such a way as to suggest that they might escape lightly, that their constitutions would stand it ; there was only one person in whom there showed no taint at all. Minna and Dury were the two. Minna, God knows, was idle ; but she was completely without arrogance, and her idleness was coupled with such energy that it seemed like the flourish of a vitality too rich to be contained in any doing, a stream too impetuous to turn any mill-wheel. As for Dury, his arrogance was intolerable ; but as Ingelbrecht had said, no peasant slaved on his small holding more savagely than Dury laboured his canvases. Even in conversation his gaze drudged over one's face, harrowed the posture of one's hands, or scythed an expanse of wall, the colour of a curtain, the light falling upon a wine-glass and an apple-paring. There was no advantage too petty for him to take, his pinch-farthing husbandry would wring advantage out of a dirty glove or a cotton reel.

The one wholly untainted was Ingelbrecht. Whatever the sickness, there was no taint of it on him, whatever happened he, resolute, discreet, self-contained, alert, would trot like some secret busy badger along his own path.

The tour was ended, and the gains divided. In Raoul's studio, it was a stable really, she put up her hair and tied on her bonnet, eyeing herself in a speckled mirror that reflected the dirty window, the straggling vine-branch that crossed it, the splendid russet haunches of the dray-horse which was being backed into the shafts outside.

' There's a behind for you,' she exclaimed, landing another unwomanly blow. 'Better than these incessant human bottoms. Why don't sculptors do more animals ? '

' They lack soul,' he replied. ' There would be no market except in England. May I offer you a little beer ? It is thirsty weather.'

They drank in the amity of professional fellowship, and when the beer was finished parted as cleanly as a cup and saucer which have been rinsed and set apart till they are next needed in conjunction.

For it would not do, they had decided, for her blonde plaits to be exhibited in the rue de la Carabine. Apart from the censorious Cotons, such a display would be bad for business. As a lady she left Minna's dwelling, as a lady she returned to it, as a lady embellished with five francs seventy-five, as a lady footsore but lighthearted. Five francs seventy-five was not too bad, considering the times and the nature of her wares, the limited appeal of Dr Watts' hymns to a Parisian public; though it was not the winning number which she promised herself to bring back one fine day: the vindictive rapture of having squalled attention, if nothing more, from a strolling Frederick.

The baseness of this aspiration had shocked Minna. There was no doubt that Frederick's late mistress had more elevation of soul than Frederick's late wife.

Sophia had never had much elevation of soul; and that the life she was now leading released her so thoroughly into a low way of living was perhaps one of the main reasons why she was so intensely happy. Like some child who has toppled full-clothed into a stream and, taking to the sensation, only returns to the bank to strip off boots, hat, stockings, petti-coats, she who had arrived at the rue de la Carabine with all her prejudices girt about her now only recalled her former life in order to discover that another prejudice was a hamper, and could be discarded.

She had been brought up (and had brought up her own children) to consider the chiefest part of mankind as an inferior race, people to be addressed in a selected tone of voice and with a selected brand of language. Towards the extreme youth and age of the lower classes one adopted a certain geniality, to the rest one spoke with politeness. But to none of them did one display oneself as oneself; be it for

approving pat or chastising blow one never, never, removed
one's gloves.

Now, in addition to singing in the street she shopped in
the street also. The decent veil of shopping in a foreign
tongue and under conditions which made such shopping an
adventure and a fantasy had soon ravelled away. With her
whole soul she walked from stall to stall, countering the wiles
of those who sell with the wiles of those who purchase,
pinching the flesh of chickens, turning over mackerel, com-
menting disadvantageously upon the false bloom of revived
radishes. Her fine nostrils quivered above cheeses and sniffed
into pickle-tubs and the defencelessly open bellies of long
pale rabbits. Her glance pried out flaws, the under-ripe or
the over-ripe, and her tongue denounced them.

Those who displeased her learned of it ; not in the old
tongue, the lofty cold-shouldering of Blandamer days, but
roundly. Where she had found good bargains she put forth
wiles without conscience, with flattery, exhortations, or
shameless appeals to better nature extorting better goods or
lower prices. She became—highest boast of those who
market—a recognised customer, a person whose tastes and
whims were known. Bunches of asparagus were put aside
for her, and the one-eyed Madame Lefanu held out to her,
above the heads of the crowd, a richly drooping garland of
black puddings.

All round her were faces of the kind she liked to see ;
sharp clear glances, lips taut with cupidity, brows sharply
furrowed with exact thought. When people justled her it
was not because she was a fine woman, but because she stood
in the way of a fine duckling. All her life she had been more

or less accustomed to finding herself the first, now she tasted the rapture of being first among peers. When all was bought, the bag filled, the purse pocketed, and a bunch of flowers for Minna brought intact from the crowd, she would find herself approving with passionate affection the people she had quitted, the buyers and the sellers, whose sea-gull voices still echoed on in the narrow sounding-board alley of the rue Mouffetard.

With a queer glance, now, she looked on people of her own class. Not many such came into their quarter; but on forays into 'that other Paris,' as she learned to think of it, she saw them, elegant and lifeless as she had been; and sometimes, when she was singing in the streets, such a one would pause for a moment, a fish-like wavering, a stare with glassy eyes, a compassionate glove, maybe, advanced. And her body would tighten with malice, her ribs arch over the singing breath, the corner of her due singer's smile twitch a little further up, as her spirit made long noses at them.

The decorum of class had gone, the probity of class had gone too. At intervals she searched Minna's purse for bad money (none came into hers) and used it for seats in parks, seats in omnibuses, or to bestow on beggars for religious purposes who could not be fobbed off otherwise. Gladly would she have swindled on a larger scale, had she been able to. But she could not invent cheats by herself, and Minna, coming to her aid, swiftly enskied any project into impracticality.

With a step she had ranged herself among the *mauvais sujets*, the outlaws of society who live for their own way and by their own wits. There had been no tedium about her fall, and with a flash every false obligation was gone.

Even the prudence of her class had shrivelled. Day by day they grew poorer, every week they pawned something more, money was a continual preoccupation with her, whether she beat down the price of a sausage, or sat laughing with Minna over their grandiose projects for cozenage. But now the question of how to live seemed no more than some sort of gymnastic, in which daily she suppled herself, sharpening her wits in the same arrogant combat towards perfection as that with which a runner or a wrestler keeps his body in trim. Bread and lodging and the outward adorning might be threatened, but she could feel no menace to her happiness. And anyhow we shall all be dead in six months' time, she repeated to herself; and with the next thought visited an unexplored wineshop where there was a white cat and a very cheap *vin rosé*.

Her happiness, blossoming in her so late and so defiantly, seemed of an immortal kind. One day, looking over a second-hand bookstall with Minna, she opened a snuffy volume that had English poems in it. Her eye fell on the verse :

> ' My love is of a birth as rare
> As 'tis of object strange and high,
> It was begotten by despair
> Upon impossibility.'

' Look,' she said, pointing on the withered page.

Minna began to glance about for the vendor.

' No. Let me look at the other poems. It is silly to buy a book just for the sake of a verse which one can learn by heart.' It seemed to her that the other poems were wilfully annoying, and she would have put down the book, but Minna clung to it, absorbed, her lips fumbling at the English syllables.

' *Un objet bizarre et élevé.* Sophia, I must buy this book. I feel an obligation towards it. Besides, it will improve my English.'

To please her Sophia spent some time beating down the bookstall man.

Whatever it did for Minna's English, Sophia did not open the book again; but that one verse, rapidly memorised, stayed in her head, and seemed in some way to sum up the quality of her improbable happiness, just as Minna's absurd *bizarre et élevé* hit off the odd mixture of nobility and extravagance which was the core of the Minna she loved.

Minna was not beautiful, nor young. Her principles were so inconsistent that to all intents and purposes she had no principles at all. Her character was a character of extremes : magnanimous and unscrupulous, fickle, ardent, and interfering. Her speaking voice was exquisite and her talent of words exquisitely cultivated, but she frequently talked great nonsense. Similarly, her wits were sharp and her artfulness consummate, and for all that she was maddeningly gullible. She offered nothing that Sophia had been brought up to consider as love-worthy or estimable, for what good qualities she had must be accepted with their opposites, in an inconsequential pell-mell of wheat and tares.

Sophia had been brought up in a world policed by oughts. One ought to venerate age, one ought to admire the beautiful. One ought to love ugly Mary Thompson because she was so clean, God because he was so good, prating Mr Scarby because he was so honest and paid all his son's debts, scolding cousin Arabella because she was so capable, Mamma because she was so kind, Frederick because he was her husband. One ought to devote oneself to one's children because, if well brought up, they would be a comfort in one's old age. Behind every love or respect stood a monitorial reason, and one's emotions were the expression of a bargaining between demand and supply, a sort of political economy. At a stroke, Minna had freed her from all this. Unbeautiful and middle-aged, unprincipled and not intellectual, vain, unreposeful, and with a complexion that could look greasy, she offered her one flower, liberty. One could love her freely, unadmonished and unblackmailed by any merits of body or mind. She made no more demands upon one's moral approval than a cat, she was not even a good mouser. One could love her for the only sufficient reason that one chose to.

She pleased or entertained or moved one without an extortion upon one's sense of gratitude. Like the work of art, her artfulness was for art's sake, and her flashes of goodness were as painless as an animal's. Calculating with unscrupled cunning upon the effect she might have, her calculations stopped short there, she was unconcerned as to whether the effect of the effect would advantage her or no, receiving with the same brief convention of astonishment the news that she had been charming, had been infuriating. If the effect miscarried, was no effect at all, the astonishment was more genuine. A bruised look would settle upon her face for a minute or two. Then, bearing no more malice than a fountain, she would begin again.

In fact, if one came to examine it, she summed up everything that Sophia had previously disapproved. *My love is of a birth as rare.* . . . She hummed the verse softly to herself, fitting it to the tune of the Old Hundredth which she had lately been intoning in the rue Monge . . . which was a good place to sing in, for at midday the men from the tanneries came out for a snack and a stroll, in spite of the stink of hides she felt a friendliness to the neighbourhood. The sun was shining, the flavour of the beer she had drunk floated agreeably over her singing thirst, in this shabby merry quarter of Paris the prevalent republican shabbiness could be forgotten. And however shabby, cautious, and downcast, Paris was the Paris of May. Wherever one looked there was a demonstration of green, a tree, a lilac-bush with its heart-shaped petals falling back as though in admiration from the spikes of blossom, a trail of vine leaves dangling from the farther side of some courtyard arch, looped there between the shadow and the sun, playing their trick of green stained-glass and tracery. The houses with their pale dirty faces had the vivacious appearance of town children. This one was trimmed with lemon colour, that with blue, beyond the arabesqued façade of the wineshop was the sober nut-coloured door of the watchmaker. All his clocks were ticking, but one could scarcely hear them for the song of the canaries caged in the first-floor window under the scroll saying *Midwife.* From the watchmaker's darted a very small kitten, prancing sideways on stiff legs. Sophia stooped to caress it, and noticed that attached to the tartan ribbon round its neck was a tin medal dedicating it to the care of the Virgin and Saint Joseph. But it escaped from her hand and capered on towards the butcher's shop where a woman wearing a claret-coloured shawl stood conversing with the grey-haired proprietress over whose solid bosom and heliotrope gown was tied a muffler of the brightest acid-blue.

In the air was a smell mingled of woodsmoke, wine, coffee, garlic, horsedung, and beeswax. A dray left standing blocked the entrance to the rue de la Carabine, the other vehicles went round it with shouts, insults, and the clatter of hooves, beneath it a white hen moved to and fro, pecking at the chaff which lay among the cobbles. And beyond this, and, so it seemed to her, in some way belonging to it, like a demesne, like a park, curved the stately river, stood the avenues, the statues, the palaces of the other Paris, where the grandees strolled in their silk and their broadcloth. There too, universal as the bland voluminous white clouds overhead, were those volumes of greenery, the clipped and bulging alleys, the volleys of green shot from courtyard and soaring above blank walls. Everywhere this brag of green seemed like an assurance, a consenting signal wagged to her from every quarter of Paris, that it was May, that she was, for the first time in her life, intensely happy, and that she should be so.

In the rue de la Carabine, as though stored there as in a reservoir, her passion of happiness seemed to burst upon her a hundredfold. In one of Minna's windows stood the potted rosebush, and it seemed to her that a rose had come out since the morning; from another swelled the houri-like curves of the feather bed. Catching her breath she dived into the dark entry, ran up the twirling stairs.

Minna had company. Some one was strumming a guitar. The company, as Minna's company so often did, had brought its little luggage with it—a small and cheap valise.

The company turned round at her entrance, dropped the

guitar, and forestalling Minna's speech of introduction, ran towards her with a cry of joy, and was Caspar.

He had changed almost beyond recognition : to her conscience, accusingly changed. He was lanky and overgrown ; his clothes would have been too small for him if they had not given at every seam. His hair had been vilely chopped, and had outgrown the chopping in grotesque tufts and drakes-tails ; his knuckles were discoloured, his nails were broken, one of his teeth had been knocked out, the dusky grape-like bloom which had sat on his skin had been rubbed off, leaving nothing but a sallow complexion with spots. Only his honeyed voice and his rolling eyes declared him to be the Caspar who had played so prettily with Damian and Augusta, ridden the bay mare, confounded the rector, enchanted the house with his presence and antagonised all the servants.

'It is a romance,' said Minna, 'how this child has come to us ! '

Caspar's rough paws stroked her skirts, he was kissing her hand with his dried lips. Behind him, anxious and moved, stroking her breast, stood Minna. That gesture, hand reassuring heart, those looks of embarrassment and tenderness, it was easy to know on whose account they were. Not for the poor blackamoor, starved and travel-stained ; but for her who had dismissed him to such a state, and for her to whom his trust in her had brought him.

'I would not be so vile now,' she murmured.

It was as though Minna received the words only with her eyes. But as they were spoken the twining fingers lay still, the look was of tenderness unmixed.

'Such adventures,' continued Minna, 'such homing-pigeon adventures! He came over in a fishing boat, and for the rest of the way he has walked or had lifts in waggons.'

Impossible to tell how much of this statement as to the behaviour of homing-pigeons was genuine, was dexterity. And the grimace which followed the speech told nothing either.

'From Cornwall? O Caspar, what a long, long journey.'

'From Cornwall. And from Blandamer too. I went there first, after I had run away from the Academy. For I had to leave the Academy,' he added swaggering. 'It was no place for my father's son.'

'Blandamer! Did they look after you properly, did Saunders——'

'There was no one there. The house was shut up.'

'*No one there?*'

'No! Not a soul. I went to the door, I went to all the doors. I could not look in at the windows, the shutters were up. There was no sound, no smoke from the chimneys—and yet it looked as though the house had people in it, for in the rubbish-pit there were fresh potato peelings, quite new cinders. I stayed a long time—I was tired—looking at the house. Then I went to the stables. They were empty too, but the smell of horses was still there. I walked about the garden, the kitchen garden, pulling up spring onions and young carrots and eating them. And I picked a bunch of flowers, to put on Damian and Augusta's grave. Then I heard a shout, and a dog barking, and there was the gardener and Pilot. Pilot knew me, and jumped on me. And I asked the gardener where you were, and he said you were in France with Mr Willoughby, and that two days before an order had come from Mr Willoughby that the house was to be shut up, and the servants dismissed, and everything taken away. He had come up, he said, just to walk round and keep an eye on things. But everything in the hot-houses would die, your flowers and the nectarines. And he said it was unfortunate that I had come just then.'

(And Frederick could shut up her house, dismiss her servants.)

' Did Brewster look after you ? '

' Yes, he took me to his sisters in the village. And they both said, What was to be done with me, and they must write to you. But when I had got your address I came away. It was melancholy staying there. They did nothing but sigh and wonder. And Pilot did nothing but scratch. He has got a skin disease.'

' What address did they give you ? '

' 16, Place Bellechasse. But they sent me on here. They stared at me, I can tell you.'

' They ? '

' Célestin and Madeleine.'

He pulled out a crumpled cigarette and lit it. That ruined young hand still kept some of its intuitive airs and graces ; and leaning back on the pink sofa, pouting his lips in an attempt to blow smoke-rings, he showed still through his ungainliness some of the old suavity of movement. Every way debauched, she thought ; his softness gone to a mess, like a bruised lettuce. Those tatters of childishness, of self-confident grace, had survived only to become somehow morbid and disquieting, just as it was disquieting to see those eyelashes, their silk unimpaired, flourishing in that jaded sickly countenance.

To Minna she said,

'It is my fault that he is like this. I should not have sent him to that place. But you cannot expect me to like him any better because of that.'

'He wants food and sleep, then he will be all right. Food, and sleep, and a little luxury—some scented hair-oil—and a quiet wholesome life.'

'Will he get that with us, Minna?'

'Certainly. My dear, I assure you, after two or three days of soap and water you will find him as loveable as ever.'

'Soap and oil him as you please. You won't get rid of that look, that—that unhealthy look. As if he'd curdled.'

'His blood is poor. He wants water-cress and spinach and a tisane of young nut-leaves.'

'Tisane of dog-grass!

'The truth is—' she burst out—'I am jealous, already.'

'But it is *you*. It is you he adores.'

'Jealous of him. Jealous because he takes up your time, jealous because he is in our way. It is intolerable to me, when I think how rude I have been about your lame dogs, about your poor Claras and your Macgusties, that I should be the one to encumber you with the lamest dog of all.'

Minna spoke truly. All Caspar's love, all his solicitous adulation, was for Sophia. Taking it for granted that Minna should wait on him hand and foot, feed him, groom him, tune the guitar for him, he would leap out of his cushions to pick up Sophia's handkerchief or fold her shawl. In her presence, he wheedled, postured, strutted, charmed—and all the while his black eyes watched her with humble desperate anxiety. For all her nonconcurrence, his conversation attached itself to subjects wherein she might be magnified : the splendour of Blandamer, the beauty of Damian and Augusta, the immensity of her bereavement. Even the Trebennick Academy he suppled into a compliment—exclaiming on the audacity of a Mr Gulliver who could so ill-use the ward of such a patroness, or picturing how Mr Gulliver would grovel before the wrath of that patroness aroused.

All his wits had been bruised out of him, his one idea was to please and he had no ideas as to how it should be done. If she snubbed him he only redoubled his flatteries, and borrowing money from Minna went out to buy propitiating gifts—stale flowers, bad sweets, execrable gimcrack ornaments with their exorbitant price tickets still proudly dangling from them—for he was always cheated.

To their visitors he was invariably rude, loftily chattering in his snatched-up slangy French about the glories of Blandamer, the beauty of Damian and Augusta, the condescension of their mother in living in the rue de la Carabine. Because they had no room for him he slept with the Cotons. Every night he woke bitterly weeping from dreams of the Trebennick Academy. Madame Coton, hugging him in her scrawny arms, comforting him against her yellow flannel bedgown, deepened her grudge against the English and warned him to beware of the Jewess.

It was not until he had made ten days miserable that Sophia came to her senses and remembered Uncle Julius Rathbone. The shock of emerging from her state of muddle

and fury into common sense was so great that she could not
contain herself until morning.

' Minna ! Minna ! I have just realised that I am a fool.'

' No, no ! ' With a soothing murmur, with a warm un-
certainly aimed caress, Minna would have sidled back into
sleep.

' A flat damned fool. That boy has got a father.'

' Yes, you told me. So did he. In the West Indies. But
the West Indies '—her voice indicated the utmost limits of
space—' are a long way off.'

If it were possible, her yawn propelled them even farther.

' And it is his money that pays for Caspar, not mine.
Frederick cannot possibly lay claim to that.'

In the darkness there was a majestic and cat-like stir :
Minna rousing, reassembling her pillows, propping herself to
sit up and attend. The body that by day was heavy, ill-
framed and faintly grotesque, at night achieved an extra-
ordinary harmoniousness with its bed, became in suavity and
sober resilience the sister of that exemplary mattress.

' Well ? No, wait a moment ! I think I must have a
biscuit. Well ? '

' So that all we need do is to find somewhere to put him,
and have the bills sent to Frederick. Uncle Julius sends over
a remittance twice a year, the money's in the bank at this
moment. And Frederick spending it, no doubt. My God,
what a fool I've been ! '

' Where would you put him ? '

' In a school. A boarding-school. There must be plenty
in the suburbs. To-morrow I will go out and find one.
Uncle Julius only stipulated that the school should give a

commercial education. One can get that in any language, I imagine.'

' Wouldn't a day-school be better ? '

' And have him back here every evening ? Dangling round our heels and being rude to your friends ? Eat another biscuit, you aren't properly awake, you don't understand what this means. Think how happy we were before he arrived, think how glad we shall be to be rid of him.'

' But you should consult your uncle.'

' I'll write to him, of course, and say what I've done. But there is no need to wait, he gave me *carte blanche*. All he wants is for Caspar to be at school. No ! Uncle Julius would be the last person to keep the boy hanging on our petticoat tails.'

' Rather than send that child as he is now to another school I would let him sell newspapers, run errands for the wineshop, apprentice him to any trade—*any* trade.'

' A sound commercial education, in fact. Unfortunately, his father wants him schooled. And anyhow, in this flourishing republic no trade can afford apprentices.'

' Poor child ! '

' Tiresome cub ! '

' So unhappy in one school that he runs away. To you. And now you put him in another.'

' Minna. Apart from the fact that we don't want him and can't afford him, can you seriously maintain that Caspar is benefiting by his stay with us ? '

' Better than a school.'

Sophia leaped up in a fury.

' I shall write to Uncle Julius *now*.'

The letter took a little while to compose. She was in the mood, trembling with midnight and angry excitement, to dash off something incisive and eloquent, it was irritating to have to choose words carefully, compose a prudent epistle which would skirt round the facts that Caspar had run away from the Trebennick Academy, that she had run away from Frederick. And darkening over this was her wrath against Minna, her indigation that this solution of the problem of Caspar should be so grudgingly, so doubtfully received.

Signing the letter, laying down the pen, she looked sulkily in front of her. Over the writing-table hung a mirror, and there she saw reflected the half-open door into the bedroom, and Minna candle-lit in bed. Her hand had just conveyed another biscuit to her mouth. Her eyes were full of tears and she was munching slowly. Seeing that face, melancholy and gluttonous, Sophia forgot the anger of the one who is in the wrong. Her whole being was ravaged with love and tenderness. Still holding the pen she sat and stared into the mirror, beholding as though for a first and a last time the creature who, but a few paces away, hung in the mirror as though in the innocence of a different world.

She felt an intricate repentance. That jibe against the republic was a hit below the belt : not by any fair means would Minna's resources of tongue and temper be so easily put out of action. On this she now heaped the equally illegitimate assault of love. Nevertheless, when the morning came she excused herself from hymn-singing, looked up a number of suburban schools in a directory, arrayed herself in the remains of her best clothes and set out to find another Trebennick Academy.

In one thing she had reckoned without her host. For though there were any number of obliging establishments, cheap, suitable, ruralised with vines and acacias, and yet not too far beyond the Barriers, not one of these would receive a pupil on the strength of her appearance and word only. There must be money paid down.

'These troubled days,' said Professor Jaricot, 'these menacing horizons, destroy that confidence which is at once so typical of civilisation and so necessary to it. No one regrets this more than I.'

His parlour, so tidy, so bare, so polished, so lofty and so shady—for the window was screened with another of those vines—reverberated the noise of three blue-bottles circling high above his bald head. Modulating through their conversation came a heavenly smell of onion soup, a solid middle-class proclamation that though May weather, wafts of lilac, tilted summer parasols, cooing of doves, beckoning of blossomed trees, were all very well, yet the stomach demanded more of midday than flowers and flowery exhalations and the squeak of shears snipping suburban lawns to a neat edge.

My God, she thought, how hungry I am. I could lie down and fawn for a bowl of that soup, for a day of this assured middle-class comfort and sober repletion. So much emotion in the middle of the night, so much activity since, had made her indeed appallingly hungry. And while Professor Jaricot continued to expatiate on the political situation, explaining how his fatherly heart grieved for those whose most sensitive years must be exposed to an epoch so tumultuous and subversive, she passed her handkerchief across her lips to conceal the languishing yawns of appetite.

These Englishwomen, thought he, sprinkling a few parting reverences on her retreating flounces, how shameless they are! One would say that she had no maternal feeling, no warmth at all. And yet she had had an illegitimate child by a negro. Strange! Strange of the negro, too. Sophia's type of beauty had no appeal for Professor Jaricot, so little impression had it made on him in their first encounter that he did not recognise her as the hymn-singing beggar to whom, in an irresistible impulse of sentiment, he had given a five centime bit. And as Professor Jaricot's type of beauty had no appeal for Sophia either, they parted in ignorance that they had met before.

Money must be paid down. Well, there was nothing else for it. Frederick who was responsible, must be invoked.

'It would be surer, it would be far less painful, to write to your lawyer.'

'It would be much slower. And now that I have made up my mind to get Caspar off my hands, and now that you have made up your mind to disagree with me, the sooner it is settled the better. Besides, Minna, Caspar is not so utterly to be pitied. If you had smelled that soup . . .'

'Smelled that soup? I have smelled it a thousand times! There is scarcely a city in Europe where I have not smelled that persuasive, that fatal soup. What is it made of?—ledgers, prayer-books, dividends, death-sentences, the bones of the poor, the flesh of the young, the tears of prisoners, mouldy bread and black beans; and when it is scummed and cleared and flavoured they serve it up in a plated soup tureen. And you hankered for it. Shameful!'

'A good nourishing soup—not a metaphor in it. And,

Minna—Can you look at those people there and tell me that they too are not hankering for Professor Jaricot's soup, that a bondage to a regular dinner would not mean a great deal more to them than the liberation of Poland?'

A straggling procession of demonstrators was moving slowly down the street. The cross-traffic halted them, and the outmost man heard Sophia's words. He turned towards her a placard which he was carrying. Scrawled on it in large characters were the words, *Bread or Lead*.

'As you say, Madame.'

His voice was dry and fatigued, the voice of a schoolmaster nearing the end of a lesson. Hunger had painted him of any age, but he was probably young. He had small adder-coloured eyes, pungently bright.

'A regular dinner, soup without metaphors. That is what the workers want, is it not? The ten-hour day, two francs a day from the National Workshops, the blessing of Marie and a little organisation from Thomas—that is a prospect to keep them peaceable, eh?'

'Two francs?' said Sophia.

'If there *is* work, naturally. We are told that perhaps, in time, with organisation, with the good-heartedness of employers, there may even be work every other day.'

'I cannot understand,' she exclaimed, 'why there is no work. For though an old lady and her spiritual director in the Faubourg St Germain assured me that the republic was doomed to ruin because no one would have sufficient confidence to buy jewellery or have their window-boxes repainted, I cannot be ninny enough to believe *that*. Work! The paving of this street alone and the repair of these houses should be enough to employ a hundred men. And the city has got to go on, hasn't it?—people be fed, and clothed, whether it is a republic or a kingdom?'

She spoke excitedly, forgetting that she was addressing a perfect stranger; it seemed to her that this wry fellow with the adder-coloured eyes was the sort of person she wanted to question, and that she could get from him tougher answers than Minna's circle could supply. For though it is no affair of mine, she said to herself, yet here I am in the middle of this vaunted republic which is so obviously going wrong; and at least I might know why.

'However, your friends in the Faubourg St Germain might have given you an inkling,' he said. 'They assured you that the republic was doomed to ruin—that is to say, they meant to ruin it. They were even frank enough to inform you how they meant to bring that ruin about. Really, Madame, for an Englishwoman, reared at the very hearth of political economy, you have been a little dense.'

While he was speaking the procession had been released, and moved on, he with it. It went the faster for having been stemmed, she had some ado to keep up with him, hauling Minna along with her.

'But their trumpery patronage, their twopenny-halfpenny effect on trade—what difference can that make? And anyhow, they must still buy essentials, they must still buy bread.'

'So must others, with shallower purses . . . (*Bread or Lead*,' he shouted, displaying his placard). 'Have you never heard of a lock-out, Madame? It is a simple enough system. There is a difference of opinion between the workers and their employer, and the employer says, in effect, Since I can afford to go without my profits longer than you can afford to go without your wages I will close the manufactory until such time as hunger shall compel you to agree with me. The employing class, not only of France but of Europe, the investors, the manufacturers, the middlemen, the banks, the officials, mislike the republic. And so they are using the lock-out against it.'

' Charmingly clear, is it not ? ' said the boy beyond him, gazing on Sophia with fatherly interest. Not even want had dimmed his good-hearted impertinence, he was one of those Gallic radishes like the porter who had so much pleased her at Calais. Suddenly she recollected the man who had drawn on the wall, the tree, hung with dimpled fruits of the Orléans dynasty, the working-man whose axe was laid to its root, and the crowd, giggles rising through their intent excitement like bubbles rising through wine. Joy was it in that dawn to be alive. She also had been pleased with herself that morning, rocking on her toes with the sense of an adventure before her ; and her adventure too had miscarried very oddly.

' Yes, I know about lock-outs. It is a device often used in England. But are you going to stand it ? ' she enquired.

' No ! ' said the man.

' No,' said Minna beside her—a thoughtful echo.

' Decision is a great deal,' pondered Sophia. ' But not quite sufficient. I should think you would do well to get rid of some of your ridiculous leaders, for a start.'

' That idea has occurred to us also, as it happens. The more so, since we do not consider them our leaders. At first, our go-betweens; and now, for some time, our betrayers.'

Léocadie to the life, she thought, tingling with an odd sort of pleasure at the rap of his snub.

' And so . . . ? '

Before she could finish the question the boy cried out with a brisk cock-a-doodling voice,

' Bread or lead ! '

His voice, so young and impudent, uttering those grim words, fetched from Minna a sudden sigh, a tightening of the hand ; and from a Civil Guard who was sourly prowling on the edge of the march, a shouted admonishment to hold his tongue or it would be the worse for him. Other voices took up the cry, the Civil Guard flushed angrily among his whiskers.

Pitching her voice carefully, aiming it to travel under the uproar, Sophia asked,

' Have you got the lead ? '

He turned and gave her a full glance of those pungent eyes—long, searching, and ruthless. Then, suddenly casting aside his schoolmaster's voice for the twang of the gutter, he replied,

' That's telling, ain't it ? '

The glance, leaving her, discarded her too. They slackened step, dawdled to watch the rest of the demonstration go by, remembered that they must purchase salami. Not till some time had gone by did Minna remark,

' Did you know you were talking to a Communist ? '

' Of course.'

Grabbing the end of that advantage, she added,

' And, Minna—How did you know ? '

' Oh, as you did.   By the way he spoke.'

' Yes.   He reminded me of Ingelbrecht.   So—so lucid.'

' You are lucid too, Sophia.   You always know your own mind.   It is one of your qualities that most delights me.'

The affable mendacity of this tilted Sophia's thoughts back to the question of Caspar, of how soon he could be deposited with Professor Jaricot and Minna's delight given full scope.   The sooner the better, undoubtedly.   It was a dubious deed, all her dealings with that luckless mulatto were shoddy enough.   But testing, as it were, the resilience of her conscience, she knew that once he was out of the way, and the dubious transaction signed and delivered as her act and deed, she would be able to forget about it, and go forward with enough impetus to carry the gainsaying Minna with her.

Only the method, then, remained to be settled.   Discreetest, most dignified, would be to write to Mr Wilcox, sitting, the soul of dignity and discretion, behind his green-shaded windows, his copper-plated brass name-plate, his Georgian housefront, demurely set back a pace or two from the narrow Dorchester street.   There he sat, among his documentary band-boxes, his few quiet spiders ; and sometimes his eyes, so round and clear and empty of expression that they seemed very much akin to his bald forehead, might rest on the deed-box where *Aspen* in white letters had been cancelled with a line and *Willoughby* painted below.   Discreetest, most dignified course.   Unfortunately it would also be the slowest.

At the other extreme was an appeal to that Willoughby who had cancelled her Aspen.   And mid-way, just where she would be, agile and timeless trimmer, was great-aunt Léocadie, who would, no doubt, welcome any opportunity to display her mediating talents, do another little family job. One would show oneself a swine before a pearl not to invoke Léocadie at this juncture.

The decision was speeded-up by Caspar's greeting, and his news that during their absence a wretched Jew—a Jew with a hump-back, moreover—had come to the door, enquiring for Minna, but had been routed by Caspar's assurance that there were no old clothes for sale to-day.

His eyes of black velvet travelled from Sophia's rigidly unobserving face to the bunch of lilies of the valley arranged on the table, and piteously back again.

'What lovely lilies! I smelled them the moment I came in. Did you get them, Caspar? Are they for us?'

'I got them for Mrs Willoughby.'

Slowly turning herself from Caspar to Sophia, Minna lifted her shoulders, displayed her emptied hands with the gesture of the advocate whose best plea for his client is the admission that there is nothing to be said for him.

With a sensation that the cat was cajoling on behalf of its kitten and that she did not like cats, Sophia carried the salami into the kitchen. She pulled open the little safe and scrutinised a platter. Yes, exactly! The kitten thieved, into the bargain.

'This brat must go, and soon,' she murmured, raging, slicing the salami with the deftness of fury. 'If I am to be driven into counting anchovies! . . .

'And of course he's hungry,' she added, whisking dry the lettuces, mounting on the wings of her fury into the further aether of fair-mindedness. 'We've not had a respectable meal for a week, no wonder he has to filch anchovies. What he needs is that reliable onion soup. He shall have it.'

So great-aunt Léocadie was dismissed with Mr Wilcox. Those mediating talents of hers might withhold the Caspar claim until some favourable moment, when one was that age time was nothing to one, ripeness, all. Moreover, a demand transmitted through her to Frederick might afford Frederick a good excuse for pretending it had never reached him. Frederick should be directly approached; and since so much depended on it, the treaty letter should be inoffensively, reasonably, tactfully constructed.

It was difficult to write tactful letters from a heart pounding with fury, from a stomach whose void was only taunted by scraps of salami and a flourish of salad, and to the accompaniment of a woman of generous disposition and great dramatic talent teaching an over-excited boy how to dance a bolero and click his own stimulus from castanets. Seven drafts were composed, and pensively corrected, and wholeheartedly torn up.

'Are you going out, Sophia?'

'Yes. To the Catacombs. For a little peace and quiet.'

'To the Catacombs? Where all the skeletons are? Oh, Mrs Willoughby, may I come too? You promised I should see the Catacombs.'

Minna, putting away the castanets, said maternally,

'Unfortunately the Catacombs are always shut on the second Thursday of May. For spring-cleaning. But I will ask Monsieur Macgusty to take you there to-morrow.'

It was not till the evening, when Caspar had retired to the

flannel bosom of Madame Coton, there to be comforted and warned afresh against the Jewess, that she had time to say,

'I have decided that the best thing to do is to write a tactful letter to Frederick. Here it is.'

Minna read it, with the attention, part solicitous, part admiring, which she gave to all Sophia's doings.

'Yes, it is tactful. Perhaps it is a little like a tactful proclamation. But then the grand manner suits you—and it is certainly tactful.'

'But yet you disapprove?'

'No. No, I don't disapprove.'

'You disapprove sentimentally, you think he will be unhappy?'

'Not more unhappy than he is here. And to be candid, I must consider my own happiness also, and I find the poor little wretch a great burden, and we do nothing but fall out about him. . . . I have no wish to keep him, God knows.'

'Minna, what is it?'

She wrinkled her broad forehead, drooped her lower lip, put on a look sulky and innocent, the look of an animal driven towards the bloody smell of the slaughterhouse.

'A misgiving, Sophia. An intuition, a feeling that this is something we shall have to regret. Do you never have such feelings?'

'Often. Constantly. But I have never found them come to anything.'

She knew she was lying. She had never known an intuition in her life, blundering unwarned from one mischance to another.

' And when I have analysed them they have always turned out to be colds coming on or a change in the weather.'

' *Enfin !* '   Minna rose.   ' What will be, will be.'

As though these time-worn words were a sort of music her body yielded, melted itself like the snake's heavy coils beginning to shimmer with movement at the sound of the Indian's flute.   Leaning her cheek on her clasped hands she began to revolve about the room in a waltz, staring down at the floor, vaguely smiling.   The air still pulsated with the heat of the long day, the scent of Caspar's cheap dying lilies filled the room.

' When I remember that you have always been like this, and that I have only known you for the last three months I could bite off my fingers.'

Minna did not answer.   But now, as she revolved, her wide-open black eyes floated their glance upon Sophia, and wisely, pensively, she nodded her head.

IV

To the letter that might also have been a proclamation Frederick replied with a letter that was all, and no more than, a letter should be. He quite agreed that since Caspar had found his way to Paris, Professor Jaricot's was the place for him. He was sure that in choosing Professor Jaricot's establishment Sophia had chosen the best possible establishment, and only regretted that she should have been put to the inconvenience—an inconvenience which he would gladly have spared her—of hunting it out. He had paid all the necessary fees in advance. And since it seemed probable that Caspar would be the better of a new outfit before departing (the sooner the better, no doubt) he proposed calling at the rue de la Carabine on Monday, a little before noon, to take Caspar out to lunch and then on to the tailors and the hairdresser. And he was, bridging an awkward passage, hers to a cinder, as the Yankees say, and really it is exceptionally hot for this time of year, Frederick.

' Beautifully curled, isn't it ? Especially that little frizz of the tongs just at the end,' said Sophia, handing over the letter. On this unfortunate matter of Frederick she would allow no subterfuge, no vulgar discretion.

Minna read the letter without comment. Her caution, the way in which, the letter finished, she refolded it and laid it down without once raising her eyelids or wavering from her air of melancholy self-control suddenly irritated Sophia. It was the look Minna had worn on the night of the twenty-

third of February, pinned against the doorway in the boule-
vard des Capucines. Then it had been that affair of Gaston
and the dray. Now it was Frederick. That look, that
plaintive scapegoat air of oppression accepted, of accusations
meekly unanswered, Minna sheltered behind it whenever
she felt a situation becoming awkward. And according to
Sophia's view of the situation, these retreats were melting or
infuriating.

'Isn't it?' she repeated sharply.

The eyelids flew up, as though the voice had shaken them.

'I've a letter too, a—a delightful letter. It's from a lawyer
in Rouen, saying that I have been left a little property.

'Very small,' she added hastily. 'A small farm. Think!
Fancy me a landed proprietor.'

'Who left it to you?'

'An old gentleman.'

'How very grateful of him!'

'As a matter of fact,' said Minna, colouring furiously,
bouncing to her feet with a stamp, 'he was one of the few
people I haven't lain with. So there!'

She swept into a flood of tears, and simultaneously Caspar
and Wlodomir Macgusty entered the room, exclaiming that
the Catacombs had been memorable, had been great fun.

'Min-na!' exclaimed Macgusty, bounding across the room
between one syllable and the next, throwing down his hat
and falling on one knee beside the pink sofa. 'Minna!
Unfortunate child, what distresses you? What catastrophe
is this? Why do you weep?'

Fumbling in his pocket he drew out a paper bag of sweets
and a small flask of smelling-salts. 'I use them myself,' he

said persuasively, holding the smelling-salts to Minna's eye.

Caspar sniggered.

' Heartless boy ! Fresh from the Catacombs you laugh at human woe. Can nothing move you ? '

'. I can,' said Sophia, pushing Caspar out of the room and shutting the door on him. It seemed to her that she would have given a fortune to remain on the farther side of the door herself. But on second thoughts nothing, except to explode, would have been adequate, so she stalked back to the sofa again and stood looking down on Minna's heaving shoulders, on Wlodomir's waving paws.

Shifting distractedly from knee to knee, drawing long breaths of smelling-salts and offering the flask again to Minna, he continued to implore her to share her griefs with him, to exclaim that sorrow was sacred, to ask why she wept and to suggest various good reasons why she should do so. Suddenly, out of this tumult and flurry, Sophia became aware that Minna was looking at her with one eye, an eye streaming with tears but at the same time bright with intelligence. Then the handkerchief covered it and there was another interval of tears and entreaties. At last, with a long, increasingly determined snuffle, Minna emerged from the entreaties and said,

' I weep for a benefactor, Wlodomir. For a good old man.'

' Well may you weep then. They are few,' answered he sympathetically.

' I had almost forgotten him,' continued Minna. ' For one grows heartless as one grows old.'

' No, no ! '

' Lately I have not even asked myself if he was dead or

alive. Now I learn that he is dead. A lawyer's letter tells
me, cold and formal. He is dead. But with a better heart
than mine, he remembered me, and has left me a legacy.'

Her head was raised, her eyes fixed on the cornice. She
was well off on the concerto now.

Oh, you baggage, you audacity! cried out Sophia's heart
in admiration.

' A small farm,' she said, feeling that there was now some-
thing for her to say. Do as she would, she could not prevent
a note of congratulation and approval creeping into the words.
Two glances were shot at her from the sofa—Wlodomir's a
glance of reprobation towards such a mercenary frame of
mind, Minna's a flash of intimate gratitude, triumph, and trust.
Presently, with the lavishness of the virtuoso, Minna had
played another trick and so modulated the situation that it
was Wlodomir who needed comfort and soothing; and the
balm for his sensitive feelings, still quivering from the shock
of another's woe, turned out to be lemonade, biscuits, de-
scriptions of the old gentleman, speculations about the farm,
and praise of country life in general. They were all picking
buttercups and daisies and making cream cheeses (and here
Sophia with her practical experience of country life could be
most usefully invoked) before Caspar occurred to any of their
recollections. As usual he had gone to Madame Coton.
But it was agreed that he should make one in the excursion to
Treilles—a name already so much a place to them that each
speaker had a mind's-eye view of it, Minna and Wlodomir
already at a misunderstanding over poplars and willow-trees,
and Sophia privately deciding that the pig-sties must be
reroofed.

The farm, a small-holding really, since only one family worked it, was occupied ; and for many years had brought in a rent of 700 francs. As for old Daniel Boileau, he visited it twice a year, in order to collect the rent, and for the rest lived in a hotel in Rouen, making notes for a book which was to prove that the Jews were the great impediment to civilisation. It had been a tract preliminary on this subject which had sent a younger and more impassioned Minna (so she said, pensively folding and refolding a sopping handkerchief) to visit the old Sisera. He had been delighted with her pleading, and perfectly unconvinced by her arguments, a balance of mind, he remarked, impossible to any Jew, lop-sided with monotheism ; and at parting he had presented her with the pseudo-Watteau which still hung on the wall.

This account of the benefactor was rather astringent to the veneration which Wlodomir was prepared to feel for the shade of the departed. He hurried back into his willows again, and planted some rustic graves there, an orphan or two, a weeping widow. Death, he said, in a country churchyard, seemed a different, a humaner thing. Minna must keep a green enclosure in her mind wherein to inhume the thought of the late Daniel Boileau, and shed there only tranquil tears. And with renewed entreaties that she should only weep tranquilly he took his leave, promising to supply, against the excursion, some very superior pâté, made by a wonderful old woman who lived, quite unsuspected by epicures, in the rue de la Roquette.

' As if I didn't know his wonderful old women and his wonderful old wineshops,' said Minna. ' They stew their own bones, and bottle . . . Sophia ! '

Sophia's back was turned, she was examining Daniel Boileau's Watteau. It was a pretty, a harmless fake, plump cat-faced music-makers under autumnal trees. Such gilding poisoned no gingerbread, fell off as easily, as naturally, as the trees' brief gold.

'When I saw that ridiculous Macgusty,' she said, still staring into the picture, 'I began to be ashamed of myself. He keeps a perpetual cistern of pumped-up feeling, one has only to turn the tap and it flows by force of gravity. I don't propose to let loose any more jealousy. I suspect it of being pumped-up, too. Much better to play away on our fiddles, since we shall all be dead so soon.'

She turned from the picture to Minna, who stood behind her, pale and tear-stained, her eyes blackening as though with fear.

'*So soon*. I do not know how you can say it so calmly. Whether I die first or survive you, I lose you.'

'I haven't any feeling of immortality whatsoever, have you?'

'Not for years. When I was a child, perhaps. Sometimes I think that those who die young may have immortality, but it perishes in us long before we are thirty.'

'My father used to say that the younger the rabbit, the longer it kicked and leaped after it had been shot dead. That is about as much immortality as we can presume on, I suppose. Does it grieve you?'

'Bitterly!'

She spoke in a voice passionately unreconciled.

'But why is death so much in your mind to-day? Because of Daniel Boileau?'

' No, no ! He is well out of it. No. Because of a hundred things which touch us more nearly. Because of this.'

Out of her reticule she pulled a small crumpled note, written on a slip of paper with a printed heading.

' It was handed to me in the street yesterday, while you were out singing. I have kept it back all this time, but you must see it, there's no escape.'

The heading said, *The Alpine Laundry. 29, rue Javotte. Proprietress Madame Amélie Goulet. All branches of fine laundry-work, moderate terms, bag-wash and gentlemen's shirts a speciality.* Under this was written, in pale commercial ink, ' If your friend will call at this establishment on Monday morning about 10.30, and enquire for Mademoiselle Martin, she will learn if we have the alternative to bread.'

While she was still knitting her brows over this, Minna took the paper from her and tore it up.

' The man who said, *Bread or Lead.* Don't you remember him ? '

' But . . . but why should he write to *me* ? And from a laundry ? And why *should* he write to me ? He doesn't suppose I am a Communist, does he ? '

' I really can't say, my dearest. But it seems unlikely.'

' Well, then, why does he send this extraordinary invitation ? Is he mad ? '

' It doesn't read like the letter of a madman.'

' Minna, you know a great deal more about this than you let on about. I can see you do. A mystery is a mouse to you, and you've put on your cat-face. Now tell me how long you've known this fellow.'

'I don't know him. I've seen him, and heard him speak. But I have never exchanged a word with him.'

'Where did you see him?'

'With Ingelbrecht. It was in March, about a fortnight before I met you at the fountain. That was one reason why I was so terribly unhappy then. I could not forget his words, and I could not deny their truth. But with every word he rent all the beliefs I had, made all my enthusiasm for liberty seem a paper garland, and my idea of a republic a child's Utopia, a house built on a quicksand.'

'But Communists are all for liberty and republics.'

'Not of my kind, Sophia.'

'And so he gave you this note?'

'No, not he. The boy who was with him. He was in the rue de la Carabine with a handcart, collecting rags and bones and bottles and old iron—every sort of rubbish—when I went out to do some errands yesterday. And he gave me a handbill, and this with it. Then he went on with his barrow, down the street.'

'But why should I be the one to receive this invitation?'

'I don't know. I say to myself, Because I love you, and so, with every movement I make I must be bound to endanger you; stab you if I fasten your brooch, poison you if I cook for you, offer you a death-warrant if I show you this. Already I have lost you your money, your world, your friends——'

'I never had any.'

'—hauled you down into this shabby Bohemia, which is all I have to offer you now, where you go hungry, wear holes in your slippers, sing in the streets——'

' I have never been so happy in my life and you know it.'

' —and now, seeing you happy, knowing that in spite of my fatal influence you have never been so happy in your life, now, it seems to me that I am doomed to direct you and your happiness towards what must endanger it, what may endanger you. That is what I say to myself, Sophia. But if you ask me for a reasonable answer as to why you should be invited to the Alpine Laundry, then I am at a loss.'

' I like your unreasonable answers much better. I hope you have a *quid pro quo* preference for my reasonable questions. For I must ask you, Minna, what there is so very hazardous about a Communist? What do you know about them ? '

' Scarcely anything. Nobody does. But I know they are dangerous, deadly.'

' But why? Why more deadly than any of the other species in your menagerie ? '

' There are so few of them. Ten here—another ten there— saying so little but all saying the same thing. So few of them. And all knowing their own mind. And all of them dead in earnest. There must be death,' she cried out vehemently, ' in any such earnestness !

' Look at Ingelbrecht,' she continued, lowering her voice to a whisper. ' So tranquil, so bald, so resolute. How he goes his own way, keeps his own counsel ! When I meet him in the street I feel as though I had met the nose of a steel screw, boring up through the pavement from underground. Think of all the prisons he's bored his way out of. Though I have not dreaded *him* on your account, I knew he didn't want you. But this one . . .'

'Minna.   Do you ask me not to go?'

She paused, shook her head.

'No.   I make it a rule never to impose my will on other people.   Besides, to turn you back now, when we both anticipate so much . . . we should die of a galloping curiosity.   And from the moment I read this, I knew it was a destiny.'

It was not till some while later that it occurred to them that Sophia might not have returned from the laundry before Frederick called for Caspar.

'Never mind.'   Minna spoke soothingly.   'At least it will spare him the anguish of seeing us together.'

'I suppose he hopes to worm a good deal out of Caspar.'

'Of course.   Why else should he trouble to take him out to lunch?   Has that only just occurred to you?   I saw that at once, I meant to point it out, but then my sorrow for poor Daniel drove it from my mind.   Yes, he will get a lot out of Caspar.   Who we see, who we don't see, if we quarrel, how much we have to eat, if we wear each other's petticoats, etc.   Frederick likes domestic details.   I have never met a man of good breeding who didn't.   Whereas your Martin— Caspar could pipe to him all day about the holes in our stockings and never get an encouraging word.'

'Oh, well, he can pipe and be damned.'

'Yes, isn't it a comfort to feel that we are not going to do anything about it?—that one can't do anything about it?   Such serenity!   One feels like the angels in heaven or poor Monsieur Thomas being kidnapped in his cab.'

The abduction of that functionary was still news, and to a certain extent, comic relief.   Hardening towards the prospect of a much greater degree of violence, the mind of Paris saw in the fate of M. Thomas the rather insignificant horseplay of the clowns who only open the circus—unless one took the view of Égisippe Coton, who said in a tone of gloomy longing, ' It might happen to any one of us now.' Raoul, who piqued himself on the sensitive ear which he turned to the demands of their public, had indeed suggested to Sophia that the hymns might be dropped in favour of *Partant pour la Syrie*, and anything she knew about exiles ; but this change of programme did nothing to improve their takings, which were now steadily diminishing.

' Why can't you come on Monday, Sophia ? ' he asked. ' I always consider Monday one of our favourable days, and for this Monday I was working out . . .'

She shook her head, firmly binding up her plaits, her mouth full of hairpins.

' Why don't you take Minna for a change ? '

' No ! Minna is a collector's piece now. She's lost any knack she may have had for street-work. In another ten years, yes. Then she would be magnificent as a crone, as a destitute grandmother reduced to hawking improper albums. But for the moment Minna is decidedly between-tides.'

' How old is Minna ? ' she said.

' God knows !—the old Medusa ! '

How odd, she thought, walking homeward, that I felt no impulse to knock him down and dance on him. It is unlike me to be so reasonable. Nor was there any baseness in my question, however loudly my upbringing must shout to me that such questions are base. It was a practical question. For if Minna is—is old, then I ought to know it. Towards the old, the ageing, one observes a certain line of conduct. One respects them, defers to them, spares them. Translated into action, this entails not contradicting them, concealing from them one's private opinions and seeing to it that they sit in the easiest chairs. On this last count, at any rate, she had nothing to reproach herself with. Suavely as any cat Minna always planted herself in the best chair—unless she reposed on the floor; and though dividing the food with scrupulous equity, if there happened to be any unclaimed *bonne bouche* she would crunch it up with the greatest goodwill, mop up the sauce with bread, with thoughtful greed lick out the dish.

Suavely as any cat. Even cats age, though so imperceptibly that no one agrees on the natural span of a cat's life, some saying ten, some twelve, some a score of years. But age and die they do, dying of heart-failure, dying in their sleep before the kitchen embers as a ripe apple falls on a windless afternoon, or throwing themselves down exhausted, after a rat-hunt through the barton, never to rise up and hunt again. For all their nine lives, their guardian cunning and their whiskers, the wariest, the sleekest cats grow old and die. Or of a sudden, in their practised prime, a sore on the neck will make them peevish with life, they will turn from their food, exploit their wholesome talent of vomiting, spew up in the end nothing but froth and slime, sit gasping for breath with their blackened gaze fixed on some familiar piece of furniture as though, at long last, they recognised in it the furtive enemy of a lifetime, the unmasked foe.

'I can be sick whenever I please,' was Minna's boast. 'Like a cat, Sophia.'

After all, one need not wait for age—how long was it since she, turning from the imitation Watteau, had spoken so seriously with Minna about death, speaking as though under its shadow? But they had spoken together, with every admission re-establishing their liveliness, their power to speak, hear, communicate. It is one thing to speak of death with those one loves; but to think of it alone, walking through the streets, one does that at a different temperature.

Speaking of death had led them to speak about Martin and the Communists. Now she was thinking again of death, and every step of her thought went with a step leading her towards the Alpine Laundry. She had left Minna at her most exasperating: plunged into a martyrdom of domesticity, counting and darning Caspar's underclothes, washing his handkerchiefs, gloomily bruising her fingers in an attempt to hammer the heel more firmly on his boot. Over her shoulders, despite the heat of the day, she had pinned a little shawl, unbecomingly too skimpy for them. From her ears dangled a pair of disgustingly meagre and lack-lustre jet ear-rings, ear-rings which, since they had never appeared there before, it was tempting to suppose had been borrowed from Madame Coton—that soul of sour domestic virtues—for dressing this particular part.

And all this, as Sophia knew quite well, was because not Minna but she had been bidden so mysteriously to visit the Alpine Laundry. Thither she could go, flourishing her heels, the child of good fortune, destiny's pet. Whereas Minna, the daylong labourer in the vineyard, Minna the nursing-mother of revolutions, must stay at home, devoting her slighted talents to Caspar's socks. In this mood Frederick would find her.   Then God help Frederick !

She was immoderately early for her appointment, Minna's grand renunciation had begun with the smarting punctuality of any attack at dawn, and despite the muddle which her efficiency bred on every hand it had been impossible not to leave the rue de la Carabine at least half an hour too soon. She leaned her elbows on the parapet of the bridge, staring at the barges below her, watching with approval a man who came out of a cabin with a little mat, and shook out its dust into the river. It was obvious that such a man kept house alone.

A hundred times she had injured Minna intentionally, dealt shamelessly blows below the belt, cuffed her vanity, trapped her into the wrong, trampled over her wishes and her principles—and all without a pang. Now, when really for no fault of hers, Minna was thrusting her breast against the thorns of wounded vanity, and caterwauling beyond the powers of any impassioned nightingale, she must feel her heart, wrung with sympathy and a conviction of guilt, cry out, ' The poor angel ! ' But long, long ago, she had thrown her reason into this river flowing beneath her—perhaps even on that winter's afternoon when crossing from the other bank to visit great-aunt Léocadie she had wished that she could hold Madame Lemuel beneath the cold flood until she came up gasping, and having revised her metaphors.

Meanwhile, whatever might or might not comfort Minna, to turn back from the Alpine Laundry certainly would not do so.

Thanks to Minna, who knew her way through Paris very

much as a mongrel might, she had her directions. But now, staring at the decrepit fortress of the Marais, it seemed to her that she would never disentangle her way thither. But why did the word fortress come to mind? Rat's Castle rather—a quarter even more entangled, tattered, secretive of everything except stinks, than that which lay behind her. They did not even look historical, those tall jostling house-blocks, with their stooping gables and crooked roofs. They were past mark of mouth.

'If I stay here much longer,' she said to herself, ' I shall begin to feel courageous.'

This she had determined not to feel. And with a last glance at the river's clear highway she set forward for the Alpine Laundry.

Before she found it she had grown sufficiently accustomed to the Rat's Castle to be observing the prices of the food on the open shop-counters, and thinking that this would be an even more advantageous place to shop than the rue Mouffetard. The language of the country too was extraordinarily grand, never had she read such lofty sentences in cookshop windows nor seen such flowery recommendations of wine and butter. It was as though they had picked their phrases from the second-hand shops, she thought, running her eye over a dusty interior where chairs and gilded bedposts in the grandest manner struggled pell-mell with broken mangles, gaping concertinas, old mattresses and odd coffee-cups. It was from shops like these that Minna liked a fairing. But it would be better to take her something clean ; and from a shoemaker's window she selected a pair of magnificent slippers, made of spotted crimson plush and trimmed with sparkling tinfoil Cupids. Each slipper cost rather more than the result of a morning of song, and she was, as she agreed with the woman who sold them, highly favoured to buy such slippers so cheap.

This transaction emptied her of time as well as of money. Reaching the Alpine Laundry, a hasty glance told her no more of the exterior than that it was painted blue and white, that the paint was thin but well-scrubbed, that in the window two highly gauffered infant's long petticoats flanked a man's shirt, whose starched arms extended towards the baby-clothes as though in a gesture of family affection.

Inside also the little office was all that honest poverty should be—well-scrubbed, orderly, a chastened senti-mentality manifesting itself in a vase of marguerites on the counter. The air had the bitter-sweet almond tang of starch, and behind a glass-panelled door the top part of some piece of machinery rose slowly, and dropped, and rose and dropped again, and with every rise and fall there was a sighing whistle and a gush of water released.

The woman sitting behind the counter was making-up accounts. Her thick red fingers held the pen clumsily, her right hand was ink-stained. As Sophia entered the shop she glanced up with a look at once placid and earnest, and it was obvious that she was holding a thread of addition in her mind.

' *Vous désirez, Madame*——? '

Sophia spoke her wish. The woman made a little tick on the column of her addition, noted a sum on the blotting-paper, rose and opened the door, calling for Mademoiselle Martin.

' This lady wishes to inspect the laundry.'

Mademoiselle Martin was lame, she threw out her hip as she walked, and with each halting step a cordlike muscle stood out in her neck. Her eyes were dark and beady, her face was pinched, dutiful, and industrious. Her arms below her rolled-up sleeves were extraordinarily full and muscular.

Behind the glass-panelled door there was only whitewash and scabby iron for the blue and white paint of the office. There was a great deal of steam, the squelch of wet clothes, the hissing of irons. Four women were at work, their faces shining with sweat, their skirts bunched round their hips. Moving on pattens over the wet floor they seemed in their bunched white pinafores like the creatures of some queer aviary. They looked at Sophia no more mysteriously than any other washerwomen might, good-dayed her in affable voices.

Limping beside her, glancing up sometimes with her beady mouse's eyes, Mademoiselle Martin showed off to Sophia the washing tubs, the mechanical pump, the mangles, the stove where the irons stood heating, the racks of clean linen. Sophia asked questions, examined, approved; and in the moist heat of the workroom her ears sang, her heart pounded.

'One moment, Victoire.'

The woman at the heavy ironing-block stood aside. Thrusting with her strong arms, Mademoiselle Martin swung back the ironing-block; and there was a hole in the floor, a dark square, the tips of two iron uprights just showing.

'If you will go down the ladder—' she said. 'It is quite easy. Nine rungs. No one will observe you from below.'

I am glad it is so decent, thought Sophia, holding on to the uprights, feeling the well-oiled darkness overhead move back into place again. Still, I should like to have some idea of what to expect next.

Rats, said reason promptly.

Standing in the darkness at the foot of the ladder, snuffing up the natural mouldy smell of cellar and with it a queer, a Spanish-Inquisition-like tang of red-hot pokers, waiting for her senses to reassemble themselves, her eyes to gather patches of dusk from patches of darkness, her ears to disentangle the rats below from the clatter of the laundry, the far-off continuing whine and gush of water overhead, it was extraordinary to remember that in this position she was wearing a bonnet, a still quite ladylike bonnet.

' Though really,' she said to the rats, ' there is nothing extraordinary about it. Considering the matter rationally, it would be more remarkable if I were not wearing a bonnet.'

' True,' said a voice, the same voice which had cried *Bread or Lead.* And at the same moment she heard a door open and close behind her.

' I am sorry to have kept you waiting. I was delayed for a moment. But there was no wish to be dramatic, we are not freemasons.'

' I don't like drama either.'

' If you will step this way? Can you see better now? There is nothing to trip over, no steps.'

His voice was brittle and businesslike. In the darkness she remembered those bright adder-coloured eyes.

' You do trust me? '

For answer he pulled open a door, stood back for her to enter.

The cellar was lit by a couple of oil lanterns. It was an

old wine-cellar, its walls were arcaded for casks, but in the niches where the casks had been were heaps of scrap-metal, old fire-irons, pots and kettles, a bird-cage, chains and bolts, broken tools, lengths of piping, clock-weights and trivets. Against one wall where a gas-pipe ran there was a roughly set-up bench, and on this, tapping the gas-supply, were half a dozen little tubed stands, each with its gas-jet hissing and flaring. Over these they were melting down the lead, like so many intent toffee-makers. The table was strewn with moulds, tools, neat little heaps of bullets and ball. For all that it was crowded and makeshift, it was orderly. And the look of a busy kitchen was enforced by the bottles of cheap wine, the assemblages of food, which stood here and there on the bench.

Other workers were squatting on the floor, sorting the scrap, sawing it up for melting. They were of all ages, as many women as men, and their intent and weary expressions gave her the impression that they were all of the same cast of features, that, however long she stayed and looked at them, she would not be able to distinguish between one and another, carry away with her the recollection of any face that was not a composite face.

The gas-jets flared against this general colouring of drab and dusky with the imperious hue of another element ; and over all the room hovered the taint of metal smoke. In this lighting, pale faces, red hands, seemed alike livid and unreal. Glancing back at Martin she saw that his face wore the stamp of all the other faces, was intent and weary, and insignificant.

Catching her eye, ' Our bakery,' he said, with a little bow. ' I hope you will give us your custom.'

The quip sounded hollow and conscientious. It was clear that he had thought of it some time before, had decided to say it, had forgotten it till this moment when it bolted from his lips. No one laughed. The moulders, the men squatting on the floor, went on with their work, still cutting her dead.

How awful for him, she thought. He has got me here, God knows why, and now he doesn't know how to get rid of me.

And she felt a profound uneasiness, a painful sense of guilt. It seemed terrible to her that this man, so resilient and peremptory, should stand there looking awkward, making jokes that fell flat. For the first time in her life she found no comfort in her sense of the ridiculous. For nearly a week she had been thinking, on and off, of Martin, and always thinking highly of him, more and more highly. Now the bubble was to be pricked; and it was as though she awaited the end of a world.

Well, there was no use in hanging about, waiting to be assured that he was a weakling, just like all the other people in this revolution. She must say something tactful, tactful and feminine, and get away as soon as possible.

'I understand why your young friend goes round with a rag-and-bone barrow.'

'Yes. But it is not a perfect method. The scrap has to be paid for—and we have other things to buy, things that must be bought. Besides, he has to accept a lot of other rubbish, that is inconvenient too.'

'I know. Whatever one wants, one always has to accept a great deal of rubbish along with it.'

'How strong are you?' he asked. 'Could you carry that basket there?'

It was astonishingly weighty. As she lifted it she saw a woman turn from her work and watch her superciliously. Mettled, she gave herself more carefully to balancing the basket, walked across the cellar with it, and had the pleasure of seeing the woman's expression change to surprise.

'In your quarter,' he continued, 'there must be a great deal of scrap lying about. A bit picked up here, a bit there—between the two of you in a week you could collect a passable deal.'

He watched her silence.

'I don't see why you shouldn't change your laundry. The Alpine Laundry does excellent work.

'Don't carry too much to begin with,' he recommended. 'And don't let Madame Lemuel accompany you. She would probably wish to tie a handkerchief over her head and walk barefoot. That sort of thing would estrange the other clients of the laundry.'

Meanwhile she was still holding the basket of scrap, and on her hand the veins were standing out blue and swollen. The set indifference of her countenance, too, was rapidly turning into a glare. Now he took the basket from her, saying, 'Don't attempt to carry as much as that. You don't want chivalrous strangers offering to help you.'

'When shall I come?' she said.

'As soon as you please. But come regularly. And wrap up the stuff so that it doesn't clatter. And call for the clean clothes four days later. We will leave you to supply your own basket.'

'Thank you,' she said, already with the sourness of the conscript.

' Thank *you*. I assure you, you will be doing us a considerable service. We are abominably short of helpers, or it would not have occurred to me to ask you.'

' I understand. Now I think I had better go. I don't want to waste your time.'

' I will see you up the ladder.'

His tone was bland, he was working like a well-oiled machine, smoothly, swiftly, powerfully.

As long as you never make another joke—she said to herself. At the foot of the ladder, ' What shall I do at the top ? ' she enquired childishly.

' They're waiting for you,' he said. ' Nine rungs.'

And he was politely removing himself from her ankles when she demanded,

' Do you all come up and down this ladder ? '

' Good Lord, no ! '

The trap swung open, the smell of steam, the whistle and gush of the pump, came about her once more. Mademoiselle Martin brushed her skirts down, looked over them attentively for any cobwebs or filings.

' I have decided to bring my linen to your laundry. Will you please tell the proprietress ? '

' I am so glad,' answered Mademoiselle Martin. ' If you will leave the linen with Madame Goulet in the shop she will see to it.'

In the office she looked at the clock (her watch had been pawned some while since). It was eleven—there was time to get back to the rue de la Carabine before Frederick should arrive. But instead she went and sat in the church of St Paul, trying, among the shuffling Masses, the in-and-out of worshippers, to settle her thoughts. Instead, she fell asleep, and did not get to the rue de la Carabine until well after midday.

But though her thoughts were unsettled still, sleep had perfectly tidied up her sensations. And there was no affectation, only a genuine tactlessness, in the calm with which she walked in and said,

'Well, I have had a very interesting morning.'

'And a nice cup of tea? For pity's sake, Sophia, do ruffle your hair a little. Frederick has only just gone, spare me any more English phlegm.'

'How is he?'

'Oh, very sleek. Very manly, too. He didn't bring any flowers this time, not for either of us. But I shouldn't be surprised if he sends us each a magnanimous shawl. The way he let his eyes stray round this room, Sophia . . . the hole in the sofa, the hole in my stocking, the patches on the wall where the trophies were—every glance a fig-leaf.'

'Is that why you brought in the sausage-paper and left it on the table?'

'Yes. But I got into my best clothes before he arrived, except the stockings, he interrupted me there. But I wore gloves all through the interview. I hope you think I look well?—And do you see how beautifully I've polished the mirror and the chairs? Well, in he came, and pretended to be sorry to miss seeing you, but really he was immensely relieved. And, Sophia! He's a Bonapartist now.'

'No doubt that will make a great difference to Europe. Has he changed his hatter too?'

'No, you're wrong. It's more significant than that. People like Frederick, people who are perfectly secure and never do anything, never range themselves on one side or another, are good guessers. Just as when you are very rich you always win in the lottery. I don't like it at all, Frederick being a Bonapartist.'

'Minna. Does it never occur to you that I am one of those people who never do anything, never range themselves on one side or another?'

'No. If you were, you would never have been so angry on the night of the twenty-third of February.'

It was the first time either of them had spoken of that night, tact, sometimes, or prudence, at other times the inattention which happiness has for its past, turning away their talk from the subject.

'I was angry with you, disillusioned with you.'

'Not only with me. For you have forgiven me, but you have never forgiven the Revolution. If you were one of those people who never take sides, it would have been all one to you whether that volley was stage-managed or no.'

'Should it have been?'

Minna's hands washed themselves.

'How can I answer? How can one tell? But I can assure you that those Communists you have been among would not hesitate at much more drastic dealings. Tell me, what did Martin say, what happened?'

'He asked me to change my laundry. And to collect bits of old iron we found lying about.'

'Oh! For ammunition!'

In her exclamation was excitement, pleasure at the device, pride at so instantly unriddling it; and at the same time an after-sigh of resignation, despairing acceptance.

' So it will come to that.'

She rose, walked about the room, went to the window and stared out as though already there were blood on the cobbles. Then she came back, took Sophia's hand, kissed her gravely.

' You have not asked what I said to his suggestion.'

' I need not, my dear. It is exactly what would suit you, it is practical, arduous, and rather dangerous. What intuition he has, that Martin ! '

She walked about again, sighing, shaking her head. Then she put on her bonnet, took down the shopping bag.

' What do you want, where are you going ? '

' To look for scrap iron. I seem to remember an old bell-pull that some children were playing with in the square.'

' You can't do it in broad daylight.'

Minna winked. ' Can't I ? When I was young I could have stolen the hem off your petticoat.'

Thieving did Minna a great deal of good. She began to resume those sleek and sumptuous airs which she had worn as by right on the evening when Sophia first arrived at the rue de la Carabine, but since then only fitfully and incompletely. My poor darling, thought Sophia, I must have been constraining her to respectability without knowing it—all this time she has been pining in my bleak northern climate. For it seemed to her that Minna was thieving for theft's sake, and with very little attention to the claims of the Alpine Laundry; and sometimes she speculated on the odd concatenation between Minna's beaming delight over some especially neat filch and the end appointed for these unconsidered trifles—their billet in limb or heart or brain.

She thought too, seeing Minna thieve with such industry

and *savoir-faire*, that there had been no justification for that taunt about walking barefoot and tying on a handkerchief, for Minna's technique was essentially serious.   However, she went alone twice a week to carry their gains to the Alpine Laundry, grinning to herself as she remembered all those little ministering Christians of the goody-goody books, the Misses Lucy and Emily Fairchild visiting a deserving tenantry with a basket of viands and bibles, trimly covered over with a white towel.

The deserving tenantry were not up to tradition.   However well-laden the basket it was received with a flat impervious civility, and without a word said the woman behind the desk made it clear to her that, the load deposited, the next thing for her to do was to get away immediately. It was only on her third visit that Madame Amélie Goulet looked up with anything like a smile of acquaintanceship, and feared that she must find walking in such heat fatiguing.

'What I don't like is being stared at.   You seem to live in a very observant street.'

'I am so sorry,' said Madame Goulet, as though she would have it put right in the next wash.   'The truth is, to be so tall, and if I may say it, so elegant, must make one somewhat conspicuous.   In this quarter, we do not see many ladies. And to be patronised by a lady so clearly a lady is a most convincing proof of the respectability of my establishment. One can see at a glance that you would not be connected with anything—with anything unusual.'

'But is it not unusual for ladies to carry their own washing?'

' One can see, too, that you are English. It is well known that English ladies are energetic.'

And not a word of thanks, thought Sophia on the way back, furtively rubbing an aching arm—just to be told that one is conspicuous and eccentric, and that that will do nicely. My God, how patronising they are !

Still irate, she retailed this interview to Minna. Minna listened in silence, looked properly awed and pained—perhaps a trifle too much so, but then she was always pitching herself to an imaginary gallery.

' And she said that you looked respectable !—that any one could see you would have nothing to do with low Communists ! No, that is going too far. I don't wonder that you are annoyed.

' By the way,' she added rapidly. ' You remember Égisippe handing out the dog-chains ? No doubt he has more—he would not empty himself at one gush, our Égisippe. To-night I mean to explore downstairs. I shall probably walk in my sleep.'

However worthless and neglected other people's property might be there was no doubt that she preferred it to her own. Letters, increasingly long and noble, came from the lawyer in Rouen, but Sophia had to answer them, frowning over the complications of legal terms in another language, sourly quoting to herself, ' But mine own vineyard have I not kept.' For it seemed to her shameful and ridiculous that she should be taking so much trouble over Minna's affairs, and writing so painstakingly to Minna's lawyer whilst, in all this lapse of time, she had not written to her own Mr Wilcox to enquire how much income, if any, Frederick's assumption of the

husband had left her; but for all that, she still could not
bring herself to that letter, still too fastidiously furious to
risk Mr Wilcox's polite confirmation of Frederick's slap in
the face.

How Ingelbrecht would scorn me, she thought. Here am
I, hanging round pawnshops, sponging on Minna, living
from hand to mouth—and all because I have not the moral
courage to write to Mr Wilcox. Her state was the more
pressing since she went out singing no longer. Raoul had
said there was no money in it, things must wait until he had
another good idea. And it seemed to her that if Ingelbrecht
were to appear he would read at one glance her slatternly
shame, and that no amount of well-doing in the old-iron
business would exculpate her.

He had not visited them for some time—not since Caspar
had left them. Apart from her private guilt she could have
wished with all her heart that he would come soon, for he
might be able to make Minna take her legacy seriously. To
Sophia it seemed that a property, however small, however
worthless, was a thing to attend to. Its few acres should be
walked over with thoughts of crop rotation and manure, its
fences examined, its barn ascertained to be rat-proof and
rain-proof. 'If you will do nothing,' she exclaimed, 'I shall
have to go there myself.' Minna replied by forecasting the
pleasures of a first visit together, the wild flowers, the swallows
building their nests, young lambs, wild strawberries, etc.
While she was in this frame of mind the visit might as well
be postponed. A few injudicious warblings on the beauties
of nature to a tenant-farmer might set back the rent for a
quarter.

So she held her tongue for another few days, or only used it to supply assents to Minna's fancy sketches of lambs bounding in the hayfield. When next she gave herself to the serious duty of looking after one's property, she got the answer,

'I wonder if I need go yet. You see, I have talked about it so much, that if we were to go there and find everything as dreadful as you say it will be, pigs dying and the roof falling in, it would be more than I could bear. Perhaps it would be better never to go there at all, but just to take the rent and keep it as a beautiful dream.'

Ingelbrecht was what she needed. Perhaps he thought that Caspar was still with them, a thought which might well keep him away. Surely he would have heard from some one? But whom? For lately they had been singularly unvisited, even Wlodomir Macgusty had come but once, and then—so now it struck her—with a rather forgiving and magnanimous air.

Now that the thought was in her head, it would not out. They were being dropped. In any other society poverty would have been explanation enough, but here the excuse would not run. Minna's rapscallionly circle would not leave a board because it had grown bare. And what else they can find to object to, she said to herself, God knows. They are all so outrageously broadminded.

It was broadminded of her, too, to be fretting like this. How often, formerly, her wishes had swept the room clear of them, silenced their chatter ! They were Minna's friends, not hers, except for Ingelbrecht she would miss little if she never set eyes on them again. They were Minna's friends. And now that the thought was in her head and would not out, she knew she must do something about it. Maybe a little decisiveness here would serve to drape over that continued indecision over Mr Wilcox. When any one does turn up, she determined, I will somehow manage to speak about it.

No one turned up. Then, from the window seeing Dury in the street, she was ready to repent her determination, for no one could be more obdurate to a tactful handling than Dury. But he walked past the door and went on into the wineshop further down.

Snatching up an excuse she descended in chase of him, ran him to earth. It seemed to her that his answer to her greeting was unwilling, and that he looked at her with antagonism.

'It is a long while since we have seen you. I am afraid that tiresome Caspar was enough to keep any of our friends away.'

'He wasn't so bad.'

'He's gone now, you know.'

'Yes, I know.'

Staring at her with solemn dislike and disapproval, he said,

'We think it a pity that you sent him into the Gardes Mobiles.'

'Into the . . . ?' She stopped, and remained with her mouth open as this neat piece of trickery by Frederick unfolded itself before her. Two francs a day and keep in the Gardes Mobiles was certainly a better bargain than paying fees to Monsieur Jaricot.

She felt rage flooding her face with scarlet. To gloss things over she ordered a bottle of wine which cost more

than the money in her purse. Her bonnet's term of credit
was long ago ended, and she had to counter-order it for a
cheaper bottle. Turning, she found the bovine young man
still breathing on the back of her neck. Imperious with loss
of temper she planted the bottle in his hands and marched out
of the wineshop.

Would he think it a gift and walk off with it? But he
followed her in silence to the entry, to the foot of the stairs.

His face was a great deal redder than hers as she took
back the bottle.

'It was a pardonable mistake. Raoul saw him among them,
in full fig. It seemed a serious pity, at such a time as this.'

'And so you all instantly believed it?'

'The air is full of mistrust, every one's nerves are on
edge. . . .'

'It is a pity you are all so idle,' she remarked, thinking of
the old-iron trade.

'That's true.'

But at that moment his busy eye was at work on her, his
attention wandering among the tubes in his palette box.
From the landing above she called down, forgivingly,

'I arranged for him to go to a boarding-school.'

One by one they came back, a little sheepish some of them,
at their first entrance, soon rehabilitated by Minna's un-
suspicious greetings. For Sophia had kept her own counsel,
even about Caspar and the Gardes Mobiles, sucking her paws
in silence over this. One and another, they all reappeared,
except Ingelbrecht. And since Minna had no suspicion, and
all the rest of them were coming as usual, Sophia could remark
in safety,

' It's a long while since Ingelbrecht's been here. I wonder where he is.'

' Buried himself,' was the answer.

No sooner were they back than Sophia began to curse herself for a marplot—for the worst of marplots; for it was her own plot she had marred. During that unvisited interval she had begun to build up a sort of daily routine, as though the constitution of her relationship with Minna needed an iron tincture which routine would supply. With horror she saw them lost, those habits of the two sprigged coffee-cups on the table by the window, the clock set by the compline bell, the paired plates and glasses that her hand could with certainty take down from the shelf and replace there.

Trained all her life long to look upon order and regularity as convenient, in the last few months she had come to regard them with an almost mystical admiration—and in this change of aspect perspective might have played a part, since to live with Minna swept order and regularity far away. But her plot had gone beyond the pleasure of regular coffee-cups and a reliable timepiece, and it was with more than the disapprobation of a character naturally orderly and precise that she saw it marred. Habit, method, the facets of a daily routine, she had been amassing them against the menace of that day when everything would fall to pieces, when the roof of the waiting-room would fall in.

So, quite unreasonably, she had taken hold of her regular visits to the Alpine Laundry as a reassurance against the impending ruin of that queer existence in which she knew such happiness; and while carrying material for that next revolution which must explode beneath their feet had found comfort because she carried it twice weekly. Like a hen, she told herself, like a silly hen walking along a chalked line. And yet, though it was destruction she served, it was a purposed destruction, something foreseen and deliberated; and here, if she could only get herself into the well-scrubbed fortress of the Alpine Laundry, become one of those Communists instead of an eccentric Englishwoman carrying a laundry-basket, might be a safety for the mind.

So, blindly and desperately, she had begun to build up that routine of coffee-cups and clock-setting, fastening these cobweb exactitudes round Minna like a first scaffolding of something that time (but there could not be much more time) might stiffen into a defence.

With the return of Minna's friends, the cobweb fortifications broke. They came back more distracting than ever, those friends, more filled with rumours, theories and counter-theories. Macgusty had grown very militaristic. War, he said in his melancholy, piping voice, a war of liberation, must be the next step. The people must put on their might and liberate Ireland. As he declaimed he glanced at Sophia with fury, and added that the English aristocracy should yet tremble before Smith O'Brien. In another corner of the room Raoul was babbling about a congress of arts, pavilions of industry constructed in a gothic manner of glass and iron to be erected in the Champ de Mars. For demonstrations of civilisation, he said, must be the weapons of a civilised republic, and the setting-up and subsequent demolition of the pavilions would supply the unemployed with labour and livelihood.

' And who will visit your pavilions ? ' enquired Macgusty.

'Who will inspect your inglorious machinery, your demonstration of a servile tutelage to commerce?'

'Not the Irish!' shouted Raoul. 'They can keep out of it for all I care. France for the French!'

The lovers of France, the lovers of mankind, joined in a furious quarrel, and were hauled out of it by a newcomer announcing that not only were the workless to be drafted to the wastes of the Sologne, but that the Government had framed a scheme for shipping unemployed builders and paviors to Corsica, to erect fortifications. Their wives and children would accompany them, and rear silkworms.

Now into the most outrageous rumours and theories the question of the workless penetrated, and those words, *Bread or Lead*, clanged through every conversation. Sophia found herself believing, arguing, theorising, with the rest. The spreading madness had infected her, even while scorning the disputes of the nostrum cheap-jacks she beat her brains for some panacea of her own. If only Ingelbrecht would come, or if she could see Martin again! Neither of them had said a word, she recalled, of panaceas; they had laid bare causes only; but in the certainty of that analysis there had been a promise of some remedy they could and would apply. Minna, presumably more case-hardened, sat among her noisy visitors saying little, preserving that air of inspiration which she could always radiate in company. And when she poured out coffee and carried round the dish of cherries she seemed to be dispensing something so much more actual than the substance of those she nourished that it was as though, gravely and pityingly, she dispensed an All Souls' Night meal to a tribe of ghosts.

More and more clearly, during those summer evenings, shone out her air of technique, of being a professional amongst amateurs. They, quarrelsome and excited, waited in all the fidgets of stage-fright for the rising of a curtain. She, uncommunicatively tranquil, sat wearily in an attitude that, for all her weariness, was from long learning both stately and as comfortable as circumstances would permit; nor was it possible to guess from her demeanour if she were going over her lines, or holding a mental roll-call of her greasepaints.

Had it not been for love and love's lack of faith, Sophia might have drawn from Minna the reassurance she longed to get from Martin or Ingelbrecht; and while others were present Minna's spell, her infallible sense of when to speak and how to move, stayed her. But as soon as they were left alone, solicitude undermined the stately idol, and Minna was once again a creature to ward and think for.

Since it was impossible to guess where safety lay, speaking of danger was idle. They continued to collect their scraps of metal, enjoy the green peas and wood-strawberries that the season had brought into the scope of their means, and discuss the management of Minna's property.

For a while that property had seemed to Sophia the way to safety. She set herself to encourage Minna's peculiar views on country life and to repress her own. Yes, there would be young lambs bounding in the hayfields, nightingales singing in a greengage tree, a vine-shaded dairy, sheets coarse but lavendered, a gnatless willow bower by a brook. Yes, there would be beehives, and nothing is easier than taking the honey. Everything would be as in Minna's childhood, only cleaner, greener, more fertile.

Nothing came of these conversations save more conversations. She was trying a new line of approach, speaking of the neglect of roofs, the disrepair of fences, the inordinate negligence and inordinate demands of tenant-farmers, and feeling rather more sanguine as to the effect of it until the hunchback, Guitermann, walked in one evening.

It was some time since they had seen him, and in the interval he had changed a great deal. Just as the flesh had wasted from his bones it had wasted from his manner. . . . Aloof, with glittering eyes, he stared at the company, speaking little, haughtily rebuffing all attempts to draw him into the talk. It was his flouted music, she guessed, working in him, frustrated and corroding; and she recognised the authenticity of the talent by the authenticity of the rage. When he did speak, it was with sneers and bitterness, and the coughing-fits that followed were like defiant cock-crowings. With a herd animosity the others put him in Coventry, patently rallying round Minna as though to protect her from such a guest.

So general a manifestation of dislike must needs include Sophia also, for now she was definitely unpopular among Minna's friends. There was nothing for it but to talk to Guitermann, and she did so, wishing with all her heart that she had never given buns to any one so capable of resentment, or at any rate that he would not recollect the buns.

'How do you think Minna looks?'

'Badly,' said he. 'Dulled and stupefied.'

Blinking under this, she spoke of country air, Minna's legacy, the project of a visit of inspection.

'I suppose you like the country. Minna would not. An

assault of clod-hoppers, rural conversation about the culture of beetroot and the swine disease would be the last blow to her talent. Who would she find to talk to, in the country ? '

' Minna's talent is in herself, not in her listeners,' she answered.

' Talent ! ' he exclaimed bitterly.

Hunting her wits for a tolerable subject for conversation she could find not one. So she told him how Caspar, sent to a school, had joined the Gardes Mobiles.

But later in the evening he had sought her out, saying, his manner furious as before, but coloured with concern and a kind of despairing trust,

' Don't let Minna go into the country. It's too dangerous.'

' Why ?   How ? '

' The peasants may rise at any moment—a counter-revolution. They are enraged against any one from Paris, any one suspected of liberal ideas. None of us dare say it, but it's true. Here, at any rate, she would have some friends. In the country, none.'

' When do you think it will happen, the next outbreak ? '

' At any moment, now. Perhaps even while I am still alive.'

His youth, grandiose and dramatic, flowered in those words. As he went out it seemed as though his deformity were too great a weight for those threadbare limbs to carry, those wounded lungs to lift. She had seen too many of her tenant's children die in a galloping consumption to have any doubts as to his ending.

From that night she said no more of country pleasures or cheating tenants. Whether she blew from the east or the west, her words had made little impression. A property in Normandy was not so real to Minna as a forest and a heath in Lithuania. Of them she spoke inexhaustibly, able to recall every hour of her childhood.

For now, just when Sophia had trampled out her last illusion of anything to be gained through routine, Dury was actually making his picture of them, a canvas long debated and long postponed. It was easier to paint in summer, he said. Living was cheaper then, it was possible to buy all the paints one needed. The picture, which he persisted in referring to as *Mes Odalisques*, was in truth to be called A Conversation between Two Women. His design seated them upon the pink sofa, their backs to the window. Sophia must listen, hers was a countenance most characteristic in attention. Minna, to give her something to listen to, must talk.

It was curious to sit there in the charmed circle of his watchfulness, hearing the breeze fluttering the curtains, the living noises of the street reared up to them. There was a kind of precarious immortality in this studied repose, and his painter's aloofness quickened the sense of being for an hour's forever in another world. Minna, inexhaustibly recounting, telling with all her art of incidents grotesque or intimidating, piteous or indecent, might have been a bird singing for all the notice he took of her words ; and across her narrative would fall his short commands for the redressing of her head's tilt, the loosening of Sophia's hands that the course of the narrative had tautened one against the other, his murmured blasphemies, or the thoughtful click of his tongue against the roof of his mouth. What his painting left of him was rudimentary. It was as though one overheard the monologue of a small boy, of an exceedingly stupid and exceedingly self-satisfied small boy, who was spending an afternoon fishing with a bent pin or possibly catching frogs and tearing them in pieces. This scum of words, slowly rising from the simmering of his intent, and Minna's idle noble flow of narrative mixed in Sophia's hearing, and touched as though with a bodily impact her sensations of chill and languor and stiffness.

To sit still and listen—this was a child's part. Towards the end of each sitting a profound self-pity would overcome her, a sentiment of weakness and dependence. Like a religious sentiment, she supposed. The religious, who trust in a God, who lie in His hands and never stir themselves to question the future or combat it, must feel so . . . a shameful and a shameless emotion. But still this meek melancholy, this quietism, would well up in her like the rising of a pure tepid water ; and through all the irk of her body her spirit clung, lamenting and satisfied, to these hours of precarious immortality, islanded on the pink sofa.

Out of these sojourns in immortality she would come weakened, even more inept for speech or decisive thinking. To-morrow, bringing nearer a revolution with all its God-knows-what of what would happen then, would bring another sitting.

Every afternoon Dury lugged off his canvas. They were not to see it, he would have no comments muddying his own view of it. And having dreamed of the finished canvas, the dream persisted in Sophia's mind, so that her unscrutinised thoughts beheld it as it had been in the dream : a picture of two swans floating on a pink lake.

It had grown very hot. An acrid dust flew in the streets, drains and gutters stank, windows open on the street level showed summer vistas of tumbled beds, fading salad in basins, women sweating in camisoles. Marketing was no pleasure now. The midsummer richness of the wares was sullied by town conditions into stickiness and greasiness, buyers and sellers looked at each other with the unglossed antagonism of the war to live, or exchanged bad money and bad bargains in a lethargic truce.

There were more crowds in the streets but there was less talking; and the decree against out-door assemblies kept the people in a dreary purposeless trudging. Through their sullen to-and-fro the sharp squawk and rattle of the Gardes Mobiles, parading to music, cut like a vinegared knife. It was said that in the politer quarters the Gardes were cheered and fêted. Among the workers one needed an extra dose of sentimentality to have any feeling other than annoyance, and the vague dread that ageing or wearied flesh feels for youth in the mass, for these prancing youngsters.

Twice it seemed to Sophia that she recognised Caspar. And this was likely enough, since Frederick would most probably have deposited him in some Left Bank detachment. But an angry unwillingness kept her from looking too closely, for this was another of Frederick's lucky cannons, and she was in no mood now to appreciate such.

With a stale sense of ignominy she had at length written to Mr Wilcox, enquiring how her finances stood. Whatever was to befall, lack of money would make it worse. She expected the answer any day, and hoped in her heart that it would not come. Whatever the answer, it must establish her as a fool. A fool to hope anything; a fool not to have written before, and saved herself the discomfort of a needless penury. Above all, a fool to know so little of what had been for so long her own affairs that Frederick could put her, or gull her, into this state.

And he had stolen that five-pound note out of her dressing-case, too. To think that there had ever been a time (four months ago, no more) when five pounds was merely a fitting in a dressing-case, like a nail-file or an eyebrow tweezer! Now she hesitated over a twopenny nosegay, thinking how soon the flowers would die, thinking shame to herself for such thoughts. That fancy about the 'good old-gentlemanly vice' was bidding fast to grow into a fact, and the return of Minna's useless eating guests made the husbanding of their money even more pressing. At midsummer, she supposed, there should be some rent from Treilles, and midsummer was near, now; but till the money was in Minna's hands (and how soon out of them again?) she must walk by flower-baskets and toyshops. Passing the shop where she had bought the slippers trimmed with tin Cupids she shook her head and walked on. But the thought was only a tremble of the mind; her arm chafed by the weight of the basket, the cobbles under foot, the stinks of human living that poured heavily into the narrow street, took up the chief of her attention. And her first sensation was relief when Madame Goulet said to her,

'I regret that we shall not be able to accept your washing next week.

'We are moving to new premises,' she added. 'There will be a little interruption.'

Staring at the vase on the counter where marguerites had given place to sweet-williams, Sophia felt the earth begin to shake under her feet. There would be a little interruption. She thought what this traffic had meant to her, pride, assertion of performance, a steady prosaic rhythm to rivet together her days.

'You are exhausted. It is the heat,' said Madame Goulet firmly. 'Will you not wait here a little and repose yourself? It is cool in my parlour—at any rate cooler than in the street.'

She opened a door behind the counter and showed Sophia into a minute room, with a waxed floor, walls painted to resemble nut-wood, a horsehair couch, a group of plaster fruit under a glass shade.

In this prim apartment Sophia sat primly, her throbbing hands folded on her lap. This, which she felt as a disaster, must not be thought so. Better to reflect on the cool room, the refreshment of sitting still. The door opened, and Mademoiselle Martin limped in, smelling of starch, carrying a glass of water.

'How is your brother?' asked Sophia.

'He is very grateful to you. He asked me to express his thanks if I should see you.'

Damned casual, thought Sophia, downing the instant upleap of her heart. And she said,

'I suppose if you want me to do anything more you will let me know?'

'Yes, you may depend upon it.'

The beady timid eyes rested upon her with a queer look of confidence. Mademoiselle Martin appeared to be unconscious of any humiliation to Sophia which such words might impose.

'As though,' said Sophia, recounting the interview to Minna, 'she also were a glass of pure cold water.'

'Yes, you can appreciate that sort of thing better than I. I should find it very difficult to exist without some wine in my water, some tincture of passion or duplicity. It is a flaw in my character, I admit—but there it is. Ah, Sophia! Your laundry would be too Alpine for me. But I envy you that you can be at home on such heights, breathe that air without a shawl over your nose.'

'Well, I shall not breathe any more of it, I am afraid. Unless one of them cuts my throat, this is likely to be my last encounter with the Communists.

'And this, too, I owe to you, Minna. There is no end to the extraordinary things you bring out of your horn of plenty.'

'It has been worth it?'

She spoke hastily, with a passionate unguarded anxiety. They looked at each other, startled, as though truth had been a lightning in the air.

'Yes, Minna. It has been worth it. . . . So you too think that it is nearly over, that we have reached the time when we can reckon up and say, *It has been worth it*?'

'Sophia, I know no more than any one else. I only know this feeling of something in the air or underfoot, a new day or a disaster. All over Europe, maybe, people are feeling like this. But here's Dury. Now we will sit on our island and be princesses.'

'Guitermann's dying,' said Dury, setting up his canvas.

'Dead,' said Minna, settling into her pose, leaning forward to arrange Sophia's hand.

'I went there this morning, while you were out, Sophia.
He moved last week, you know, to a cheaper room after that
last quarrel with his parents. It is unusual for Jews to quarrel,
the family bond is strong with them. But the elder Guiter-
manns suddenly had a little stroke of prosperity, an order
from some army furnisher to make so many badges, a piece
of work any tradesman might do, but by some chance it fell
into the hands of old Guitermann, a skilled goldsmith.
There was work at last, a great deal of work, and to be done
swiftly. They called David to share in it and in the money it
would bring. And he refused. He would not work for the
army, he said. He had had enough of their trumpets, he had
his own music to attend to. There was a bitter quarrel, and
David, wrapping himself in a bloodspitting as in a royal
mantle, walked out of the place.'

'If I can do nothing else, I can paint a cheap brocade and
make it look like a cheap brocade. It's those blistered high-
lights. Go on, Minna.'

'To be young, and a genius, and dying, makes people
exceedingly kingly. "He spoke to us like a prince," the
woman said. And she looked back over her shoulder as
though she still feared to disturb him. They had two rooms,
she and her husband and her children, and David had rented
the larger of them. It was small enough. And it looked the
smaller for being still crowded with their belongings, a child's
go-cart, a ladder, pails and brushes. Her husband was a
house-painter, she said. They were hoping to keep these
things of his trade in case he found work again.

'The bed took up most of the rest of the room, and she
had spread a sheet over the body, and lit a candle. But all

round the bed were bloodied rags, the floor was moist and smeary where she had been trying to scrub the bloodstains off the boards. She had shut the window, she said, because of the flies. The room was suffocatingly hot, and smelt like a shambles. And for all her precautions, flies darted over the bed, to and fro, as though death were some sort of magnetic attraction to them, twitching them back, willy-nilly, into its orbit.

'I asked her if he had died alone. She told me, yes. They had heard him, his choking and his death-rattle, but they had not dared to move, they were afraid of waking their baby. It cried so loud, she said. There had been already so many complaints of its cries, and threats to turn them out. On the floor were some sheets of music paper, scrabbled over in pencil, written in every kind of haste. But one could not read them, they were soaked in blood, stuck together with blood.

' " Please look at him," the woman said. " I did my best for the poor body, after he was gone." His hair was singed, he had fallen forward against the candle-flame, I suppose, when the last bleeding began. It gave to that side of his face a curious resemblance to a clown . . . the frizzy top-knot and the estuary of bald scalp beside it. He was like a clown who had whitened his face and forgotten the dab of red on nose and eye-sockets. His expression was snarling and malevolent. For on some faces, Sophia, death descends like a thick snowfall, smoothing every contour, so that we look on the face of the dead as on a landscape made unfamiliar by a fall of snow. But here death had fallen like a scanty rime. She had folded his hands on his breast, and put a shred of dusty palm beneath them. His nails were long, long as a wolf's. It seemed as though they were already sprouting under the impulse of death.'

'Sophia, your hair is drooping. Stay still, let Minna put it back for you. Keep your lips like that. They are admirable.'

'As I was coming away, I looked at the woman. I saw that she was quite young, five-and-twenty may be, no older. As I looked, her expression of sympathy and decorum seemed to be snatched off her face. Tears of anger began to stream down her cheeks. "It is just our luck!" she exclaimed. "Just our luck that he should move in and die! I told my man that he had paid the rent in advance, but he had only paid me one-half of it. Now where am I to get the money? And his blood is all over the floor, I must buy soap to scour it off, and I cannot afford to buy food for my children even. It is our luck all over. Though people come here to die, for us there is nothing but living. We are tough, we cannot die so easily as these artists."'

Dury looked up.

'I wonder if that's true. I suppose it is. My God, I don't want to die before I've finished this.'

'And so I gave her what money I had and came away. I am sorry, Sophia. I ought to have kept it for our own rent, I suppose. I gave her nine francs fifty.'

'I begin to think we must all be damned,' said Sophia. 'The way we can endure to hear of these things.'

'No sisters of charity flocking to that death-bed,' said Dury. 'No discriminating philanthropists bringing jellies. Presently, no doubt, we shall see some lover of art bringing round the subscription list for a memorial tablet. Was his music good, Minna?'

'I don't know. I have heard so little of it, only the fragments he played me. And I can't read music in score.'

'Sophia's going to faint. We had better break off for a minute or two.'

'No, go on! It is only in my mind that I feel faint. I think of all the money I used to have, and what I did with it. New cushions for the pulpit, subscriptions to memorial tablets and Bible Societies.'

'When I had money,' said Minna, 'I gave it away to the poor and to the sick, to artists and beggars and frauds, all in the name of charity. But when I was a child in my father's house I learned some Hebrew, and one of the things I learned was, that in our Hebrew language there was no word for charity. The word I must use, my father said, was Justice. This libertine word, charity! . . . I have used it often enough since, to my shame. But I still sometimes remember what my father taught me. While we cannot give justice, Sophia, it is idle to debate whether or no we have given charity.'

'I have heard old Ingelbrecht make the same point,' observed Dury.

'Yes, I dare say,' answered Minna with gentle pride. 'He got it from me.'

They were silent. Dury went on painting. Things were not going so well for him now, he grunted, and cursed dejectedly. They were relieved when there was a knock at the door.

'Some one for you, Sophia.'

On the landing was Mademoiselle Martin, holding a band-box. Her face shone with sweat, she had white cotton gloves on her large hands. She gave Sophia a note.

'I am to wait for an answer, Madame.'

'*Dear Sophia*,' wrote Ingelbrecht in his clear stiff hand-writing. '*You are a good carrier pigeon, I know, punctual and reliable. I have heard you highly praised. May I ask your long legs to do me this favour? Here are five packets, and I want four of them delivered into the hands of the addressees before to-morrow night. They contain tracts, explosive only in the intelligence. As for the fifth packet, I leave it to your wits to scatter the contents about with modesty. Do this on your way back only. The addressed packets are the essential. I am much obliged to you. Josquin Ingelbrecht.*'

She crumpled up the note, saw Mademoiselle Martin's beady eyes fix and sharpen. Tearing it to pieces, carefully sifting the shreds from hand to hand, she said in her Mrs Willoughby of Blandamer voice,

'That will do admirably. I will see to it to-morrow. Do you want the box back?'

'If you please, Madame,'

Plotting on a stairhead, she said to herself. Nursing Ingelbrecht's neat packets under her arm, listening to Mademoiselle Martin's uneven footsteps on the stairs and the empty bandbox banging against the rails, she remembered Minna's greeting of the man called Gaston. Here am I, she thought —as gullible as she, for all I know.

The addresses for the packets were on a separate sheet of paper, to be learned by heart, she presumed. It took all Minna's mongrel-dog knowledge of Paris to work out the

itinerary; as for the address in La Villette, even Minna had
to admit herself baffled.

'I should leave it to the last, if I were you. Work up that
way by the address in the rue des Vinaigriers, and then across
to the canal to the Cité Lepage, and after that northward.
And come back by those sturdy *Dames Réunies.*'

'Who are they?'

'An omnibus. And if you get into any sort of fix, or
think you are being followed, remember that the arms of the
Church are always open, and that a Christian is safest on his
knees. I took part in a full-length funeral once; and I assure
you, my grief was an adornment to it. Poor gentleman, they
had never suspected him of keeping such a devoted mistress.'

'I wish it were you, Minna. You would do it with a great
deal more style.'

'Would it were!'

Looking back at the house she saw Minna leaning from the
balcony, her black hair glittering in the morning sunlight, her
large hand waving, and every line of her body expressing an
invincible sense of drama.

And I might have taken her after all, she thought, as the
omnibus rattled over the cobbles. There was nothing to
prevent it, no word of going unaccompanied. With half of
her mind she turned back to the rue de la Carabine. But the
ticket had been paid for; and when she descended into the
boulevard Poissonnière, the sun struck on her with such
brutality that she was thankful for the thrifty impulse which
had stayed her from haling Minna out for such a day's
discomfort.

She had decided to start as early as possible, for the sake

of what freshness there might be in the morning air. But there was no freshness, only the same nervous tension which marked every morning now. Those who loitered looked restless, and the walkers hurried. Above the rumble and jangle of the omnibus she had heard the *rappel* beaten, a noise in these days of not much more significance than the chiming of a cuckoo-clock.

Even Minna's sense of drama would have flagged under this. The route so lightly undertaken was another thing under the realism of the midsummer sun. Two packets had been delivered over, one to a frowsy woman in a gunshop, another to the lean proprietor of a lean café. Behind his dusty grove of privet she sat down to rest and drink a glass of tepid beer. Over and over she perused the painted advertisement on the house-front opposite. Walk without Fear, it said. Attach the celebrated metal rings of Beaufoin to your heels and save shoe-leather. Walk without Fear. The air shook with a vehement hot panting, the noise of some heavy machine or other. Through the gap in the privet she could see the clustered garments dangling outside the second-hand clothes shop, and among all the other smells of the street she distinguished their sour taint of dried sweat extorted by the sun. The man of the café leaned in his doorway with looks that bade her begone. She was the wrong sort of customer for him, no doubt of it.

She got up, and joined her footsteps to the other footsteps that lagged by. Like every one else on these pavements she was down at heel and too heavily clothed for the season.

It was a quarter of tall factories and warehouses, cowed and shabby dwellings. The windows had paper shades, the food exposed for sale was meagre and unenterprising. On stall after stall she noticed the same platters of sliced cooked meats, the same ready-bunched assortments of salad : a head of chicory, a lettuce, six radishes, some spears of spring onions, a sprig of fennel. As though for prison meals, she thought. So much and no more, and for every one the same. *The Institution of Labour*. . . . Somewhere she must have heard that phrase, and now her steps trudged it out on the pavement. Somewhere between prisoners in a jail, paupers in an institution, the workers were pent in the Institution of Labour, to do their stint and get their ration. They could no more escape than grow wings, at a dreary best the best-conducted might hope to become sub-warders over their fellows. Sometimes, as now, the running of the Institution failed : there was a shortage of work and a shortage of food. But that would not break down the walls, within the Institution of Labour they must remain—kick their heels, and starve, and breed on.

What idiocy, what futility, to be carrying revolutionary tracts through these streets ! The succession of little grasping shops, butcher, baker, candlestick-maker, butcher, baker, candlestick-maker, the factories like ill-kept barracks, the warren-like *cités* badged with the spiritless ensigns of family washing, what written word, what thought exploding in the mind, could leaven them ? A woman in a gunshop, a man in a café, and between them a mile of mean streets, streets wavering between shabby-sordid and crass-sordid. . . . At least, she had assured herself, Ingelbrecht was not an idealist ; but she must revise that opinion now. And it was with something like satisfaction that she took from the receiver of the third packet a mistrusting glare, a word of abuse, a door slammed in her face.

It was not consoling to be told in the rue Furet, La Villette, that Monsieur Georges was out, would not be back until three o'clock at the earliest.

Over the counter, heaped with cheap drugs, ointments for sores and skin diseases, elixirs for the middle-aged, soothing syrup for infants, the chemist's assistant blinked at her wearily through pale eyelashes. He was pale all over, his voice was pale, his eyes had pink rims. Everything of his physique was noxious and debased, and out of his blinking eyes looked a character of helpless anxious integrity. Scratching his head, stirring his limp straight hair, he repeated,

' No, certainly he will not be back before three. I am very sorry. But it would not do for me to mislead you.'

It was a little before noon. The sensible course would be to go back. No woman in her senses would wish to dangle herself in La Villette for three mortal midday hours. Equally, no woman in her senses would perform the journey to La Villette twice in one midsummer day.

I am bound to be a fool anyhow, she said to herself. I will eat something, and pull myself together.

The meal was cheap, gross, highly-flavoured. It made her sleepy, and heavier-witted than before. From the cheap restaurant she went to a cheap church, and sat there yawning, too vacant even to open the fifth packet and find out with what doctrines Ingelbrecht proposed to kindle men's minds. While she sat there, two christenings took place. Between the christenings she dawdled round the building, examined the stations of the cross and read a number of obituary cards pinned up on a notice-board. They hung in tattering sheaves, one pinned over another. Death had covered death; few people would come to the church of Our Lady of Perpetual Succour with leisure enough to pray their way through to the bottom-most yellowing pasteboard. The holy water smelled, the church smelled too—the smell of raw new plaster warring with the odour, already antique, of a dirty congregation.

At three she returned to the chemist's shop, where the pale young man, looking pleased, informed her that Monsieur Georges had just come in. Monsieur Georges also looked pleased. His was the first face that day to express anything like vigour. He was a fat little man, middle-aged and jaunty, he apologised for delaying her and offered her a glass of wine, which he handed across the counter. While she drank he talked to her about the elixirs and syrups. They were all traditional remedies, he said, perfectly harmless and perfectly useless.

' My professional hours,' said he, ' are spent in the vilest cheating and charlatanry. My leisure, on the other hand, I lay out to good account.' And he winked at her as he refilled her glass.

Revived by the wine, she walked uncomplainingly to the omnibus stop, and watched the horses munching from their nose-bags, the driver combing his whiskers and counting over his money. She had been carried some way before she recollected that the fifth packet remained to be distributed, and had been left behind in the church of Our Lady of Perpetual Succour.

Cursing herself and Ingelbrecht, and the perpetual sun, she went back. It was there right enough, but the time was now quarter past four and Minna would be anxious, and her purse was growing empty. Taking out a hairpin she wasted some time fishing for coins in the collecting-boxes. She had only extracted seven sous, inadequate even as a tip for the cab she meant to take from the Barrier, when a sniffing woman and a talking child entered the church. For exchange, she tore open the last packet, slipped one of the tracts into the rack of pious booklets, and dropped another on the bench outside the church. She spent no time in reading them, she was in a hurry.

In the chemist's shop she explained her predicament, and her poor success at church-robbery. He laughed, and lent her five francs with a gesture that went near to being a chuck under the chin. As she was leaving the shop he whistled her back, came to the door and looked up the street.

'I thought so!' he exclaimed. 'You get to know a trot like that in La Villette. It's a blood-horse. Hi, Carrabas! You give this lady a lift down as far as the Barrier.'

The young man addressed as Carrabas was driving a light cart hung with tin-ware. An ancient wild-eyed chestnut was in the shafts.

'Take care of her,' said Monsieur Georges fervently. 'She's just been robbing Holy Church.'

Carrabas flushed to his ears. He seemed unable to speak except to his horse, and as the animal jerked into a trot the clatter of tin-ware seemed to Sophia a sufficient reason to be silent also. However, after about half a mile of swallowing and glancing sideways, he said,

'How far have you to go?'

'Across the river, to the Latin Quarter.'

'You'll get there all right,' he answered. 'Keep round to the west a little, then you'll get through.'

'Get through?'

'The fighting has started, you know.'

Near the Barrier the streets began to fill up. People stood in their doorways and on the pavement, silent mostly, looking towards Paris. Outside a café she noticed a group of men singing. They sat comfortably behind their table spread with bocks and dominoes, and sang *Mourir pour la Patrie* with gusto, leaning back in their chairs, opening their lungs, waving their shirt-sleeved arms. Beside them stood a young waiter, patient and furious, his bill-tab in his hand, and a fat dog, tied to the table-leg, barked furiously.

'That sort can sing,' observed Carrabas. 'They'll burst their tripes, singing!'

At the Barrier he helped her down, apologising that he could take her no further. And again he told her to keep to the west. Here the street was crowded also, but with a moving crowd. She went with it, towards a noise of firing and the smell of gunpowder. The *rappel* was being beaten hither and thither, a dry bony noise on the stifling air.

The crowd closed about her, thickened, came to a standstill. There was a barricade further along, some one said. Where she stood there was nothing to be seen, but word came back from those in the front, carried from mouth to mouth. Meanwhile the people behind amassed, and pressed forward, and a vacant-faced woman, far gone in pregnancy, kept digging her elbow into Sophia's ribs, and enquiring, 'What is it, what is it?'

'Twins, mother,' a voice replied. There was a guffaw of

laughter, and a bickering. In this heat no one is going to keep his temper for long, thought Sophia, uneasily combating her impulse to beat a way out of the crowd; and it was with a feeling of doing something dangerous that she wriggled and pleaded her way to the right, and escaped into a side street.

She had little idea where she was, and no idea which way to go. But she continued to work westward, guiding herself by the sound of firing and the flux of people in the streets.

After nearly two hours, looking down a side street, she recognised the profile of Notre Dame de Lorette. Up the street, howling, and holding his hand to his cheek, ran a boy; and as he passed, she saw there was blood dripping on to his shoulder. She flattened herself against the wall to let him go by. He ran past without seeming to notice her and hurried on, howling still. The street became full of voices, women leaning out of windows to stare and exclaim, walkers suddenly materialising and turning to run in the boy's track.

As far as was possible, she would not allow herself to think, bending all her powers to be an animal, an animal that twists and turns and keeps on its way. But she could not prevent herself from comparing the afternoon of this interminable summer day with the evening of the twenty-third of February. People had talked then, questioning and exclaiming. Every one had talked, knit together by a common excitement. These crowds were almost silent, if they spoke it was under their breath, bitterly or fearfully. And at a screaming bugle-call a man, a clerk perhaps or a shop assistant, walking a little in front of Sophia, threw up his hand and clasped his forehead, as though the noise had been an agony to him.

As she overtook him he came closer to her, bade her an endearing good-evening, and tried to put his arm round her waist. Looking into his face she saw that his teeth were chattering with terror. And she struck back his hands with fury, as though terror were a plague, and his touch might infect her.

Even here she could hear shots behind her, and the smell of gunpowder hung on the air, pungent and autumnal. But she had outflanked the fighting, and could cross the boulevard des Italiens and be among the streets she knew. The sky had clouded over, a few large drops of rain fell, and the trees along the boulevard stirred their leaves uneasily. She crossed the river. She was on her old track, soon she would be passing below great-aunt Léocadie's windows. The house-fronts were shuttered, cautiously impassive. She went up the rue de Grenelle and the noise of fighting roused up again, and the smell of powder.

From the turning into the rue de la Carabine she could see Minna's windows. They stood open, the curtains swayed to and fro. She began to run.

The echo of her feet on the stairs sounded like some one pursuing her, turned into the footsteps of Madame Coton, holding out the key. She unlocked the door and went into the empty room.

On the table was a plate of sandwiches and some wine, a letter addressed to her with an English stamp on it, and a small box of polished walnut, plain and solid. She lifted the lid, saw the blue velvet lining, and the scrolled label saying,

J. Watson, Gunsmith, Piccadilly. One of the pistols was gone, and in its cradle lay a folded slip of paper.

She carried it to the window, and read.

My well-loved,

You will not blame me that I have gone on. I cannot sit here any longer, in this room full of the echoes of all my speeches about liberty.

Ask for me at the Maison du Four aux Brindilles—you remember, that shop where we bought the very good pâté. But you are to eat and drink first.

Minna.

Shaking with fatigue, moving with rigid concentration, she pulled a chair to the table, and poured out a glass of wine. All the time a hollow voice seemed to be prompting her, saying, Now the chair. Now the wine. That's right. Presently the collaborating voice was helping her to change her shoes and put on a wrap, and look to the pistol.

Leaving the house she left the voice behind. ' Yet another promenade ? ' remarked Égisippe Coton. The taunt, and the voice wizened with rancour, gave her the fillip she needed, and blandly she condoled with him that he could not also allow himself a little stroll to see how things were going. One is very possibly safer out of doors, she observed.

For a while that seemed true enough, unless it were for the risk of breaking one's ankle. Paving-stones and blocks of cobbles had been hacked up at random, and in the half-light it was easy enough to stumble into the gaps that remained.

Out of an alley darted the wood-seller's little girl. Her pallor of town-life, her skinniness of under-nourishment, gave her a resemblance to Augusta, whom neither good air

nor good food had forwarded ; and she had, too, something
of Augusta's elfish decisiveness of diction. Poverty, though,
had freed her from any nursery airs. And like a grown
woman she greeted Sophia, and stretching upwards, linked
arms.

'You are late, Madame Vilobie. You have missed a
magnificent spectacle ! Such barricades I have never seen
before.'

Looking more closely at this experienced veteran, Sophia
saw that she had a patch of plaster on her nose.

'Were you wounded, Armandine ? '

'Nothing, nothing,' said the child. 'A scratch, a graze
from a piece of stone sent flying. However, I can say that I
have been wounded in the people's defence.'

'And the others ? '

In her voice of a businesslike bird, Armandine detailed
the dead and wounded : the butcher's boy, the pastrycook,
the sweep, the wine-merchant's two nephews, and Monsieur
Allin, saddler and National Guard.

'They also are with us,' she said with a sweep of her hand.

It seemed as though this child knew the defenders of the
local barricades as well as she knew her father's clients.
These were not disembodied revolutionaries, these men
behind the barricades, but the workers of the neighbourhood,
figures seen every day. The actual barricades were almost as
intimately known to Armandine. In this one was Aunt
Zélie's great wardrobe, in that the cornchandler's bins, in a
third cords of wood from Armandine's papa and a great mass
of books carried out by an old gentleman whom no one had
ever set eyes on previously.

' Look,' she exclaimed.   ' There they are ! '

Dark and regular, the barricades traversed the vista of the rue St Jacques like waves rolling in upon a lee-shore.

' That is Monsieur Allin's barricade,' said the child.   ' He came to attack it, but the sweep harangued him, and in a twinkling he was among the defenders.   And there, do you see it, is the umbrella of the old gentleman who brought the books.   He seems to be a little delicate.'

Like a guide finishing his course, Armandine walked away.

Augusta, gloved and wrapped in wool and cherished, might have been like this, Augusta walking staidly intrepid into the waves on Weymouth beach.   But convention and riches had made of Augusta a rather dull and didactic child. Frederick had understood her best, calling her The Twopenny Piece.   These men behind the barricades had children they loved, wives with whom they were in amity.   Unglorified, undisciplined, under the windows of their own homes they walked out to die.

' I have no place here,' she said to herself, ashamed to the soul.   And her hand fell back from the knocker on the door of the cooked-meats shop.   The Maison du Four aux Brindilles stood in a quiet by-street near the river, a street of ancient and overhanging houses.   The burst of cannonading echoed through it as though from another world.

Cannon !   The stature of that sound reared up above the height of the barricades, the minnikin height of man.   She banged on the door.

' Is Madame Lemuel . . . ? '

The old man had a serious face, large and pale and wrinkled.   He trod with the cautious dignity of some one suffering from corns, and on his hand was a wide wedding-ring.

' This way, if you please.'

Beyond the kitchen, spotless and orderly, abundant with looped black puddings, casks of brined pork, bunches of herbs and jars of spices, was a woodhouse opening into a small courtyard. Across the courtyard was another back-door, another shed, a room where, in semi-darkness, people were sitting round a table eating and a child whimpered. The shop beyond, shuttered and obscure, smelled of blood ; putting out her hand Sophia touched something cold and sticky.

' It is only horse-flesh,' said her guide. ' Never fear.'

She heard a door being unbarred, stepped through it, stood in a street. It was almost as though she had entered another courtyard, so tall was the barricade. She looked for Minna, and in an instant recognised her. And her first impulse was an irresistible impulse to laugh, for Minna was holding a gun.

The impulse to laugh was succeeded by a feeling of acute anxiety when she observed more closely how the weapon was handled. She hurried forward.

' Sophia ! You are safe ! ' exclaimed Minna, and levelled the gun at Sophia's bosom.

' How many people have you killed with that ? '

' None ! But I have wounded several.'

' I can well believe it.'

There was a crowd of people, a great noise of conversation. An old man, red-nosed and serious, with military medals pinned on his coat, was tying up a boy's wounded hand. The boy was sitting on the ground, his back against the barricade, tears running down his furious rigid face. An old soldier, three National Guards, several students, artisans, small shopkeepers, many ragged and workless, many women . . . for a moment it seemed to Sophia that a young officer was also among the defenders of the barricade.

‘ Our prisoner,’ said Minna.

He was seated on a doorstep, his long thin legs sprawling, on his long thin face a look of bewilderment and dejection. Beside him, and seemingly in charge of him, was a very stout old lady with a hairy chin and a magnificent cap. She was haranguing him, emphatically wagging her head, creasing her double chins. Sophia edged a little nearer and heard her say,

‘ And that is how one gets piles.’

The young officer shut his eyes and swallowed.

The attack which he had led so much too spectacularly (‘ He came clambering over the barricades, waving a sword, so there was nothing for it but to let him in,’) had been repulsed. The old man with the medals snorted at this. It was a wretched piece of work, he said, he would have been ashamed to be seen dead in it. It was obvious that he spoke with intent, careful to discourage too much elation among the defenders. At every thud of the cannon he cocked his head, made a wry grimace as though he were trying some bitter flavour on his palate. The cannon, Minna said, was firing from the hospital, the Hôtel Dieu. And she made a joke about pills which had obviously not originated with her.

She had completely assimilated the colour of her surroundings, identifying herself with the barricade, knowing all the news, all the rumours, all the nicknames. It was quite genuine, but slightly overdone, and the effect was as though she were a little tipsy. To Sophia, arriving cold and raw in the midst of this scene already warmed with blood and powder, Minna's demeanour was embarrassing and painful, she could not help feeling that Minna knew every one behind the barricade much better than she knew her.

' How long have you been here ? '

' Three hours.'

If I were here as many days, thought Sophia, I should still be out of it. If only there were something for me to do !

As time went on this feeling was augmented by a searching wish that there might be something to eat. And she had her first moment of identification with those around her when the door of the horse-flesh shop opened, and the old man who had let her in to the Maison du Four aux Brindilles came out, treading with his cautious suffering dignity, and carrying wine and bread and slices of pickled pork.

Then, thinking that these refreshments were for those who had fought, whereas she had done nothing but arrive late, hang about, and look on, she stood back, proud and miserable.

' You look so tired.'

Minna was at her elbow with a glass and a hunch of bread and meat.

' Do you know, those are the first words you ever spoke to me.'

' When you came that evening to the rue de la Carabine ? '

' Yes.'

In the shabby remains of daylight they stared at each other, startled into recognition.

' To arms ! To the barricades ! '

A barricade to the southward was being attacked. A moment later the noise of firing broke out in the next street.

' They are doing it in style,' said the old soldier. ' Keep down, damn you ! ' he shouted to those who had mounted the barricade and were watching the fighting, and shouting encouragement ; and he grabbed the leg of a red-haired boy and hauled him down.

' Oh, but I say ! We've got to see how it goes, down there.'

' We shall know soon enough. Now listen ! If they carry it, it'll be our turn. Wait till they come close. Long shots are no good in this cat-light, nothing but waste of powder. Let them come close, and then give them a real peppering. And don't try any fancy shooting. This is fighting, not target-practice. Aim fair and square at their middles.'

His bellowing harangue over, he climbed heavily up the barricade, and peered down the street. They listened for his report. He clicked his tongue against the roof of his mouth and climbed down again. Stumping grandly to and fro, he trod on Sophia's foot.

' Hey ! Can *you* shoot ? '

His voice was so contemptuous that the prisoner vented a sound of protest. Turning her back on this champion, Sophia answered,

' I can load.'

' Load, then ! Here, Clément, Dujau, Laimable ! This lady will load for you.

'As for you, Captain—you'll see some fighting presently, maybe.'

The prisoner flinched as though the old man's wrath had caught him a buffet. Then, biting his lip and bridling, he tried to reassert his superior dignity, tossed his head, put on a sneering and haughty expression. The old woman on the camp-stool continued her inflexible narrative. She was trudging through a death in childbed now. If she could keep him an hour or two longer, thought Sophia, she would make mincemeat of him.

It seemed as though they would stand for ever in this smoky dusk, under this confused hubbub of firing and shouting. The echoes rang and rattled through the gully of the narrow street, and a cage of canaries in a window overhead trilled frantically. Suddenly, as though answering the canaries, there was an outburst of shrill cheering.

'Those damned brats!' exclaimed the old soldier. And another voice, snarling and agitated, began to speak of the Gardes Mobiles, trained by the government to savagery like a pack of trained hunting-dogs, until a third voice, solid and peremptory, silenced the recital.

The man called Laimable, not turning his head, remarked, 'The worst of it is, they ought to be fighting with us.'

His tone was philosophical, the flat voice of an intellect, the voice of one accustomed to receive no answers to his statements. There was no answer to this one, either.

The cooked-meat-shop man, having carried in his tray and his bottles, now came out again with a long carving-knife.

'The best I can do,' he apologised. 'My two boys have

taken all the firearms, and everything else they can lay
hands on. However, they are making good use of them,
no doubt.'

Without a pause in her monologue the stout old woman
fumbled under her petticoats, produced a chopper, and laid
it across her knees.

It seemed that the noise around them constrained them to
keep silence. With one accord they moved cautiously, spoke
in undertones, coughed under their breaths as though in
church. A deepening seriousness pressed on them one and
all, and there was scarcely a stir in the common mood when
the noise from the barricade down the street changed its
tune, was traversed by shrieks and crashes, when the clatter
of running feet approached.

Panting and bloodied, a man scrambled up the barricade,
was helped over.

' Give me a gun ! Mine's jammed.'

In a moment Minna had given him hers. There was an
unmistakable renunciation in the gesture, and an equally un-
mistakable triumph in the movement with which she pulled
the duelling pistol by J. Watson of Piccadilly, London, from
her bosom. Sophia could imagine that melancholy voice
remarking with suavity,

' One must be prepared for emergencies.'

It was likely to be her last clear impression of Minna, for
more runners were being helped over the barricade, and
already she was busy loading, comparing with rage the
smoothness of Frederick's well-oiled pieces which she had
handled in the Blandamer preserves, and the cranky unkempt
weapons which must serve now. For we shall all be killed,

she said to herself—a purely formal movement of the mind.
For hours now, under this imminence of death, the idea of
death had been unmeaning, unrealisable. And even when the
red-headed boy fell back with a cry and lay struggling beside
her she went on loading, knowing that the wetness on
her hand was blood exactly as she knew that her legs were
cramped with kneeling on cobbles, that her ears were hum-
ming like stretched wires, that a cold sweat of excitement
had broken out all over her.

But this isolation was no longer an isolation setting her
apart from those around her, she was not cased up now in that
feeling of being out of it, an anomaly, an intruder. This
furious detachment, she had it in common with every other
fighter on the barricade. It was the mood of battle.

Bread or Lead. Before long, the ammunition would be
running short. This was how one felt when one's children
were starving, when there was no more bread in the cup-
board, no more milk in the breast. The fighters were lessen-
ing too. She had noticed that one particular musket was no
longer thrust down to her, and now it fell clattering ; and
slowly, like an ebb, the body of Laimable drooped from its
meditative attitude, the head pillowed on one arm, and fell
also.

This barricade was not holding out so well as the other,
or maybe the time of fighting went more swiftly than the
time of waiting. Yet, when the assailants rushed it, the
hand-to-hand fighting revived a fierceness that the failing
ammunition had belied, and for a minute or two it seemed as
though they might be driven back. Then, in the street
running parallel, the sound of cannonading burst out, and as

though this jarred the rhythm of fighting here, there was a wavering, a pause; and like a swarm of bees the Gardes Mobiles came over, yelling and jeering.

Caspar is one of these, she thought. She was able to think now, there was nothing more she could do. With the certainty of a bad dream, there, when she looked up, was Caspar's profile outlined against the smoky dusk, tilted, just as it had been on those summer evenings at Blandamer House, when he played his guitar, leaning against the balustrade. Lightly he leaped down within a hand's-breadth of her, crying *Surrender*.

On the farther side of the barricade a house had been broken into. Trampling steps were heard, shouts and cries. Suddenly the shutters of an upper room were thrown open, and a woman leant out, shrieking with terror, crying that she was going to throw herself down. The gaslight shone out into the street, a livid square of light falling like a trap. She saw Caspar recognise her, and for an instant his face wore a look of sheepish devotion.

' Why, it's Caspar ! '

It was Minna's voice, warm, inveterately hospitable. He glanced round. With a howl of rage he sprang forward, thrust with his bayonet, drove it into Minna's breast.

' Drab ! ' he cried out. ' Jewess ! This is the end of you.'

A hand was clapped on Sophia's shoulder, a voice told her she was a prisoner.

' One moment,' she replied, inattentively. With her free arm she pulled out the pistol and cocked it, and fired at Caspar's mouth as though she would have struck that mouth with her hand. Having looked to aim, she looked no further. But she saw the bayonet jerk in Minna's breast, and the blood rush out.

Even when her hands were caught behind her and tied there, she did not realise that she was a prisoner. Thumped with a musket-butt, kicked and hauled and shouted at, she remained motionless and uncomprehending. And dragged away by force, marching with the other prisoners, she thought she was yet standing by the barricade with Minna lying at her feet.

It was the clatter of the pistol, falling from her numbed grasp, that roused her. She awoke, looked round to see where she was, and who was with her. They were going by the Hôtel de Cluny. Its windows were lit up, a stretcher was being carried in through the doorway.

' We could have some fun in there.'

It was one of the escort who spoke ; and they began to quarrel amongst themselves, the blither spirits canvassing the project of hunting through the wounded to see if they could lay hands on any notorious revolutionaries, the duller saying that they had better get rid of this lot first.

' That's easy enough. Shoot them now.'

' Excuse me,' said a voice, precise and anxious. ' Such were not our instructions.'

And they were halted, while the dispute continued. In some near-by belfry church-bells were ringing the tocsin, the peal running its scale backwards, the topmost bell smiting back the ascending jangle.

' Orders are orders,' persisted the doctrinaire.

' Quite right ! ' the old soldier interposed. ' Orders are

orders, prisoners are shot at dawn. I've been in the army, I know.'

While the wrangling continued he added softly,

'Maybe things will have changed again by then.'

The boy with the wounded hand looked up.

'Do you think so? Yes, why shouldn't they? Listen! The fighting goes on.'

With his bright feverish eyes he stared into the old soldier's face, interrogating it for a look of hope. There was no trace of hope on that bleak countenance, only a great deal of obdurate cunning.

Meanwhile the Gardes Mobiles had taken themselves off into the Hôtel de Cluny. The remaining escort were getting under way, the conscientious National Guard scratching his head, and glancing at the old soldier as though for guidance, when another batch of prisoners came past. This was a very different turnout. The escorting men were regulars, an officer was in charge. With a sigh of relief the doctrinaire shepherded his flock into their wake.

There had been nothing in that moment of revived attention to justify coming to life. Sophia made no further attempts to attend, and when they were halted in a courtyard, she sat down on the pavement, leaned against some one's legs, and fell asleep.

When she woke it was morning, the sun already high, the noise of fighting still continuing. She woke with a perfect uncommenting recollection of everything that had happened, and a raging thirst. Others had woken thirsty too. All round her she heard complaints, voices begging for water. Cramped, parched, aching all over, sullen and dull-witted, her only feeling was one of dissatisfaction because there were two facts to which her mind woke unadjusted. One was that it had seemed to her overnight that they had been brought to the courtyard of a massive and stately building; whereas this was no building at all, but the tattered skeleton of a building in demolition, all gaps, and jagged edges, and papery broken walls. The other new aspect of the morning was that her acquaintances of overnight were exchanged for perfect strangers.

She had to look at them several times to make sure of this. They were exactly the same sort of people as those behind the barricade, wearing that general badge of being pale, underfed, shabby and serious. Here were hands exactly like the hands she had touched, receiving and giving back the guns she loaded—hands scarred and discoloured, with the dirty nails and enlarged dusky knuckles of labour. Here were heads that had gone uncovered in all weathers, the hair strong and coarse like a pelt. There, peering into the world through his dirty spectacles, was just such a timid, short-sighted student as he of overnight, and there was another red-headed boy, and there, tormented with a hiccough, resigned and un-compromising, was Laimable, who had fallen back dead from the barricade.

So powerful was this weaving between the dead of over-night, the living of the morning, that when she recognised Martin she supposed that the Martin she knew must be dead also; and this impression was the stronger since, happening to turn his head in her direction, he looked at her without any alteration of his harsh and thoughtful visage. Yet that peremptory turn of the head, and those adder-coloured eyes stabbed through her illusion, and she admitted that he, at least, was real and living.

' You are looking for your friends, no doubt ? '

It was a rather squeaky voice that made this enquiry, one of those voices which, being used seldom, and diffidently, acquire a false note of patronage. It came from the short-sighted student.

' It is possible that they may be among those who have been shot.'

Making conversation, he continued,

' What barricade were you on ? '

' Do you know, I cannot remember the name of the street.'

' I was on the barricade of the Place Cambrai. Ah! I think it may be our turn now.'

Suddenly his hand touched hers. It was impossible to guess, so cold was that hand, whether it sought in that contact to reassure or to be reassured.

' It is curious, isn't it, how clumsily one's mind adapts itself to the thought of death ? '

' Very curious, Madame.'

They were being shouted to their feet, ranged closely together, as though they were inferior exhibits on the back-staging of a flower-show. A sergeant of the Republican Guard reckoned them over with a wagging forefinger. There was one above the reckoning, and with a rapid contemptuous movement of his hand he dismissed him from the group, as though flicking off a grain of dust. The firing-squad marched up and fell into position. Behind them an officer walked to and fro, soaping his hands, staring with a vaguely critical glance at the sky.

Suddenly he pricked up his ears, became animated, came down from the heavens to the earth.

' What's that ?   What's that ? '

' Wants a priest, sir.   Wants to make his confession.'

' Certainly ! Certainly ! A very edifying desire. I could only wish that more of these miserable wretches had such an impulse. Fetch a priest at once.'

And advancing on the religious young man who, already isolated from his fellows by this movement of piety, was now in tears, the officer remarked with a noble blitheness,

' Quite right, my poor young fellow ! Such a wish I will always grant with pleasure. We do not combat against souls, quite the contrary.

' Stand at ease,' he added, to the firing-squad. And crossing himself withdrew, to walk to and fro and consider the heavens once again.

A very awkward pause ensued. The religious young man continued to weep, those on either side of him drew away as much as they could, somebody whistled softly, some one else gave a disapproving cough. Sophia could hear the student beside her grinding his teeth.

Slowly, his acrid voice most skilfully modulated to the tone of one who, out of courtesy only, seems to be persuading others to an opinion which he knows they hold already, Martin began to speak.

' Some one calls for a priest ; and immediately, at this cautious provision for another life, this invocation of eternity we, who have so little of this life left to us, feel any prolongation of it as an intolerable burden. That seems odd, does it not ? Unreasonable, to feel so acutely about so small a fret.

If we were to revolt against living, we might well have done so earlier. Our lives have been bitter enough, joyless, imperilled, ignominious, the lives of working-people. We have laboured, and never tasted the fruits of our labours. If we have loved, that love has only compelled us to a more anxious hate. The married man, the man who loves his wife and children, in our class that one love cuts him off from the love of his kind. He sees in his fellows only enemies and supplanters, rivals, who may do him out of a job, outbid him with a lower wage, steal the bread from the mouths of his children.

'How often we have declared that our lives were intolerable! How much more often, not even troubled to declare it! And yet, having endured such lives, we feel now that it is beyond the resistance of our nerves to endure the delay of five minutes while a priest is sent for. Here we stand, as in our old days we have often enough wished to stand— idle for once, able to stand about in the sun as though it were a holiday. Here we stand as we have wished often enough, too, to stand—on the brink of the grave, our labour and mistrust and weariness almost at an end.

'But after all, what is this five minutes' burden? The weight of a husk, of a dead leaf. For our lives are over. What purpose we had—and we had, many of us, a purpose— is taken out of our hands. What we had to do and to say, is said and done. The word is with others now, and our purpose in other hands. And so this weight of time upon us, it is only the weight of a husk, of the dry wisp that remains and withers after the fruit has been gathered, or the seed fallen into the ground. It is no more substantial than that. And really it seems to me that we ought to bear it with more patience.'

He shook his head, a gentle rebuke. Then his bright eyes perused the faces of the firing-squad, and he continued,

' But that is how this delay affects *us*. For you, who are here to execute us, it is probably more tedious, certainly more embarrassing. For this break in the common routine, it lets in a draught of cold air, it gives an inconvenient leisure in which to reflect on this odd business of killing one's fellow-men, one's country-men, and people of the same class as oneself, at a word of command. For after all, you and we have much more in common than you and your officer, you and the ruling class whose orders your officer orders you to carry out. That ruling class—you would not marry their daughters, sit at their table. You and they are different nations. And if you reflect on it, you will see that you and they are constantly at war with each other, and have been during all your lives and the lives of your forefathers. But as it is a war in which, so far, they have always won, you have failed to notice that it is a war.

' And here we wait, face to face, people of the same class, fellow-combatants in this profound war in which, so far, we have never gained a victory—waiting for that word of command at which you kill us. Not that I speak against words of command, to be able to carry out an order is admirable and essential—provided that the order does not come from the enemy. But as things are—no! And it seems to me, a prisoner, that you are pretty much prisoners yourselves, and likely, sooner or later, to die very much as we are going to die—blown to bits because some one of the ruling class has ordered it. You are disciplined and courageous prisoners, I grant it. But we have a boast too in our ragged regiment, and it seems to me better than yours. We know what we are dying for, we have fought and will die at our own word of command, not the enemy's.'

The priest had been brought, and Martin fell silent, retiring, as the defending counsel might, to listen impassively to the speech of the prosecuting counsel. Professional as the lick of a mother-cat's tongue the absolution was given, and the officer, hovering in the background, crossed himself more and more devoutly, soaped his hands in an increasing ecstasy of sentiment and grand self-approbation.

It was over, this satisfying interlude, the soul was saved, and the order to prepare given. Suddenly his eye lighted upon Sophia.

' I cannot consent to the death of a woman.'

' Death of a woman ! ' she cried out furiously. ' Death of a woman ! And how many women are dead already, and how many more will be, with your consent and complaisance ? Dead in besieged towns, and towns taken by storm. Dead in insurrections and massacres. Dead of starvation, dead of the cholera that follows starvation, dead in childbed, dead in the workhouse and the hospital for venereal diseases. You are not the man to boggle at the death of a woman.'

It seemed to her, and she was glad, that she had screamed this out like a virago of the streets.

But with a bow he reasserted,

' I cannot consent to the death *of a lady*.'

Bitterly humiliated, she found herself taken out of the rank of the doomed. As she stumbled forward the student leaned after her.

'I am to tell you that Martin feels great satisfaction to think you will remain alive.'

While they were untying her hands she heard the words of command, and the volley. Then the priest was at her side, saying something about mercies and thankfulness, and the dangerous state of the streets. She ran out of the courtyard, not glancing behind her.

She was her own creature again—flipped back into the farewelled world, to fend for herself, sink or swim.

Martin had not much to congratulate himself upon that she was still alive. Never was there a woman with less heart to live. And maybe I shall be killed yet, she said to herself as a bullet went past her. But there was no conviction in the words. No life so charmed as the life that would be laid down. Creaky doors hang longest.

Probably I shall live to a profound old age. And people will say of me, ' Do you know, old Mrs Willoughby went through the Revolution of '48 in Paris ? ' And some one else will answer, ' How extraordinary ! One would never think it.'

With a sleep-walking obstinacy her body was taking her back to the barricade. Murderers go back. And if it comes to that, I may be said to have murdered Caspar. ' Do you know, in the year '48 old Mrs Willoughby murdered her uncle's illegitimate son—a boy of fifteen, a poor stupid blackamoor who worshipped the ground she trod on ? ' ' No, really ? One would never think it.' ' Such a dull old woman. Rather cold-hearted, don't you think ? ' This icy pain in her bosom, this pain of a heart becolded, it would go on and on, she supposed, the counterpart to that flowering crimson on

Minna's white muslin gown, that flowering of her warm and generous blood.

It was difficult to get back. Where there was not fighting, there was ruin—houses gutted, streets impassable. Crowds of people had settled upon the ruins, like bluebottles. She could hear their buzzing voices, their crawling exploring footsteps. People thrust their heads through broken windows, recounting what they had found within, holding out a bloodied rag, a musket, a broken chamber-pot, as testimony.

She flinched aside from these, wary as a hunted animal. These carrion sight-seers, they might settle on her if she gave them the chance.

There was the place she sought, and there, too, another crawling inspecting crowd. She tried to drive herself forward, began to sicken and tremble, could not go on. Then she remembered the quiet by-street, the stone-hooded door which had let her in. She made her way back, and found the narrow turning. Above a high stone wall a tree, an aspen, whispered and sighed. Paris was full of trees—all those Maytime trees which had waved their vivid greeting to her happiness. And actually she must have seen the aspen on the day when they walked together down the narrow by-street and found the unexpected shop with its romantic name of an old-fashioned provinciality, and bought that remarkably good potted hare; but happy and companioned, she had ignored the aspen tree, sighing then as it sighed now, for from the moment the leaves put out the tree utters its whispering plaint. She had not noticed the tree till now.

She reached the stone-hooded porch. The door had been broken, and roughly boarded up. Through the gaps in the boarding she could discern the dusky shop, dishevelled and pillaged. She sat down on the step and buried her face in her hands.

It was nothing out of the way to see a woman in despair. She heard a child's trotting step go by, never pausing, and heavier footsteps went by too, and did not pause either. Yet when at last a heavy and slippered treading stopped beside her, she thought it better to be left alone, and resolutely hid her face.

The slippers shuffled as their wearer eased her weight from one leg to another. Sometimes a staybone creaked, petticoats dragged over the cobbles. With these slight movements a smell detached itself, a humble smell, mixed of oil, and yellow soap, and garlic, and calico. At last, sullenly enough, she raised her head, and looked into the face of the stout old woman who had sat on a camp-stool haranguing the young officer.

'There!'

Her voice was a sort of soft rumble, her expression compassionate. With her hands folded over her stomach she stood slowly shaking her head, easing her weight from one leg to another.

'I thought it was you. You aren't the sort of person one is mistaken about. Well, we didn't think it would go like this, did we?'

A sort of cloud, a look of more immediate, more compassionate concern, crossed her face.

'I suppose you've come back about that other poor lady. You were friends, I reckon.'

Minna dead. *On some faces, Sophia, death falls like a fall of snow*. Minna sitting up in bed, weeping and munching biscuits. Minna dead.

' Where——'

' She's not here now, my dear.'

' What ! '

This lance-thrust of hope jerked her to her feet, sent the echo of her voice, hoarse and shrieking, down the alley.

' She's dead, my dear. Don't let yourself think otherwise. Her body's gone, but she was dead for certain sure before that. I saw her with my living eyes, and I wouldn't deceive you.'

It was as though she were proffering a comfort, the way she insisted that Minna was dead.

Afterwards, sitting on a small chair in a very small room, and looking at Madame Guy's enormous bed, Sophia began to think that for all her kindness the old woman was not to be trusted ; that for all her protestations she knew, and would conceal, that Minna was still alive.

Instantly she began to tremble again, to drown in an icy faintness. For, having been so sure of dying, now to return to life and uncertainty was an agony like the bodily agony of the thawing-out of a frostbitten limb. ' And I shan't come back till I hear you having a good cry,' the old woman had said, ' for that's what you need.' Not a tear had come. But for all that Madame Guy presently walked in, her survivor's gregariousness too strong for her good resolutions. I will let her talk, thought Sophia. She's the sort that lets out the truth by accident.

Watchful and antagonised, she listened to the old woman's babble, that flowed on innocent as a brook. But just as a

brook may flow, innocent and tinkling, and through the
limpidity of its waters one may see on the bed of the stream
broken tins, a foul old boot, the jawbone of a dead animal,
so under Madame Guy's guileless chatter was death, misery
and exploitation. As she said, she had seen a lot of trouble
in her time.

'And it's a terrible thing, you know, to see your good
neighbours killed and chopped about, or taken off to prison
to be transported maybe. Particularly at my time of life.
For though new families may move in—you may be sure of
that, for as Jesus said, The poor you shall have always with
you, and living in a poor neighbourhood like this, I can
vouch for the truth of it—I shan't be able to feel the same
interest in them, I'm too old now to make new friends.

'And another thing I can't get over, is taking those boys
and teaching them to act like so many young demons. When
I saw them scrambling over the barricade last night like
wicked monkeys it came over me like a thunderclap that the
rich have no mortal right or justice to turn boys into demons
just because boys are poor and plentiful. Your poor friend,
too, dead and gone! I could see she was a kind-hearted
lady. Stuck through by one of them, wasn't she?'

'I tried to kill him. Did I?'

'I can't tell you, my dear. I was running, by then. And
don't my legs know it this morning? But I dare say you did.
They carried off several of their dead, so I hear. They didn't
carry off our dead, though. Left the poor bodies to lie in
the street till their own folk came and found them.'

'Where is her body, then?'

'They took it, they took it—maybe because she was a

lady. Now, my dear, don't you go and get it into your head that she is still alive. She was dead before they took her, I can swear to it, I saw her lying dead with my own eyes.'

'But you were running away. . . . Why do you lie to me like this? She is alive and you know it.'

Madame Guy turned pale. Tears began to run down her large face.

'Oh, this world of misery! One can do nothing to better it.'

That was all she would say, offering her great wet countenance to Sophia's furious questions as to a succession of blows. At last she turned and walked out of the room.

'You shan't get away from me without an answer.'

Madame Guy walked on, walked into the courtyard at the back of the house, and through it, and knocked softly on a door.

'Monsieur Guillaume, Monsieur Guillaume! It's me, it's the old Virginie.'

The door opened a very little. They went in. There was the cooked-meat-shop man, with his head bandaged. He was covered with cobwebs and dirt, as though he had been hiding in a cellar.

'Monsieur Guillaume, this lady—you remember her—has come back asking for her friend. For her friend who was killed. I tell her and I tell her, but she won't believe me. You, you tell her that the lady was certainly dead.'

'I assure you, she was dead.'

There was a heavy groan from Madame Guy. On his lips it became so palpably a lie.

'Aha! They are lying to you just as they lied to me!

She was alive enough when they carried her off, alive enough to cry out with pain, for I heard her. They are sparing your feelings, that's all.'

It was a woman's voice, young, speaking in a tone of such imperious despair that it seemed to Sophia that it might well have been her own voice speaking.

'She was alive, right enough! She was alive, for I heard her scream as they hauled her up from the ground where she lay. But whether she's alive now, that's another matter. For maybe they grew tired of pulling her along, and knocked her over the head like a dog. Or threw her into the river. Or sabred her, as they did that good Ingelbrecht. But dead or alive, they took her and they've got her. And if she's still alive, then God help her, I say, for then she's herded into some barracks, or some prison, or some cellar, yes, with hundreds of others, mad with thirst, mad with pain, suffo-cating in this heat, or else down in the vaults below the river level, with the water rising, the filthy stagnant water, and the rats galloping overhead, and . . .'

'Mathilde!' exclaimed the old man imploringly.

'She is my daughter-in-law,' he said. 'She is half dis-tracted, poor creature. For my son is missing since yester-day, and we fear he may have been taken prisoner. And now she has heard these rumours. There are already these rumours. They spring up, they are everywhere, one cannot prove or disprove them. . . .'

'One cannot prove them?' She came forward, clapping her hands together, taut as a lightning-flash. 'One cannot prove them? But if one has seen these things happening, if one has stood outside a building and heard within the shriek-

ing and the shooting ?—If one has seen the cobbles spattered
with blood, covered with bits of bones as though bottles
had been broken there, as it is in the rue des Mathurins,
where they shot the twenty-six prisoners ?—One cannot
prove these rumours ? And if they are only rumours, why
do you hide in the cellar ? '

She beat her hands together, and stared at them,
contemptuously.

' What else could I do ? ' asked Madame Guy. ' Knowing
all this, how could I have the heart to tell you she was alive
when, after all, it is possible that she is dead ? '

' Come with me.   Show me where to look for her.'

She saw them hang back.   After all, it was not their affair.
With a last effort of the mind she admitted the light of reason,
viewed herself insignificant and powerless, one straw among
the thousand straws that danced in the grip of the whirlpool.
She sat down on a bench by the door and said humbly,

' Will you keep me a little longer ? I can't go on. I am at
my wit's end.'

For three days she lay in Madame Guy's great bed, awake,
and sensible, but powerless to direct her will into her body.
She would put out her hand, as she thought, to lift the glass of
water by the bedside, and see it instead move wanderingly to
and fro, paw at this and that, and fall on the coverlet again.
With a perfect intention of what to say, other words would
impose themselves upon her tongue ; and an hour afterwards,
carefully pondering as to how and where the speech failed of
its aim, she would realise that instead of asking Madame Guy
if there were any news of Mathilde's husband, she had asked
what time the chimney sweep might be expected. Every

night Madame Guy, her head tied up in a bandanna, would climb into the bed beside her, and lie there, a warm mountain, remote in slumber.

On the morning of the twenty-seventh, body and will came together again. She got up, and made the bed, and went into the kitchen to say goodbye to Madame Guy.

' Are you going to look for your friend ? '

' Yes.'

' It is better that you should not go alone. As a matter of fact, while you were ill we thought of this. And Monsieur Guillaume has found a very suitable person who will accompany you—a Monsieur Paille, a notary.'

' There is one thing I must warn you of,' said Monsieur Paille. ' You have been ill, I understand, you have not been in the streets since the first days. You will find a great change of temper since then, a very great change of temper. There is no sympathy now for the insurrection. I feel it my duty to prepare you for this.'

He seemed to apprehend that she would be a dangerously demonstrative companion. But by the end of their search she admired him the more for this lack of courage, since it made the courage he had so much more remarkable. He had prepared a list of all the places where enquiries might be made ; and as they went from one rebuff to another, and entry after entry was crossed off in pencil, he remained dry and un-flustered and dutiful ; and though at every enquiry it was quite clear that no one in authority cared to answer, or indeed was capable of answering, he renewed the same persuasive tones, and even remodelled his phrases from time to time, as though he feared they might pall on her.

His mood, his moderate unenthusiastic stoicism, still tinctured hers as she walked up the rue de la Carabine. Madame Coton came forward from the lodge, carrying a new piece of knitting which was already more than half finished. No doubt she had added on many more rows to her ruminating hatred also, but that she kept to herself.

'Ah! It is Madame Willoughby. There is some one waiting for you upstairs.'

Who could be waiting for her, who was there left to wait for her? Not Minna. It could not be Minna. She allowed her fatigue to go as slowly as it pleased up the winding stairs, neither hastened nor hesitated at the door.

'Sophie, what a joy, what a relief! . . . My poor child, I never thought I should see you looking like this.'

In that shocked cry, in that wondering abhorring glance, Léocadie was for a moment perfectly genuine.

'On the contrary, I think you should congratulate me that I have been through these last few days and retained not only my head, but my bonnet.'

'I have not even glanced at your clothes, my dear. But to see you looking so tired, so strained, so pale . . .'

'So old, so dirty . . .'

'Goes to my heart,' continued Léocadie. 'Ah, Sophie, I cannot express how anxious I have been, how often I have reproached myself for submitting to this estrangement between us. For the last three days I have come here, sat here waiting for you. That odious good woman downstairs is growing quite accustomed to me.'

'I'm afraid you must have been very uncomfortable.'

'I do not wonder that you speak coldly, after all that you

have been through. You are like me in that. I have always
found that catastrophes leave me positively frigid. But where
have you been ever since ? '

' Ever since when, great-aunt Léocadie ? '

' No, there is no need to spare my feelings. I have had
four days, my child, in which to accustom myself to the idea
of you being lined up for execution. I still do not quite
understand by what providence you escaped.'

' Because I had been brought up as a lady.'

' Thank God ! ' she exclaimed devoutly.

' But now it is my turn not quite to understand. How did
you come to hear of this ? '

' Through Père Hyacinthe. The priest who was fetched
for that unfortunate misguided young man described to him
this lady, so tall and distinguished, so astonishing an object
among that crew. He was immensely struck by you,
described you with such detail that Père Hyacinthe recog-
nised you immediately. Especially since he noticed that you
had a slight, a very slight English accent. And ever since then
we have been moving heaven and earth to find you. Poor
Père Hyacinthe ! He was immensely concerned about you,
almost as concerned as I was.'

' And was poor Frederick also immensely concerned
about me ? '

' Poor Frederick, my dear Sophie, poor Frederick . . . he
is certainly in a very perturbed state. But at this moment he is
not in Paris. A certain Irish lady, a Mrs Kelly, very beautiful,
I believe, and immensely witty, became so agitated at the
prospect of being killed in her bed that she left Paris. And
Frederick went with her.'

With a flush of delight on her withered cheeks, with her eyes dancing and her lips pursed, she gazed at Sophia in an ecstasy of amusement and serene ill-nature.

'Ah, Sophie, what a pleasure to hear you laugh again! You admirable creature, I can forgive you all your vagaries for such a laugh, so candid, so free from affectation. And seriously, my love, I feel I may congratulate you on being— how shall I put it?—on being again released from a bad bargain. For you know perfectly well that I have never considered Frederick fit to black your shoes.'

'Yes. I have suspected you felt like that.'

'Moreover,' continued great-aunt Léocadie smoothly, 'I congratulate myself. For now I think you will forget all this shocking business about money, and allow me the pleasure of being both your bank and your hotel. I have always looked on you as a daughter, you know. Except that I have never found you tedious.'

'I think I should be very glad of some money. But if you give it to me, you must give it to an ingrate. For I cannot possibly return to the Place Bellechasse, or to anything like my old manner of living.'

'Nonsense, my dear. You are overwrought, you see things in an exaggerated light. A little soap and water, if you will let me be so frank, a visit to the hairdresser and to the dressmaker, and you can return to the Place Bellechasse without a scruple.'

'No.'

'And why not?'

'I have changed my ideas. I do not think as I did.'

'Now, my dear Sophie, do not become a prig just because

you have been a revolutionary. I have not said, I shall not
say, one word about your ideas. Think exactly as you please.
Add only this to your thinking : the possibility that other
people may even think a little as you do. For myself, I am
perfectly disgusted with the spirit shown by some people.
Only to-day I had that upstart Eugénie de Morin assuring
me that four hundred criminals have been shot daily in the
Luxembourg gardens. Four hundred criminals ! Forty mis-
guided working-men, more likely. I detest this fouling of
our own nest. It is not patriotic. It is not French. For me,
I am heartily sorry for the poor fellows.'

' Yes, I am sure you would feel sorry for them, after they
had been shot. Death is always an ingratiating act, and we
could manage to agree quite nicely over the dead. But we
should still disagree over the living.'

' For what reason ? '

' For one reason, the conditions under which you are
prepared to let them live.'

' There you go, my poor child, flying away after another
fallacy. Naturally, I do not say that we can run in and out
of each other's houses like brothers and sisters. But I recog-
nise that we are all the children of one Father. And since I
had the advantage of being one of a large family, an advantage
so unfortunately denied to you, I can also recognise that in
every family some will be more able, some more beautiful,
some more fortunate than others. Meanwhile, if I am one
of the more fortunate, I perform my obligations, I do what
I can for the less fortunate. And I count myself particularly
fortunate, particularly obliged to a universal Father, that I
happen to be born of a family which has always honoured

such obligations. When my dear father lost his estates in
1792 his first cry was, "Now I can do nothing more for my
poor peasants!"'

'But his peasants were poor?'

'Naturally. It is the order of the universe. And let me
tell you—I am an old woman, I permit myself to speak my
mind—that it is the people of my way of thinking who do
most for the poor. While people like your new friends are
making indignant speeches about the wickedness of a society
in which Madame Dupont lies freezing to death in an attic,
people like me, without making any speeches whatever, see
to it that she is given a good load of firing.'

'Unfortunately, your system does not relieve Madame
Dupont from the anxiety of wondering how she will keep
warm when your load of firing is burned up.'

'It is not impossible that I may send her another load.
And in any case, I assure you she does not wonder. It is
people like you and me, Sophie, who have never done a
day's work in our lives, who wonder, and meditate on
society, and ask ourselves what good we can do in the world.
But I won't argue with you about these things. I have no
arguments, no theories. All this while I have been hobbling
along on what I could recall of your own arguments, when
we used to discuss your tenants at Blandamer. There! That
was a pretty little rap, wasn't it? But seriously, my Sophie,
on this matter I have no arguments, no theories. I only
know the teaching of religion, I hear only the dictates of my
heart. And where you are concerned, my religion tells me
to clothe the naked, relieve the destitute. And my heart . . .
My dearest child, you will come with an old woman?'

'I will see you home.   Then I shall return here.'

Great-aunt Léocadie sighed, rose nimbly, gave her a tranquil, a philosophic embrace.   On the threshold she turned, surveyed Sophia from head to foot.

'No, my dear.   On second thoughts, I refuse your escort. You look too tired.'

And too shabby.

Ah, here in this empty room where she had felt such impassioned happiness, such freedom, such release, she was already feeling exactly as she had felt before she loved Minna, and wrapping herself as of old in that coward's comfort of irony, of cautious disillusionment!   How soon her blood had run cold, how ready she was to slink back into ignominy of thought, ignominy of feeling!   And probably only the pleasure of disagreeing, the pique of being thought shabby and deplorable, had kept her from a return to the Place Bellechasse.   She looked round her, dragging her gaze over the empty, the soiled and forlorn apartment.   There was the wine that Minna had left for her, the slippers she had tossed off, sprawling, one here, one there, and on the table where she had thrown it down and forgotten it, the fifth of the packets which Ingelbrecht (yes, he was dead too) had entrusted to her.   She took up one of the copies, fingered the cheap paper, sniffed the heavy odour of printers' ink, began to read.

'*A spectre is haunting Europe—the spectre of Communism. All the powers of old Europe have united in a holy alliance to exorcise this spectre.   The Pope and the Czar, Metternich and Guizot, the radicals of France, and the police-spies of Germany.*

'*Where is the opposition party that has not been accused of*

Communism by its opponents in power ?   Where is the opposition party that has not, in its turn, hurled back at its adversaries, progressive or reactionary, the branding epithet of Communism ?

   ' *Two things result from these facts :*

   ' *Communism is now recognised by all European Powers to be itself a power.*

   ' *It is high time that Communists should lay before the whole world their point of view, their aims and tendencies, and set against this spectre of Communism a Manifesto of the Party itself.*'

   She seated herself ; and leaning her elbows on the table, and sinking her head in her hands, went on reading, obdurately attentive and by degrees absorbed.